THE BODY MAN

ALSO BY ERIC P. BISHOP

The Body Man

Ransomed Daughter

Breach Of Trust (Coming in 2024)

The Omega Group (Coming in 2024)

For more info about Eric, please visit his website:

www.ericpbishop.com

or

You can contact him at eric@ericpbishop.com

THE BODY MAN

A THRILLER

ERIC P. BISHOP

BRUNOE MEDIA PUBLISHING

eBook ISBN-979-8-9888360-3-2

Paperback ISBN-979-8-9888360-4-9

Hardcover ISBN-979-8-9888360-5-6

Library of Congress Cataloging-in-Publication Identifiers: LCCN: 2024900999

Book Cover by Momir Borocki

Book Formatting by Atticus

First Edition November 2021

Second Edition January 2024

Printed in The United States of America

10 9 8 7 6 5 4 3 2

— • —

PRAISE FOR THE BODY MAN & RANSOMED DAUGHTER

—◆◇◆—

"Thriller readers take note: there's a new sheriff in town."
--Ben Coes, New York Times Bestselling Author

"In a world of tired cliches, Eric has crafted the rip-roaring world of Troy Evans. This novella is a pure shot of intellectual adrenaline!"
--John Guarnieri, Security Director, Former USSS

"In a crowded field of today's political thrillers, The Body Man will keep you guessing until the final page."
--Don Bentley, NYT Bestselling Author of Tom Clancy's Target Acquired

"Action and intrigue abound in this fast-paced, one-two punch from the author who gave us The Body Man."
--A.M. Adair, Author of the Elle Anderson Series

"Heart pounding intensity, action filled, and heart-felt."
--Steve Stratton, Author of the Shadow Tier Series

DEDICATION

For my Mom, Patty
My most ardent supporter
I love you, always

In Memorial
My Nanny, Hilda Dewhurst
11/11/1917 --- 03/08/2010

"In every powerful organization, there's always someone who knows where the bodies are buried..."

1

WASHINGTON, D.C.

The Body Man closed the front door of his townhouse and crossed the tiled landing of the porch. A stiff breeze pushed against him as he approached the top step. His eyes looked down at his Rolex Oyster Perpetual, the watch a gift from the most unlikely of sources.

Fifteen minutes. Plenty of time.

Cast iron gas lamps stood like sentries in front of each residence, dotting the tree-lined street. Like a hunter in search of its prey, he glanced left, then right. Keen eyes probed both sides of the road. The meticulous stare searched for the slightest anomaly but revealed nothing out of place.

Habit led his right hand to slide under the black leather coat. His fingertips brushed against the smooth belt he bought last year in Florence until his thumb bumped into the reassuring polymer of the Glock.

Confident of his surroundings, he descended the steps to the sidewalk and approached the four-door black Audi A8 sedan. Tonight, invisibility was an ally, discretion a trusted friend. Without breaking stride, he climbed into the vehicle, started the engine, and pulled away from the curb. The Body Man accelerated quickly to make a meeting with a reporter he preferred not to attend. He knew it had to be done, but he was also keenly aware a firestorm would erupt once he brought the reporter into the mix and revealed the damning intel only he possessed.

Yet, he had no choice.

The drive from Vienna to Mclean paralleled Route 123 and would only take ten minutes.

The Body Man ran heavy on the gas to shave off a precious minute or two. His eyes darted from the rearview to the side mirrors.

All clear.

Up ahead, the traffic light turned yellow, then red as he braked hard to slow the vehicle. With a slight chirp, the car came to a sudden stop just short of the white line. His fingers struck the steering wheel in a rhythmic beat that sounded like taps. Another vehicle, a canary yellow four-door sedan opposite him, idled and inched up past the white line like an impatient toddler not keen on being told no.

As the light turned green, the yellow car lurched forward at the same moment a blue pickup truck careened through the intersection. The sound of grinding metal pierced the still night as the two vehicles slammed into and then bounced off each other. Glass sprayed across the intersection as they both came to a sudden and violent stop.

The Body Man was out of his car and moving towards the yellow sedan, the vehicle closest to him. His role of protector was worn like a badge.

As he approached the driver's side door, a male figure was visible. The man slumped against the steering wheel appeared unconscious with no other passengers inside the car. The Body Man yanked at the door, but it didn't give with the first pull. Undeterred, he gripped the door handle harder and strained his muscles as he jerked with overwhelming force; on the second tug, the metal groaned and finally released its steel grip.

With the door ajar, he leaned into the car and reached towards the driver's neck to check for a pulse. As his index and middle fingers pressed against the carotid artery, the driver's head jerked from the steering wheel, and the closed eyes sprang to life.

The Body Man knew that look. Empty, and devoid of emotion, only darkness.

Survival instinct and years of training took over as his hand pulled away from the driver's neck and shot towards his belt. However, before The Body Man's hand reached under his leather coat to grip the Glock, the driver's balled fist shot out from the steering wheel and struck him in the solar plexus. The unexpected blow caused him to stumble and fall away from the doorframe.

Staying upright, he felt a presence behind him. He wasn't alone and now understood this wasn't a mere accident.

It was a takedown,

And he was the target.

His brain connected the dots as a white box van stopped to the right of the yellow vehicle, its side door slid open with a high pierced squeak indicating the track needed lubrication. The van caught his attention as he pivoted to face a towering figure. At close to six feet seven inches tall, the imposing man wore all black, his face concealed behind a mask with slits that revealed dilated eyes.

The Body Man gripped the butt of the Glock from under his coat and drew his weapon.

Target acquired.

He didn't get the chance to pull the trigger as his attacker delivered a roundhouse kick, striking his wrist, sending the Glock free of his hand and across the asphalt. His best form of self-defense slid twenty feet away far out of reach.

Surprised by the move, but undeterred, The Body Man dropped to the ground and twisted in midair to face the pavement. He did what looked almost like a squat thrust as his body went perpendicular. His right foot shot out, and the sole of his shoe met the imposing figure's left knee, causing a sharp snap and popping sound as heel met cartilage.

Not surprisingly, the heel won.

The sound made a sickening crunch, like a wishbone pulled apart. As the man dressed in all black let out a moan he dropped to the ground, grabbed his knee, and writhed in agony.

Without pause, The Body Man jumped to his feet as a set of muscular arms reached around his chest. The driver of the car was on him and squeezed his torso like a python. Using his height and weight advantage, The Body Man pushed off with the ball of his feet, propelling both bodies back toward the car's door frame.

Flesh met steel and as expected steel won. An exaggerated grunt came from the driver as he collapsed into the car.

The Glock lay less than twenty feet away, and The Body Man made his move; the weapon his only chance of survival. He closed the distance in less than two seconds as his hand swooped down and touched the polymer grip with his extended fingertips. Searing pain caused his arm to recoil from the weapon as a chunk of lead tore his flesh between the wrist and elbow. A stream of crimson flowed out of his sleeve as blood droplets splattered on the ground in a circular pattern. Undeterred, his eye darted towards the Glock as it lay just out of reach.

He saw the muzzle flash as a second-round came from deep within the interior of the white van, and the bullet whizzed by his ear.

A warning shot.

Don't go for the gun.

As he considered his next move, the force of a body slammed into him like an NFL linebacker sacking a quarterback. The surprising hit drove his body into the asphalt. Disoriented by the sudden blow, he felt a sharp wince as a needle entered his neck near the seventh vertebrae.

A burning sensation followed, and it flashed from the base of his skull and soon encapsulated his whole body. It felt like a heavy shroud suffocated him as someone, or something turned him over, face up.

Two burly men stood over his immobilized body and dragged him to the rear of his car.

They the hunters, he the fresh kill.

The last thing The Body Man remembered was being stuffed into his trunk while one man wrapped the wound on his arm with a thick piece of white gauze. Next, one of them placed a thick hood over his head.

Then the trunk was shut closed with a loud thud.

Lights out.

2

WASHINGTON, D.C.

FBI WASHINGTON FIELD OFFICE (WFO)

Eli Payne hung up the phone, a look of disgust plastered over his face. "Can you believe this horseshit?"

His squad supervisor, Wes Russell, who sat across the field-office bullpen, looked up from the case file spread across the desk, rolled his eyes after he looked towards Eli, and glanced back at the papers. "What is it now, Payne? Your team lose another wide receiver?" He asked it with more than a hint of exasperation.

Eli pursed his lips. "Not funny. They want me to head out to Vienna for some missing person call."

"Sounds like a Virginia State Police matter," Wes said.

"That's what I told them."

"And?"

"The woman who called it in insists the missing person is a fed." An annoyed expression hung on Eli's face like a thin veil.

This caused the supervisor to perk up. "One of ours?"

Eli shook his head. "No. The White House."

"Well now, that could be interesting."

"Hardly. I'm having a football party at the house tonight."

Wes rolled his eyes. "Of course you are."

"Can I dump this thing back on the state turds?" Eli asked.

"No, and I doubt the state police would like to know you call them turds. This one is all you, Payne."

Eli responded with a pleading look. "Come on, Wes. There's gotta be someone else around here who can take this." He paused for a moment before he added. "How about Miller?"

"Nope, Chris's wife has an ultrasound today. He's AWOL. The baby is due next week."

"Not fair."

"Stop whining, Payne. It should be quick. After all, Vienna isn't far away. With any luck, the woman has dementia, and nobody is missing. You know what? Take Stone with you. She needs some experience."

Eli sighed. "The new chick fresh out of Quantico? What do I look like a babysitting service?"

"She's not a 'chick.' Jeez, Payne, you're a walking sexual harassment lawsuit waiting to happen. Yes, she's new, but that's more reason to get her feet wet. She doesn't have a field training agent yet. Be better than the complaint agent desk she's working this week. Just don't screw her up on her first assignment."

"What's that supposed to mean?"

"You don't have a stellar track record with the newbies."

"You're crazy; I'm a brilliant teacher."

"Umm, you brilliant?" Wes rolled his eyes. "Guess you forgot all about Special Agent Calvin."

"Oh, I see how it is. You're going to bring that up?"

"You'll never live down the noodle incident, bud."

Eli shot Wes a dirty look before heading to the far end of the bullpen, where Probationary Agent Katherine Stone quietly sat. Her back was to him, and she had white earbuds firmly implanted in her ears.

"Kat," Eli said as he cleared his throat and tapped her on the shoulder.

Startled, she turned around and locked eyes with him as she removed one of her earbuds. "Yeah. What's up?"

"Eli Payne. We met on your first day."

Kat was attractive, not model beauty, but she certainly gave off a girl-next-door quality. Her auburn hair came down to her shoulders, pulled back in a ponytail to reveal a narrow face, small nose, high cheekbones, and large brown eyes.

As she stared at Eli, her eyes narrowed. "Yeah, I know who you are."

"Glad to hear it."

"I also heard you avoided new agents like the plague."

Eli knew he had a reputation within the WFO for being an asshole. Something he did little to dispel. He would readily admit that playing nice, especially with the new agents, wasn't his forte. "Well, today I'm bending the rules."

"Lucky me, I guess," Kat said as her voice trailed off.

Eli just looked at her, his face expressionless.

"Also heard you're a big football fan," Kat said.

His stoic glare faltered, and a slight smile appeared at the corner of his lips. "Guilty as charged."

Kat shrugged. "Not me. I think it's barbaric."

"You hate apple pie and your momma too?" Eli asked in a sharp tone as his smile faded.

"Excuse me?" Kat's eyebrows raised as she removed the second earbud. Her body visibly tensed.

Eli decided getting into a pissing match with the newbie wasn't in his best interests. "Never mind. I got a case, and Wes told me to bring you along."

"You mean I get to stop taking these complaint calls?"

"That's right. At least for a few hours."

"Count me in. I've never talked to this many crazy people in my life."

"Grab whatever you need."

Kat opened the bottom desk drawer and removed her purse. "What type of case?" she asked without looking up.

"A missing person."

"Isn't that for the police?"

"Already tried that line of reasoning, and it didn't work."

"Where we headed?"

"Vienna. The missing person supposedly works at the White House, and we're going to interview the elderly lady who called it in. Follow me." Eli turned and walked away as Kat stood and had to double-time it to keep up.

He led her to the bank of elevators without looking back.

As they stepped inside and the metal doors closed, Kat asked, "Victim's name?"

Eli frowned. "Well, he's not a victim. At least not yet. We're not even sure he's missing. But the name the caller provided is Ralph Webb. He lives in the townhouse across the street from her."

"Did you call the White House? Confirm he's missing?"

"Easy, girl," Eli said as the elevator came to a stop, and he stepped out. "First things first. We need to interview the woman. If her story's credible, we'll start running down leads."

"And if it's not?"

"Well, you go back to the complaint desk, and I head home to watch football." Eli walked fast as they left the building and approached his car.

Kat opened the passenger side door and climbed in and let out an audible, drawn-out whistle. The floorboard was covered in an array of receipts, crumpled up napkins, paperback books, and discarded wrappers. She pushed the trash around, trying to find a clean spot with her left foot.

"What's the whistle for?" Eli asked, his eyebrows turning downward as his nose scrunched up.

"Your car is an absolute pigsty."

"Says who?"

"Me."

"Well, I'm used to working alone."

"I take it there's no Mrs. Payne?"

"That's kind of personal, isn't it?"

Kat looked down. "And I think I have my answer."

"I like my stuff just the way it is, thank you very much."

"Pretty sure the Bureau has some rules on keeping the appearance of your car presentable."

"And I'm pretty sure I've got a finger," Eli said as he raised his middle one in her direction before slamming his car door shut.

Kat laughed out loud and pointed toward the mess on the floor. "I see you like to read thrillers."

"You noticed?"

"I'm surprised I saw them with all the trash on the floor, but relieved you can read something not filled with pictures."

"Yeah, that's funny because I keep the nudie magazines at home under my mattress."

"You're clearly a classy guy, Payne." Kat rolled her eyes as she uttered the phrase. "But you still need to clean out the car."

"Uh-huh."

Eli started the car and pressed the gas pedal, giving the engine a not-too-subtle *roar* as the RPM's jumped. Whitesnake's *Here I Go Again* erupted from the speakers at an ungodly level.

Kat covered her ears. "Jeez, this is my dad's music," she yelled, reaching over and turning off the stereo.

Eli cocked his head, his eyes narrowed, and his lip curled into a snarl. "Well, at least your dad has good taste in music."

Before Kat could respond, he slammed the car into drive and floored it. The lurch forward pushed her against the headrest as the car shot out of the parking space. Eli didn't take his foot off the gas as the vehicle barreled away from the underground garage.

3

WASHINGTON, D.C.

Merci De Atta settled into the comfortable first-class Air France seat. Her exhausted body sank into the plush faux leather. She already slipped her shoes off, her standard custom when on a flight. A few hours after she completed a hit was tough on her physically. During the actual act of taking a life, she stayed focused, determined, as little distracted her from finishing the job. However, once done, the inevitable adrenaline rush abated. Now on the plane at cruising altitude leaving the United States, she finally reached that place mentally where she could take a step back and breathe.

The flight attendant stopped at her row long enough to take her drink order before disappearing into the front galley. Two minutes later, the woman in a dark blue skirt and white blouse with a dangling silver crucifix hanging from her neck reappeared and placed the glass in the cupholder. Merci nodded to the woman and picked up the tall crystal glass. She took two sips from the Long Island Iced Tea. As the alcohol entered her bloodstream, she relaxed, and her mind turned back to the events six hours earlier.

A husky male voice emanated from the transceiver hidden deep within Merci's right ear. "He's about to emerge from the curve. Be ready. You've got less than five seconds."

Along the Mt. Vernon Trail, the Potomac River glistened blood-red with the reflection of the sunrise. To Merci's right was the river, while to her left the George Washington Memorial Parkway moved steady, the morning traffic not yet at a standstill.

Merci knew what to do. Like a gymnast who'd spent years honing their abilities, Merci's skills were innate. Keeping a steady pace, she picked out the spot further down the trail.

The voice crackled again in her ear. "He's visible. I repeat. He can see you."

Merci counted to ten, and at the designated spot, she pushed her right foot toward her left. The unnatural motion caused her to miss a step as her body weight shifted to the right and sent her down hard. At the last second, she raised her arms, preventing serious injury.

As Merci hit the ground palms first, her hands slipped, and most of her body landed on the grass lining the side of the trail. She slid several feet along the dew-soaked grass, rolling onto her stomach.

She lay motionless on the ground, slowed her breathing, and waited. Merci studied the mark's file intently and anticipated his reactions. He didn't disappoint. They talked for a minute after he helped her up. Unlike many of her marks, Merci sensed he wasn't just some self-absorbed asshole; but appeared to genuinely care for her wellbeing after she took the hard fall.

A pity.

After a minute of back and forth, Merci insisted he continue to jog. Finally, he relented, and as soon as he turned away, Merci's left hand moved across her body in one smooth motion and reached inside the fanny pack. Her right hand reached into the opening. A suppressor would have been preferable, but speed trumped stealth. She raised the weapon toward his back and took a measured breath.

Merci applied pressure to the trigger, but waited until she completed her exhale. At the end of the breath, she made two smooth consecutive trigger pulls without the slightest hesitation.

She watched as the first slug struck his back like a sledgehammer hitting thin concrete. The subsequent second round struck with an equal concussive force an inch from the first bullet.

As the mark crumpled to the ground, his face landed flush against the gravel of the trail. Merci stood over him with the barrel of her Sig Sauer P320 pointed at the back of his head. In the distance, a piercing scream, almost like a banshee, disturbed her trigger pull. Out of the corner of her eye, Merci saw movement atop the Arlington Bridge. Her imperceptible flinch a moment before the slide lurched back caused the third bullet to miss its intended target by centimeters. But it didn't matter; the shot had drilled a hole in the back of his skull.

Confident the mark was dead; she took off in a full sprint towards the roadway, sure to keep her head down and not give the frantic woman screaming on the bridge a look at her face.

Merci darted into the open door of the waiting van as it came to a skidding halt on the side of the parkway. She slammed the passenger door shut, and the driver peeled out, leaving lines of rubber on the asphalt. As the van passed beneath the bridge, it accelerated away from the scene.

The man driving the van said nothing. A mile down the road, he slowed, and only then did he look over.

"We good?" The man asked.

"Yes."

"You sure he's dead?"

"Two in the back, one on the head."

"Good girl."

Merci's body stiffened at his comment. *You sanctimonious asshole.* "Take me to Dulles," she said.

"Not yet." The driver shook his head. "We have an additional stop."

Her eyes narrowed, and she gripped the Sig in her right hand tighter. For the briefest of moments, she considered putting a bullet right in his forehead as he darted between traffic. "That wasn't part of the arrangement," she said through gritted teeth. "Do I need to call my handler?"

"No, he doesn't know anything about this. Look, I'm the messenger telling you the plan's changed. That's it. I don't call the shots."

"Like hell, the plan's changed. By whose authority?"

The driver raised his bushy eyebrows. "By his authority."

Shit. Things just got complicated.

***

Merci sensed the person next to her even before she opened her eyes.

"You pressed the call button," said the attractive flight attendant who now stood at her side and pointed to the illuminated light on the bulkhead above Merci's seat.

Merci smiled and held up the crystal glass. "I did, would be so kind as to pour me another? Maybe a double this time?"

"Hard day, girlfriend?"

A narrow smile emanated from the side of her lips. "The hardest."

The flight attendant smiled. "It would be my pleasure," she replied and removed the glass from Merci's extended hand.

Five minutes later, with the second glass of liquid emptied and the alcohol pulsating through her bloodstream, Merci closed her eyes once more, but this time her mind focused on the new task.

She had a job, one that was told to her, not requested, a big difference from her typical modus operandi. Merci never enjoyed being told what to do. It rubbed her all the wrong way. She agreed to do it, but only because the man who summoned her didn't ask, he told, and she felt like she had no choice. Merci was cornered, trapped. And any animal such as Merci, when backed into a corner, only responds one way.

4

— · —

Manassas, Virginia

Manassas Regional Airport

The Body Man awoke to the taste of a metallic flavor. He knew it must be his dried blood. Darkness engulfed him, but he heard the sounds of the car and felt the vibrations of a moving vehicle. He felt an extreme desire to throw up, but swallowed hard, pushing the bile down with a forceful gulp.

The car came to a halt with a shudder, and next the engine stopped.

A minute later, the trunk opened, and what felt like two sets of powerful hands grabbed him and yanked him out. The hands let go of him, and he struck the concrete hard, making the same sound as a bag of flour hitting a tile floor.

He saw a glimmer of light from where the hood met his shirt around the chest.

The light and what it might reveal became short-lived as the vicious beating commenced.

The Body Man had received his fair share of ass whooping's in his younger years, but often, he gave them out. Even during his darkest of times, he never dared beat anyone with the ferocity his abductors railed on him.

This was personal.

Calculated.

At first, he tried to deflect and block the strikes, but they came from every direction, and besides, he couldn't see them on account of the hood. Instinctively, he curled up in a ball and waited for the next strike to come. And it did, one after another.

He suffered for minutes before he blacked out.

The unmistakable smell of piss and shit greeted The Body Man as he awoke hours later. Lying in his own filth, he shuddered at the stench. Two men came for him. He knew they were men by the sound of their steps. Men walk with a different gait than women, which he knew from years of experience on the job watching people, studying them.

One of them shuffled his feet, while the other walked with an audible limp. One foot came down with a different intensity than the other. The two men stood on either side, yanked him to his feet, and carried him down a flight of stairs.

Neither man said a word.

With his clothes cut off, a garden hose sprayed ice-cold water over his body. The chilly water felt good on his skin, although it burned in places where open wounds covered his body. With fresh clothes pulled over his damp, naked body, the shirt and pants clung to his moist skin.

A pair of oversized hands lifted the hood high enough to force-feed him Vienna sausages, a strawberry pop tart, and a Snickers candy bar. Contrary to the advertisements, the Snickers didn't satisfy.

Five minutes later, they led The Body Man to an adjacent bathroom, pulled down his pants, and sat him on the toilet. He didn't like pissing like a woman, but it was far better than the alternative of warm urine running down his leg. After he finished, the two men placed him inside a vehicle. Relieved it wasn't his trunk; the door sounded like a van as it slid along a crooked track and slammed closed. Someone pushed him to the floorboard, and the vehicle sped off.

The Body Man counted. He reached 420, which meant seven to eight minutes when the vehicle came to an abrupt stop. Once the door slid open, he knew they were at an airport because he recognized the distinct sound of an auxiliary power unit from the idling plane.

It must be late. The tower is probably closed. Perfect time to get someone on a plane without anyone seeing. I'd do the same thing.

Strong hands grabbed him, pulled him out of the vehicle, and led him onto the waiting plane.

One word came to mind.

Rendition.

Spooks? A foreign agency?

The Body Man's mind raced.

He knew he would die before any secrets would seep from his lips. *The capsule.* His tongue went back to the top right molar.

It was gone.

But how did they know about it?

The realization struck him like a cue ball stuffed into a long sock and swung with pinpoint accuracy into an unsuspecting skull.

I'm fucked.

His mind spun like a centrifuge, but with the capsule missing, his life no longer rested in his own hands. Others with unknown intentions held his fate. That pissed him off more than knowing he would likely die soon. Death was a part of life, and he didn't fear it. What he did fear was the lack of control. For the first time since his youth, he felt vulnerable, and the taste of bile filled his mouth as he considered his dark fate.

Geoff Watson heard a loud noise. He left the office in the building's rear and made his way through the darkened hangar. His boots squeaked on the freshly polished floor.

It was late, and nobody should have been around.

His wife, Ann, had spent most of the day on all fours over the porcelain pony. A nasty stomach bug had made its way through the family, and Geoff was hoping it would continue to skip him. With Ann unable to clean the offices at Dibaco Aviation, the responsibility fell to him.

The vibration caused by the jet engines near the metal building shook the walls, while the high-pitched noise from the idling turbines filled the hangar. The sound startled him. Geoff walked quickly through the vast space, and the noise grew louder as he reached the front of the building.

Near the hangar doors, he moved towards the large window that overlooked the tarmac. With the blinds drawn, only the faintest amount of light from the exterior motion sensor lamps made its way through the gaps in the slats.

Geoff pulled up one of the wide slats and peered outside.

Less than thirty feet away, an executive style jet sat on the tarmac. With the airstairs lowered, Geoff could see part of the interior of the plane. Ann had told him she rarely saw anyone around on the nights she worked.

What the hell is going on?

Two men emerged from the plane, descended the airstairs, and waited on the tarmac. They didn't look friendly. The hairs on Geoff's arms stood up as a slight shiver ran through his body.

Several minutes later, a set of headlights pierced the darkness beyond the idling plane, and a van pulled between the hangar and the aircraft, obstructing most of Geoff's view.

Two burly men emerged from the van and pulled a figure out of the vehicle. They half-carried the person, who wore a hood and had both hands and feet bound. A powerful gust of wind blew off the covering, which landed twenty feet away from the van.

The man looked around. His face appeared stoic.

Geoff did a double-take. The hooded man looked like someone beat the shit out of him.

What the hell?

Geoff quickly removed his phone from the clip on his right hip and activated his cell phone's camera. He took one picture after another in rapid succession.

One of the burly men jogged over, grabbed the hood from the ground, ran back to the bound man, and yanked the hood over the bound man's head.

Geoff continued to take pictures as the three men disappeared inside the plane. He zoomed in close enough to get a picture of the plane's tail number.

Two men descended the airstairs and removed several bags from the van. They spoke loudly enough over the sound of the idling jet engines for Geoff to make out both voices. As soon as they opened their mouths, he knew they weren't speaking English. His first guess was Russian, although truth be told, he didn't recognize one accent over another.

His heart raced as he stood frozen.

Should I call the cops?

Immobilized by abject fear, he did nothing but watch.

Two minutes later, the van pulled away as the plane taxied down the runway and disappeared into the pitch-dark sky.

Silence returned to the hangar.

Geoff stood motionless, lost in his own thoughts. After a few minutes, he glanced back at his phone and looked through the photo gallery at the photos he took.

5

VIENNA, VIRGINIA

Eli's thick knuckles struck three times on the red door.

"There's a doorbell, you know," Kat said.

"I don't like them," Eli said. His eyes narrowed and lips pursed as he stared at Kat. "I prefer the feel of wood against my skin."

"Figures," she replied and blatantly rolled her eyes.

A minute later, the door opened only a few inches, the security chain still attached. An older woman glared at them through the slim gap between the door and its frame.

"Rose Lewis?" Eli asked. His inflection sounded harsh.

Kat poked him in the side with her pointer finger. As Eli glanced back, the look on Kat's face could best be described as, *What the hell?*

"Yes," came the timid reply from behind the door.

Eli's gaze swung back to Rose as he dialed back the sternness in his voice. "FBI, ma'am. You called us about a missing person." He displayed his badge and held it out towards the door.

The door closed with no response, and the sound of metal sliding against metal filled the silence. As the door opened, an older woman emerged. Rose Lewis had an elegant look about her. She wore her white hair pulled back in a bun and had a pale complexion. About Kat's height, Rose wore a tan-colored floral printed dress that flowed to her ankles while a pair of red shoes, like Dorothy wore in Oz, adorned her feet.

"I'm Special Agent Eli Payne," he paused and turned towards Kat. "And this is Agent Katherine Stone. May we come in and ask you a few questions?"

"Of course," Rose said as she stepped aside and opened the door fully.

Rose led Eli and Kat through the tastefully decorated foyer and into the living room. The room contained two taupe colored couches with a glass coffee table between them. A catty-cornered fireplace with an ornate mantle and a large oil painting of El Capitan was in one corner of the room, while floor-to-ceiling bookshelves lined the wall behind one couch. The shelves held not only books, but photos and dozens of trinkets of various sizes. Several curio cabinets dotted the room, also filled with items, mostly small but surely collectible. Eli noticed the little details, and a story formed in his mind of Rose's life.

"My husband, Charlie, traveled extensively for work. He brought me back a little something each time he returned home," Rose said as she watched Eli scan the room.

Eli nodded. "I see that. Is he away now?"

A forlorn look formed on Rose's face. "Unfortunately, he passed many years ago."

"I'm sorry for your loss."

As quickly as the look came, it dissipated. "So am I."

Rose directed Eli and Kat to the couch on her right while she took the other. "Would you care for something to drink?"

"Thank you, but we're fine," Eli said.

"Let me know if you change your mind."

"We will." Eli, not one to waste time, jumped straight to the chase. "Can you tell us when you discovered your neighbor, Mr. Webb, had gone missing?"

"Today, when he didn't show up for our morning coffee."

Eli looked at Kat with a bemused expression.

Kat shrugged her shoulders in response.

"And that's unusual?" Eli asked as he turned back to face Rose.

"Highly," she replied. "Ralph always comes over in the morning, seven days a week, unless he's traveling."

"Any chance he took a trip without you knowing?"

"No. Ralph was supposed to leave later this morning for a day trip and was coming back tonight. Plus, there's an upcoming trip overseas in a few weeks, one of those G-some-number meetings the president attends."

Eli couldn't hide his smirk at the G-some-number comment. "I'll be honest; we don't normally assume someone is missing if they happen to be late for morning coffee, Mrs. Lewis. A missing child, I could see. But as for a grown adult, there are too many variables. The person really must be gone for more than a few hours before we assume they're missing. Unless, of course, there is some evidence of them disappearing or an eyewitness to an abduction. Are either of those the case?"

"Well, no, but I'm sure he's gone. He assured me he would be here today."

Eli let out a sigh. He tried not to make it visible, but he did it anyway. He needed to switch up the line of questioning. "Sounds like you know his schedule pretty well."

"Of course. After all, I feed Ralph's cat while he's out of town."

"Can you describe your relationship with Mr. Webb?" Kat asked.

Eli turned and gave her a slight frown. They had agreed before they got out of the car; he would do all the talking.

Like Eli, Kat had trouble following the rules.

"Well, Katherine, it's nothing romantic, if that's what you're implying," Rose said as her voice raised an octave.

"It's Kat."

Rose continued. "Lookie, dear, I have grandchildren your age. Ralph is over thirty years younger than I am, and our relationship is purely platonic. He became a trusted friend over the past two years, but nothing more. Ever since he saved me, he comes over at 6:30 a.m. sharp for coffee seven days a week before he heads to work."

"Saved you?" Eli asked.

"Yes, Ralph stopped two young men from attacking me one night while I was on a walk. I used to do that all the time in the neighborhood. Sadly, times aren't what they used to be."

"What happened?"

"Ralph came around the corner as one of the men grabbed me. Ralph moved like lightning. With one punch, he laid that fella out cold. The others, well, they ran off when their friend hit the ground. Ralph let them go and focused on me."

"Sounds like he was your hero that night."

"He was."

"And when did Ralph tell you he worked at the White House?" Eli made notes on a small black notepad as Rose spoke.

"About a year ago. I asked about his frequent travel, and Ralph admitted where he worked. Up until then, Ralph talked in vague terms about a job that required him to be on the road."

"Why did he tell you he worked for the White House?"

"Not sure. Maybe I finally earned his trust. Ralph Webb is an extremely private man. In almost four years of living across the street from him, I've rarely known him to have visitors. He has no family to speak of; it's only him and the cat."

"And what does he do at the White House?"

"He works for the president."

"Can you be more specific?" Eli asked.

Rose grew silent for a moment. "No, I can't," she finally said. "It's pretty secretive stuff. I don't ask, and he doesn't tell. I respect Ralph's privacy too much. And frankly, it's none of my business."

"It's common for friends to discuss what they do at work."

"Correct, but his job isn't typical."

"But he told you he works directly for the president?"

"Yes."

"He's part of the presidential staff?"

"No."

"Then, is he a Secret Service agent?"

Rose frowned. "I know he protects the president, but that is all. Look, I've told you what I know, Agent Payne."

He scribbled a few more lines on his notepad before he looked up. "So, Ralph doesn't show up, and you call us first because he works for the White House? Correct?"

"Yes."

"Why not call the local police department?"

"I may be old, Mr. Payne, but I'm no dummy. I know how things work. The FBI is the premier organization for finding missing people. Ralph's a federal government employee. You're a federal agency. It's simple."

"I appreciate the compliment, Rose, truly, but the FBI works closely with local law enforcement in these types of matters as well."

"Yes, I understand that, but based on what Ralph does for a living, I felt calling the FBI first was prudent."

"Fair enough. Back to the timeline. What happened after Ralph didn't show up this morning?"

"I went to his townhouse across the street to see if he was OK. Make sure nothing happened to him."

"You have a key?"

"Of course. I told you I feed his cat, Italia when he's out of town."

"His cat is named Italia?" Kat asked.

"Yes. Ralph said he got her on a trip to Rome last year. A gift from the Pope."

Eli's eyebrows raised. "And you believe him?"

"Ralph is not a man to tell tall tales, Agent Payne. 'His word is his bond,' he always says."

"OK, you went over there this morning to feed Italia and noticed he was gone …"

Rose cut him off. "Yes, but there's more than that."

Eli looked at her. His eyes narrowed, and his brow furrowed. "How so?"

"Things were out of place."

"What do you mean by out of place?"

"Books stacked on the floor, papers were lying on the couch. Even the rug in his living room appeared rolled up."

"Maybe Ralph had to go out of town suddenly, and he was looking for something before he left?"

Rose shook her head back and forth as Eli spoke. "I don't think so. I've never seen anything out of place at his home. Ralph's what you might call anal-retentive about his stuff. And if his schedule had changed, he would have told me."

Eli didn't want to get hung up on the condition of the man's house. "Did you think to call the White House directly if that's where he works?" he asked.

"No."

"Maybe they could have confirmed he left town earlier than expected for work?"

Rose said nothing in response.

Eli realized arguing with her would get them nowhere. "You don't have a photo of Ralph by chance, do you?"

"Sure, I do," Rose said as her expression changed to a smile. "Let me go grab it from the other room. Ralph wasn't keen on taking pictures, but I asked for one from time to time." She left the room and returned a moment later, clutching a four by six photo. "Here you go."

Eli looked at the photo carefully. The man didn't look familiar. He knew a few people who worked at the White House but not many. "Good looking guy."

Rose blushed. "He reminds me of my Charlie when he was younger."

"Thanks for the photo. I'll get it back to you as soon as I can."

"I'd appreciate that."

Eli looked over his notes and thought for a moment. "Rose, I know you said Ralph is private and doesn't discuss what he does at the White House, but did you notice anything different about him lately? Has he acted out of sorts, not like himself?"

Rose lowered her eyes but remained silent.

Eli could see her eyes flutter back and forth.

After a long pause, Rose said, "Well, he has been a little distant recently."

"Since when?" Eli asked.

"The past few weeks."

"Anything in particular that stands out?"

Rose stood up and paced the room. "He made comments about what I should do if anything happened to him."

Eli watched as he moved around. "And was that out of character?"

"Highly. He's never said anything like before."

"And?"

"He asked if I would take care of Italia."

"That's it?" asked Eli.

"It's the only thing I can think of, yes."

"Thank you for telling us," Eli said.

"Do you think he knew he might be in danger?"

Eli shrugged. "I don't know."

"Please find him, Agent Payne."

"We'll do our best, Rose," Eli said.

The conversation carried on for several more minutes. Eli took meticulous notes during the time they talked. He and Kat thanked Rose for her time and assured her they would be in touch soon. The last thing Eli did was give Rose his card and tell her to call anytime if she thought of something else that might help.

As Eli and Kat left the house and walked toward the car, he couldn't shake the feeling someone had eyes on him. Eli paused in the middle of the road, the hair on the back of his neck stood up. His eyes scanned the street in a grid pattern, looking for anything out of the ordinary. Nothing stood out, and the road appeared quiet.

His senses told him otherwise.

Something was off.

Kat took several steps past him, then came to a stop. She turned back. "What is it?"

"Nothing," he said after a few seconds. "Just a feeling."

"Good or bad?"

"I'm not sure."

They continued to the car, and Eli scanned the block once more as he stood next to the car door.

"What about Rose? Is she bat-shit crazy, or is this Ralph Webb missing?" Kat asked as she climbed into the car.

Eli pulled away as he shook his head. "I think she was sincere in her answers, but I do think she is holding out on us."

"How so?"

"Just her body language when she told us about him asking her to keep the cat."

"What about it?"

"There's something she didn't tell us."

"Thoughts on what it is?"

Eli shook his head. "Not yet."

"What's next?"

Eli smirked. "We head to the White House."

"Seriously?"

"Yes, I can't discount her story offhand. I need to see if this Ralph Webb exists."

"And you're going to march up to the front door of the White House?"

"Well, not the front door, no. More like the side door."

"You know what I mean. Why go there?"

"No reason to beat around the bush. We go to the source and see what we can find out."

Kat didn't respond to the comment but instead handed him the photo Rose provided. "Something is wrong with this picture."

"How so?"

"The man in this photo. He isn't a Ralph."

"Huh?"

"His name isn't Ralph," said Kat. "I'm telling you. He doesn't look like a Ralph."

Eli's cheeks moved toward his eyes. The motion caused his pronounced crow's feet to stand out as his eyes squinted. "And what does a person with the name Ralph look like exactly?"

Kat pointed at the photo. "Not that."

Eli rolled his eyes. "Whatever."

"You don't think people can look like their names?"

"Never really thought about it, I guess," Eli said.

"What if I introduced myself as Jasmine when we met earlier today?"

Eli let out a chuckle. "Well. I'd say you were either a stripper or your parents were Disney freaks."

She rolled her eyes. "I think you just made my point."

"Or I gave you a not too subtle ribbing."

Kat ignored the statement. "Look, I'm telling you it isn't his real name," came her retort as she pulled her phone out.

"Who are you calling, your parents?"

"No smartass. I'm confirming if Ralph Webb owns the townhouse across the street. I'll have Jessie back at the office run the property info down. And while he's at it, I'll have him see if Mr. Webb owns a vehicle and get the make and model."

"Who's Jessie?"

"Jessie James works on the second floor. He's the guy to contact if I needed any data from our sister agencies, places like the DMV."

"You're saying we have a guy named Jessie James at the office?"

"Yes."

"We have a William H. Bonney who works bank robbery cases as well?"

"Who's that?"

"You serious?"

"I am."

"Billy the Kid. Ever heard of him?"

"Didn't Emilio Estevez play him in that 1980's movie Young Guns?" Kat asked.

"You've seen that movie?"

"Sure, my dad enjoyed watching it when I was a kid."

Eli shook his head. "Who said to go to Jessie?"

"My first day on the job, I was given a list of resources by the special agent who taught the new recruit class."

"Huh, imagine that."

"I take it you didn't get a list when you started?"

"Not that I recall."

"And what do you do when you need something?"

"I yell, really loud."

"At?"

"Everyone. Until someone gets off their ass and gets me what I need."

"I guess that's why no one likes you."

Eli smiled. "Sweet. My charm offensive is working."

———◆———

A man sat slumped down in the car at the end of the street. His ball cap pulled low. He sat up after Eli pulled away. Pulled out his phone and dialed a number.

"Yes?" The person who answered said.

"We may have a problem."

"What type of problem?"

"The old woman." He said.

"You referring to the neighbor?" The person asked.

"Yes."

"What about her?"

"She called the Feds."

"Old news. We are aware of that already."

"They left her house."

"And?"

"I used the directional microphone and was able to listen to some of their conversations."

"What did she say?"

"The old woman knew something was wrong inside the house. That we went through his stuff."

"We don't need any complications."

"I understand. What do you want me to do?"

A pause occurred before the man responded. "Sit tight. Keep an eye on her, and let me make some calls."

"I need to get back into his house. We didn't find it yet."

"Negative, too much heat right now. We have to wait until things die down."

"And in the meantime?"

"Observe and report. When that changes, I'll let you know."

"There's another thing."

"Yes?" He asked.

"The two FBI agents are headed for the White House." The man said.

"What's your point?"

"Shouldn't we warn someone?"

"No. That's not our problem either. It's HIS problem."

6

WASHINGTON, D.C.

THE WHITE HOUSE

President Charles Steele sunk into his favorite Chesterfield leather chair and let out a deep sigh as his body relaxed. He reached up with his left hand and rubbed his temples. His right hand held a tumbler of Woodford Reserve, the amber liquid drowned quarter-sized ice balls. Charles loosened the red tie he wore since seven in the morning. He placed his feet on the walnut desk and leaned back. The chair had been a gift from Queen Elizabeth II when she had visited the previous fall. Six months before her trip to the United States, the president had traveled to England and stayed as a guest in Buckingham Palace. He loved the ornate furniture and spent many hours touring the palace. During his stay, he took an interest in one of her antique chairs, commenting on it several times. After the visit, the queen had commissioned a replica made for the president, which he accepted during her state visit to the White House.

His day had started at 5:30 a.m., as it had every day since he took the oath of office. The full presidential entourage had left Joint Base Andrews at 11:00 a.m. for midterm election campaign stops and had arrived back at the White House around 6:00 p.m. In the Oval, the president had signed paperwork and reviewed three executive orders before a late dinner with his wife in the residential dining room.

The president had retreated to the private study adjoining the Oval after dinner. Charles needed comfort and an element of normalcy, and his private office offered him both things. When he closed the study door, everybody in his administration knew to leave him alone. Those who didn't listen learned a lesson the hard way.

Tonight, he made the mistake of leaving the door cracked. Not fully shut, but certainly not wide open.

The president had two files on his desk. One on top was a red folder that contained an intel report brought earlier from the secretary of defense. The one on the bottom was jet black, and nobody, not even the senior members of his staff, touched it. With his family name embossed on the top in bold golden letters, the contents were for the president's eyes only.

Although the information inside the black folder gnawed at him, he decided to open the red file. The president leaned back in the chair and stretched his arms back over his head; a distinct cracking sound filled the room as his back popped.

The loud knock on the door startled him. The president leaned forward, and his feet came off the desk and onto the floor as the door crept inward.

"Yes," said the president in an irritated tone as his head snapped towards the door.

His chief of staff poked his head inside. "Sorry to bother you, Mr. President, but the door was slightly ajar."

"Yes, well, I meant to close that damn thing."

"My apologies, sir."

"It had better be important, Jacob."

Jacob Sterns cleared his throat. "I have an update for you, sir."

"Regarding?"

"It's about Danny, sir."

President Steele's scowl softened. "I'm all ears. Is he out of surgery?"

"The hospital called. Well, I should say the surgeon himself called."

"And?"

"He's alive. The doctor is not sure how he made it through the surgery, but the initial post-op scans appear promising."

"Permanent damage?"

"Too early to tell. But according to the doctor, the slug missed the internal carotid artery by a few millimeters."

"Meaning?"

"He's one lucky son of a bitch, Mr. President," Jacob said.

"Will he recover?"

"No way to know yet. He's on a ventilator and in a medically induced coma. The doctor said he had a 10 percent chance of surviving the surgery based on the trauma he sustained."

"How about the other wounds on his back?"

"Amazingly, the two bullets did no damage to his internal organs. They tore him up, but the surgeon said they were non-fatal injuries."

The president nodded. "The Secret Service attracts a unique breed, don't they?"

"I agree. The best of the best, Mr. President."

"Danny's a fighter. If anyone can beat this, he can."

"You're right, sir."

"Was the witness who saw the attack able to provide any useful feedback?"

"Not much. She believed the shooter was female, but the description applies to most joggers running along the Potomac. The eyewitness said the shooter jumped into a waiting van and fled the scene. D.C. Metro found the van torched in the Navy Yard a few hours ago." Jacob grew quiet but lingered even though the president said nothing.

An awkward moment passed.

"Is that all?" The president asked.

"No, sir. "

"What is it?"

"Wanted to talk with you about The Body Man, Mr. President."

"Has he been found?" The concern clear in the president's tone.

"No," came the reply. "But aren't you bothered he goes missing, and someone tries to kill his apprentice on the same day? I mean, they happened within hours of each other."

The president frowned; questions about how he felt irritated him. He exhaled a deep breath. "Yes, of course, I'm troubled," he said.

"They must be related," Jacob said.

"I don't believe in coincidences," the president answered, "but we must have more facts before jumping to any conclusions."

"Have you spoken with David?"

"Not since earlier today on Air Force One, but I can assure you the director of the Secret Service is taking today's incidents seriously, as he should."

"And in the meantime, is he appointing someone to take The Body Man's place?"

"I think that's a little premature, don't you?"

"We need a Body Man, Mr. President."

The president's eyes visibly rolled. "'Need' may be a bit of a stretch, Jacob."

Jacob bristled at the president's nonchalant remark. "Well, I'd feel better if we had one."

"No president had a Body Man before Kennedy," said the president as an indignant look crept over his face.

"And all of them have had one since, sir."

"You do your job, Jacob; let David and his team do theirs."

The president turned his head away and looked at the wall where a painting of John D. Rockefeller hung.

Jacob recognized the sign that the president had had enough of the conversation. "I'll let you be, Mr. President. Enjoy the rest of your night."

"Goodnight, Jacob. Don't work too late. Get home to Amy and the kids."

Jacob smiled. "Yes, sir."

The president's private phone rang, and he looked at the number with no change in expression. "I need to take this, Jacob. I'll see you tomorrow."

Jacob nodded, turned, and left, careful to pull the door fully closed on his way out by making sure he heard the distinct clicking sound.

As the door shut, the president picked up the black folder and then reached for the phone.

7

WASHINGTON, D.C.

It should have been an easy hit.

Even a two-bit thug from the streets could pull it off.

The handler vouched for her, even going as far as stating she was the best female assassin in the world. However, shooting Danny Frazier hadn't been enough; he needed to die, and there was no excuse for failure.

The man growled audibly, his frustration growing stronger as each second passed. His hands rolled into balls, and he struck the table several times in anger. Finally, after he collected his thoughts and compartmentalized his emotions, he reached into the drawer and pulled out a new burner phone.

The recipient answered on the second ring.

"You've got a problem," said the man, not even waiting for the person to answer.

"I have a problem, or we have a problem?"

"The asset fucked up. Now you have a problem."

"What are you talking about?"

"The mark is still alive."

Silence greeted the statement for almost ten seconds before the reply. "That's not possible. He took two slugs in his back and one in his skull at point-blank range. Nobody survives that."

"Well, Danny Frazier did."

"How?"

"I don't know how he fucking survived, but he's still sucking air, albeit through a plastic tube." The man's displeasure practically oozed from the other end of the phone.

"And what do you want me to do about it?"

"Where is she?" The man asked.

"Who?"

"Merci. The best female assassin in the world according to you. Is she still in the States?"

"You know better than to use actual names on cell calls. The NSA can ..."

"I don't give a flying fuck about the NSA or their PRISM capabilities. And besides, I'm on a burner."

"That is irrelevant; it doesn't ..."

The man's anger rose, and he cut the other person off. "What I care about is the job being done and done right. So, answer my damn question."

"No. She boarded a flight from Dulles several hours ago."

"Why?"

"She was given another task at the last minute."

"By whom?"

"HIM."

"You spoke with HIM personally?"

"No. But she did."

"He didn't inform me." The man said.

"Is he in the habit of excluding you?"

The man ignored the question. "Well, clearly he chose her for another task before he knew of her failure."

"What do you want me to do about it? What's done is done."

"She needs to be neutralized."

"That's out of the question."

"And how do you know she won't fail at the next task?"

"She won't."

"And if you're wrong?" The man asked.

"I'll put two slugs between her eyes myself."

The man considered the statement. "Fine. For now, she lives. But ..." His voice lingered without finishing the thought.

"But what?"

"We still have the apprentice to deal with."

"We?"

The man paused, "Well, by we, I mean you."

The person on the other end of the line sighed. "Where is he?"

"George Washington University Hospital."

"And what do you want me to do about it?"

"Finish the fuckin' job she started."

"What's his condition?"

"He's in a medically induced coma."

"Sounds like he's pretty well taken care of."

"If he has breath in his lungs, he's a threat to us." The man paused and added, "All of us."

"I thought he hadn't spoken with The Body Man?"

"We can't be sure what Danny knows, so finish the damn job."

"Is he guarded?"

"Heavily. The Secret Service isn't too keen on one of their agents getting gunned down in cold blood."

"Getting to Danny alone on the running trail was straightforward. Killing him now won't be."

"Your assassin should have done it right the first time, and we wouldn't be having this conversation, now would we?"

"This will take some planning."

"If he wakes up and starts talking, the morgue will get additional guests. You're smart enough to realize who it will be."

"Look, I'll get to him, but I need to be creative."

"And fast."

"I get it. I won't fail you."

"That's the spirit. See, you catch on fast."

With that, the line went dead.

———◇———

Several minutes of silence passed as Marcus Rollings held the phone in his hand.

Shit.

He picked up a clean burner phone and made a call across the pond. He didn't wait for the man who answered to say anything. "What time does her plane land?"

"Three hours," the voice on the other end said.

"And where is she staying?" Marcus asked.

"One of the safe houses in the countryside. Her target is currently in Reims."

"I need to speak with her as soon as possible. Tell her to call in when she gets a secure line."

"We both know she marches to her own drum."

"Trust me; I know that better than most. But I still need to pass along time-sensitive information."

"I'll have her call you as soon as she checks in."

Marcus clicked off the line and fired up his laptop. Within a few minutes, he had a detailed map showing the layout of the George Washington University Hospital.

It was going to be a late night.

No rest for the wicked, thought Marcus as he typed keywords into the search engine.

8

AT CRUISING ALTITUDE

The steady hum from the engines and heavily accented voices of his captors filled The Body Man's head once the plane took off. Thirty minutes had passed since they'd shoved him in the seat. At least that's what his internal clock told him.

With his head covered by a hood, his sense of hearing became more acute. If he moved his head far enough back, the bottom part of the hood expanded to reveal his waist, part of his legs, and his hands. Using his limited peripheral vision, he saw the flex cuffs his captors had used to bind his hands. The thick black plastic handcuffs looked like standard-issue double restraints with pull loops, the kind used by police forces and military units around the world. Simple yet efficient, they were easily purchased on countless websites for a few dollars apiece. A thin zip tie ran through the thick plastic and under the seat, keeping his hands from moving over six inches in any direction.

If only I had a piece of Kevlar cord to cut through them.

The Body Man knew he would have to use his ingenuity or brawn instead to attain freedom.

The noises changed, and the voices trailed off, moving away until only the engine noise rang in his ears. A distinct *click* sound indicated a door closed.

He glimpsed the outline of the plane on the tarmac as his hood blew off, but felt certain his abductors used a Bombardier Challenger 350. A jet enthusiast, he knew the configuration of most private planes. As a Secret Service agent, he had the added perk of flying on many airplanes in the US government fleet.

If I could only break free from these restraints and block the galley door somehow, I might have a chance to breach the cockpit and take control of the aircraft. Maybe force it to land somewhere and make a play for my freedom.

But first, before he could act on his impulse, The Body Man needed his hands free.

One task at a time, he reminded himself.

He pulled his flexed biceps toward his chest like he was doing an imaginary curl. Using all his strength, applied maximum pressure to the flex cuffs and the thin zip tie that connected them to the seat. He let out a muffled grunt, and the sudden *pop* sound as plastic snapped let him know the zip tie broke. His restrained hands hit hard against his chest, and he stayed still. The Body Man listened intently, wondering if anyone heard the noise.

With his hands able to move, he reached up and pulled off the hood. It took several seconds for his eyes to adjust to the sudden onslaught of light, but once they'd focused, he looked around for anything useful to remove the flex cuffs. His eyes zeroed in on a piece of metal that protruded from under the leather seat facing his own.

Reaching down, he sawed at the plastic flex cuffs, using the exposed metal. The process was slow and arduous, but within two minutes he had both hands free. He stood up and suddenly froze. Two rows up, a bald head cleared the top of a seat.

How didn't he hear me?

With slow, measured steps he approached the seated man and without giving him time to react, had his large arms wrapped around the man's neck. The Body Man performed a perfect carotid restraint, also known as a sleeper hold, and the bald man slumped over unconscious within seconds.

He quickly scanned the rest of the fuselage and found no one else. His eyes darted back and forth as he looked for something, anything he could use to block the rear door leading to the galley, where he believed the other captors must be. The fold-out executive table caught his eye. He moved toward it and, reaching underneath, found a release switch. The table came off its pedestal, and he hurried to the aft of the plane. Two high-backed captain chairs rested directly against the rear wall on either side of the galley door. The Body Man figured he could wedge the table between the seats and the wall, locking the door in a closed position and trapping any other captors.

Time worked against him, and he knew once he made a move, he was committed. With the galley door secured, he needed to breach the closed cockpit door and take control of the jet.

He picked up the table and jammed it down between the seats and the wall. Confident it was secure, he turned and barreled down the aisle toward the closed cockpit. Behind him, he immediately heard someone trying to open the jammed galley door to no avail.

He knew firsthand that private planes didn't have hardened doors like commercial airliners. The cockpit doors on the major carriers can withstand an immense amount of pressure, but that's not the case with small jets.

Five feet from the cockpit door, he lowered his right arm and turned his body slightly, leading with the thickest part of his shoulder. The Body Man slammed into the door with his full body mass, and the door gave way. A loud splintering sound indicated he shattered the structure as the door slid to his side and his body breached the narrow cockpit.

The co-pilot, who sat to the right, reached down to his side. He drew and leveled a Smith and Wesson .40-caliber pistol at The Body Man's chest. The co-pilot was fast, but his skills paled in comparison to The Body Man's abilities. Before the copilot could depress the trigger, The Body Man grabbed the gun and in one lightning fast motion spun the weapon around in the man's hands and trained it on him instead.

While the copilot's eyes grew wide with surprise, The Body Man didn't hesitate.

Rage pulsated through his cells like a rush of adrenaline.

The Body Man wrapped his finger around the trigger, angled the gun down in case the rounds went through since they were in a compressed air fuselage, and pulled twice in rapid succession. Two loud retorts filled the cockpit, and his ears felt like they might explode. The slugs slammed into the man's chest, and in an instant, two growing crimson spots spread over his pressed white shirt just left of his black tie. He watched as the life departed from the copilot's eyes.

Momentarily deaf, he spun toward the pilot.

The Body Man suddenly felt the ground drop out from beneath him as his body lurched toward the roof of the flight deck. For the briefest of seconds, he felt weightless, almost like the feeling of freefall when he used to skydive in his early twenties for the pure adrenaline rush.

As he smacked hard against the roof, his downward glance revealed the pilot pushing the control column forward, toward the flight control panel.

The jet entered a nosedive, and he plummeted back to the ground after the initial lurch upward.

If the pilot's goal was to throw him for a loop, he succeeded. But he didn't realize The Body Man worked best under the most extreme circumstances and possessed an unrivaled ability to adjust when others faltered. As the pilot pulled back to level off the plane, they had dropped over five thousand feet in a matter of seconds, far enough to put your stomach in a knot and expel whatever it held. Like a cat, The Body Man landed on his feet and wrapped his left arm around the pilot's neck.

With flesh pressed against flesh, he started a slow squeeze, like a python overcoming its prey. "Put this bird on the ground," he screamed, still partially deaf from the gunshot in close quarters. His voice sounded harsh, gravelly. "Because if I have to, it won't end well for any of us."

Under extreme duress, the pilot gave a subtle and strained head nod. His free hand reached down into the pocket hanging on the side of the chair. The pilot slowly removed a fixed-blade serrated knife but kept it low, hidden from view.

The Body Man continued to apply pressure but turned to check his six when he thought he heard a sound, despite his ringing ears. The pilot saw his head movement and with his left hand swung the blade wildly toward The Body Man's arm. He punctured the top of his bicep, pushed the knife into flesh and twisted.

His head snapped back toward the pilot, and he screamed out in pain as he cocked back his arm. His natural reflex to deliver a vicious blow on the side of the pilot's face.

The blade protruded from his left bicep, it wiggled back and forth from his raised arm.

He never got the chance to strike.

A thick black Maglite struck the top of his head with the force of a major-league slugger's thick bat on a helpless ball. He saw nothing but instant black as the ringing in his ears subsided, and everything faded.

Two burly captors dragged The Body Man's unconscious body out of the cockpit, where they tied him to a different chair. Unwilling to make the same mistake twice, they ignored the flex cuffs this time and used more suitable, escape-resistant bindings. Once secured, they yanked the knife protruding from his arm and wrapped the bleeding wound.

9

WASHINGTON, D.C.

Eli could see Kat glare at him out of the corner of his eye as he pulled off Interstate 66 onto the E Street Expressway. "What?" he asked.

"Are you going to share your plan with me, or are we walking up to the White House unannounced?"

"Relax. I know what I'm doing."

Kat shot him a glance that made it clear she wasn't convinced. "And that is?"

"I'm following a lead."

"Straight to the front door of the White House?"

"It's the people's house. So, it's our casa too."

"Uh-huh." Kat pursed her lips.

"Look, if this guy worked for the Department of Motor Vehicles, we'd head to the DMV. If he worked at Domino's, we'd go there, eat a shitty pizza, and spend the rest of the day on the shitter. But this Ralph Webb guy supposedly works at 1600 Pennsylvania Avenue. That's where we go. It's simple, really."

"You sure they'll even let us on the property?"

"Nope. But there's only one way to find out."

"You'd better not derail my career before it starts, Payne."

Eli smiled and made a clicking sound as he popped his tongue off the top of his mouth. "Trust me. I know what I'm doing."

"My ex-boyfriend tried that line once."

"And?"

"You heard what title it earned him."

"You're funny, Stone." Eli threw her a sideways glance. "And I'm not surprised you're single."

"Guess it takes a ballbuster to know one," she said.

As he took the turn onto 15th Street NW, the entrance to the White House grounds on E Street NW was on the left. His body tensed as he pulled in behind a silver Mercedes with D.C. plates.

The man at the checkpoint waved him forward as the Mercedes moved on. "Can I help you, sir?"

Eli displayed his badge, as did Kat.

The man's eyes narrowed as he scrutinized both FBI badges.

"Special Agent Eli Payne and Agent Katherine Stone. We're working a missing-person case."

"And the purpose of your visit to the White House?" the uniformed officer asked without looking up from the IDs.

"We have reason to believe the missing person works at the White House."

"Which department?"

Eli paused, knowing the words about to come out of his mouth would set off alarm bells. At least he figured they would. "Secret Service."

The uniformed officer visibly stiffened at the two words, his head jerked up, and eyes narrowed as he stared at Eli. "Hold tight for a minute, Agent Payne." The man turned, entered the small building, and picked up a phone. He turned back several times and leered at Eli and Kat as he spoke into the receiver.

A minute later, he returned and handed the ID's back. "Pull forward. Take your first right, and park in an open space on the left-hand side. An agent will meet you at your vehicle."

Eli nodded and did as instructed.

"Well, made it past the front gate," Eli said as he pulled forward.

"Guess you piqued their curiosity," Kat replied.

"We'll see what it does beyond that."

"You having second thoughts?"

"No. But I have a sneaking suspicion we won't be getting a big welcome committee."

"Story of your life?" Kat asked.

Eli chuckled. "Yeah, Kat. That would be the story of my life."

An imposing man dressed in a navy-blue suit with a white curly wire leading from his ear to his collar was at the side of the car within seconds of Eli putting the car in park.

Eli stepped out, and the man extended his hand. "Brandon Walker, Special Agent in Charge."

"Special Agent Eli Payne, and this is Agent Katherine Stone."

Agent Walker shook Eli's hand. The first thing Eli noticed was the man had a grip that could crush rocks. Next, he observed the man's stare; it was not friendly.

"Please follow me so we can speak in private," Agent Walker said.

"Of course."

Eli and Kat followed a step behind the towering figure. As they approached the building from the east, Eli recalled taking the White House tour as a teenager, back when it was easy to get tickets pre-9/11 and before the world and D.C. security changed forever.

Times are different now, and not really for the better, Eli thought.

He hesitated as they crossed the threshold to the east entrance. Memories of her raced through his mind. He hadn't expected this reaction, not after so much time had passed. Always good at compartmentalizing, Eli had believed the feelings were locked away where they belonged.

Not so.

Kat noticed the hesitation. "You good?"

"Yeah," Eli said, "just thinking."

"I know. I saw the steam."

As Eli and Kat stepped inside the building, they found four large men with serious expressions and physical builds similar to Agent Walker. A metal detector blocked the way forward, while an x-ray machine stood to its right.

"I'll need to ask both of you to surrender your weapons," Agent Walker said in a forceful tone.

"You got it, boss." Eli removed his Glock 22 from his side holster, pulled up his pant leg, and unstrapped a Walther PK380. He passed them over, and Kat did the same with her Bureau-issued Glock 23.

Once through security, and with visitor passes prominently displayed, Eli and Kat were led by Agent Walker down the Center Hall and past the North Hall, where they took a right and entered the Secret Service offices. Guiding them through several rooms, he turned into a conference room and closed the door behind them.

He pointed to two seats. "Please," he said as he gestured to the chairs.

Eli and Kat did as they were asked.

"I hear you're working a missing-person case. Is that the purpose of your visit?"

"It is," Eli said.

"And you believe the person in question works for the Secret Service?"

"That's correct."

Agent Walker looked back and forth between Eli and Kat, and settled his gaze on Eli. "What's his or her name?"

"Ralph Webb," Eli said.

Barely a second passed before Walker responded. "Never heard of him."

"You sure?"

"I know all my guys, Agent Payne, and I can assure you there's no Ralph Webb at the White House. Maybe he's over at Treasury or assigned somewhere else?"

Eli looked at Kat.

She raised her eyebrows and nodded subtly.

"We have reason to believe the name is a fake," Eli said. "I'm working on a hunch, but the elderly neighbor that made the missing-person call might have been provided an alias to protect his true identity."

"Or the neighbor is mistaken," Walker countered.

"Of course, that's a possibility as well."

"Let me run the name through our database. Like I said, maybe this Ralph Webb works at another location. I'll be right back."

Agent Walker left the room in a rush and closed the door.

"Not often you find yourself in the White House," Kat said.

"And piss off the Secret Service at the same time," Eli replied with an eye roll.

"He did look mad, didn't he?"

"These guys are wired pretty tight. And trust me, they don't like it when the Bureau shows up on the property."

"A little fed rivalry?"

"Something like that," Eli said.

The conference room door opened three minutes later, and Agent Walker stepped inside.

"Well, I hate that you drove down here, but there's no Ralph Webb in our system. So, if there's nothing else." Walker stepped toward the door.

That was quick, Eli thought.

Kat didn't move.

"One more thing." Eli removed the picture from his pocket and slid it across the table.

Agent Walker stepped toward the table, leaned over and looked down at the picture, his eyes blinking faster than before.

He watched the reaction on Walker's face. "Have you ever seen that man?" Eli asked.

"Never." Agent Walker looked up and to the right.

Eli noticed the tell.

As did Kat.

"You're sure?"

"Positive. I take it this is Mr. Webb?"

"It is," Eli said.

"He doesn't work for me or at the White House in any capacity. I can assure you of that."

Eli retrieved the picture and stood up. "I appreciate your time. Sorry if you feel we wasted it."

"Merely doing your job, Agent Payne. Trust me; I get it. And I hope this Ralph Webb turns up safe and sound really soon."

"As do I." Eli paused at the door. "Oh, one more question."

"What?" There was no mistaking the perturbed tone from Agent Walker.

"Do you have any missing agents?"

"Of course not. All my people are accounted for."

"Thanks," Eli said.

—◦—

Mila Hall stepped out of the Palm Room and entered the Center Hall on her way to the Secret Service offices on the ground floor for a venue assessment meeting. She was late. Mila hated being late. Several steps into the Center Hall, her body jerked to a stop as she saw the distinct profile of a man taking a left-hand turn and walking in the opposite direction. Even though it had happened in a split second, she had no doubts who she saw.

What is he doing here?

Her heart rate doubled, and the muscles in her shoulders constricted as she watched him walk side by side down the Center Hall with a woman she didn't recognize. They took a sharp left at the end of the corridor and disappeared.

Once he was out of sight, Mila quickened her pace and entered the small waiting area in the Secret Service office suite.

"Sandy," she asked the woman who sat behind the reception desk. "Who was the man and woman who just left?"

"Two FBI agents," Sandy said.

"What were they here for?"

"They met with Agent Walker."

"Was it about him?" Mila asked, a touch of concern in her voice.

Sandy nodded silently.

Mila turned and looked at her watch. The meeting was about to start. *I wonder how much Eli knows?*

Once they were inside the car with the doors closed, Eli started the engine, and they looked at each other.

"He lied to us," Kat said. "Besides being a total asshole."

"I agree on both counts."

"You could see it in his eyes."

"Yeah, as soon as he saw that picture. But did you notice he didn't recognize the name?" Eli asked.

"Yes, I picked up on that."

"Interesting." Eli stroked his chin.

"Rumor around the office is that you're a pretty well-connected guy," Kat said. "Know people in almost every agency."

"True."

"But, no Secret Service contacts?"

"I had one." Eli didn't elaborate.

"And?" Kat asked.

"It soured."

"You piss the guy off with your world-class charm?" she asked with a faint smile.

Eli raised his eyebrows. "I never said it was he, did I?"

"Ah, the plot thickens. What's next, Casanova?"

Eli stuck his middle finger up. "We need to get inside Webb's townhouse. Or whatever the hell his name is."

"Tonight?"

Eli looked at his watch. "I'd prefer first thing in the a.m. since it'll be dark by the time we get there. I would rather work a scene in the daylight with a fresh set of eyes."

Kat smirked. "And it has nothing to do with the fact that the football game starts in less than an hour?"

"Never crossed my mind," Eli said with a wry grin.

"You lie as well as Agent Walker."

They rode in silence for a minute before Kat's cell phone rang.

Eli only heard one side of the brief conversation.

"Sounds like you got an update?"

"Yes, that was Jessie," Kat said. "He ran the property records, and the townhouse is registered under the name Ralph Webb. Looks like he bought it about four years ago, and also has a black Audi A8 registered under the same name.

Eli nodded. "Good work, and that's a sweet ride. Not many Secret Service agents can swing the payments on a car like that."

She ignored the compliment on the type of car Ralph drove. "It's still not his real name," Kat said. "No matter what the property records or DMV might say."

"I agree."

"Plan of attack tomorrow?" she asked.

"We need to confirm if he's missing or not. And figuring out his real identity would be a good start as well."

"Sounds pretty straightforward, right?"

"Not exactly. Things may seem easy, but those often take the longest time."

"Guess I have a lot to learn."

"It never stops, Kat. Once you think you've got it all figured out, something invariably helps pull the rug out from under you."

"So cynical," Kat said.

"I prefer to be thought of as a realist."

Kat smiled. "Ok. Really cynical."

10

— · —

THE GULF OF MEXICO

The jet's tires screeched as rubber met concrete, and a shudder through the fuselage which jostled The Body Man awake.

He tried to move, but his captors had restrained his upper body and legs after the incident in the cockpit. Slumped to one side, he fought a wave of nausea. His head felt like a drummer had placed a snare against the crown of his skull and played a Metallica song in an endless loop. Swallowing hard, he pushed down the urge to vomit and forced himself upright. His arm throbbed from the knife wound, and he wondered which hurt worse: his head or arm.

With the hood once again keeping him in relative darkness, he cocked his head slightly and listened. Several voices spoke nearby, but their muted tones prevented him from making out specific words.

He didn't know how long he had been out.

The voices grew louder as someone approached and he made out a few words from at least two men. They both spoke English, but with heavy accents that sounded Eastern European.

Russian maybe? One of the Baltic States?

Someone forcefully grabbed his leg and cut the restraint that kept his feet bound together. For the briefest of moments, it felt good to move his feet back and forth independent of each other. The freedom of movement was short-lived though, as one of the captors jerked him upwards.

His feet didn't touch the floor as the two men carried him sideways down the narrow aisle of the plane. His knees hit the seats as they hauled him toward the front. At the top of the airstairs, the unmistakable thumping sound of rotor wash filled his ears.

From a plane to a chopper?

Once inside the helicopter, his captors restrained him once again. Within seconds, the helicopter ascended rapidly, and his ears popped from the pressure. The sound of the rotors meant he couldn't make out any voices. The only noise he heard was the rhythmic beat of the helicopter.

With nothing else to do, he counted. Time slowed to a snail's pace as the chopper moved toward the unknown. Fortunately, his years in the Secret Service had taught him invaluable skills, the primary one being patience.

As they descended and finally touched down, he calculated they had traveled for roughly ten minutes.

The door to the left slid open, and he immediately recognized the smell wafting past his nose. Having grown up in Kill Devil Hills on the Outer Banks of North Carolina, he knew the unmistakable scent from miles away.

Saltwater.

The Body Man lived the salt life for much of his adolescence and missed the ocean. He rarely saw it now that he lived in Washington. Kayak trips in the Chesapeake Bay with members of the Secret Service weren't the same as his childhood ocean adventures.

Now outside, his senses went into overdrive.

He felt the moisture against his exposed skin and breathed the salt air through his hood in deep gasps. A gust of wind caused by the rotors sprayed him with a fine mist of water and he felt the ground shift slightly under his feet. The shudder was subtle, but he noticed the tremor.

Wait. Are we on a boat in the ocean?

His mind reeled as he immediately thought about the *Ark*.

In the early 2000's during the height of the war on terror, the Bush administration turned a former cargo ship into an off-the-books mobile prison. Known as a black site, clandestine agencies conducted extreme rendition activities on the ship far from the media or anyone else. With a name like the *Ark*, someone in the administration either had a wicked sense of humor or took the Bible way too literally.

It can't be, he thought. *The Ark's been shut down for almost a decade.*

Plus, he knew black sites no longer existed. The last president had seen to that. A not-too-subtle dig at the CIA, which he despised. Publicly, the president praised the agency, while privately he attempted to gut their clandestine services. Still, rumors persisted, and some believed black sites still existed with no ties to the United States government.

The Body Man didn't have time to dwell on the idea as his captors had him off the ground as he moved forward. He heard a metallic sound with each step.

Then they stopped. One man grabbed his ankles and forcefully separated them slightly. He felt the cool steel on his skin, then heard the unmistakable sound of leg cuffs tightening around his ankles.

His hands remained flex-cuffed behind his back.

One man shoved him forward. He stumbled slightly but maintained his balance and shuffled along as fast as he could, considering the restraints.

A firm grip grabbed his shoulders and stopped him with a jostle.

The sound of an electronic buzzer and the release of a lock followed by the screech of steel sliding on steel indicated a door of some sort had opened. The same firm hand squeezed his shoulder and directed him forward. They passed through two more electronic doors before coming to a stop.

A raspy voice before him said, "Prisoner's name?"

"I'm not a priso ..." he said.

A vicious punch to the side of his head mid-word dropped him to the ground. Not knowing he was about to get hammered had made it worse. He had no way to brace himself for the brutal impact. Lying on his back, he felt a trickle of liquid flow from his ear.

One of his captors grabbed him by his shirt and with two hands pulled him back to his feet.

"You don't speak unless spoken to. Do you get that, prisoner?" asked a man with a heavy Eastern European accent only inches from his bleeding and ringing ear.

Prisoner. There was the word again. What the hell? He thought.

Not interested in getting struck again, he said, "Got it."

Next, an eerie silence as his ear simultaneously throbbed and rang.

The man to his right said in a thick accent, "Prisoner is known as The Body Man."

Fuck, he muttered under his breath. *Did he just say what I thought he said?*

"We've been expecting this prisoner. He's late."

"We delayed," the man said in broken English. "Just sign him in and take off our hands."

"Patience," cautioned the man with the raspy voice. "The Sanctum has rules for these types of transfers. Rules everyone adheres to."

A few minutes of silence followed. Finally, the raspy-voiced man said, "Everything appears in order."

Another buzzing sound as a door opened down the hallway to The Body Man's right. He could make out multiple footfalls as two people approached.

"These men will take possession of the prisoner. You can leave now."

One of his captors gave him a parting punch in the kidney. He doubled over, the pain intense.

"Fuck you, Body Man," said the voice in a vitriolic tone. "That was for Boris, my friend you killed on the plane."

A moment later, two men led him down a long hallway and through one more secured door into a room. They sat him on a hard, metallic chair in front of a table. The guard cut the flex cuffs, which released his hands from behind his back. He rolled his wrists around, grateful for the sudden relief from his bonds, but he didn't get a chance to enjoy the freedom long as both wrists were pulled in front of his body and handcuffed. The guard ran the restraints through a large steel ring connected to the top of the table. Then he did the same with the leg cuffs, affixing them to a ring welded to the floor under the table.

From the frying pan to the fire, he thought.

Once secured, the guard removed the hood. His eyes involuntarily squinted at the bright light from the fixture hanging above the stainless-steel table, and it took a minute before they adjusted.

When he could finally see, he looked around the stark room. Everything in the room, which only comprised a table and two chairs facing each other, was metal.

The Body Man sat in silence.

He tried to shift his weight and move the chair, but it didn't budge. With his hands bound, he tried to move the table without luck, since everything appeared bolted in place. The space contained a door to his left and mirrored glass on the wall across from him. He figured it was a two-way mirror. The other walls were barren, painted a gunmetal gray color.

Ten minutes passed. He stared at the mirror and wondered how many people watched him from the other side. Like a caged animal on display.

He looked at his reflection, and it confirmed he looked like hell. Dried blood covered much of his face, caked up around his nose and ears. But he didn't care about his appearance.

The door buzzed and opened.

In walked a man dressed in khaki pants with a blue dress shirt and brown loafers. The Body Man stared at the man as he moved toward the table. He looked to be about five feet, eleven inches and probably about one hundred and seventy-five pounds. The man walked with a slight limp on the right leg. He wore black round rimmed glasses and had brown hair parted from right to left. His hair was graying around the temples, and The Body Man guessed the man was likely in his early sixties. His face appeared expressionless as he stared back.

The man took a seat in the chair across, his back to the mirror. In his hand was a thick manila folder. He removed the contents and placed the papers down on the table to his right.

"Greetings, prisoner," he said in a flat tone as he looked directly into The Body Man's eyes.

"I have a name."

"That's right, and here in this facility your name is prisoner."

The Body Man paused for a moment. He spent enough time with his counterparts at Camp Peary, also known as "The Farm," and knew what to expect. He considered his words before he replied. "And what do I call you?"

"You may call me 'Sir.'"

"I take it you know who I am, Sir?" The Body Man said.

"Yes, I do, prisoner."

"Then you know who I work for?"

Sir smiled and rapped his knuckles against the file. "I know who you worked for, prisoner, past tense. I know more about you than you realize."

"I was taken against my will. I have rights as an American citizen."

"Wards of the Sanctum no longer have rights."

That was the second time he heard that word since he entered the facility.

What in the hell is the Sanctum?

"I don't know what you're talking about. And what is the Sanctum?"

Sir didn't respond.

"Where am I?"

Again, the question only produced silence.

"What do you want?" The Body Man asked.

Finally, after about a minute without response, Sir said, "Those are all relevant questions for you, I'm sure. But I'm not here to answer your questions. You're here to answer mine."

With his mouth open slightly, The Body Man's tongue reached back to his missing molar.

Sir saw the movement and smirked.

"Like a good soldier, willing to die instead of revealing what he knows. I respect your dedication to honor death over compromise."

"I'll never talk. You should know that."

The man leaned in closer. "That's what they all say. Eventually, they talk. Every man has his breaking point."

The Body Man stared back in defiance. His eyes squinted, revealing deep crow's feet. "Not me," he replied.

"I heard about the incident on the plane."

No response.

"Why did you shoot him?" Sir asked.

"He tried to kill me, and I reacted."

"You felt killing him was justified?"

His eyes narrowed, his gaze piercing. "Without question."

"You like to operate in a world of black and white, don't you, prisoner?"

"No, I live in the gray area. I exist in the space between both right and wrong."

Sir nodded. "Well, you've had a long day, and by the look on your face, you've been roughed up. My men will escort you to a room, and you will get some rest, prisoner. We'll start fresh after you've recovered some strength."

The Body Man said nothing. The door buzzed, and two men entered. They removed his restraints from the hooks on the table and floor and pulled him out of the chair roughly.

"Till we speak again, prisoner," said Sir. "Get some rest."

The Body Man stared back at him with an icy glare, but said nothing.

"You're going to need it," Sir said.

Ever since his captors had stuffed him in his Audi and he realized the capsule was gone, The Body Man's mind had never stopped calculating probabilities and ways of escape. As the two guards pushed him into his cell, he saw an opportunity. Whether it was the best chance or not didn't matter; he knew that to survive, he must first escape.

As the guard closest to him undid his leg shackles and reached for his wrist cuffs, The Body Man twisted his body 180 degrees and landed a vicious round-house kick to the sternum of the guard behind him near the door. The sound of a heavy foot meeting bone echoed a cringe-worthy cracking sound in the small space as the man's breastbone cracked.

Startled, the remaining guard who held his wrist drew his right hand back to strike. The motion proved much too late as he pulled back his extended leg and swiped the other guard's legs out from under him.

Down on the ground, The Body Man was on the man in an instant. With his hands still bound by the wrist cuffs, he climbed atop the man lying prostrate and slid the cold steel under the man's face until it touched the warm flesh of the guard's neck. He pulled his bound hands toward him and applied a tremendous amount of pressure, enough to crush the guard's windpipe in mere seconds.

He would have done that if two other guards hadn't arrived.

The electric jolt from the taser turned his body rigid as the 200,000 volts provided the intended consequence. He convulsed and fell forward, landing on top of the guard below him.

Dropping the taser, the guard removed a baton that hung from his belt loop and delivered non-stop blows to The Body Man's stunned body.

11

PALO ALTO, CALIFORNIA

Jase Marshall looked down at his watch. For once he was early. Not a common feat for a man who struggled with being on time every day of his life. Fortunately, he chose a profession that didn't concern itself with punctuality.

As a programmer for Apple, Jase found the work rewarding financially while dull intellectually. Most days, life felt like the movie *Groundhog Day*.

Jase wrote code for the newest iOS software updates Monday through Friday. Weekends were a blur, and a new week arrived way too fast. His life was in one word, boring. But everything changed when a fellow programmer introduced him to the dark web. The more he learned about the Internet not seen through standard search engines, the more the hidden world fascinated him.

He entered chat rooms and met enigmatic people, willingly immersing himself in a hidden culture few lusers, a tech term for an unsophisticated Internet user, experienced. Then late one night he stumbled upon a person who went by the screen name Mammon. Their interaction started innocently enough until one day, the mysterious person made a request. Jase thought it was a joke at first but soon wondered if maybe Mammon was a Fed trying to entrap him.

The request was highly illegal and even frightened him at first. But before long, the thought of pulling it off made him feel alive in some sick, twisted way. Butterflies flooded his stomach, and the hair on his neck stood up as Mammon discussed specifics weeks later, offering assurances he was no Fed. The promise of a large sum of money followed, but Jase didn't accept the job for the money; he did it for the thrill.

He did it to feel alive.

It took him almost a month, yet somehow the government never even knew he cracked into one of their most secure servers. The thrill of succeeding overwhelmed any feeling of guilt he encountered as he downloaded the documents and schematics. Jase half expected men in black outfits to burst into his room when he downloaded the last file, but nothing happened. Only the sound of his air purifier broke the silence of the room.

For a few hours, he felt on top of the world. When he reached out to Mammon, he received a set of specific instructions.

Forty-eight hours later, he sat in his car. Jase felt nervous, more than when he had stolen the actual data. His eyes darted from one face to another as he looked down the road and into the rearview mirror.

Too late for second thoughts.

He reached over and cranked the air conditioning on his Tesla Model S to its highest setting. The icy cold air chilled his stressed body.

His car idled on the side of Alma Street, one block from Stanford University. Nervously, he tapped the steering wheel to the beat of ACDC's song *Shoot to Thrill* as the catchy tune played through his Bose speakers. The sudden rap on the passenger window startled him. Jase's eyes darted to his right, and he saw a figure hunched over wearing a dark brown hoodie. The person wore dark pants; a gray satchel hung over his shoulder exactly as Mammon had described.

Jase unlocked the doors and turned off the music. His heart pounded in deep pulses and felt as if it would burst from his chest.

The stranger climbed in and pointed forward. "Drive," he said.

"First, I need to confirm who you are," Jase said.

The man in the hoodie pulled out a gun from under his sweatshirt, cocked back the exposed hammer and pointed it at Jase's head. The tip of the cold steel pressed against his forehead. "I'm Mark Zuckerberg, bitch," said the hooded man as he removed the gun from Jase's head and stuffed it back under his clothes. "Now drive the damn car."

"Where to?" Jase asked as he gulped hard.

"Drive. I'll tell you when to turn."

They drove in silence for forty minutes except for the occasional instruction to turn. As they pulled off Highway 9 into Castle Rock State Park, the man indicated where to pull off the side of the road. Dusk arrived as the sun disappeared into the waters of the Pacific.

Once Jase had the car turned off, they sat for a minute in dead silence. His heart raced, and he tugged his shirt collar away from his neck while beads of sweat formed on his brow.

"Over there," the man said as he pointed to an outcropping of rocks.

"I'm comfortable right here," Jase replied as he tapped his leather seat.

"Too bad. We'll conclude our business out there." The words uttered in a forceful tone.

Stay in the car, Jase's mind screamed.

He should have listened to his inner muse.

The man in the hoodie climbed out of the Tesla and led the way. Jase reluctantly followed at a slower pace.

As they neared the edge of the steep drop off the man in the hoodie turned. "You got the zip drive?"

"Yes."

"Let me see it," the man growled.

"I want my money first."

The man's eyes squinted, and the look of displeasure grew on his face.

Jase continued, "Mammon said I get paid, and then I give you the drive. A deal is a deal." It took all the courage Jase had to utter the words.

The man in the hoodie grunted but didn't reply. He walked past Jase, away from the edge of the drop off and stopped. Pulling out his smartphone he opened an app and typed a few characters before showing it to Jase, who initially took a step back and got closer to the edge.

"Transfer is complete."

Jase looked skeptical.

"Check your account," the man said. "I insist."

Jase took out his phone and went to the website of the offshore bank account he set up a few weeks before. A few clicks later he confirmed it was all there.

"We good?" the man asked.

"Yes," Jase said.

"Give me the zip drive."

"It's encrypted."

"It'd better be. Your instructions were specific."

Jase handed over the zip drive as the man in the brown hoodie pulled a tablet from his gray satchel. Inserting the stick into the tablet, he keyed in the eighteen-digit agreed-upon encryption key.

Curiosity got the best of Jase. "Are you Mammon?" he asked.

The man in the hoodie looked up from the tablet's screen. His eyes bore inside Jase's soul. "No."

"But you work for him?"

"I'm here," came the reply. "That's all you need to know." The man looked back at the screen and perused the documents from the zip drive. Satisfied everything was included, he nodded his head. "It's all here."

"I told Mammon it would be," Jase said.

"And he appreciates your attention to detail." The man in the hoodie reached back into his satchel and removed a Walther PPQ M2 with a suppressor. It was a different weapon than he pulled on Jase inside the Tesla.

"Hey, wait ..." Before Jase could finish the statement, two suppressed muzzle flashes exploded from the end of the gun, illuminating the night.

Both bullets found their target between Jase's eyes as his body crumpled and fell off the edge of the rock outcropping. His lifeless corpse landed two hundred feet onto the rocks below.

———— ◆◇◆ ————

The man in the brown hoodie stepped to the edge and peered over the side of the drop-off. Barely visible below, he made out the outline of a motionless body on top of a massive boulder. Satisfied Jase was dead, he stuffed the gun back in his bag and walked toward the Tesla. He wiped down the seat and door handle as another vehicle arrived.

He climbed into the passenger seat as the driver of the car nodded but said nothing. The instructions were explicit. Drive and don't speak.

The vehicle sped away from the scene and a minute later took Highway 9 headed east. Once the car reached Highway 35, the man in the brown hoodie placed a call. "I've got it," he said.

"You sure it's all there?" The voice on the other end asked.

"Yes. We have everything."

"Good. There's a jet waiting for you at the Palo Alto Airport. Hurry up. I'm needed back east, and you've got another job."

"I'm on my way."

12

———— • ————

VIENNA, VIRGINIA

A small stream of drool ran down the tinted glass, pooling on the rubber seal lining the door frame. The sudden ringing of the cell phone startled the driver from his momentary slumber as the phone display read 3:33 a.m.

The driver swiped his finger to the right and answered the call. "Hello," he said in a groggy voice as he rolled his neck back and forth until it cracked multiple times.

"Are you both asleep?" A stern voice asked. It sounded like a father scolding a child who disobeyed him one too many times.

"No, of course not. We've been taking shifts." The driver lied with ease as he threw a hard elbow at the man to his right who was curled up in the passenger seat and snored loudly.

With a loud grunt followed by an audible, "what the hell?" the passenger stirred.

The driver ignored the outburst and continued talking to the man on the phone. "She fell asleep around 10:00 p.m. The streets have been quiet. A bunch of middle-aged people with grown kids and retirees live around here."

"Well, it's time to get to work."

"Where we headed?" The driver asked.

"Inside his townhouse."

"But I thought with all the heat we had to lay low?"

"Change of plans. You need to get in there and find it before dawn."

"Clean or dirty?" The driver asked.

"Dirty is fine, but don't wake the neighbors. It may be your last chance before the feds show up. No excuses this time, and if the heat shows up, you're on your own."

He ignored the comment. "But when the feds arrive, they'll know someone tossed it."

"That's not our concern. Find the damn thing. No excuses."

"Roger that."

"Damn, that hurt," Don said as he held his ribcage.

"Boss says it's time to work, and I had to wake your fat ass up," Ryan said.

"Next time shake my shoulders or something. You don't need to be a dick."

"Stop whining. Grab the two duffel bags from the trunk and get inside. Dawn is in a few hours, and we need to wrap up by the time the sun rises."

Two minutes later, Ryan stood before the thick oak front door painted forest green. He used the same snap gun as earlier and within fifteen seconds, had the tumbler lock disengaged. Once inside, he carefully closed the door and re-engaged the lock.

Both men slipped on LED headlamps to keep their hands free.

"I'll take the main floor. You start on the second level," Ryan said as he handed Don one of the duffel bags. "Keep the house lights off and the blinds closed. We don't need to attract any unwanted attention."

"Got it."

Once Don headed for the stairs, Ryan started his search in the living room. Earlier he checked behind all the paintings and photographs, finding nothing. "Dirty" meant he could ransack the place without any repercussions. Ryan removed a claw hammer from the bag and started wrenching several of the bookshelves away from the walls. He checked the walls and punctured the sheetrock in several places.

Nothing.

Next, he started tapping on the floor in a grid pattern, listening for any empty or hollow spots. The noise upstairs indicated Don must've been doing the same. Using the hammer, he pulled up dozens of hardwood floor pieces.

Still nothing.

After thirty minutes, the only thing he found was a cat under the couch. But even that was short lived as the feline quickly retreated to another room after giving him a distinct hiss. Ryan wrapped up the search in the living room and moved to the kitchen and pantry. He knew from years of experience that crafty people hid important items in the most obscure spots.

He removed every drawer, moved the appliances, and even popped off tiles from the backsplash. An hour later, frustration set in as he hadn't located any secret compartment or hiding place.

Don's frantic call from upstairs over the two-way radio interrupted his train of thought.

"Get up here. I think I found something in the master," Don said.

Ryan dropped his hammer and made his way upstairs two steps at a time.

He entered the master bedroom and found Don next to a large mahogany bookshelf.

Beside the bookshelf, the large room contained a cherry-colored king-sized sleigh bed, matching armoire, and a long six-drawer dresser. Thick ivory carpet covered the floor, which was pulled up in several places.

"What do you got?" Ryan asked.

"Worked my way through the upstairs and found jack shit. After starting in his room, I came across this bookshelf."

"What about it?"

"Tried to pry it from the wall with no luck. I cleared all the shelves and looked for mounting screws but couldn't find any. Then I found this. Check it out."

Don crouched low to the ground on the left side of the bookshelf and showed Ryan the hidden pivot hinge concealed where the ivory carpet met the baseboard.

"I felt something metal when I rubbed my hands through the carpet. When I pulled it back and saw the hinge, I figured I'd better call you."

"Smart move," Ryan said.

"You think if we both use the big crowbars, we can pop it open?" Don asked.

Ryan shook his head. "No need. Give me a minute. There must be a release somewhere. This isn't a shitty do-it-yourself cabinet from that IKEA hellhole. Someone crafted this bookshelf by hand. He had to have a talented carpenter custom make this thing. It must have cost a pretty penny."

He started low and worked his way up the right side until he found it. A small indent no bigger than a postage stamp that felt different from the rest of the smooth wood. Pushing the spot hard with his index finger, he heard the distinct *click* sound as the mechanism keeping the shelf adhered to the wall disengaged.

Ryan grabbed one of the middle shelves and gave a firm tug. The door swung open, and a whoosh of air passed through the room.

As Ryan stepped inside, he found a light switch on the right side of the entryway. He flipped the switch and illuminated the room. The space was narrow, no more than five feet wide, but the length appeared to be the entire size of the master bedroom, some twenty feet long.

He looked back at Don and frowned. "Didn't I tell you to check the measurements of all the rooms?" Ryan asked.

"Yeah, and I did," Don said with a bewildered look on his face.

Ryan pulled up the house schematic from his iPad. The master bedroom showed twenty-five by twenty on the diagram. He stepped out of the hidden room and removed his laser distance measuring tool from his back pocket. Within ten seconds he had his numbers. Twenty by twenty. "Well, asshole. If you did what I said instead of lying to me, we'd have found this hidden room an hour ago."

Don's upper lip turned to a snarl. "We found it now, didn't we?"

Ryan knew to argue the point made no sense. He shook his head and walked back into the room. As he looked to the right, he noticed one entire wall was lined with pegboard and hooks holding various firearms: semi-automatic rifles, some with suppressors; two sniper rifles; shotguns; and handguns. Ammo of varying calibers lined the opposite wall.

"Jesus," Don said as he stepped in behind Ryan and glanced to his right. "Is this dude a Secret Service agent or a prepper?"

"Don't touch the bang bang's," Ryan said as he threw his head to the left and pointed to the opposite end of the room. "That's what we came for, after all."

At the end of the narrow room, a black safe with a twelve-digit keypad built into the wall about four feet off the ground beckoned.

Don smiled. "Pay dirt."

"Can you open it?"

Don walked to the far side of the room and examined the safe. "No problem. It's pretty run of the mill. This model costs around two grand. Might be rated for burglary and fire, but anyone that knows their way around a safe can crack it quickly with minimal tools."

"How long?" Ryan asked.

"Ten minutes, max. Let me grab my gear."

"Hurry up."

Eight minutes later, the safe door opened.

The top shelf held several stacks of documents and bundles of cash. The middle shelf had a gun, two mags, and more papers, while the bottom contained only a thick manila envelope.

Ryan grabbed the envelope and slid the contents out.

He smiled.

"We got it," Ryan said.

"Are we done?" Don asked.

"First, put that stuff he gave us into the safe with the other papers, then let's clear out before we overstay our welcome and the heat shows up."

"Understood."

"On the way out, we need to grab his laptop and printer from the downstairs office."

"I'm on it."

Ryan left the safe door open, turned, and walked away.

"Whoa, hold on," Don grabbed Ryan's shoulder. "What about the cash? There's got to be a hundred grand in Benjamins on that shelf."

Ryan frowned. "You know the rules. Leave it. We got what we came for. Don't be greedy."

"Boss don't need to know."

"I'll know," Ryan said. "Shut your damn mouth and collect our gear. We're outta here in five. And push the hidden door closed on your way out."

13

VIENNA, VIRGINIA

Eli met Kat at 7:30 a.m. sharp in the WFO employee parking lot.

As she climbed into the vehicle, he had a shit-eating smile plastered all over his face. "You saw the score last night, right?" Eli asked.

Kat shook her head. "Good morning, Eli. I slept great last night. Thanks for asking. How about you?"

He ignored her snarky response. "Five touchdowns by the GOAT. Count them, five. It was a hell of a game, Kat. Sure you didn't watch any of it?"

"No, Eli, I was too busy staying up late watching the Lifetime network, eating bonbons, and braiding my girlfriend's hair."

"Girl, you missed it. There was one pass that … wait, did you say 'girlfriend?'" His eyes opened wide enough to almost pop out of their sockets. "Seriously?"

Kat rolled her eyes. "Sure, that got your attention. Guys are all the same."

"I mean …" Eli tried to backpedal. "I didn't know you were a lezbo. That's cool and all. Like, really cool, actually."

"Uhh," Kat said as she exhaled a drawn-out breath and smacked him across the chest with the back of her hand. "I'm not a lesbian you asshole. I was trying to stop your stupid story about the football game."

"Jeez, now I'm bummed."

"And … it worked," she said and rolled her eyes. As her eyes glanced down at the floorboard, she noticed only the paperback novels remained. The wrappers and papers were all gone. "I see you cleaned up the car. Or the cleaning fairy visited you."

"Took your insult to heart. Figured I'd better straighten out my ride a little bit."

"You tell Wes about what we found yesterday?" Kat asked.

"No, not yet. I rarely bring the squad supervisor into the loop until I have something a little more concrete to go on."

"But what else do you need?"

"You tell me what we have."

Kat paused and considered the question. "Well, the lady who lives across the street from Ralph Webb says he is missing ..."

"Which we can't prove," Eli interrupted.

Kat continued. "We go to the White House and a Secret Service agent recognized his photo but lied about him working at the White House."

"Possibly lied, again we can't prove that. It's hearsay."

Kat sighed. "You're right, it sounds thin."

"No. It doesn't sound thin, it is thin. We have no corroborating evidence. Only a nosy neighbor who may or may not know that the man across the street is missing. And a Secret Service agent who told us he didn't recognize the man in the picture and said no one by that name works at the White House."

"But you believed Rose yesterday and agreed Agent Walker lied to us."

"Absolutely, but that was my gut talking. It isn't admissible in court. I need cold, hard evidence to make this into a full-blown investigation. Pure supposition doesn't cut it with the Bureau."

"What type of evidence are you hoping to find?"

"Something that confirms he worked at the White House for starters. Plus, evidence that he's missing."

"And you hope to find it at his place?"

"Yes," Eli said. "Mr. Webb, well, whatever his name is must have left something behind that indicated where he worked."

"But how do we get into his place?" Kat asked.

Eli removed a piece of paper from his black notebook resting on the front seat of the car. "With this."

Kat unfolded the piece of paper and her eyes bulged. "How the hell did you get a warrant? You just agreed the evidence was thin, well actually you said there wasn't any."

Eli smiled. "I have a few connections. Made a few calls at half time and pulled a few strings to have it ready by dawn."

"Even though we don't know what we will find?"

Eli shrugged, "Yeah."

Kat didn't press the issue. "OK, we have a warrant. I guess you're smarter than I thought, Payne."

His eyebrows lowered. "I guess I should take that as a compliment."

She smiled and looked away quickly. "And for the record, I do like guys."

Eli smirked.

"Normal guys," she added. "Not pervs."

His smirk turned into a low, guttural laugh.

⸺◇⸺

As his car came to a stop in front of Rose's house, Eli's cell phone buzzed. The new text icon showed on his phone's display. The first thing he noticed was a number displayed with no name. It meant he didn't have the number of whomever sent the text in his address book. Not unheard of but also not common. Most texts he received were from friends or colleagues.

He read the message, and a bewildered expression formed on his face.

Kat watched his expression change. "What does it say?"

Eli turned the screen so she could see it and said, "What the hell does this mean?"

Eli. You must find The Body Man.

"No clue," Kat said. "Who sent it?"

"No name on the caller ID. It's just a number. The area code is 202. It came from the D.C. metro area."

"The Body Man is a strange term. Is it a case you worked?"

Eli shook his head. "Not that I recall. Never heard that phrase before."

"Text them back."

Eli nodded. *Who is this?* He typed. He waited a few seconds, but the reply wasn't an answer to the question.

Find HIM, Eli. You must recover The Body Man.

Eli typed back a few more texts without any response.

"Can you call your buddy Jessie? See if he can backtrace who the number belongs to?"

"Sure," Kat said. She placed a quick call. The call lasted no more than a minute. "Jessie's running late, he'll be at the office in an hour and will run the number for us then."

Eli looked out the windshield and toward the townhouse. "Time to get to work."

Rose wore a simple yellow dress with her hair pulled back into a tight bun. Her wrinkled face displayed a warm smile as she opened the door for Eli and Kat. "Good to see you both so soon. Do you have news to report on Ralph?"

Eli smiled back but shook his head. "Still gathering info but nothing concrete."

"Did you visit the White House?"

"We did."

"And let me guess. Whoever you spoke with said they didn't know him and claimed Ralph didn't work there, correct?"

"That's right. They denied having any Ralph Webb at the White House or with the Secret Service."

"It must be an alias," Rose said as she gently stroked her cheek. "His name."

The statement surprised Eli. He stared at Rose with a determined gaze. "Did you know he used a fake name?"

"No," she said and shook her head, "but I'm not surprised."

"Does that bother you?" Eli watched intently for her reaction. "That he gave you a fake name?"

Rose shook her head forcefully. "Not at all. Ralph had to protect his identity. I understand. Did you show them the picture?"

"Yes."

"And?" Rose asked.

"The agent we spoke with claimed to not recognize the man in the photo, although Kat and I believe he was being less than forthright."

"Figures," Rose said. "They're circling the wagons."

Eli didn't expect this response but had to admit Rose was correct. "How so?" he asked, playing dumb.

Her voice, even though frail, gained strength, and she became animated. "Government agencies don't like others to get in their business. I learned that from my husband, Charlie. After all, he was an agency man his whole life. You get my drift?"

"Loud and clear."

"The agency always hated when other government entities, as in the FBI or anyone else, put their nose where it didn't belong. I'm sure that is the case with the Secret Service. If Ralph is missing, you can bet a pretty penny they want to find him themselves and not have an FBI agent track him down."

Eli rubbed his chin. Her theory had merit. "Pretty astute observation, Rose," he said.

Her face lit up. "You pick up a few things when you're married to a spy for most of your adult life, Agent Payne. Especially when he never truly admitted what he did for a living."

"No doubt." Eli said.

"Well, I'm sure you didn't come by merely to tell me you've not found anything yet. So, what do you need?"

"We would like to get a look inside Ralph's townhouse. Have a look around. I was able to get a warrant. It's limited in scope, but hopefully a cursory walk through of Ralph's house will uncover some evidence he is missing."

"Would you like my key?"

"Yes, please. If it's not too much trouble." Eli asked.

Rose turned and disappeared into the kitchen. A minute later, she returned. "Here you go." She handed Eli the key ring. "Do you mind feeding the cat when you go over there? The food is in the pantry."

Eli looked over at Kat with a slightly annoyed expression on his face. Like many guys, he hated cats.

Kat read his expression. "We would be glad to feed Italia, Rose," Kat said as she nudged Eli with her elbow.

"Thank you, dear," Rose replied with a warm smile.

"We'll bring the key back once we're done," Eli said.

———— ◆O◆ ————

As the door closed and they turned to leave, Kat gave Eli an icy glare. "Older woman like cats, you know?"

"I'm not an elderly woman, in case you didn't notice."

"Yes, but you want something from her, meaning you need to play nice."

"What?" Eli asked. "I know how to play nice."

"Your facial expressions didn't convey that."

"But I don't like ..."

Kat cut him off. "The point is not whether you like cats or not. You may be a great investigator, but I'm good at reading people. Like it or not, Payne we're working together, and we need to be on the same page. Trust me. A woman's intuition is more powerful than a man's obstinance."

Eli stopped before he dug too deep of a hole. "I got it."

"Good. Now let's see what Mr. Webb may be hiding," Kat said as she playfully smacked his shoulder.

14

LOS ANGELES, CALIFORNIA

PORT OF LOS ANGELES

The tropical turquoise El Camino came to a stop alongside South Seaside Drive as Peter Casha reached inside his Italian leather jacket. He unsnapped the safety strap and removed the .45-caliber Kimber 1911 hanging from his vertical shoulder holster. Peter stared at the spartan engraving on the grip of the heavy pistol and rubbed the faded image in a circular motion with his thumb. He ejected the magazine, confirmed it was fully loaded, and slammed it back into the grip. With his left hand, he racked the slide, chambering a Barnes TAC-XPD hollow-point bullet. Peter didn't expect to use the weapon, but could never be too careful.

He rolled down his window and waited. With the temperature hovering around fifty-eight degrees, the cool breeze felt refreshing. Five minutes later, a black cargo van approached from the opposite side of the road.

Peter looked at his Tag Heuer watch. With an hour and fifteen minutes before the cargo ship arrived, he still had plenty of time.

As the van pulled alongside, the driver eyed him suspiciously.

With the driver's side window down the man said, "Get in." The van's side door slid open.

Peter grabbed the large green canvas duffel bag from the passenger seat, slung the thick strap over his broad shoulder, and climbed out of the car. As he entered the van, he sat in silence in the third row. Beside the driver, another man sat in the passenger seat but said nothing.

The van weaved its way through several abandoned parking lots at the port. A couple of minutes later, the driver pulled onto Earl Street and stopped in front of a large white warehouse. All three men exited the van and headed to a side door of the building.

They walked in silence down a long, narrow hall. Several fluorescent lights that lined the hallway flickered. The whole setup gave off a vibe of being straight out of a horror movie. They arrived at the second to last door as the van driver gestured for Peter and the other man to enter.

Peter stepped into the room and looked from one side to the other cautiously. He already figured the best route out of the building if the meeting went south, and he clutched the green duffel bag tightly. There was a lot of money in there and even though he could handle himself, he would rather things go according to the plan.

The sparse room had a linoleum-covered floor, wood-paneled walls, and looked like someone had designed it in the 1970s. It reeked of mold, and several ceiling panels had dark spots indicating a perpetual water leak. With little in the way of office furniture, the room contained two metal folding tables pushed together and a total of eight folding chairs surrounding them. In the corner, an old water cooler sat empty, its plastic water jug missing, and a large whiteboard hung on the wall opposite the table. That was it.

Peter took a seat and placed the duffel bag on the ground near his feet. The other men stood next to the door.

"You going to sit?" Peter asked.

"No," the driver of the van replied. "We'll wait right here."

"Suit yourself."

The two men pulled phones from their pockets, and several minutes passed.

Peter sat in silence; he watched the two men, studied their body language, and listened to their occasional banter. For their part, they ignored his stares. Ten minutes later, sounds echoed down the hall indicating more than one person had entered the warehouse. Peter watched as five men shuffled into the room. They all appeared tired. Another long night on the graveyard shift at the docks will do that to anyone. Each of them looked unhappy to be there.

"Take a seat," said Peter to the seven men as they congregated near the door.

The men looked at the van driver, who nodded. "You heard him."

Peter looked across the table to the van driver, Hector, who had been his main point of contact for the past several weeks. "How we looking?"

"Everything's on schedule," Hector said.

"When did the eight containers arrive?"

"The semis pulled in from Rancho Bernardo about 2:00 a.m."

"Heavily guarded?"

Hector nodded. "General Atomics doesn't fuck around, E*se*, and they never let the containers out of their sight. They even inspect the ship after it's loaded and wait on the dock until it sets sail before they leave."

"And you're sure everything is in place to make the switch?"

Another head nod. "Juan and Pablo know what to do." Hector turned and looked at two of the men at the table.

The two men who must be Juan and Pablo both acknowledged with a "*sí.*"

"I'd like you to go over the plan with me one more time. I want to make sure we all hear it together," Peter said. "We only have one shot at this, and it can't fail."

A perturbed look plastered over Hector's face. "If that's what you want."

"I do."

Hector meticulously laid out the plan for almost thirty minutes.

Pleased with the attention to detail, Peter said, "I'll need an overwatch position."

"I already have a spot picked out for you."

"Good. Now the reason you're all here." Peter reached deep into the green duffel bag and removed stacks of currency held together with mustard-colored straps. Each bound stack contained one hundred bills predominately displaying the face of Benjamin Franklin. He lined them up on the metal table, seven individual stacks totaling fifty thousand dollars each.

With the money arranged in a symmetric shape, he couldn't help but notice the sudden smiles of each man. Peter pulled out two additional bound stacks of money equaling twenty thousand dollars and placed them on the far-right stack.

Peter suspected the local liquor stores and jiggle joints would see an influx of crisp, new C notes in the coming weeks.

He looked over at Hector, then back at the stack on his right. "This one is for you, Hector."

Peter pulled the stack away from the others. Set it apart.

Hector shook his head back and forth. "We agreed on an equal share."

"My employer decided you deserved extra for all your additional efforts."

"That's not necessary. An equal share is all I want."

Peter's eyes narrowed. "It's not up for discussion."

Hector frowned, knowing full well additional money would put a target on his back with the other six men.

Peter knew this too. The overpayment was intentional. It was all his idea, not his employers. Money divides, and he wanted to keep the men on edge. If they had some animosity toward Hector, it would only work in his favor. "Come get it," Peter said as he tapped the stacks of bills one by one.

He grabbed brown paper bags from his duffel and placed them on the table. Unlike when they'd first shuffled in, the men practically stumbled all over each other as they approached. Everyone but Hector, that is. He stayed back and let the others get their money. Once the men had collected their money and stuffed it into the brown bags, they sat back down. Several of the men pulled out the bound stacks of bills and flipped through them quickly, making the sound of a fan.

"You are being paid handsomely due to the sensitive nature of what we are doing here," Peter said. Next, he reached into his jacket, pulled out the .45-caliber Kimber and placed it on the table. The barrel pointed straight ahead toward Hector. "My employer expects your silence." Peter paused. "Or should I say demands it." He looked at each man one by one as he spoke the words. "There're seven of you, and if word leaks out, it won't be hard to figure out who squealed."

He reached down and cradled the weapon in his hand. As he talked, he slowly tapped the end of the barrel on the metal table one time after another, progressively getting louder with each strike. "And if one of you talks, all of you pay."

The expression on each man's face changed, including Hector. A palpable fear passed through the room.

"But I have nothing to worry about, do I?" Peter took the .45 and slid it back into his shoulder holster. "You will all perform your tasks and keep your mouths shut. Right?"

All seven heads nodded in unison.

"Perfect. Exactly what I expected." Peter looked at his watch. The time had arrived. "Time to start the hustle and earn your pay, gentlemen."

15

VIENNA, VIRGINIA

Eli turned the key and pushed the dark green painted door open slightly as his right hand reached down to his holstered Glock 22. His fingers curled around the polymer grip.

"You know something I don't?" Kat asked.

Eli shrugged. "Force of habit when I walk into the unknown."

He pushed the door fully open, and they stepped into the townhouse. The telltale signs someone ransacked the place were impossible to miss.

Kat pulled her Glock 23 and pointed it straight ahead.

Eli already had his gun raised.

"Maybe your habits aren't all that bad," she said in a whisper.

Eli raised his finger to his lips.

She leaned in close. "Backup?"

Eli shook his head. With a few hand gestures, he indicated they needed to clear the house. Staying near each other, they started on the lower level and moved room by room in a slow, methodical process.

All the rooms were in disarray, and it took five minutes to clear the entire lower level. Next, they went upstairs and followed the same process. As they made their way through the spare bedroom and closet, Eli called out, "Clear!"

They both had perspiration on their faces.

"You ever cleared a house before?" Eli asked.

Kat shook her head. "Only what we did during NATs in Quantico."

Eli holstered his weapon. "Well, you did a pretty damn good job, especially for your first time."

Kat smirked and followed his lead by putting her gun away as well. "Thanks, I guess. Where do we begin?"

"Since we're already upstairs, I say right here," Eli said.

Even though they cleared the house Eli's body remained rigid. His senses remained on high alert, not knowing if whoever ransacked the place might come back. "Don't let your guard down," he said to Kat, "and be ready to draw your weapon if you hear any noises."

"But we're alone," she said with a perplexed look forming on her face.

"At the moment, yes."

"Do you think whoever did this will return?" Kat asked.

Eli pursed his lips. "I'm not sure, but if they do, I want to make sure they are the ones who have the bad day and not us."

"Want to call for backup now?"

Eli's gaze narrowed, and he spoke with a confident tone, "I'm not really a backup kind of guy."

Kat ignored his snark. "They tossed this place good."

"Agreed. But did they do it before or after Ralph went missing?"

She shrugged as her cell phone rang. "It's Jessie," she said and walked out of the room. She returned a minute later.

"What did he say about the number?" Eli asked even before she ended the call.

"There was no name on the account. Whoever texted you bought a prepaid phone from the 7-Eleven on Rhode Island Ave."

"No way to track them? They must have used a credit card to pay for it."

"Sorry, but according to what Jessie found, it was a cash transaction. One of these phones you buy, go online, and add more minutes. The phone has only been used to send those text messages to your number. That's it."

"So, it's a burner phone?"

"Yes."

"Well, that got us nowhere," Eli replied with an audible sigh.

"Maybe whoever sent the text will use it again."

"Guess we'll see. For now, back to work."

The search began in the spare bedroom. Besides a queen-sized bed and dresser, the room contained little. Opening each drawer, they found no personal effects.

"It feels sterile in here," Kat said. "Almost as if the room has never been used."

"Agreed."

Attached to the bedroom was a half bath that they found completely empty besides a hand towel and bar of soap in a glass dish on the sink.

"Guess this guy qualifies as a minimalist."

Eli nodded. "If he works for the Secret Service, I doubt he's home much. And with no family, he probably doesn't have many visitors."

The bedroom held a large walk-in closet. One much larger than you find in most spare bedrooms. Kat stepped inside first and observed the meticulously organized clothes that lined the wooden shelves on both sides. Clearly, Ralph used this as a changing room of sorts. Over a dozen pairs of properly shined dress shoes, sneakers, and hiking boots lined the left side of the closet, while the right side was full of clothes. Pristine folded t-shirts on one shelf of various colors while dress shirts, pants, and numerous suits on cherry-colored hangers. The collection of Hawaiian flower printed style type shirts to the far right of the suits caught her attention.

"Not what I expected," she said and pointed to the Hawaiian shirts.

Eli grinned, "Guess he thinks he's an 80's television star living in Oahu."

"Hey, Tom Selleck was hot," Kat said.

Eli shrugged, "Guy certainly had a good stache and a kick ass car."

She rolled her eyes, exited the closet, and walked down the hall to the master bedroom. Eli was right on her heels but paused at the threshold.

"Hold up," he said.

"What is it?" Kat asked.

"Footprints."

Kat scanned the room. "We've been in here."

Eli nodded. "But not over there." He pointed toward the large mahogany bookshelf on the far wall.

"It's a shelf. Big whoop."

"Not the shelf. Look at the marks on the carpet."

"What marks?"

Eli walked over to the spot in front of the shelf and traced the marks on the carpet. "These marks. This bookshelf pivots out from the wall."

Kat joined him and grabbed the shelf, giving it a firm tug. It didn't budge. "Looks pretty solid."

"There must be a release somewhere." Eli ran his hand up the side of the shelf and found the spot thirty seconds later.

Kat gave the shelf another tug, and this time it pivoted open. She looked at Eli. "Clever. Good eyes."

"I'm more than just a set of muscular hands," he quipped.

"Is that how you sweet talk all your female partners?" she said with a laugh.

Eli smiled as he pulled out his tactical LED flashlight. "Ladies first," he said as he shined the light into the darkened space.

"Well, how gallant of you." Kat stepped into the hidden room and quickly found the light switch to the right of the opening.

She looked to her right, while Eli glanced to the left.

"Whoa. That's a lot of guns," Kat said as she saw the arsenal that lined the wall.

"It is," Eli answered.

Kat turned to the left. "Ooh, a safe."

"And it's open." Eli's eyes narrowed as he stared at the ajar door.

"That's not normal."

"No, it's not. Someone either cracked it, or Ralph left in a hurry."

"Nobody hiding something leaves a safe wide open."

"I agree."

"But did whoever ransacked the house find what they wanted?"

Eli shook his head. "Safe doesn't appear to be empty. Let's see what they left behind."

As they got close enough to observe the contents, they both noticed what sat on the top shelf.

"Who leaves stacks of cash in an open safe?" Kat asked.

"Someone not interested in money," Eli said.

16

WASHINGTON, D.C.

GEORGE WASHINGTON UNIVERSITY HOSPITAL

Google stores data in exabytes, and while much of the data is harmless, in the wrong hands, any data has the potential to be utilized for nefarious purposes.

Marcus Rollings knew firsthand that information is power and expertly used it as leverage any chance he got. For twenty-four hours straight, he downloaded a tremendous amount of data about the George Washington University Hospital. Marcus had even paid a hacker to crack the hospital's servers to know which ICU room held Danny Frazier. He studied the floor plans and compiled intel until he felt certain he could navigate the hospital better than most workers.

But it wasn't enough. He needed something no floor plan or diagram could provide.

Marcus left his apartment in Adams Morgan and drove eleven minutes to downtown Washington. He walked into an apartment on K Street as a white male in his early thirties, and less than twenty minutes later, emerged dramatically different. Gone was his close-cropped hair, light complexion, and narrow nose. Instead, the man who approached the McPherson Square metro station had bronzed skin, wavy hair, and a slightly oversized nose that propped up thick-framed black glasses.

As he boarded the Blue Line train, a heavyset man brushed against him, deftly depositing a hospital badge into the left front pocket of his scrubs. When the train left the station, he carefully removed the ID from his pocket and attached it to his outfit. The patient care technician badge for the ICU would fool even the most thorough examination, although Marcus didn't plan on being stopped or questioned.

Two stations later, the train jerked to a stop, and as he exited the Foggy Bottom-GWU station, Marcus turned left and took the escalator to the street level.

Before he walked through the front door, he pressed the left side of the thick black glasses near the front of the frames. Unbeknownst to anyone who might watch him, the movement activated a video camera. The images were sent to his phone and uploaded to a secure server.

Marcus moved his head from side to side in a slow motion, careful not to attract any unwanted attention. He walked with a confident step as he made his way to the bank of elevators. Before he arrived, he recognized three Secret Service agents scattered around the lobby, marked their positions, and stepped onto the waiting elevator.

"What floor, sir?" A small Hispanic boy asked. He was only six years old and stood by the control panel. He wore blue jeans and a cartoonish Iron Man t-shirt. His wide smile revealed the distinct scar from a cleft lip.

Marcus looked down. "The fifth floor, please," he said as he gave the boy a wink and an enormous grin.

"Thanks for helping everyone who comes in here," the boy said as he looked at the badge hanging from Marcus's scrubs.

"My pleasure," Marcus replied.

The doors opened, and Marcus stepped off the elevator. The police and Secret Service presence was unmistakable, with numbers heavier than expected.

Two agents stopped Marcus along the way as he proceeded down the hall. After examining his badge, both agents let him pass.

His pace slowed as he approached room 306, where two Secret Service agents stood on either side of the door. They both eyed him suspiciously as he walked past, but neither man stopped him. Out of the corner of his eye, Marcus stole a glance through the glass door. In less than the fraction of a second it took to pass, he observed a person lying in bed. Tubes appeared to protrude from every part of his body, and three nurses scurried around the room.

Danny Frazier, thought Marcus.

His shoulders tensed as he continued down the hall and made his way down another set of stairs that led to the fourth floor. Marcus focused on his escape route. Fifteen minutes later, he exited the front of the hospital and took the Blue Line back toward downtown.

An hour later and back in his apartment, he looked at his watch. *Why hadn't she called?*

The phone on his computer desk rang, and his heart rate quickened.

"Why the hell did you wait so long to call?" he asked with a flustered tone as he answered the call.

"Excuse me?" A distinctly male voice asked.

It wasn't the person Marcus expected. "Sorry," he said. "Wrong person."

"Is everything ok?"

"Yes," Marcus lied with ease.

"The FBI agents are going through the townhouse right now."

"I thought you said the FBI wasn't our problem?" Marcus asked.

"They're not," said the other man, "per se."

"Meaning?"

"They'll find the planted evidence and hopefully chase their tails," the man on the phone said. He paused for an elongated moment. "But ..."

"But what?" Marcus asked.

"It would be in our best interest if we slowed them down a little."

"How so?"

"You know ..." The man's voice trailed off.

"Like put a fucking hit on them? Are you insane? Do you know how much of a spotlight it would shine on the case?"

"No, not a hit. Do you think I'm some damn fool or something? Nothing like that. I'm talking about a traffic accident, something to startle the two agents looking into his disappearance. Like a good martini, I want them shaken. But it needs to look like an accident."

"And how should I facilitate that? I'm stretched pretty thin right now." Marcus did little to hide his frustration.

"I'm sure you know someone who can orchestrate a motor vehicle incident."

Marcus stayed quiet for a moment; his mind raced. Finally, he answered, "I might know someone I can get in a pinch."

"Perfect. Again, it doesn't need to be serious. Just put the fear of God in them. You know, give them a distraction and slow down their investigation."

"Understood."

"And no matter what, whoever you call, make sure they don't get caught."

Marcus had played the game long enough to know this wasn't a request. "Trust me; I'll take care of it."

"Perfect."

The line clicked off and left Marcus with only his thoughts.

Where is she?

17

— • —

VIENNA, VIRGINIA

Eli took pictures of the safe from various angles. Next, he handed Kat a pair of latex gloves. "The tech guys may get prints off whatever is in here. Let's glove up, and you take what's on the top shelf. I've got the middle."

"OK," Kat said. "By the way, do you think it's odd that the bottom shelf is empty?"

"Yeah. But maybe whoever left the safe open only cleared out that shelf. Or it's always been empty. There's no way for us to know." Eli reached in and grabbed the gun, two mags, and a stack of documents. "We can sort through the contents on the bed."

Kat removed everything from the top shelf and followed him into the bedroom and lay everything she collected out on the plush king-sized bed.

Eli examined the handgun he removed from the safe with great interest.

"What are you doing?"

"Checking this out." Eli raised the weapon. "It's a thing of beauty."

"Why would he have a gun in a safe? I mean, he had an entire wall of guns. What's the big deal with this one?"

Eli shook his head. "You're not a gun nut, I take it."

"Hardly. It's a tool. Nothing more, nothing less."

"Jesus. You don't like football. Not impressed with guns. What do you like?" Kat smirked, clicked her tongue and winked.

"Forget I asked. You'll probably say either crocheting or being a dominatrix."

"Maybe I do both," she said, "at the same time."

Eli raised his hands. "I don't want to know what kind of kink you're into."

"Doubt that's true, but tell me, Mr. Gun nerd. What's the big deal about this piece? Looks to be a 1911 model, right?"

"Well, I'll give you credit for that at least." Eli removed the mag and checked the chamber. Sure the weapon wasn't loaded, he held out the gun. "Here. Take this."

Kat grabbed the weapon, surprised by the weight and perfect balance.

"This magnificent piece of craftsmanship," Eli said, "is called an SVI Tiki-T."

"Say what?" she asked as she examined the weapon.

"It's a high-end, custom-made weapon crafted in the great state of Texas by men that are not only gunsmiths, but patriots. They create works of art."

"And ... it fires bullets."

Eli frowned. "Yes, it also happens to fire bullets."

"How much would this set you back?"

"They start at $4,500, but that's only for the base model."

"You're saying this thing is the price of a used Honda Civic?"

"Yeah."

"How the hell does a Secret Service agent afford one?"

Eli shook his head and pointed toward the stack of currency in front of her. "Great question. And I might answer it once we figure out where he got that much dough. How much is it?"

"Haven't counted it all yet." Kat flipped through the neatly bundled stacks and let out a long, drawn-out whistle. "One hundred and forty thousand big ones!"

"That's a lot of money." Eli examined as he flipped through the papers he collected. Most looked to be tax statements and insurance documents.

"And what do you make of this?" Kat asked as she held up a ring found on the shelf next to the gun.

Eli reached out as Kat placed the ring in his large palm. He examined the item. It appeared to be a custom-made signet ring; the weight alone impressed him. Eli rolled it around in his palm as he analyzed all the sides. The distinct black colored shield with a red knife and gray background made it a unique piece.

"Any idea where it's from?" Kat asked.

Eli shook his head. "Could be a college ring. But clearly, it's something with special significance. I'm not familiar with the design, but it appeared to be custom made."

"Bag it and tag it." Kat commented with a sly grin formed on the corner of her lips.

"You're picking it up fast," Eli said as he went back to the papers in front of him.

Then he found it.

He rubbed his chin. "Well, this is interesting."

"What is it?"

"A numbered Swiss bank account. It was opened at Lombard Odier, one of the oldest private Swiss banks."

"Let me guess. You're an expert in Swiss banks?"

Eli chuckled. "Actually, I took some international business classes in college and even had an internship in Switzerland during my last year."

"Well, you're full of surprises."

"Aren't we all?"

"Well, he has passports too. Lots of them." Kat held up the stack she found between some papers.

"How many?" Eli asked.

"Ten."

"What countries?"

"Britain, France, Spain, Germany, and several others."

"Any from the US?"

Kat nodded. "Just one." She held up the blue passport and handed it to Eli. "Name says Nick Jordan. It's the same guy in all the photos, even though he wears a disguise in several of them."

Eli grabbed the US passport and thumbed through it. "Pretty sure this backs up your hunch the Ralph Webb name is a fake."

"Agreed. But which one is his real name?"

"I'd go with Nick Jordan. At least for now."

"Who the hell is this guy? Is he Jason Bourne or something?"

"Nah, but maybe he's Matt Damon."

She rolled her eyes and said, "Hardy, har, har."

Eli looked back down at the papers and flipped to the next one.

Kat's raised voice and tone caused his head to jerk back up. "Holy shit!" she exclaimed.

"What is it?"

Between her fingers was an ID badge slightly larger than a credit card.

Eli could only see the backside, which was all white. "Let me see it."

The White House ID showed the same face as the passports. Printed below the picture was the name "Nick Jordan." The color code of the badge confirmed Nick worked for the Secret Service. Eli knew the badges well and immediately realized it was legit.

"Looks like Rose was right."

Eli nodded. "I agree, and it also proves Brandon Walker lied to us."

"That's not a shocker, but what do we do next?"

Eli handed over his camera. "Take pictures of it all. Every page. Each passport. Get digital proof of everything we've found."

"But we have to turn all this in as evidence."

"Sure do. After I call Wes, the next call will be for an evidence response team. But before I place either call, you need to realize the shit is about to hit the fan. Big time."

"How so?"

"We have some pretty damning evidence of a Secret Service agent with cash, passports, and bank accounts that he likely shouldn't have. God only knows what else is going on here."

"And?"

"If he's crooked, the old Potomac two-step will kick into high gear."

"Meaning what?" Kat asked.

"Jeez, did you never see the movie *Clear and Present Danger*?"

"No, it was before my time."

"Did you at least read the book by Tom Clancy?"

"Um, no. My dad probably did. He has all of Clancy's books," Kat said. "Old farts read Clancy."

Eli ignored the clear dig at his age. "What it means is people with real power may try to bury this investigation. Especially if it drags any of them into it."

"By 'people in power' are you saying the White House?"

"Possibly, but I'm not sure yet."

"So, what do we do?"

"Take the pictures, catalog the evidence," Eli said. "I'll figure out our next move."

Kat took over two hundred photos, and Eli counted over a dozen bank statements for various accounts worldwide. Some were in the name Nick Jordan, but most were not. After he took the photos, he flipped the side of his camera open and inserted a secondary memory card. After the photos were copied to the card, he removed a small device and placed the card inside. Next, he moved all the photos to his phone where he sent the photos to a secure server.

"What are you doing?" Kat asked.

"Covering our ass."

"From what?"

Eli looked toward the double windows on the far wall. For several seconds, he was lost in his thoughts. Finally, he responded. "I'm not sure yet, but covering it anyway."

"You sure that's legal? Sending those photos to wherever you did?"

"Is what legal?" Eli smirked.

"That."

"I have no idea what you're talking about."

A thorough examination of the house revealed little else. While downstairs, Eli pointed out that the office looked as if equipment was missing. He showed Kat the empty stand next to the computer desk. "Printer is missing."

"How do you know he had one?"

"Cables are still there, but they aren't connected to anything. Also, I think he probably had a laptop as well, based on the mouse pad and other cables."

"So, who took them? The same folks that ransacked the place?"

"Maybe."

Finally, they ended up in the garage. The Audi registered to Ralph Webb wasn't there. Eli pulled out his phone.

"Who are you calling?" Kat asked.

"I'm putting out a BOLO for his car."

"You think whoever took him may still have it?"

"Possibly."

"You realize he could have left on his own, right?"

Eli nodded. "Of course, but if he did, I don't imagine he would have left the cash and passports. Look around the house; does a guy who lives this way strike you as someone careless enough to leave town in a rush and leave damning evidence behind? And did he trash his own house to throw off whoever came looking for him?"

"Doubtful, but you never know."

"Highly unlikely, based on my experience. Nick Jordan is probably in a lot of trouble right now. And that's if he's still alive."

Kat's eyes narrowed as she glared at Eli. "And here I thought you were taking me across town to meet an old lady with dementia."

"Welcome officially to the Bureau; nothing is ever as it seems."

"Thanks," she said as an enormous sigh passed from her lips. "Thanks a lot."

18

— · —

REIMS, FRANCE

The piercing sound of trumpets filled the festive Bar La Rotonde within Domaine Les Crayères. A luxurious hotel located inside a grand chateau, Les Crayères attracted an affluent crowd accustomed to the finer things.

Merci De Atta sauntered into the bar, an elegant series of adjoining rooms decorated with British accents. Four large oil paintings with regal figures adorned the wall facing the glass-enclosed sunroom. A half dozen rounded tables with leather upholstered chairs lined the room. Jazz music played from the embedded speakers, the rhythmic sounds added to the ambiance.

Most eyes in the room, regardless of their sexual orientation, focused on the stunning woman as she made her way into the lively bar.

The black skin-tight cocktail dress with a plunging neckline hugged her curves and accentuated her partially exposed breasts. Merci knew how to draw attention when the need arose yet could blend into any crowd just as easily. These skills, something she worked tirelessly to hone, served her well in her chosen line of work. A chameleon by trade, Merci integrated into any environment depending on what role she needed to play.

Out of the corner of her eye, she singled out one man ogling her. His lust was evident as his eyes narrowed and he pulled back on the collar of his shirt with his curled index finger.

Merci knew that look.

A slight smile formed at the corner of her mouth as she sensed what would happen next. Without warning, the woman to his left smacked his chest loud enough to elicit a grunt and muttered several words in rapid French. His eyes quickly darted away from Merci and back toward her.

Merci turned toward the mahogany bar in the center of the room. It looked like something out of a James Bond film. Five leather stools followed the elegant curves of the antique bar, the thick wood milled in the Amazon circa 1900. With four stools occupied, only the second one to the left remained open. A sign before it read "*Réservé.*"

She glanced at the bartender, who subtly nodded.

As Merci sat, the bartender removed the reserved sign. The hundred Euro note she slipped into his pants pocket an hour before had made her job a little easier. The fact she let her hand wander for a few seconds in his pocket had sealed the deal.

Experience had taught her all too well. *Men are weak, easily manipulated.*

"Un pinor noir," she said to the bartender, who wore a white shirt with black bow tie. He winked and returned a minute later with an expensive glass of red wine.

To her left, a tall man with black- and gray-speckled hair glanced in her direction as the bartender placed the glass of red liquid in front of her.

His eyes lingered on her ample chest before he looked up, making eye contact. If he was embarrassed by his stare, it didn't show.

Merci gave him a warm smile and rubbed the top of the wine glass in a counter-clockwise manner with her index finger. She spun the liquid around in the glass several times before she smelled the aroma of the wine. Then she took a small sip.

"Well, how do you do, mademoiselle?" The man asked.

"Very well, monsieur, and you?"

For several minutes they engaged in small talk. He made her laugh, which caused him to take a greater interest in her. He continued to provide witty comments, and with each of her laughs, he inched closer. They both finished their drinks at the same time.

He drank a whiskey sour.

"And what do you do?" he asked as the bartender brought them both another round.

A devilish grin formed at the corner of Merci's lips. She brushed a finger along the contour of her cheek and said, "Oh, a little of this and a bit of that." She waved her other hand in the air. "Mainly, I travel and enjoy the finer things in life. And yourself?"

"I'm in the banking industry," the man said with an air of authority.

"Really? Do you manage one?"

He chuckled. "No, my dear, I own them."

"More than one?"

"Yes, my business is global."

"How interesting." She bit her bottom lip. "And is business good?"

With that, he was off to the races. A beautiful young woman had caught his eye and took an interest in his line of work. He could blather on ad nauseum, and he did all the while the drinks flowed. As the alcohol in his system increased, his defenses, which weren't high to start with, waned by the minute.

After an hour, Merci and her new gentlemen friend moved away from the bar to a red couch in the adjacent sunroom. Their conversation remained jovial as he peppered her with sporadic questions while mainly discussing his own interests. Merci turned the attention back to him without fail.

With his ego stroked, he rubbed her knee. Slowly, he moved his hand toward her upper thigh.

The time had arrived.

Merci pulled out her room key from her purse. "Care to join me upstairs?" she asked as her tongue brushed against the top of her upper lip.

"Thought you'd never ask, my dear."

"I should warn you, my room is on the smallish side," she said.

He removed his key. "Mine isn't. It's quite sizable. I have the largest one you'll find in the castle."

Merci winked. "Still talking only about your room, aren't we?"

"Guess you're about to find out."

Five minutes later, they were in his room. He had his hands all over, and she did nothing to slow things down. As he whipped off his belt and unzipped his pants, she said she needed to freshen up. He protested, but she insisted.

She won.

Merci always won.

She disappeared into the bathroom and pushed the door closed with her heel.

Coming out several minutes later, she wore only a black bra and matching thong-style panties. She asked if he wanted a nightcap. He nodded and pointed toward the wet bar. The black thong left little to the imagination as she moved away from the bed. The bra intentionally two sizes too small.

As she walked toward the bar, he said, "You know by now what I like."

Merci nodded and swayed her hips, sure his gaze watched each step.

How in the hell is this guy still standing? She plied him with so many drinks, even she lost count. And still he threw them down like they were little more than water on the rocks.

She returned with two glasses and handed him the one from her right hand.

He downed the glass of single malt scotch in one gulp and turned his attention back to her.

Seconds later, the thick glass fell from his hand and shattered hard on the hand-scraped hardwood floor, sending shards in every direction.

His body turned rigid as his eyes fixated on the half-naked woman before him. Her warm smile turned sinister as she reached out and pushed him backward.

The bed caught his stiff body, and he lay there in a paralyzed state. He attempted to talk, but no words formed.

Merci walked over to her purse and removed three devices. She took the first device and digitally scanned each hand, connecting the device to a small seven-inch tablet.

Next, she straddled him and brought the other device up to his face. A look of fear resonated in his eyes as his gaze darted around the room.

"This won't hurt a bit," she said in a reassuring tone.

With the device two inches from his retina, she took a digital image of his right eye followed by the left. As she completed the scan, she climbed off him and moved back to the far side of the bed, connecting the device to the tablet. Within thirty seconds, she had uploaded the images.

The stiffness in his body turned into pain as he felt his internal organs burn.

Merci could see the suffering in his eyes. With her job completed, there was no reason to extend the man's agony.

She was an assassin, not a sadist.

As she removed the glass vial from her purse and raised it above his gaping mouth, she said, "There, there, it's almost done. Thank you for a most wonderful evening, James."

Merci leaned in close to his ear. Her voice dripped with sarcasm as she turned the vial horizontal. "You-know-who says he'll see you in hell, but you'll get there first."

James's eyes grew big. As the droplets touched his tongue, the pain radiating inside his body exploded in a fury of fire that started in his mouth. Like a match to gasoline, the fire spread in an instant throughout his body before the agonizing pain gave way to a cold shudder. Finally, the darkness enveloped him.

Merci located his briefcase and poured out its contents on the bed next to his still warm corpse. She found the key in less than a minute and stuffed it inside her purse.

⚬

Merci walked to her rental car ten minutes later. Before she opened the door, she made a single call. "It's done," she said to the man who answered the call. "I got the biometric markings."

"That's great, but you have a problem."

"What kind of problem?" she asked. "I literally just left his room."

"The issue is not with him."

"Then what?"

"Make your way to the safe house. Marcus needs to talk to you immediately."

"I know. He's been trying to reach me since yesterday. You told him I was finishing this other job, right?" Merci's voice changed, and she spoke the last few words in a harsh tone.

"Look, don't shoot the messenger. I told him, but he kept calling. Said you had to check in ASAP. He sounds pretty pissed."

"Yeah, well, he can get in line," Merci said. "I'll be there in thirty minutes."

The call ended as Merci took a deep breath. She let it out slowly before starting the engine of the exotic rental car.

Shit. Guess I can't delay this any longer. What the hell is going on?

19

THE GULF OF MEXICO

Nick Jordan closed his eyes. All he wanted was sleep.

The man everyone referred to as The Body Man ached from head to toe from his most recent beating.

As his head bobbed, the sandman's comforting touch pulled him closer to slumber. That is until Sir's heavy fist crashed down on the stainless-steel table, jostling him awake. After the assault on the guards, Sir had let Nick stay unconscious for forty-five minutes before they'd dragged him back to the interrogation room.

Sir had questioned him for almost four hours straight. He had been relentless, like a used-car salesman behind on his quota. Desperate to close a deal. "One more time, prisoner. Who else knows?"

Nick shook his head back and forth. His exhausted start wore down his resolve. "I've told you. Nobody else knows."

"And I think you're lying." Sir paused. He tapped a finger in a rhythmic tone, then opened the large folder before him and pulled out a single sheet from the stack of neatly organized papers. "Maybe we have the wrong person after all. Maybe we should talk to Danny Frazier instead."

Nick didn't flinch. In fact, he watched Sir's movements and contemplated what the file must hold. *It can't be much. Mainly blank pages. After all, if they had solid intel, they wouldn't need me alive.*

He stayed stoically quiet.

"Nothing, huh?" Sir asked.

Nick stared right back at him but said nothing.

Sir pressed harder. "And if we grab Danny Frazier. What will he say?"

"Cut the bullshit," Nick said. "You already have Danny."

"Do I?"

"Yes, and you're probably beating him senseless in the next room."

Sir scoffed. "We don't handle things like that here."

"Pardon me if I don't believe you." Nick raised his bound hands as high as they would go until the steel made a metallic clinging sound. "But your goons sure did a number on me."

"You had that coming after you attacked them."

"Excuse me for trying to fucking escape," Nick said.

Sir ignored the statement. "If I had Danny, what would I learn from him?" he asked.

"Danny knows nothing, You're wasting your time."

"I have firm evidence that says otherwise." Sir tapped his index finger once more on the thick file before him.

"Then you need nothing from me."

"Oh, but I need you. We have plenty of questions that need answers. Answers that I don't believe Danny has."

"The Sanctum or whatever the hell you call yourselves probably already killed Danny."

Sir's body visibly tensed. His right hand balled into a fist and he slowly tapped it against the table. He took a deep breath and opened his hand, placing his open palm on the cool surface of the metal table. "And why would we kill him?" Sir asked.

"Maybe because you're fucking psychopaths."

Sir's fist once again clenched. This time he didn't release his fingers into an open position. "I can assure you Danny is very much alive."

Nick didn't believe a word. "Danny may be alive, or he may be dead rotting in some ditch somewhere. Either way, I don't give a shit."

"I think you do care. You were Danny's mentor."

"Look, I'm sure you interrogate all kinds of people here. But you've not had many people like me. I know how this works. You know how this works. We both know you can't use Danny as leverage. You either have him, or you don't. He's either alive or dead. But either way, it won't change what I'll tell you, which is jack shit. You'll have to step up your game and move me on to the next level of interrogative methods if you want me to squeal like a pig."

"As in?"

"Got any electric drills?" Nick paused as his eyes narrowed. "How about pliers?"

"I do, in fact."

"Sounds like fun, but you and I both know those enhanced interrogation methods don't work either. I'll talk, but you won't know what's real versus what's incoherent babble from a lunatic writhing in agony."

"Is that so?"

"That being the case, I'll offer you a concession."

"And what would that be?"

"Put a bullet in my head right now and we can both get some rest. Or give me back my cyanide capsule, and I'll end it myself." Nick leaned down toward the table, tapping his forehead with his raised index finger as he spoke the last words.

"Not afraid to die, are you, prisoner?"

Nick didn't reply.

"Far be it from me to cut your journey short. And I'd never want to help a man take the easy way out." Sir stood and paced the room, he stopped right next to Nick. "I do think we've hit a little snag here, but I'll grant your wish."

Nick smirked. "Yippee ki yay, mutha ..."

Sir cut him off mid-Die-Hard phrase as he delivered a brutal punch to the bridge of Nick's nose, sending his head backward.

Lights out.

Two guards dragged Nick's unconscious body out of the room and down the hall, a steady stream of blood from his nose leaving a crimson streak behind them.

Sir paced the interrogation room. Adrenaline rushed through his veins. His hand hurt like hell and swelled.

A tall, poised woman with mocha skin stepped into the room. "I thought you avoided violence?"

Sir shook his head from side to side. "He pissed me the fuck off. Nick Jordan is too smart for his own damn good. And besides, he didn't give me much choice. We need actionable intel, and we need it now."

"He flustered you. I've never seen someone get under your skin that quickly."

"Nick Jordan was trained by the best to resist interrogation methods. But I can't keep going around and around with him. I've got to take it to the next level."

The woman tapped her wrist and the watch that hung loosely from her smooth skin. "Time to use the narcs?"

"I think so. We both know it will take time to decipher fact from fiction after we inject him, but at this point it's our best option."

"Then we'd better get a move on it."

"Get the Chemist up to room three." Sir said.

"What should he bring?" The woman asked.

"Everything."

20

---·---

WASHINGTON, D.C.

Eli felt a skull-splitting headache form in the back of his head as he and Kat left Vienna. The acute migraine slowly followed the contour of his skull and made its way behind his left eye socket. He popped three Advil and washed them down with a sugar-free Red Bull, hoping the chemical-laden combo would do the trick.

He looked over at Kat who sat stoic in the seat next to him. "I was serious earlier. You did a good job clearing the house," he said.

"Well, can't say you were too shabby yourself. You learn to clear rooms at the academy?"

He looked taken aback. "No, the military."

"You served?" Kat asked.

Eli nodded. "Yeah. Six years."

"SEALs or CAG?"

"Why does everyone ask me that?"

"Well, I mean you look the type. Your physique, how you walk and talk. Plus, I heard you think you're a badass."

Eli frowned. "Jesus, not every guy that served was in an elite unit. Hollywood and thriller novels have given people a warped view of modern soldiers." The expression turned into a slight smirk as he stated, "But sure, I can be a badass. It's good to know at least part of my reputation is intact."

"Who were you with?"

"Rangers, Third Battalion," Eli said.

"Well, then you were part of Special Operations. Rangers are pretty badass."

A subtle grin formed at the corner of his lips. "True, and we had our moments, but I was mainly a door kicker. I never went on to Special Forces or Delta."

"Why not?"

"I got out." Eli said.

Kat raised her shoulders. "Because?"

"I blew out my knee on a training exercise. Nothing glamorous. Shit happens when you train. Decided during the recovery from the ACL surgery maybe I needed to rethink my career aspirations."

"And?"

"I made the hard decision to not re-enlist. Life in the sandbox can be hell on earth, and I needed a change of pace. Used the GI bill and went back to finish college. Applied with the Bureau the year I graduated."

"And another layer is revealed."

"I'm not that complicated."

Kat frowned. "Everyone's complicated."

Eli ignored the comment and focused on the road.

He headed east on Interstate 66 and followed his typical pedal to the floor driving pattern as he darted into the left lane. Kat ignored his speed and talked about what they'd found at the townhouse, while up ahead, a car in the fast lane drove much too slowly for Eli's taste. This prompted him to move into the middle lane.

With a glance in the rearview mirror, he saw something that made his muscles tense. A Green Chevy Tahoe barreled down the left lane at a high rate of speed. Kat kept talking, but Eli didn't hear a word of it. The Tahoe drove erratically; the driver had a difficult time keeping the oversized vehicle in its lane. Eli's fingers gripped the steering wheel tight which caused their tips to turn white. When the Tahoe closed within thirty feet, Eli saw the driver's face. He looked Hispanic, with a thick black goatee and a bandana covering his head.

Sure, it was a stereotype, but Eli thought he looked like a gangbanger. Not an uncommon sight in the greater D.C. metro area.

As the Tahoe pulled parallel with his car, Eli's entire body was on high alert, his senses on overdrive. The driver suddenly jerked into his lane. Instinct kicked in, and Eli's brain processed several commands in a fraction of a second. Faster than he could even articulate. Out of his peripheral vision, Eli saw the minivan in the slow lane on his right. Cutting the wheel hard toward the minivan wasn't an option. He only had one choice. His foot came off the gas pedal and applied pressure to the brakes, which caused the car to decelerate just as the Tahoe crossed the broken white line.

Eli knew a sideswipe at that speed might prove fatal and it certainly would cause a spectacular crash.

Kat had just enough time to utter, "What the fu ..."

Eli's relief didn't last as the Tahoe continued past his front bumper, missing by mere inches, and darted toward the slow lane. The Tahoe slammed into the side of the minivan with a loud crunch sound as sheet metal crumpled into sheet metal, followed by the high-pitch screech of rubber on pavement.

Everything happened so fast, but oddly enough it felt like slow motion in Eli's mind. He watched the minivan as it flew off the side of the road and slammed against the concrete barrier lining the interstate. In the split second of the crash, Eli saw the frantic look on the face of the woman driving the minivan. Next, he noticed a car seat facing backward in the second row of seats.

Rage overtook Eli as the driver of the Tahoe recovered from the erratic swerve, straightened out his vehicle, and sped forward. Every fiber of Eli's being wanted to slam his foot onto the gas pedal and chase down the Tahoe. He could envision himself beating the ever-loving shit out of the gangbanger with his bare knuckles. But as he watched the minivan slide up the concrete barrier and tip over, it slammed into a green power box and flipped several times.

Three words flashed in his mind.

Mother.

Child.

Help.

Without a second thought, he jerked the wheel hard to the right and pushed the brake pedal to the floor as hard as possible.

Kat braced her hands on the dashboard as the car came to a halt. Without a word, Eli opened the door even before he fully slammed the gear shift into park and sprinted to the smoking minivan. The unmistakable smell of gasoline wafted through the air, and his heart raced as adrenaline coursed through his body.

The van sat right side up. Eli approached it and yanked hard at the driver's side door with Kat on his heels. After several intense tugs, the door gave way and opened.

"Free the mother," he screamed as he reached for the handle on the side of the van. Eli pulled at the sliding door, but the force of the collision had jammed it shut. He gripped the handle with both hands and pushed the door along the track with all his strength. His muscles strained and by pure brute force he made the guide bar navigate the twisted metal track. The door ground open as he forcefully slid it along the track. Once open enough to lean in, he grabbed the car seat and looked inside. A child, no older than three months, wailed uncontrollably.

Screaming is good, Eli thought. *The baby is alive.*

Eli reached for the seat harness holding the child, but it wouldn't release, no matter how hard he pushed the red button. He didn't know how the hell to work the latch, but he pulled out his pocketknife and cut the seatbelt with one cut to the top belt and another to the lap belt, freeing the car seat.

He looked at the rest of the van and saw no other children as he dropped the knife and grabbed the seat with both hands.

Kat already had the mother out, who was in hysterics yelling, "My baby, my baby," over and over.

"Run," Eli screamed as he neared Kat and the mother.

Kat grabbed the woman by the arm and yanked her away from the vehicle.

All three ran before a deafening roar and a concussive blast knocked them to the ground as the minivan exploded.

Three hours later, Eli and Kat sat in the conference room at the WFO.

The conference room table held the evidence they found at Nick's townhouse. Meticulously collected by the evidence response team after they left the townhouse. Eli's eyes focused on one thing, his precision glance laser sharp.

Two of the four special agents in charge assigned to the WFO sat across from them at the table. The assistant director in charge was traveling overseas, or he would have been in the thick of the discussions. Eli's squad supervisor, Wes Russell, attended as well, his normal eat-shit-and-die scowl plastered over his face.

Eli had started from the beginning and relayed the events of the past twenty-four hours. Within minutes of him opening his mouth a common game of cover-your-ass, a Washington staple, ensued. With all the passports and money found, the evidence suggested not only did the White House have a missing agent, but it had a dirty one as well. The senior brass wanted to buffer themselves and the Bureau from any fallout coming their way.

"I want you and Kat to catalog all the evidence you've collected," one of the senior agents said after Eli wrapped up his explanation of what occurred.

"But that will take hours." Eli protested. "We need to be out there looking for Nick Jordan, not buried in the evidence room up to our eyeballs in paperwork."

"Look." Wes stepped up to their defense. "Eli and Kat had one hell of a morning, and we have others who can process the evidence. I need them out there to shake the trees and see what falls out. That is if they feel up to it."

Eli looked at Kat, and they both nodded.

"We're good," Eli said.

"Stay away from the White House," Mitch Bauman, the senior agent in the room said as he was the one most concerned with covering his own ass.

Eli eyed him warily but didn't protest. Mitch has the reputation of being a dick. In fact, Eli might have told him that to his face on more than one occasion. A likely reason even with all his experience, Eli still held a low level role in the department. Swallowing his pride, Eli replied, "got it."

They hadn't exactly agreed; it was more like a truce. Everyone in the conference room moved toward the door while Eli stepped toward the conference-room table and with one quick motion, scooped up the White House badge in his right hand. His swipe included the evidence bag as well. Like a magician, he slid it into the front pocket of his pants.

Kat saw his movements and raised her eyebrows.

Eli winked.

———◦———

Two minutes later, Eli and Kat walked toward the bank of elevators.

Wes jogged up behind them. "Hold up, Eli," he said.

"Yeah, what's up, boss?"

"Tread lightly out there," Wes said.

"Meaning what?" Eli asked.

"You know what I mean. We both have been doing this long enough to know how D.C. works. Once Mitch calls the Secret Service, things will escalate quickly."

"I'm just following the evidence."

Wes frowned. "I know, and I'm telling you if we have a special agent running around investigating a missing Secret Service agent without any inter-agency cooperation, all hell will break loose."

"I don't think the hell breaking loose can be stopped, based on what we found in that townhouse."

"You're probably right, but watch your back anyway."

"I'm more worried about my front. Cause I think I know what's coming."

Wes raised his arm and put his hand on Eli's shoulder. For all the back and forth they really were buddies. Wes squeezed his shoulder. "You sure you're OK? The whole thing with the minivan could have damn near killed you."

"Yeah, we're fine." Eli said.

"And you're sure it was simply a random accident?"

"Can't be sure, but I think so. What else would it be? Kat and I were merely at the wrong place, wrong time."

"Well, for that young mother, you were the right person at the perfect time." Wes let go of Eli's shoulder as the elevator doors opened.

Eli ignored the compliment as he and Kat stepped inside the elevator.

When the doors closed and Kat and Eli were alone, she turned toward him. A fire raged in her eyes. "Why did you take it?"

Eli played coy. "Take what?"

"Don't give me that bullshit. You know the White House name badge is the most damning evidence we have."

"And?"

"You stole it. Evidence that's supposed to be logged and placed in a secure location."

"I didn't steal anything. I borrowed it. We'll bring it back."

"But why did you take it?"

"I need to show it to someone."

"Who?"

Eli raised his index finger and shook it back and forth. "Not yet. I need to work out a few details before I share."

"But they'll know you took it."

"Who? Me?"

"Are you trying to get us fired or even worse?"

"Don't worry about it, Stone. I know what I'm doing."

"You're asking me to trust you without providing me with all the facts." Kat's eyes narrowed. She wasn't about to back down and Eli could see it.

He considered her words as they stepped off the elevator and made their way to the lobby. "You know what? Fair enough, I owe you a response. I'm pretty sure I know who can give me a straight answer regarding Nick Jordan if I show them the badge."

"And who is that?"

"Someone on the inside." Eli said.

"The White House?" Kat asked.

"Yes."

"Thought that contact was a no-go?"

"I'm not sure, but with this evidence in hand, I may get past the barrier."

"And if it doesn't work out that way?"

"Nothing ventured, nothing gained."

"I hope you know what you're doing."

"Me?" Eli smiled. "Of course, I do."

As they reached the car, Kat's cell phone rang. Eli climbed in while Kat stayed outside.

When she got in, Eli looked at her with an inquisitive stare. "What do you have?"

"A hit on our BOLO."

"They found the car already?"

"Yes." Kat said.

"Where?"

"Days Inn Manassas right off exit 47 on I-66. The manager reported it this morning."

"Really?"

"You know where that is?"

"Yes, I know the area." Eli said.

"Good."

"I'm surprised it got reported so quickly."

"Manager said they make all guests register their cars due to thefts. She found a black Audi in the back of the parking lot that didn't show up on any guest registrations."

"A proactive hotel manager. I'm impressed."

"Lots of people are good at their jobs, Payne."

"Yeah, well plenty of them suck at it too, Stone."

"And you normally interact with the latter?"

"Occupational hazard, I guess."

"I'm starting to see that."

"Is the car still at the Days Inn parking lot, or did it get impounded?"

"Still there. Police told the manager they would send a tow truck, but it may be a while."

Eli started the car and pulled onto Third Street. "We can make it there in about forty minutes if we scoot," he said after looking at his watch.

"Should I call Prince William County and tell them to hold off on the tow?"

Eli shook his head. "Won't do any good. Manassas is an independent city. The county has no jurisdiction there. You'll need to call the Manassas Police Department. Ask for Sergeant Gervais."

"Friend of yours?"

Eli smiled. "We play against each other on a fantasy football team."

"You guys and your sports. I think most of you live in a fantasy world."

"Don't we wish."

"Yeah, I know, I know. If you did, there'd be more beer and chicks."

"A lot of more hot chicks with bigger boobs. Jeez, get it right."

Kat sighed. "You're hopeless, Payne."

"A-freakin'-men," Eli said.

21

PORT OF LOS ANGELES, CALIFORNIA

Peter Casha's place high atop the port afforded him an excellent vantage point. The wind blew hard from the west, gathering moisture from the Pacific, and each gust cut through the sky, sending shivers down his spine. The flimsy windbreaker he wore did little to stifle the bitter cold.

He raised his Leica Trinovid HD binoculars and watched the loading process commence. From his position, it looked like organized chaos as over a dozen cranes moved shipping containers of various sizes and colors through the morning sky like acrobats performing complex maneuvers under the big top.

For all the activity going on, he only cared about eight containers belonging to General Atomics. Peter watched as each container was offloaded from the semi-trucks and stacked next to the port side of the cargo ship, forming a pyramid shape. At eight feet wide, eight and a half feet tall and forty feet long, the stack climbed almost twenty-six feet into the air.

The security personnel stayed close to the containers, but Hector had assured Peter the decoy containers were identical. Still, he had his doubts, and if the guards discovered the switch, the whole operation would fail.

Hector's voice sounded from his two-way radio. "They're moving the containers."

"We still a go?" Peter asked.

"We're fine. My guys have got everything under control."

Two cranes worked in unison to move the eight containers two at a time.

Peter watched as a helpless bystander while Hector's men orchestrated the movements.

The plan wasn't complicated, but a shell-game switch of ten-thousand-pound metal containers right in front of security personnel required deliberate and calculated movements. Hector's men had built up containers on the port side of the ship, obstructing the view from the dock. The General Atomics security team could only see what Hector's men revealed.

Two at a time the crane operators moved the containers over the stack on the port side, but instead of lowering it on the cargo ship bound for Italy, the cranes moved past the starboard side of the ship and instead lowered the containers to another smaller container ship docked on its right.

Within ten minutes all eight containers were off the dock and safely on the adjoining ship.

Next, the dock foreman, one of Hector's men, gave the General Atomics men the all-clear signal, indicating they could board the ship and inspect the eight containers.

Peter watched the events play out, pleased with the progress.

His cell phone rang. "Yes," Peter said.

"Give me an update." A voice said.

Peter raised his voice over the gusts of wind. "The eight containers have been loaded successfully on the ship."

"And the security personnel?"

"Looks like they bought it."

"Are they still there?"

"Yes, they are inspecting the cargo ship bound for Italy now."

There was a pause on the line. "Good." The voice responded.

"Is there anything else?" Peter sensed checking up wasn't the only reason for the call.

Another pause from the person on the other side of the line. "Yes, one more thing."

"What?" Peter asked.

"It's about Hector and his men."

"Ok."

"Have they been paid?"

"Of course."

"Good, but we need to make a slight change."

"And what would that be?"

"You need to kill all of them after the container ship departs."

Peter didn't think he heard right. "Say that again?"

"Kill them all and do it today. Ditch the bodies at sea. No evidence can be left behind."

Rage welled up from deep within, but Peter fought the urge to let it overtake him. He took a deep breath. "What changed?"

"The boss decided the risk was too great that one of them would talk."

"What the hell? Is he getting paranoid or something?"

"Getting?"

"I'm pretty sure I put the fear of God in them. They're solid."

"And I'm pretty sure he didn't ask for our opinion." The person said.

Peter didn't say anything in response.

"Look," said the other person. "I know eliminating them wasn't part of the plan, but as we both know, plans go to hell all the time."

"I see."

"Boss said you could keep their take as a bonus for the extra hassle."

"You know it's not about the money."

"I know."

"It takes time to plan a hit on seven guys." Peter's mind raced. "And I don't like last-minute surprises."

"You got this?"

Peter hesitated. "Yeah, I'll be fine."

"You sure?"

"I said, I'll be fine."

"There's something else."

"What?" Peter asked.

"Marcus, or should I say Merci, screwed up."

"How so?"

"Danny Frazier is still alive."

"She didn't shoot him?"

"No, she did. But he lived."

"That will complicate things."

"Yes, it will." The person said.

"What's that mean for us?"

"Not sure yet."

Peter looked down at the ship and back at the phone. "Does he expect me to finish the job?"

"No, it's all on Marcus."

"I see."

"Look, he's here. I gotta go. The jet will be waiting for you at the Santa Monica Airport when it's done."

Before Peter could reply, the line went dead. He concentrated on the General Atomics personnel as they climbed down from the container ship, satisfied with what they'd found on board. At least that part of the plan had come together. His mind went into overdrive as he considered how best to eliminate Hector and his men. It was going to be a hell of a long day.

The shit show had officially begun.

22

NEW YORK CITY

MID-TOWN MANHATTAN

Joe Lagano rubbed the bridge of his nose with his index finger and thumb. The anxiety of the past several weeks showed in small, subtle ways as dark circles formed under his piercing blue eyes.

He looked out from the twenty-sixth floor of his Fifth Avenue office toward Central Park. From his vantage point, people looked like ants as they scurried across the streets, and yellow cabs zipped down Fifth Ave. in a never-ending rat race.

His door suddenly flung open as Junior entered his office like a wave crashing into a rocky bluff. It was Junior's second incursion in the past few minutes. He wasn't the easiest person to be around. In fact, he was a boisterous asshole, according to most people who knew him. It hadn't helped when at thirty-six, he become president of the privately owned family conglomerate and then just the previous year he acquired the title of CEO after his father divested himself from the business.

His ego was larger than the Fifth Ave. office tower, and when Junior walked into a room, he wanted all eyes on him. With an undergraduate degree from Princeton and an MBA from Wharton, his credentials were comparable to other CEOs within the industry. But those who knew him best recognized his flaws. He delegated too often, and digging into the details wasn't his specialty.

"JoJo, where we at with the shipment?" Junior asked in an annoyed tone.

Joe had picked up the nickname as a kid from those closest to him. A term of endearment when it came from family and friends. He loathed it from Junior, who knew this, which was why he said it loud and often.

"I just talked to Peter. The containers will be headed out to sea within minutes."

"Good, and the other thing?"

"It'll be done." Joe said.

"Casha's cool with it?"

"He will do what you said."

"That's what I want to hear." Junior took a seat on the brown sofa against the far wall and sunk into the plush cushions. As he placed both feet on the cherry-colored coffee table, he leaned back with arms outstretched above his head until his right shoulder popped. "The pieces are falling into place."

Joe nodded but didn't reply.

"Do you have the zip drive?" Junior asked as he fished his iPhone out of his pocket and responded to an incoming text.

Joe slid open the top drawer of the desk. There, sitting next to the Kimber 1911 .45 with the Spartan engraving on the grip, sat the tiny thumb drive he recovered the night before from Peter. "Yes," Joe said as he removed it from the drawer and handed it to his boss.

Junior turned it over in his fingers several times. A mischievous grin crept over his face.

"What does the rest of the day hold for us?" Joe asked. "I'm exhausted after the three hours' sleep on the plane last night.".

"I've got dinner reservations at Per Se." Junior said.

"Just you?"

A flustered look came over Junior. "Of course not. I'm bringing a lady friend."

"The one from the magazine?"

"Which one?" Junior asked in a braggart way.

"The one you said could suck-start a leaf blower."

A devious smile crept over Junior's face. "Yes, that's the one. She is quite impressive. Especially when her legs wrap around me and she starts to ... well, you can imagine the rest."

"A quiet night in the city after dinner?"

Junior shook his head. "No, I'll need to head back to D.C.. Wheels up by 9:00 p.m."

"Only you?"

"Since when do I fly alone?" Junior asked with an incredulous look on his face. "I need you with me."

"I'd say you got a pretty good security detail. You'll be fine without me."

Junior pursed his lips. "No, I don't need you for my security, Jo-Jo."

"Then why?"

"I've got someone I need to meet."

Joe knew where this was going. "And you can't be seen with them?"

"Precisely."

"So, I'll go in your place?"

"You catch on fast."

"I'll need to run by my apartment and pack some clothes."

"Nonsense. I'll send one of my people to your place."

"Fine."

"Anything else I need to know?" Junior asked.

Joe nodded. "The FBI is asking questions."

Junior turned his head from side to side, clenched his left hand into a fist, and slammed it onto the tabletop. "We're close, JoJo. Real close. The company needs this deal to go through and can't afford to have some assholes in the FBI or any other agency to interfere."

"Not sure we can prevent that."

A fire burned within Junior's eyes. "I disagree. Like my father always told me when I was growing up, 'Where there's a will, there's a way.'"

"And what do you expect me to do?"

"Find a way." Junior stood up fast and huffed out of the office.

Joe turned back to the view of Central Park and considered his next move.

23

— • —

THE WHITE HOUSE

THE OVAL

President Steele looked up as the last reporter left the Oval Office. The forced smile he reluctantly wore the past hour melted away and turned to a scowl. While some presidents enjoyed a love-hate relationship with the press, he simply loathed them. The feeling appeared mutual, based on the coverage he received since taking the oath of office.

The president had the Oval to himself for a few precious minutes. A rare treat since his time was accounted for down to the minute most days. He leaned back in his leather chair and looked up toward the ornate ceiling. A golden presidential seal, a decorative touch he added, stared back at him.

The chair creaked and groaned as he tipped it back farther.

He relished the moment of silence until the voice of Dolores, his secretary, came through the speakerphone.

"Mr. President," she said.

Charles rubbed his temples for the briefest of moments before he sat up. "Yes, Dolores."

"Sorry to disturb you, sir, but the director of the Secret Service would like a word."

The president sighed audibly. "Send him in."

David Kline strode into the Oval with long, measured steps. He wore a dark suit, red tie, and black wingtip shoes. His salt-and-pepper hair parted on the left side and deep wrinkles on his forehead betrayed his actual age. He became the director five years before, and the stress of the job had made him look much older than his fifty-five years.

The president didn't stand up and instead motioned to a chair to the side of the desk.

"Thank you for taking the time to meet with me, Mr. President," David said.

"Of course. I hope you come bearing some good news."

"Well, sir, I do have an update on Danny."

"I'm listening," the president said.

"I got back from a visit to the University Hospital, and Danny appears to be improving."

"Has he regained consciousness?"

"No, Mr. President. But the doctor said his brain swelling has gone down faster than they expected, which is a good sign."

"Glad to hear it, David. Any update on his prognosis?"

"No, Mr. President."

"How about the search for Nick? Anything to report?"

David shook his head. "I've got six of my best people on it, sir. But so far but he's simply gone."

"That's disconcerting," the president said.

"His townhouse appeared to have been ransacked."

"By whom?"

"We don't know, sir."

"Stay on it."

The director frowned. "There's something else, sir."

"What is it, David?"

"You mentioned yesterday you wanted this close to the vest and kept internal as best we can."

"I did."

"Well, the FBI is involved."

"I've heard that already. Something about a nosy neighbor across the street called the WFO to report him missing."

"Yes, but there's more."

"Like what?" The president asked.

"The FBI agents looking into the missing person call came by here yesterday evening."

"Really? What did they ask?"

"They wanted to know if the missing person they were looking for worked at the White House."

"And what did your people say?"

"They kept to the script, sir."

"Did it work?"

"No, sir. I've got a contact at the Bureau, and they found something in the townhouse that traces Nick back to the White House."

"What?"

"Not sure yet."

"You know my stance, David. This is our house. And I don't like someone shitting in our house."

"I know, sir."

"Can we push back, delay the Bureau while your team looks for him?" The president asked.

"I'll try."

"Do they know about Danny as well?"

"Not that I'm aware. We kept the incident under wraps. Even D.C. Metro doesn't know."

"Good. Now, regarding Nick, how about you make some calls over to the Hoover building and see if you can get them to back down."

"Now that it is an open case, I'm not sure I can do that, Mr. President."

The president leaned back in his chair, swiveled it around and looked out to the window. He thought for a moment before he spun back to face the director. "Cooperate if you must, but I'll make a few off-the-record calls and see if I can get the Bureau to keep their nose out of our business."

"Whatever you feel is best, sir." The director of the Secret Service saw his time had expired. He stood up and said, "Thank you for seeing me, Mr. President. As soon as I have any updates, I will pass them along."

"Yes, please, David. No matter what time it is, I want to know what you find."

"Of course, sir."

With that, the director walked out of the room, and the president was left alone. He pushed the intercom button on his phone.

"Yes, Mr. President," Dolores said.

"What's the rest of my schedule look like?"

"You have a meeting with the secretary of energy in twenty minutes, but that is all you have on the books, sir. Nothing planned for this evening besides dinner with the First Lady."

"OK, reschedule the meeting with the secretary. In fact, let him meet with the vice president. I need to make a few calls and get freshened up for dinner."

"Of course, Mr. President."

24

MANASSAS, VIRGINIA

Eli came within a few inches of the front bumper of the car he cut off as he darted into the fast lane on Interstate 66 headed west. The driver of the car laid on the horn in response to the aggressive move. Eli wanted to raise his middle finger in the air, but thought better of it.

"You saw that guy, right?" Kat asked as she grabbed the passenger door handle with a death grip.

"Yeah, so what?"

"You cut him off, Payne."

"And your point is what, Stone?"

"That's an asshole thing to do."

Eli took his eyes from the road long enough to glare at Kat. "You're surprised?"

"Sadly, no. But that doesn't excuse your driving skills or lack thereof."

"I drive just fine, thank you."

"Hello! We almost died earlier today."

"That wasn't my fault. Hell, if I hadn't reacted the way I did, we would have been splattered all over the interstate."

"Sure," Kat said as she rolled her eyes.

"And besides," Eli continued, "we're in a hurry. I don't want the car impounded before we get to the hotel."

"And that gives you the right to drive like a maniac?"

"Would it make you feel better if I turned on my lights and sirens?" Eli asked.

"I have a feeling you don't roll that way."

"Correct. I feel like a douche when I hit the lights."

Kat shook her head. "You've got a real way with the English language, Payne."

"Thanks," Eli said as he cocked his head and gave her an exaggerated wink. "Most people say I'm a basket of sunshine."

"It wasn't meant as a compliment. Payne."

"Oh, trust me. I know."

Two exits later, Eli swerved from the fast lane over to the offramp to catch Exit 47. He took a left onto Sudley Road and the first right into the Days Inn Manassas parking lot. Eli knew the area well and pulled into a spot near check-in. He put the car in park and approached the lobby with Kat on his heels.

The hotel manager who reported the car stood at the front desk. A middle-aged African-American wearing tan slacks and a red blouse, with her hair was pulled back into a taut bun stood behind the check-in counter. She had an inviting smile as the two agents approached. After Eli and Kat showed their badges, explained the situation, she led them behind the hotel to the back corner of the parking lot right near the Storage Sense building. The black Audi A8 sat by itself with no cars nearby.

Kat and the manager stayed near the front of the vehicle as Eli circled around it, looking for anything out of place.

"Anyone try to open it?" Eli asked.

The manager shook her head. "Not that I am aware of, no."

"You've been here the whole time?" Kat asked.

"All day honey," she said, "and my dogs are barking."

Eli smirked at the comment and surveying the area. He looked back toward the hotel and noticed a surveillance camera on the corner of the roof. It looked to be pointed in their direction. He gestured that way. "Does that camera on the roof work?"

"Sure does, sugar. We've had some theft issues over the years, and even though we aren't liable for anything in the lot, our guests wouldn't take too kindly to us saying, 'Yes, we have a camera, but no it doesn't work.'"

"You reuse the tapes?"

"It's all digital, but we keep the data for about six months."

"Can you get us a copy of the video from the past forty-eight hours?"

"Well, of course I can. You want it now?"

"Yes, please," Eli said as he turned to Kat. "Do you mind going inside and getting a copy?" Eli fished a thumb drive from his pocket and tossed it to Kat.

"I'm on it," Kat said. "What are you going to do?"

"Observe the vehicle." He said with a wink.

Kat looked at him with squinted eyes and a stern expression. She didn't need to reply.

"I'll poke around the car. See if I find anything out of place," Eli said.

"Uh-huh," Kat groaned.

Once they left, Eli walked back to his car and parked it next to the Audi. He retrieved a thin piece of metal from his trunk and approached the driver's side window. Sliding the long steel into the gap between the door frame and the glass, he shimmied it around until he heard the tell-tale *click*.

With the door open, he spent five minutes thoroughly examining the front and rear seats. He looked under the seats, pulled back the floor mats, checked out the center console and glove box.

Nothing.

The vehicle was clean. Too clean.

Finally, after looking at all the usual spots, he reached down next to the driver's door and pulled the trunk release.

Kat walked up alone as he climbed out of the front seat and closed the door.

"You get it?" Eli asked.

"Yes," Kat said as she held up the thumb drive. "You find anything?"

"Not yet. The interior is spotless. Didn't find any evidence of foul play. I was about to check the trunk."

"So, you're saying Nick Jordan knows how to maintain a car unlike ..." she cleared her throat loudly. "Some other agent I know?"

"Real funny, Stone. We both know I'm not anal retentive like other agents."

Kat smirked, "And I take it the car was unlocked?"

"Well, it is now."

"Don't ask, don't tell?"

Eli winked. "Something like that."

They walked around to the back of the car, and Eli lifted the trunk hatch. The trunk was empty. No decomposing body of Nick Jordan stuffed inside as it opened. Eli had a hunch it would be empty.

Then he saw it.

The carpet in the trunk was a dark gray, but there was a spot about the size of a grapefruit toward the left rear wheel well that looked darker and wet. Eli shined the flashlight on the spot, his intense gaze focused on what he saw.

"What is it?" Kat asked.

Eli shrugged. "Not sure." He reached down and rubbed his index finger on the matted wet spot. As he pulled it up, the tip of his finger appeared crimson.

"Is that what I think it is?"

First, he smelled it, then opened his mouth and rubbed his finger along the tip of his tongue.

Kat looked on, a shocked expression covering her face. "Ewwwww."

A metallic taste filled his mouth. "Yeah, its blood."

"I can't believe you just did that," Kat said as she turned away and put a hand up like she was about to vomit.

"Did what?"

Kat turned back, her face crinkled like a prune. "You put another person's bodily fluids in your mouth."

"And you haven't?" Eli asked with his right eyebrow raised.

"Not blood."

"Is there a difference? Bodily fluid is bodily fluid no matter what appendage or orifice it comes from."

"No, it's not. That's nasty, Payne. Plus, it's unsanitary. You don't know whose blood it is or if they have some disease or something."

Eli laughed. "Look, the military gave me so many damn shots during my career, I'm pretty much immune to anything including kryptonite. Besides, I needed to know if it was blood or ketchup. I'm not waiting around for the crime lab boys to run me an analysis. Question answered. It is, in fact, blood."

"You've got issues, Payne. Serious issues."

"Tell me something I don't know. Like what happened to Nick Jordan."

25

REIMS, FRANCE

The steaming hot water pulsated down Merci's sculpted lower back. It followed the curvature of her shapely bottom and fell to the base of the shower before disappearing down the drain. The water helped ease her strained muscles while washing away the scent of her latest mark. Using a loofah, she scrubbed at the greasy residue left on her skin by his filthy touches.

She dried off and put on a pair of brand-new silk pajamas she bought earlier in the day. All alone, she didn't bother with underwear or a bra, the au natural look fit her personality and the smooth fabric against her bare skin felt sublime. Her wet hair left dark marks along the top of the silk top after a few minutes.

Merci knew Marcus would be irate that she waited this long to return his call. But she did things her way and gave exactly zero fucks. Always had, always would. She bowed down to no man. Not unless they came at her with a shit ton of money, and even then, she often turned down high-paying jobs because she could.

With a reputation of being a bitch, an unfair assessment in her opinion, Merci never tried to dispel the criticism. She believed it added to her mystique in a world dominated by men who, more times than not, proved themselves to be assholes.

Unzipping her travel bag, she removed one of her half dozen burner phones and dialed his number.

Because it was Marcus, she would take a little grief, but anyone else could go straight to hell without collecting the standard two hundred bucks.

The phone rang several times before he picked up.

"It's me," Merci said.

"Where the fuck have you been? I've been trying to reach you for over twenty-four hours." The anger in his voice palpable.

"I told you I had another job, and it took longer than expected."

"We both know that's bullshit. You blew me off, wanted to make me wait. You get off on that type of shit."

"Please, you know all too well what gets me off. But don't start with me. I'm not in the mood. I finished the job, and I called. What's got your boxer briefs squeezing your ball sac so tight?"

"Danny Frazier."

The name startled Merci. "Yeah. What about him?"

"You failed."

"I what?"

"You screwed up the hit in D.C.."

"Like hell I did. I killed him like I was paid to do."

"No, you didn't. Danny survived."

Merci's stomach balled up like a clenched fist. It felt like she did crunches non-stop until her mid-section ached. Next, her chest tightened. "That's not possible," she said. Her voice went up an octave, the surprise clear in her tone. "I shot him point blank in the back of his fucking head as instructed."

"Look. I saw Danny Frazier in the hospital bed myself. He's alive."

Her mind raced, and she replayed the image of herself standing over him and putting the finishing bullet into his skull.

Merci felt a wave of nausea rise from within.

"Look," Marcus said, "the fact is, he survived. Now I've been tasked with cleaning up the clusterfuck you've made."

"But I ..."

Marcus cut her off. "He wanted me to kill you for the failure, but I saved your ass. At least, for now."

Shocked and unsure what to say at the moment, it took her a second before she collected herself and fired back in typical Merci style. "I'd like to see those bastards try to get me."

"Don't start the 'I'm indestructible shit' with me. You're aware I know your shortcomings."

Fight or flight kicked in. "I'm going to bug out."

Marcus grunted. "Don't try it; they'll find you."

"Don't be so sure. I can disappear if need be."

"I can't let you do that. Anyway, they'll take it all out on me if you're gone."

She ignored the statement. "What do they want?"

"Restitution."

"They want the money back?"

"No. This has nothing to do with money. They want us to make it whole."

"How?"

"Get back to D.C.."

"So, they can kill me there? No thanks. If I fucked up, fine. But I'm not coming back to face a firing squad."

"Look, if we fix this, the problem goes away," Marcus said.

Merci's first inclination was to run. She felt confident she could disappear in many places around the world. Africa, Chile, Thailand ... she had numerous contingency plans if or when the need ever arose. However, something gnawed at her and kept her from hanging up the phone, grabbing her go bag, and falling off the face of the earth.

Failure.

It was something new for her. She never screwed up a hit before now and didn't know how to tuck tail and run. No, she needed to make things right. Not for them.

Screw them.

For herself.

"Ok, I'll come back," she said.

"When?"

Merci looked at her watch. "I should be able to get a flight out of Charles de Gaulle this evening."

"Good. Together we can take out Danny."

"In the hospital?"

"Yes."

"Is he heavily guarded?"

"Of course," Marcus said. "Secret Service is crawling all over the place."

"You got a plan?"

"I do."

"See you soon." Merci disconnected the call and threw her head back. She closed her eyes and slid out of the silk pajamas. A full-length mirror hung on the wall, and she examined her flawless, naked body in the reflection.

A smile came to her face as her eyes closed. She needed the momentary distraction to calm her down.

With her eyes closed and her mind engulfed in darkness, the smile receded as the faces of each man she killed over the years flipped through her head like a pack of playing cards shuffled through an electronic deck.

All of them dead because of her.

The card with Danny flipped to the top of the deck. His lifeless face on the card came alive as his eyes opened and his gaping mouth widened as he said, "Boo!"

Her eyes sprung open.

26

MANASSAS, VIRGINIA

Eli Payne wasn't much of a runner, at least not since his ACL blowout. His right knee would ache something fierce if he ran for more than a half mile. Oddly enough, walks didn't bother him, as he could walk for hours without any repercussions.

Several years prior, he worked a missing-person case where someone had abducted a four-year-old girl from her home in the dead of night. For forty-eight hours, the FBI conducted a massive search around the D.C. metro area for the young child. Eli had found the little girl's body less than a mile from the family home. Sexually assaulted and her skull crushed, Eli visibly shook as he broke the news to her parents.

The case devastated him.

After he told the family and returned home, he hadn't been able to sleep. A rage had engulfed him, something he never felt during all the investigations during his career. That night he walked from 10:00 p.m. till 6:00 a.m. the next day until his body couldn't take another step. Eli found peace by the time he slumped onto his couch. The horrific events of that night and finding her broken body had never left his memory.

— ◦ —

Eli walked around the Audi close to fifty times.

Kat had enough. "Payne," she said in an exasperated tone. "Are you ever going to stop circling the damn car?"

Eli paused, a curious look on his face. "But I'm thinking," he said.

"Yeah, I know. Some people stand still when they think; you should try it."

"I don't work that way."

"Hello, Captain Obvious."

Somehow the exchange triggered something in his brain. "I need a map."

Kat reached into her pocket and pulled out her iPhone. She opened the app for Google maps and handed it to Eli.

He pushed her hand away and marched past her.

"What the hell?" she asked.

He disappeared inside his car. "Got it," Eli said as he walked to the front hood of the Audi and unfolded the paper map.

Kat looked dumbfounded. "What the hell is that?"

"A map, Miss Smartypants."

"And I've got one on my phone that works fine."

"Not like this one." Eli tapped the map with his index finger.

"That thing is for dinosaurs; I can't believe they still make them."

"The map on your iPhone sucks. The screen is teeny tiny. I can't see anything on it."

"Maybe it's because you're old," Kat said with a wide grin forming on her face.

"Bite me."

"You need to retake the Bureau's sexual harassment online tutorial."

"That's funny." Eli fully opened the map. It measured three feet by four feet and covered most of the car's hood. "Let's make a hypothesis."

"You first," Kat said.

"I'm working off the premise Nick Jordan was forced against his will out of his house in Vienna, placed into his trunk, and driven here. I believe this is his blood we've found."

"I agree. But is he alive?"

"Not sure, but I think he was alive when his body came out of the trunk. There's not enough blood in there to indicate he's dead."

"And did they take him out here in the parking lot? And if so, what did they do with him?"

Eli looked up and around the parking lot. "Doubtful. Even in the dead of night, there's no cover in this location. You'd have to be pretty stupid to remove a body here."

"Then you think the car was dropped here after the fact?"

"Yes."

"Why here?"

"Not sure. The proximity to Interstate 66 makes me lean toward it being a matter of convenience."

"OK, but where's Nick?"

Eli looked back at the map. "Let's assume he was brought within ten miles of this spot where we found the car." He took a pen and drew a circle around the area that he believed included the ten-mile radius.

"And what makes you say that?"

Eli shrugged. "A hunch based on the other cases I've worked over the years. It's unlikely they brought him somewhere and drove the car terribly far to dump it."

"Speaking of that, isn't this a lousy place to ditch a car?"

"Part of me says yes, but with little to go by, it's really hard to say. Maybe the kidnappers thought it wouldn't be discovered for a while since it's a heavily used parking lot. Who knows?"

"Ok, let's go down your rabbit hole," Kat said. "Ten-mile radius. What's around here? Shopping centers, businesses, lots of residential neighborhoods. So, where is he?"

"Well, he could be anywhere, but I'm pretty sure if he was abducted, it was not to bring him to Manassas."

"You're saying this location was a springboard for taking him somewhere else?"

Eli nodded. "Yes."

"Then why not drive him there in the car?"

He looked up from the map and over at Kat. Then he pointed to the map and tapped his finger repeatedly on one spot. "Good question. Maybe wherever they want to take him is not within a reasonable driving distance. There's not much here besides what you already mentioned with the exception of the Manassas Regional Airport."

"An airport. Really?"

"Yes, it's not that far away only ..."

"Six and a half miles." Kat held up her phone and touched the screen. "My Google maps serves a purpose after all, old man."

"Smartass," Eli said.

"But how likely is it someone brought him out here to take him away by plane. That would be awfully difficult."

"It would be easier than you think. Taking him against his will through Reagan or Dulles would be an impossibility. But a small regional airport like Manassas would be pretty easy if you knew what you were doing."

"Enlighten me," Kat said.

"Several charter airline companies use Manassas."

"Guess we are headed to the airport?"

"We are unless you have a better idea."

Kat shook her head. "Lead on, oh, master."

"Are you going to help me fold up my map?" Eli asked.

"No can do, gramps. I've got mine right here." Kat held up her phone.

"Ball-buster," Eli muttered.

Kat smirked. "I heard that."

27

—— · ——

THE GULF OF MEXICO

Sir brought the Marlboro up to his lips and took a deep drag. He closed his eyes and strained his head back as the smoke filled his lungs. His neck cracked as he swiveled it from side to side. Exhaling the smoke, he looked at the tranquil water below.

He didn't care for life on the platform. The Sanctum led him all around the world, but rarely did he find the assignments in desirable locations. Extravagant pay made up for the lousy locations, and only working six months a year was a sweet gig.

Two cigarettes in less than five minutes achieved the intended goal and helped calm his nerves.

Nick Jordan was a hard egg to crack.

During his career, Sir experienced a variety of people who passed through his interrogation rooms. The big strong ones, men built like tanks, often were the easiest ones to break. Physically, they could withstand discomfort, but mentally they were weak. Interrogation techniques confirmed life is ninety percent mental. Beat someone mentally, and they will crack like an egg on the edge of a countertop.

The Chemist injected Nick with the second round of engineered truth serum. The first round proved an absolute waste of time. Nick displayed anger but revealed nothing of value.

Sir gripped the metal rail with his right hand as he took one last drag and flicked the cigarette into the dark waters below. Behind him, the door creaked open.

Evelyn pulled her coat tight and walked over. "It's chilly out here," she said. "I needed some fresh air."

A gust of wind pulled her jacket, exposing her skin to the cool air. "We need to chat inside."

Sir nodded.

Evelyn opened the door, and he followed her inside. A coat rack stood to the left of the door, and they both hung up their jackets before they proceeded to the right, where two couches faced each other.

She pointed to one of the plush leather couches. "Take a seat."

Sir obliged. "What's up?"

Evelyn said nothing at first. Her dark brown eyes narrowed as she stared at him.

"You unhappy with my interrogation techniques?" Sir asked.

"No, you know what you're doing."

"Then what is it?" Sir asked.

Evelyn's gaze moved from the ground before it settled on Sir. "I got a phone call." She said.

"From?"

"You know."

Sir grunted. "What did he want?"

"You read the report about what they took from the townhouse, right?"

"Yes."

"Their IT analyst cracked into his laptop and determined Nick printed four copies."

"And they retrieved one of them from the safe."

Evelyn nodded. "That's correct."

"So, I need to determine what he did with the other three."

Evelyn nodded. "They want answers ASAP."

"We both know cracking into a person's mind can't be rushed. Not if you want solid intel."

Evelyn nodded. "Of course, but this is a valuable client, one who can greatly benefit the Sanctum due to his ..." She paused. "Contacts."

"You could come into a session and see if you can get him to talk."

"Use my feminine charms?" Evelyn asked.

Sir smirked. "Something like that."

"No, I'm content staying behind the mirror on this one."

"You think he'll recognize you?"

"I can say without a doubt I've never met him before he arrived."

Sir glanced at his watch. It was almost time. "The chemical cocktail should kick in any minute."

"Earn your pay."

"Don't I always?"

Evelyn frowned but said nothing.

⸺◆◯◆⸺

Nick stared at the mirror across from where he sat. He felt a shiver run up his spine then back down. The icy chill pulsated through his body, delivered via his bloodstream.

It's the drugs, he told himself. *They're trying to overtake you.*

His body shivered uncontrollably. It wasn't an *I'm-cold* shiver; it was a *get this out of me* shake from the tips of his toes to the crown of his head.

Fight it, Nick, he told himself. *Damn it, you can't give in.*

He tried to go back to his bedrock, what made him tick. Ignore everything else and hone his attention on why he got up every morning. It wasn't to earn a paycheck, not to make a living. His existence mattered, and he performed a role few knew existed or understood.

"I protect the office," he said out loud. He said it once, then after a few seconds passed, he repeated the statement.

He knew what Sir wanted; it had to be the reason they took him. The one thing he couldn't reveal. Nick placed the memory at the bottom of a large chasm within his mind, then he opened the flood gates of memories and emotions and let them run down into the void to bury what he could not reveal.

28

THE WHITE HOUSE

THE SITUATION ROOM

The Director of the FBI, Kendall Ludington, pushed back his chair and stood as the National Security Council (NSC) meeting finished. He pulled his navy-blue suit jacket taut to his body and buttoned the top button as he turned to leave. An invitation to the NSC was rare for the FBI director. Ever since 2005, when the Director of National Intelligence (DNI) position came into existence, the DNI got a seat at the NSC, dropping the FBI director down a notch.

With the DNI out of the country, Director Ludington attended the meeting. He would prefer to pass if possible since he and President Steele didn't exactly see eye to eye on much.

Relieved when the meeting ended, the director reached the door as the president's boisterous voice called out from behind. "Ken. Say, Ken."

He turned around and curled his lips back into a neutral expression. "Yes, Mr. President."

"Can I have a word with you?"

"Of course, sir."

Ken walked back to the chair he vacated and pulled it away from the table.

"No, not here. I'd like to speak with you somewhere a little more discreet."

More discreet than the Situation Room? Ken thought.

The director pushed the chair back toward the mahogany table. "As you wish, Mr. President."

President Steele walked past him. "Follow me," he said without looking back.

Ken took long strides to keep up with the president who, considering his size, walked at a brisk pace. After a quick left and then right, they approached a door with wood paneling made to blend in with the rest of the hallway. A Secret Service agent opened the hidden door, revealing an elevator.

Ken stepped inside with the president and two Secret Service agents. The elevator had cherry wood paneled walls and dark-brown carpet. A control panel to the left of the doors only had two buttons with letters in bold, U and D. One agent pushed the lower button.

⸺◆⸺

As the elevator descended, the president looked over at Ken. "Wondering where we are going?"

"Yes, Mr. President."

"You're in for a treat; you get to see the DUCC today."

Ken's brow furrowed as he looked back. "I thought the Deep Underground Command Center was a myth?"

The president let out a laugh of sorts. "As did I until my second day on the job."

"It's real?" Ken asked.

"You'll see," the president said. "By the way, your ears are about to pop."

Seemingly on cue, the pressure built up in Ken's ears as if he dove into a deep pool. He involuntarily yawned, which caused the tension to release.

The elevator stopped with a slight shudder.

"End of the line," the president said as the doors slid open, revealing a lobby of sorts with no chairs or furniture.

Along the wall were three biometric stations stacked vertically: a hand scanner, a microphone, and a retina scanner. The president approached the stations and placed his hand on the scanner and his eye to the retinal scanner while he said in a booming voice, "I am the great and powerful Oz," into the microphone. Two seconds later, a deep grinding sound emanated from the wall as the four-foot thick vault door slowly opened. Turning toward the director of the FBI, he said, "See?

I have a sense of humor. I'm not the self-absorbed asshole the media likes to play me up as."

Surprised by the candor, Ken wasn't sure he believed the latter part of the statement. "Of course, you aren't, sir."

The president winked. "At least not completely."

It took almost twenty seconds for the door to fully open. Once inside, President Steele led Ken down several long hallways that had numerous rooms lining each passageway. The bunker system appeared quite extensive and was only sparsely staffed by a handful of workers. At the end of the hallway, he pushed open a door. The Secret Service agents didn't follow them inside.

Ken was completely alone with the president.

The president sat at the desk. "Well, what do you think?"

"It's quite impressive. How far underground are we?"

"Let's say far enough to keep both of us out of harm's way in case of a nuclear strike," said President Steele before he added, "And then some."

"I see."

"Please take a seat," said the president as he gestured to the chair in front of his desk. "I rarely have visitors down here."

"You come often?"

"As much as possible, which is rarely enough. I find it relaxing. It's the one place I can truly get away from everyone. The residence is private, but I still get interrupted from time to time. Down here it's different. Only a couple of people outside of essential personnel have access to this bunker. Very few people can follow me down here. The first lady doesn't even have access," he said with a smirk and a wink.

"Bet that doesn't go over well," Ken said.

The president ignored the comment. "I've got an office, bathroom with shower, bedroom, and even a lounge down here with a flat television screen and cable. It's like a home away from home when I need space." For the next ten minutes, the president discussed the building of the bunker, which had taken place under a previous administration. He transitioned to why he invited the director to the bunker after an awkward pause. "If you're not aware of the investigation, I'm sure you will be soon enough."

"Which investigation is that, Mr. President?"

"We have a missing Secret Service agent."

The director sat up a little straighter in his seat. "Sir?"

The president's eyes narrowed, but he didn't respond.

"Missing as in flew the coop or missing as in abducted?" The director asked.

"We don't know, but there's evidence to indicate the latter."

"And you brought me down here to tell me this. Why?"

"I thought maybe you were already aware of the situation."

"Well, I wasn't," the director said. "Why would I be?"

"Because the FBI received a call about this missing person."

"And again, sir, I'm wondering why you brought me down here to tell me this. A simple phone call would've sufficed."

The president stood now and paced around the desk. Several times he stopped and tapped his foot on the hardwood floor. "I brought you down here because I wanted to talk with you man to man. And I thought maybe the Bureau could provide some professional courtesy."

"To whom exactly, sir?"

"The Secret Service."

"How so?"

"They have their people looking into their missing agent."

"And now that we have an active investigation, you'd like my people to what? Stand down?"

"Yes. We believe this is a Secret Service matter and would like it handled in house."

The director shook his head back and forth. "You know I can't do that, Mr. President. Once an investigation has begun, I can't tell my people to stop."

"Sure, you can ..."

Ken cut him off but dialed back his tone so as to not come across as confrontational. "Are you trying to hinder the investigation, Mr. President?"

The president raised his hands. "Of course not. I'm simply asking on behalf of the Secret Service for some additional time to let them find their agent without outside interference."

"Interference? I thought we were all on the same team. And besides, if the agent was abducted, it would be a criminal incident."

The president had a strained relationship with the director, and it didn't help he threatened to fire the director on more than one occasion. "I think the Secret Service should run point on this."

"Why wouldn't you want to work together?"

"It's not that I want the Bureau excluded; I believe the Secret Service knows their man and are well equipped to find him."

"With all due respect, Mr. President, the FBI is the premier agency in the United States government for finding missing people. I have nothing but respect for the Secret Service and Director Kline, but his staff is not on par with my people when it comes to missing persons. The FBI employs the best of the best. If anyone can find their agent, it's us."

"Look, Ken. I concede your point and am not denigrating you or your fine people. However, I feel strongly that the Secret Service needs to take the lead. I understand your qualms and agree the FBI can't discard their investigation now that it's begun. But ..." The president paused. "I would like to at least have your agents slow things down."

The director put his head in his hands and rubbed his temple. It took him several seconds before he raised his head. "What's the agent's name? The one who is missing."

"I don't think that's relevant to our discussion," the president said.

"I might know him."

"You don't," the president replied in a curt tone.

"Is he on a protective detail?"

"Yes."

"Whose?"

"Mine."

"You know him well?"

"Very much so," the president said.

"Then, Mr. President, I highly encourage you to let my team do our job and take the lead on this so we can get your man back. I'd be happy to assign anyone Director Kline requests to work alongside my team in a good faith effort of cross-agency cooperation."

"And I highly suggest that you give the Secret Service a little more time to find him."

"Suggest or demand?"

"Suggest in the most direct way possible."

The conversation stalled.

Neither one was about to budge.

As he looked down at his watch, the president stood up abruptly. "You know, Ken, I've got to head topside for a meeting."

"I don't want to make you late, sir."

"You and the exceptional folks that work for you will, of course, do the right thing."

"Yes, we will, sir."

The president walked past, exited the office, and walked down the hallway without looking back, leaving the Director alone.

Ten minutes later, the director climbed into his armored Suburban.

"Where to, sir?" His driver asked, a man with a crew cut and dark suit. He looked like an NFL linebacker, except he carried a badge and a big freaking gun.

"Is it too early to hit up a bar?"

"We both know it's five o'clock somewhere, Mr. Director."

"Don't tempt me, Will. Maybe next time. Take me back to headquarters."

"Yes, sir."

As the Suburban pulled out of the White House complex, the director placed a secure call. His assistant answered on the first ring. "Favor to ask, Annie."

"What do you need, sir?"

"Go into Sentinel and find out if we have an open case involving a missing Secret Service agent."

"Can you hold?"

"Sure."

Two minutes later, Annie came back on the line.

"We do, sir."

"Name on the file?"

"There are two names listed. Ralph Webb and Nick Jordan."

Neither name rang a bell with the director. "Who's working the case?"

"The investigation is being handled out of the WFO. Special Agent Eli Payne is lead on it; he's working with Probationary Agent Katherine Stone."

Ken smiled when he heard the name. "Payne, huh? Well, I'll be damned."

"Sir?" Annie asked.

"Oh, nothing. Can you get me a copy of the file and have it on my desk when I arrive? ETA is ten minutes."

"Of course. I'm printing it off now."

"Thanks, Annie. Oh, one more thing."

"Yes?"

"Can I get a contact number for Payne?"

"I'll include it with the file."

"Thanks, Annie. You're the best." Ken sat back in the comfortable seat and thought about the past hour. The most powerful man in the world, his boss, tried to strong-arm him into backing off of an active investigation.

Wrong move by the president.

He tapped his finger on the armrest of the door and considered his best course of action.

29

SANTA MONICA, CALIFORNIA

Peter finished lunch at Sushi Roku on Ocean Ave., wiped his mouth with a napkin, and looked around. He was always aware of his surroundings. The waitress, a cute blond with pigtails and legs that looked like they could wrap around him several times, approached and placed the bill on the round table. She gave him a warm smile, and her sideways glance as she moved past him lasted a little longer than expected.

Yeah, I still got it, he thought.

He dropped a crisp, new C-note into the leather bill folder, a fantastic tip on a forty-dollar lunch, stood up, and walked outside.

The sun beat down on Peter's face, and a strong breeze from the ocean brought the smell of saltwater to his nostrils.

His phone vibrated.

"Yeah, what's up?" Peter asked as he answered the call.

"Where are you?" A voice asked.

"Santa Monica."

"It's windy. I can't hear shit." The caller said.

Peter saw a coffee shop to his left. "Hold tight." He stepped inside and picked a seat in the far corner, away from any prying ears. He had his back to the wall where he could see the two points of entry. "OK, I'm inside. It should be better now," Peter said.

"Much better."

"What is it?"

"Do you have a plan worked out?"

"Yes," said Peter, "I'm meeting Hector and the others at four in Marina del Rey."

"What did you get for a boat?"

"A Lagoon 400 S2."

"Is that big enough?" The caller asked.

Peter sighed. "It's plenty big for what I have planned."

"And that is?"

"Doing what he told me to do."

"How?"

"Never mind that. I'll give you the details when I see you later. If he asks, tell him I'll be feeding the fishes soon enough."

"Good."

"I have a question," Peter said.

"Sure, what is it?"

"What the chance he double-crossed me?"

"Bro, seriously. You think I would let that happen?"

"He turned on Hector fast enough and might want to cut off any other loose ends."

"Hector was expendable; you're irreplaceable. You should know that."

"Everyone is replaceable, bro." Peter said.

"Not you. Besides, I got your six."

"You better. Because if he makes a play on me, I'll come after him with everything I have. I don't give a shit how powerful his family has become."

"Finish the job and catch the flight back. We'll be having a Tito's and lemonade as a celebratory drink tomorrow night. My treat."

"Well, if your cheap ass is buying, I'm in for more than one." Peter clicked the end button and stashed the phone back in his front left pocket.

30

MANASSAS, VIRGINIA

Eli turned onto Sudley Road and checked his mirrors. Although he felt paranoid the incident from earlier crept into his mind.

Everything looked clear.

The drive to the Manassas Regional Airport would only take twelve minutes. A half mile down the road, he stopped for the light as it turned red. His brow furrowed, and he felt a knot form in the pit of his stomach as he thought of Rose. Eli learned to go with his gut, and rarely did it let him down.

He glanced over at Kat, his eyes narrowed.

"What?" she asked after seeing his steely gaze.

Eli frowned. "I'm getting one of my feelings."

"And what would that be?" Kat asked.

"That I need to do something."

"There's a gas station at the next corner if you need to use the little boy's room."

"No, smartass, not that kind of feeling."

"Then what?"

Eli glanced out the window. "It's about Rose."

"What about her?"

"I need to check on her."

"Right now?" Kat asked.

"Yes."

"That's kind of hard to do when we are out here in Manassas."

"I know."

"We can swing by her place later tonight on the way back to the office."

Eli nodded, but didn't agree. "Or ..." He didn't finish his thought and instead grabbed his phone from the center console.

Wes answered on the third ring.

"Hey, numb nuts," Eli said as he turned on the speakerphone.

"Watch it, Payne. You report to me," Wes said.

"And not a day goes by that you don't remind me."

"You were born with the correct surname, Payne."

"So, I've been told."

"Did you call to bust my old, wrinkled balls, or do you have something to discuss?"

"Both."

Wes ignored the jab. "What did you learn in Manassas? Is it Jordan's car?"

"Yes, it's his car, and we found blood in the trunk."

"He dipped his finger in the blood and tasted it," Kat blurted out from the passenger seat.

Wes heard her. "You did what, Payne?"

"What she said."

Eli looked over at Kat. "Narc," he mouthed.

"Dick," she replied with a wide grin.

"You tasted someone's blood?" Wes asked.

"Well, I didn't want to send the crime lab out for strawberry preserve, now did I?"

"You're one sick bastard, Payne." Wes said.

"That's true," Eli replied. "And thanks for drudging up my awful childhood memories and reminding me I was born out of wedlock."

"Where are you now?"

"Headed to the Manassas Regional Airport."

"Why?" Wes asked.

"A hunch."

"I don't typically like your hunches. They tend to be expensive for the department."

"True, but how often are they wrong?"

"Rarely," Wes said. "Did you call me to ask permission or something?"

"No, it's something else."

"I'm all ears."

"Need you to run by the townhouses where Nick Jordan lives."

"Why? I thought the ERT recovered all the evidence?"

"It's not that; I need you to go see Rose Lewis."

"The one who reported him missing?"

"Correct."

"Why?

"I need you to check in on her." Eli said.

"Look, Payne. This is the FBI, not some check on the geritol granny service."

"Wes, I wouldn't ask if it wasn't important."

"What's wrong with her?"

"Nothing. Well, at least not that I know of."

"But you want me to do a drop by and make sure she is OK?"

"Yes."

"Well, shit, sheriff. Why didn't you say so?"

"I'm serious, Wes."

"And what do I get out of this?"

Eli thought for a second, "A Mountain Dew."

"Let me get this straight. You want me to drive to Vienna, and all I'll get is one lousy Mountain Dew? That's bullshit, and you know it. Maybe for a six-pack, and I'd consider it."

"A six-pack? Have you lost your mind?"

"Throw in a pack of smokes, and you got yourself a deal."

"I'll throw in a Dew, but I'm not buying you cancer sticks. If you don't give them up one day, those things are going to put you in an early grave."

"Payne, I've already expended my nine lives, and the good Lord has seen fit to let me double up. And besides, I'll take death by nicotine over a chunk of lead any day."

"I don't want to be part of putting you in an early grave."

"Yeah, yeah, yeah. Well, it's a Dew and a pack of smokes or no dice. You can check on granny on your own."

"Fine. It's your lungs that will pay the piper."

"Might be an hour before I make it over there."

"Do we have a deal, jarhead?" Eli asked.

"That's Mr. Jarhead to you," Wes said. "And yes, we have a deal."

"Once a Marine, always a Marine, huh?"

"Oorah," Wes said, "and don't you forget it, dogface."

31

DULLES INTERNATIONAL AIRPORT

Merci De Atta cleared US Customs and Border Patrol at Dulles International Airport in record time. It didn't hurt that the line moved at a brisk pace and appeared to be half the normal size. Also, she ended up in a line overseen by a young agent. With dark hair and a chiseled physique, he looked like he spent a lot of time in the gym when not working. The young man perked up when she stepped forward with her passport. The low-cut blouse and way she bent forward showing her ample cleavage hadn't hurt, either. Besides a few perfunctory questions, he let her pass with a warm smile, which she reciprocated.

Men are so easy.

She clutched her lone carry-on bag and walked past the large floor-to-ceiling sign that read, "Welcome to the UNITED STATES OF AMERICA and the COMMONWEALTH OF VIRGINIA."

Two minutes later, she exited baggage claim and saw the black SUV with heavily tinted windows at the curb. Merci climbed into the front passenger seat.

"How nice of you to pick me up," Merci said as she gave him a sideways glance.

Marcus Rollings ignored the snarky statement. "Flight OK?"

"What are we, some old married couple who talks about their boring-ass day?"

"No, Kramer," Marcus said, an obvious reference to Seinfeld, one of their favorite shows to watch together. Before she could reply he added, "It's prison, Jerry, prison."

Merci laughed. She had a delicate, feminine laugh. Most men found it downright sexy.

That included Marcus.

They drove in silence for about five minutes before she turned to him. "You got a plan to take out Danny Frazier?"

"I do."

"How many people?"

"Only you and me."

Merci frowned. "Do you have a death wish?"

"No. There's a heavy Secret Service footprint all over the George Washington University Hospital, but my plan is straightforward. I don't foresee any issues. When we get back to my place, I'll go over the specifics."

Merci leaned over and grabbed his right thigh and gave it a firm yet tender squeeze. "Back to your place, huh? Isn't that a little forward? What kind of gal do you think I am?"

Her playfulness threw him off. Even though they'd had a romantic relationship in the past, it had ended a few years back.

Marcus grabbed her hand and pulled it off his leg. "I think we learned our lesson in Paris, didn't we?"

"How so?" she asked, her voice taking on a sultry tone.

"You're screwing with me, right?" He shot her a glance.

"Remind me which time in Paris?" Merci asked as she threw her head back.

Marcus played along. "That time we posed as husband and wife in Vincennes and were supposed to take out the older couple."

Merci smiled from ear to ear. "Oh, yes. Right, right, right. Paris. We got caught in the wine cellar in a compromising position."

"Yeah, that's right," Marcus said. "Buck naked riding bareback. Our weapons in plain sight on top of our scattered clothes, and no way to reach them before Mr. Jenkins hit the silent alarm."

"Guess I should be grateful you have a good arm."

"My aim is what saved us." Marcus said.

"I must say I've never seen a man struck in the head with a bottle of cabernet from twenty feet," said Merci with a slight laugh. "And you didn't even break the bottle."

Marcus laughed as the full memory returned. It had turned out to be one hell of a night. Incredible sex, violence, and a lot of alcohol. A perfect combo. "Nope," he said. "I picked it up off the cellar floor, and we drank every last drop. Next, we went upstairs, capped the missus, and finished what we started."

Merci pulled her shirt away from her heaving bosom several times in a rapid motion. "Jesus, Marcus. You're getting me all hot and bothered over here."

"Good times," Marcus said.

"And that was the last time?"

"Sure was."

"What about that time in Macau?"

"Didn't count."

"How so?"

"Do I need to explain the difference?"

"You boys and your semantics. I guess we have Bill Clinton to thank for that."

"It won't happen," he said, then playfully patted her smooth, toned leg. "So get those thoughts out of your head. We've got a job to do. Not a past to rehash."

Merci shrugged. "We'll see. Could be the last time for both of us if things go to hell at the hospital."

"Let's make sure things don't."

"How far away is your place?" Merci asked.

"About ten minutes."

"After we take out Frazier how can you be sure we won't be double crossed?"

"To be honest, I'm not." Marcus said.

Merci bit her bottom lip. "You got an insurance policy? Something you can dangle out there to keep us safe?"

"Maybe."

"And?"

Marcus smiled. "And I hope I won't need to use it."

"Seriously? You won't tell me?"

"You got your secrets. I've got mine."

Merci shook her head. "And they say woman are teases."

Marcus huffed. "Oh, trust me, you are."

32

FAIRFAX, VA

Ryan tapped his index finger and thumb on the steering wheel to the rhythmic beat as "With or Without You" by U2 came on the radio. He sang along with the chorus, grateful no one heard his off-key voice. Years prior someone told him surveillance work consisted of 98 percent sitting around bored off your ass while the other 2 percent delivered little excitement.

The 2 percent seemed like a stretch as he looked around the parking lot of the Wegmans on Monument Drive. He let out an elongated breath.

God, I'm bored.

His cell phone rang. "Yeess," he said in a drawn-out manner.

"Where are you?" The caller asked.

"Wegmans."

"Weg ... what?"

"It's a grocery store, boss."

"Why are you at a grocery store? You should be watching her."

"We are. She went out, and we followed her into town."

"Well, I'm about to throw you a curveball."

"Ten four. Whatcha got?" Ryan asked.

"Do you still have those FBI jackets and badges?"

"Yep, in the trunk. Why?"

"I need you to talk with Rose. Give her a few minutes to put away her groceries, and then you and Don pay her a little visit."

"What kind of visit?"

"You idiot, I want the two of you to question her. We need intel."

Ryan was confused. "What are we going to get from her that the real FBI agents didn't find out?"

"We've confirmed from the printer and laptop you guys retrieved he printed off four copies of the documents. You recovered one from the safe, but we need to know what happened to the other three."

"And you think she knows where they are?"

"Possibly. That's what I need for you to find out."

"And if she won't talk?"

"Be persuasive. Firm. Tell her it's a matter of national security. Explain that you work with Agent Payne and, based on evidence he recovered, additional questions arose. Ask her about the documents. See what she knows, but keep it low key."

"And if she doesn't know anything?"

"Thank her for her time and leave, Sherlock."

"We can handle that. No problem."

"If I had more resources, I'd lean on them, but right now, you two are all I have."

"Won't let you down." Ryan said.

"You'd better not."

The line clicked off.

Ryan smiled from ear to ear.

Ten minutes later, Rose emerged, and a few feet behind her walked Don.

Don climbed into the car and shook his head. "Man, that old lady can shop till she drops."

"You get me the burnt peanuts like I asked?"

"Yeah, yeah, yeah. I got your shitty peanuts. You owe me five dollars and thirty-eight cents."

Ryan gave him a sideways glance. "For candied peanuts?"

"Tell me about it," Don said.

Ten minutes later, the two men climbed out of the car wearing FBI jackets.

"Remember, play it cool," Ryan said.

Don nodded. "As a cucumber."

When they reached the top of the steps, Ryan gave the door a loud rap.

After a minute of silence, an elderly sounding voice said, "Who is it?"

"FBI, ma'am. We need to have a word with you." Ryan's voice bellowed, and he spoke with an air of authority.

The door cracked open, and Rose looked out. Ryan and Don both flashed the fake badges, which were good enough for her to open the door.

She stepped toward the front steps, away from the shadows of the doorway.

"Where are Agents Payne and Stone?"

Ryan lied. "They are tied up on the case. My partner and I were asked to help them gather additional evidence."

Rose appeared hesitant. "How can I help? I gave them a full statement already. What else do they need?"

"We appreciate your participation, ma'am, but we have some follow-up questions based on the evidence we uncovered. Do you mind if we come in?"

Rose's cheeks raised slightly, and her eyes narrowed. Her eyes darted back and forth between the two men. Rose took a step back and began to close the door. "I have Special Agent Payne's card. Let me call him first."

For a lady her age, she moved fast and almost had the door shut before Don shot his leg out like a switchblade. His foot struck the door under the knob as it closed but before the latch bolt fully engaged. The force of his kick caused the worn latch to pop thrusting the door inward. It struck Rose squarely on her left side of her body; the force knocked her to the floor.

Without a thought of the consequences, Don stepped inside and straddled her, covering her mouth with one hand while the other grabbed her throat.

Ryan didn't expect the violent outburst. "What the hell are you doing?" He followed Don inside the door and pushed the door closed with his right foot.

Rose looked toward Don. An expression of absolute terror covered her face as her body balled up in a fetal position.

Don glared at her with dark eyes, an almost lifeless expression on his face. Next, he looked over his shoulder at Ryan. "What was I supposed to do? She was going to call Payne."

"So you jumped her?"

Don gritted his teeth. "I did what I had to do."

"And what do you think we should do now?" Ryan asked.

"Get the intel the boss needs."

"But he was clear. Don't touch her."

Don shook his head. "Well, he isn't here now, is he?"

Ryan's expression turned to rage as the color of his skin went from light cream to beat red in a matter of seconds. "You really fucked up this time."

"No, I didn't. She'll tell us what we need to know." Don looked down at Rose. "Won't you?"

Her heart raced, but Rose nodded her head and said, "Uh-huh," in a muffled, frail voice.

33

Pacific Ocean

A brilliant reddish hue stretched from the horizon and engulfed the late afternoon sky in majestic splendor. Peter Casha stood at the helm as he piloted the forty-foot cruising catamaran with the confidence of a man comfortable on the open sea.

They'd left Marina del Rey twenty minutes before the sun dipped below the horizon.

"Pretty sunset," Peter said as he stared ahead.

Hector looked toward Peter, then back to the crimson sky. "Yes, it's nice."

Neither man had said a word since the boat left the dock.

"Spend much time on the ocean?" Peter asked.

"Me? No, I grew up in Mexico City. We were piss poor without a pot to shit in. On the rare occasion I saw the ocean, we couldn't afford to go out on a boat. You?"

Peter knew Hector would be dead shortly, and he would be the one to usher him into eternity. He lied so often. The truth was intertwined within a web of stories and falsehoods.

Whatever I tell him will go to the bottom of the sea, thought Peter. *And since dead men tell no tales my words will perish with him.*

"I spent a lot of time on the ocean as a young man; the salt life is in my blood," Peter said.

"You from California?" Hector asked.

"No. Long Island."

"A New Yorker? But you don't have an accent."

Peter grunted. "It slips out when I'm home."

"Make it back often?"

Peter shook his head. "No."

Hector became quiet for a few minutes.

Neither man talked as the wind picked up enough to jostle the boat.

As the breeze subsided, Hector cleared his throat. "Can I ask you a question?"

"Sure, I guess," Peter said.

"What's in the containers?"

Peter looked over at Hector but didn't say anything.

Hector continued. "I get it. I'm the hired help. 'Do as you're told, wetback, and keep your fucking mouth quiet.' It's just...well, I'm curious. I'm out there every day and see a lot of crazy shit around the dock. I know General Atomics is a defense contractor, and I'm pretty sure the contents have something to do with the military. Maybe weapons? Bombs? I know where the ship is headed meaning whatever we gave them must be pretty serious."

"Good guess," Peter said. "You really want to know?"

Hector nodded.

"What if I said I'd have to kill you?"

"Then I'm not that interested," Hector said as his body tensed and he leaned away from Peter's chair.

Peter laughed. It was the first time he did it in a very long time. "I'm only playing with you, man."

Going into specific details, he explained to Hector what each container held.

Hector's eyes grew wide. "This is a pretty big deal, Ese." He used the slang term for dude. "I mean, you're in this weapons transfer business pretty deep."

"Me?" Peter scrunched his nose and pushed his lips together. "Not really. I'm a small cog in a well-oiled machine. I do what I'm told just like you and report to someone higher up the food chain. The folks with the real hard part are the ones dealing with The Body Man."

"Who's The Body Man?" asked Hector.

Peter looked off into the horizon, unsure how to answer that question. "Yeah, never mind. He's a nobody, a dead man walking. Anyway, it's complicated and not my problem. We need to get down to business and focus on the next phase."

"What we're doing in Catalina has to do with this weapons transfer?"

"Correct," Peter lied with ease.

Hector became quiet, but as Peter said the phrase "The Body Man" his posture had changed, the curvature in his spine as he slumped in his seat straightened.

Five minutes passed, and Peter looked down at his watch. The time had arrived. "You mind taking the helm for a few minutes?" he asked.

"Who me? I've never steered a boat."

"It's not complicated, kind of like a car. Keep an eye on this dial and keep the wheel steady. I'll be back in a few minutes."

"Where you going?"

"Lower deck, to hit the head."

"The head?"

"That's right; you don't know boat terminology. I've got to go take a piss, Hector."

"Ahh, yes."

"I'll be back in a few."

Hector nodded and kept his eyes on the dark horizon while he glanced at the dials as he attempted to keep the boat on course.

After climbing from the aft cockpit, Peter made his way through the main salon, where Jose slept on one of the couches. He would kill him on his way back to Hector.

One level down, Juan and Pablo were on the port side while Mateo, Felipe, and Angel were on the starboard. The seven men had pulled an all-nighter, and each of them was exhausted.

He would take out Mateo, Felipe, and Angel first.

Peter had stashed the suppressed Walther PPQ M2 inside a cabinet within the main salon before the others came on board. Jose didn't stir as Peter removed the gun and checked to make sure a round was chambered and the safety disengaged. The weapon held fifteen rounds, and he grabbed the two extra mags stacked next to the gun. It was plenty of bullets for the job, although he hoped not to need them all.

It was all a numbers game, and he wanted to eliminate the threats as quickly as possible.

Slow is smooth, smooth is fast.

He took the last few steps as quietly as possible and turned the door handle, the suppressed Walther raised in a ready-to-fire position.

Peter expected to find the three men fast asleep, but instead, Mateo, Felipe, and Angel sat around a small round table in the center of the cabin. A tall stack of cards teetered on the table, and each man held several of them. All eyes turned to Peter as he stepped into the room, the Walther extended from his body.

He didn't hesitate.

Felipe sat closest to the door, and Peter drilled a suppressed round into the back of his skull as his forehead exploded, showering Mateo with blood, brain matter, and chunks of flesh.

Movies got it all wrong. When a character uses a suppressor in Hollywood, it sounds like a dull pop, and nobody appears to hear the sound from a room away. In reality, while a suppressor helps to reduce noise, the bullet leaves the gun at over thirteen hundred feet per second. The sound is unmistakable and loud in an enclosed space.

The next bullet spat out of the barrel and found Angel's temple as he crumpled to the ground. With Mateo's face covered with Felipe's remains, he didn't see the shot that tore through his skull and sent him on the split-second journey to join his friends in the afterlife.

Peter spun around, exited the cabin, and moved across the narrow hall to the port side of the boat.

When the gun had recoiled from the first shot, he started an internal count-down, as he knew time worked against him and the slower he moved, the greater his danger.

Before Peter made it two steps, the door leading to Juan and Pablo's cabin jerked open. With the gun still raised, Peter fired twice and struck Pablo in the bridge of the nose and left cheek as the barrel of a handgun reached around the falling body.

Clever boy, but not clever enough.

Peter put two more rounds in Pablo's chest, which caused the body to jerk back, and Juan lost his balance. Pablo fell backward while Juan's head lost the cover afforded by his friend's body mass. Peter had the window he needed, and two more rounds left his Walther, eliminating Juan.

Peter heard movement from his left at the top of the stairs. With nine shots expended, he had six more in the mag.

Juan stood at the top of stairs. He cradled a handgun and pointed downward, his hand near the side of his leg.

Rookie mistake.

Peter put a shot in his chest, and one more in his head as the body fell forward and landed on the base of the stairs with a dull thud. Climbing over the mangled corpse, he proceeded to the upper level.

Six men down, and only one to go.

———◦———

Peter controlled his breathing to ensure the last shot would come from a steady hand. As he pulled himself up the stairs, the boat took a sudden sharp turn, enough for him to lose his balance. He gripped the railing, which kept him from falling off the stairs to the deck below.

What the hell is Hector doing?

Clearly, he heard the suppressed rounds.

Peter made his way through the salon and turned the corner with his Walther up, but Hector wasn't at the helm.

He sensed Hector before he saw movement. Peter lunged to his right in time to avoid the two bullets that splintered the wood decking boards right near his foot. In one quick motion, he ejected the used mag and slammed a fresh one into the weapon, not wanting to re-load in the middle of a gunfight.

Moving fast to the starboard side, he crept away from the stern and made his way forward. The nearly full moon provided enough light to illuminate the deck, leaving few places to hide.

A clanging sound to his rear caused him to turn. His eye caught the glimmer of a shiny metal object as it bounced along the wooden decking. Peter recognized his mistake a second too late.

The first bullet pierced his shirt and grazed his flesh under the rib cage, missing bone by less than an inch. He wasn't as fortunate with the next round. A searing pain tore through his left shoulder as jagged lead found bone and knocked him to the ground. Several more bullets sailed high past Peter's head and struck the deck.

Peter rolled to his left, and as he did, the pressure on his shoulder felt unbearable. With the window leading to the salon open, he rolled through it in a fraction of a second before bullets punctured the spot where he was a second before. He landed inside the floor of the salon on his right side, which spared his left shoulder additional damage and pain. His Walther never left his grip, and he raised the weapon from the floor.

Hector's leg passed by the window, but he moved slowly. With no chance for a kill shot, Peter squeezed off two rounds. The first shot grazed the shin while the second one struck in the middle of his left kneecap, turning it into a fractured, bloody mess.

A searing pain overwhelmed Hector as Peter made his move. Using all his strength, he ignored the desire to vomit and stood, making his way up the stairs to the main deck.

Hector saw the shadow, scrambled onto his one good knee, and lunged off the deck into the black ocean waters.

Peter fired four shots at the darkened silhouette as it went overboard. Next, he climbed the steps to the helm and pulled back on the throttle to slow the boat. He turned the wheel to circle back and find Hector.

A stream of blood flowed down his arm and dripped onto the wooden deck. He grabbed the large duffel bag next to the helm and removed the first aid kit. Finding what he needed he placed several large pieces of gauze on the wound and taped them in place. He knew it wouldn't hold for long, but he needed to stop the bleeding and apply pressure.

For twenty minutes, he traversed the ocean without luck as he looked for Hector. Using a handheld spotlight to cut through the darkness, he followed a grid pattern to search the sea.

Nothing.

His shoulder throbbed with pain that traveled all the way down to his tingling fingertips.

God, I hope I don't have nerve damage.

After removing the gauze, he used his teeth to tear open the package of Quick Clot and poured it into the open wound, then heavily wrapped the shoulder in fresh gauze. Next, he injected two syringes of morphine near the ball of his shoulder. The quick fix would only last so long, but given the distance to land, he had few good options available.

It took a few minutes for the morphine to kick in, but when it did, he ditched the boat. His initial plan involved weighing down the bodies and dumping them at sea, then returning to Marina del Rey with the boat. But with his left shoulder torn up, he knew there was no way he could lift the bodies and dispose of them. He needed to implement Plan B.

Peter didn't like the idea of torching the boat, but he looked at the GPS and saw they were twenty-six miles from the coast.

He inspected the dinghy attached to the stern, and after confirming its seaworthiness, spread the accelerant over the deck of the catamaran.

The trip back to the mainland would suck, but he had no other choice. As he lit the fuel and stepped onto the small boat, he untied the rope holding it to the catamaran. With the rope dropping into the ocean, he pushed off, started the engine, and steered for solid land.

As he glanced back over his bandaged shoulder, the boat became engulfed in flames. The orange and red inferno filled the horizon with a crimson glow.

Hector had learned to swim as a child in a public pool where he lived in Mexico City, and left that detail out when he spoke with Peter. Even though he had a certain level of comfort, Hector never tried to see how long he could tread water. Given the events of the night, he was surprised how long he lasted.

The pain in his knee subsided slightly, the makeshift tourniquet he fashioned out of his shirt sleeve helping to abate the bleeding. Another round had hit his upper back as he dived into the ocean, but the shot appeared to be through and through. It hurt like absolute hell, but he felt certain it hadn't hit anything vital.

He wasn't sure how Peter hadn't managed to see him, but he was grateful the beam from the bright light had never illuminated his body as he bobbed up and down in the ocean.

Peter disappeared into the lower deck, and Hector swam over to the ship and removed a life ring from the port side. His arms and legs ached, and the relief provided by the ring likely saved him from drowning.

As soon as he saw Peter pour the gas, he knew what was going to happen.

Hector didn't consider himself overly religious, but as the flames on the boat grew higher, he prayed out loud that someone would see the red silhouette and investigate.

He knew if nobody came, he would die. Either he would drown, or something would nibble on his dangling legs underwater and quickly finish him off. The idea of being a main course wasn't his idea of a way to go.

34

MANASSAS REGIONAL AIRPORT

Eli and Kat approached the last hangar on the list provided by the airport operations manager, a no-nonsense, straitlaced guy named Phil who seemed to have the personality of dry toast. Phil wore a bow tie, something that struck Eli as being not only quirky but downright odd.

The hangar sat off by itself at the farthest point from the main building.

"Well, this has been a bust," Kat said. "What happens if this last charter company isn't any help?"

"Well, we have hours of surveillance footage to pore over, and you can start going through it tonight," Eli said before he added, "you know, instead of painting your toenails. "He took a big sip of lukewarm coffee he bought from the airport terminal. It tasted like day-old burnt sludge.

Kat gave him a dirty look. "Dump on the newbie, huh?"

"Stripes aren't given; they're earned."

"Like I haven't heard that one before, Dad." Kat replied with a loud sigh.

The banter stopped as they crossed the tarmac to the most remote hangar on the property, a large steel building painted white. The sign to the right of the hangar doors read "Dibaco Aviation." Between the sign and a large bay window was a gray door with a small placard containing thick red letters that read "Employees Only."

Eli turned the doorknob, surprised to find it unlocked, and entered.

A series of offices lined the right side of the building, while the rest of the hangar contained two small planes. Along the back wall, several storage racks held airplane parts in various shapes and sizes. Two mechanics worked on the engine of the plane farthest to their left. Neither man looked up as they entered.

Eli heard a voice coming from the first office on the right. He approached and gave a loud knock on the hollow wooden door. Eli entered before any response.

A man with red hair and a bushy Duck Dynasty type beard put a finger in the air, indicating he needed a minute. Eli and Kat waited as the man finished the call.

"Can I help you with something?" The man asked as he placed the phone on the desk. He looked mildly annoyed that two people entered his office without permission.

Eli flipped open his badge. "Couple questions, if you don't mind?"

His expression changed as he saw the gold badge. "Whoa, feds. Don't see you fellas out here too often."

"Special Agent Payne, and this is Agent Stone."

"What can I do you for?"

"Were you here Wednesday?"

"Sure was. I own the place; I'm here most days unless I'm flying. My name is Darby Caldwell."

Eli approached and shook the extended hand. "And what time did you arrive and leave, Mr. Caldwell?"

Darby pointed to two chairs in front of his desk. "Please take a seat. Am I in some sort of trouble? Do I need a lawyer?"

"No, sir, it's nothing like that. Just asking some routine questions."

Darby stared at Eli for a moment, pushed a few papers around his desk and flipped open his daily planner. "Let's see, Agent Payne, our first charter flight was 7:00 a.m," he paused, "pretty sure I got in around 6:15. Last flight arrived around 8:00 p.m., and I left about twenty minutes later. Besides stepping out for lunch, I was at the airport all day."

"Did you see anything out of the ordinary?"

"Nothing that stands out," Darby said. "Pretty quiet day on Wednesday. Same old, same old, as far as I recall."

"And nothing odd happened that night?"

"Not that I am aware of. What's this all about?" Darby asked.

"We're investigating a missing-person case and have reason to believe they left via the airport," Eli said.

"Well, I'll help in any way I can. Do you think someone took this person against their will?"

Eli nodded. "Possibly."

"Damn," Darby said.

"Any surveillance cameras on the premises?" Kat asked.

"I don't have any, but the airport sure does."

"Did any of your employees stay late Wednesday night?" Eli asked.

"No, I'm the last one here most nights. The other charter services close by the time I wrap up. But there is someone here real late most Wednesdays."

Eli's expression changed. "Who is that?"

"I've got a cleaning lady here on Monday, Wednesday, and Saturday nights. She comes in late. Around ten or so. And she's here for two to three hours."

"I need her contact info."

"Sure. Her name is Ann Watson, but she didn't come this week. Had some nasty stomach bug that's been floating around."

Eli shook his head. "Sorry to hear that."

"Her husband Geoff came instead."

"Great. We'd love to speak with him."

"Ann called me in the a.m. Thursday and said she didn't make it. But I knew someone came because of the empty trash cans. Knew it must be Geoff because the toilets weren't as clean as normal. Men ain't as good when it comes to scrubbing the shitters. Ain't that right, Ms. Stone?"

"They're sure good at filling them but not cleaning them, Mr. Caldwell," Kat said with a wink and a slight smirk.

"Ain't that the damn truth." Darby's eyes lingered on Kat. After a long stare, he looked away from Kat and back to Eli. "Geoff works a mile down the road at a masonry supply store if you want to have a word with him."

"I would appreciate that. Can I have the address?"

"Sure thing." Darby jotted down the address and handed it over.

"Thank you for the cooperation, Mr. Caldwell," Kat said.

"Anytime, Ms. Stone."

As they walked away from the hangar, Eli looked over at Kat.

"I think Darby had a little thing for you," he said with a wide grin.

"Well, then he has good taste."

They pulled onto Prince William Parkway as Eli's cell phone vibrated. He forgot he turned the ringer off when they talked with Darby.

The number came up blocked, but he answered it anyway.

"Special Agent Payne," Eli said.

"Agent Payne, this is Annie Hertzell with the director's office."

Eli recognized the name but had never met the director's assistant.

Uh oh, this can't be good.

"Hello, Ms. Hertzell. What can I do for you today?"

"Please hold for the director."

"Of cour ..."

Before he could finish the second word, the line had already gone to hold. Eli looked over at Kat. The expression on his face looked dire.

"What is it?"

He held his free hand over the microphone. "Director wants to speak with me."

"The director of which department?"

"The entire FBI! *THE* director!"

"Seriously?"

"Yeah."

"Shit. Do you think they know you took the White House badge?"

"No, the director of the FBI does not know about, nor does he care about the fact I borrowed a piece of evidence. Come on now, Stone, get with the program."

"Then what does he want to talk with you about?"

Eli shrugged. "I have no clue."

The voice of the director interrupted the back and forth. "Agent Payne, thanks for taking my call."

"Pleasure is all mine, Director Ludington. To what do I owe the honor?"

"You're working the Ralph Webb/Nick Jordan case, right?"

"Yes, sir. I'm following up on a lead right now in Manassas. Is there a problem?"

A long pause followed before the director responded. "Well, I'm not sure. There might be an issue."

"Can you elaborate?"

"Not over the phone. Can you and Ms. Stone swing by headquarters after things wrap up in Manassas?"

"Of course, sir."

"You know where my office is, correct?"

"Everyone knows where your office is, sir."

"Good, I'll be here for a while. Call Annie on your way."

The line clicked off before Eli could respond. He sat there for a few seconds and looked at the phone as he placed it back in his pocket.

"Soooooo?" Kat asked as it became clear Eli wasn't going to say anything.

"He wants to talk about this case."

"What about it?"

"He didn't say. But he wants us to come to his office."

"Us? As in both of us?"

"That's typically what 'us' means, Kat. Besides, he asked for you by name."

"Have you ended my career before it started, somehow?"

Eli shrugged. "Better I ended your career than your life."

"What's that supposed to mean?"

He cocked one eyebrow higher than the other. "Didn't anyone tell you what happened to the last probationary agent they dumped on me?"

Before Kat could respond, he winked.

"Jerk," Kat said.

35

MANASSAS, VIRGINIA

Geoff Watson shifted his eyes back and forth as he sat across from Eli and Kat in the break room. The plastic Costco table and metal folding chairs might've been cheap, but they were also very uncomfortable.

He looked like a guilty man.

"Is this about Wednesday night?" Geoff asked. A bead of sweat formed on his brow and slowly trickled down the side of his face. "It is, isn't it? Because of what I saw at the airport?"

Eli and Kat shot each other furtive glances.

"That's why we are here," Eli said.

"Man, I knew I should have called the cops."

"Don't worry about that now, buddy," Eli said as he flipped open his black leather-bound notepad and clicked the top of his pen.

"But am I in some sort of trouble for not reporting it?"

"No, you're not in any trouble, but we would like to hear what you saw that night."

Geoff sucked in a big gulp of air and slowly exhaled. "A plane landed at the Manassas Airport real late Wednesday night. I saw a guy get loaded onto the plane before it took off."

Eli smirked. "I'll give you a point for being succinct, but we need more. Can you be more specific? Walk me through everything you witnessed. Even the minutest detail may be of help in our investigation."

Geoff spent about ten minutes telling them about why he was at Dibaco Aviation.

"Is it normal to have jets land that late?" Kat asked.

"My wife, Ann said it's pretty rare. She's there three nights a week. I think she knows what happens around the airport. I just fill in for her on rare occasions."

"OK, the plane pulls close to the hangar, and two suspicious guys descend the stairs?"

"Yes."

"What happened next?" Eli asked.

Geoff told about the cargo van and how two men led a hooded, bound man from the van to the plane. "But then his hood blew off."

"Did you get a good look at him?" Kat asked.

"Sure did."

"Could you identify him if I showed you a picture?"

"I can do one better," Geoff said. "I snapped some pics on my phone."

"Seriously?" Eli asked. He felt his pulse quicken.

Geoff removed his cell phone and went to the photo app. He started scrolling through the camera roll. "I took pictures of more than just the hooded guy's face." Geoff found the clearest photo. The picture wasn't sharp; it had a little grainy blur to it, but he used his fingers to zoom in and turned the phone around for Eli and Kat to see.

"That's him," Kat said, excitement in her voice impossible not to notice.

Eli knew he shouldn't be surprised. Once again, his gut proved to be right.

"Who is it?" Geoff asked.

"The man we're looking for," Eli said.

"Can you tell us the rest of what you saw?" Kat asked.

"Where was I? Oh, that's right. I left off with the hood blowing off."

Geoff continued with what happened next. On occasion, he flipped his phone around and show them pictures.

"Tell us more about the guys who went to the cargo van to retrieve the bags." Eli continued to make notes. "You said they were talking and you could make out some of their conversations?"

"Well, I heard them speaking, but like I said, I couldn't make out what they said. Sorry, I should have clarified. It wasn't because I couldn't hear them, but because I couldn't understand the language they spoke."

"It wasn't English?" Eli asked.

"No. I'm not that good with foreign accents. I only speak English. Know a few Spanish words, but mainly the dirty ones."

"Don't we all," Eli replied with a smile. "But can you venture any kind of guess as to their nationality? Maybe try to mimic what it sounded like?"

"Well," Geoff paused and pursed his lips. "If I had to guess, I'd say they sounded Russian, at least what people from Russia talk like in the movies. I saw that Jason Bourne movie last night with the wife while we were lying in bed. Those two guys sounded like that assassin who killed Jason's girlfriend on the bridge in India. You know, shot her instead of him. The vehicle goes off the bridge, and Bourne leaves her dead in the water. You know what movie I'm talking about?"

Eli nodded. "Pretty sure that's *The Bourne Supremacy*. Great flick."

"Yes, that's it. The guys had the same kind of accent."

"That helps a bunch," Kat said.

"You got a picture of the jet's tail number, which is more valuable than you realize," Eli said.

"You sure I'm not in any trouble?"

"No, you've been most helpful, Geoff."

Geoff smiled; a look of relief plastered over his face. "The whole incident made me think of that R word. Removal? No, that's not the word."

"Rendition?" Kat asked.

"Yes, that's it. Rendition. That thing the CIA does to people in the movies when they snatch them away in the middle of the night. Then they do things to them to get info."

"You thought maybe our government grabbed this guy?" Eli asked.

"Thought crossed my mind," Geoff said.

"What matters now is what you've told us and especially what you've shown us. Agent Stone and I will need a copy of all the pictures."

"I'm glad to help in any way I can."

———◄O►———

They talked for another ten minutes before Eli and Kat thanked Geoff for his time and headed to Eli's car. Kat leaned against the passenger's side door and put her hands on top of the roof. She looked toward Eli, who fumbled with his keys and tapped the top of the car to "We Will Rock You" by Queen as she waited.

"What's next?" Kat asked.

"Head to D.C. and meet with the director. On the way, I need you to send the pictures to my secure server and send a copy to the tech guys at the WFO so they can start analyzing them."

"That's it?"

"I need to make a few calls. Anytime a plane flies above 18,000 feet, they must file an IFR flight plan. We need to find out where that jet went."

"We can use the tail number to track the jet?"

"Hopefully, yes. They would have been in contact with air traffic control, and we should be able to figure out where the jet went."

"What if they didn't fly that high?"

Eli frowned. "One problem at a time."

36

— • —

THE GULF OF MEXICO

Warm turquoise water gently lapped against the soles of Nick Jordan's feet as a blazing sun spread a bronze hue across his skin.

Man, this feels good.

He lowered his hands from the beach chair into the coarse sand, and his fingers gently dug through hot granules. The sand slipped between each finger with some lodging under his nails.

A deep breath of salt air entered his lungs, and he exhaled slowly. The only sound was the waves crashing against the rocky beach. To the right of his chair a bucket of half drunk beer bottles chilled in the ice.

Curling his toes and opening them several times, he stretched his legs as far as he could into the warm water and raised his arms over his head. The stretch elicited distinct popping sounds as he twisted his body.

Nick stood up fast, but immediately felt his head spin.

Too much drink too fast? he wondered as he fell backward and landed in the beach chair. A distinct crack sounded as his full weight struck the flimsy chair and snapped the support bars.

Behind him, the sound of labored steps filled his ears. The person's feet made a squishing sound as they sank and rose in the coarse sand with each step. As he sat in the broken chair, his eyes rolled around in his head, and the slow spin when he stood now felt more like a vial inside an out-of-control centrifuge. His stomach did cartwheels inside his body, and the beers he savored made their way back up his esophagus toward his mouth, the acid burn coursing through his throat.

The vomit made its way to the top of his throat, and his hands reached to his mouth to ensure the contents of his stomach didn't spew onto the pristine beach. His hands suddenly jerked to a stop only inches from his mouth. He yanked at his hands several times and found them restrained. As he looked down, he saw the thick handcuffs wrapped around his wrists connected to a metal ring fixed to a stainless-steel table.

A set of hands grabbed his shoulders.

The sand and water disappeared. Gone was the beach, the blue skies, even the palm trees.

Nick jerked his head up to find the stern expression of Sir staring down at him.

"Well, welcome back, prisoner," said Sir. "I'm glad the Chemist finally found the right concoction. I hope your slumber was filled with champagne wishes and caviar dreams."

Nick balled his hands into a fist, but he remained quiet.

"Interesting stories you shared about Mogul," Sir said.

That name. The Secret Service's code name for the president. A quiet rage welled up from within, and he knew whatever drugs they'd given him must have caused him to crack. *No one can hold out forever*, he reminded himself. The only question running through his mind was, *What the hell did I tell him?*

———— ◆◇◆ ————

Sir exited the interrogation room and walked down the hall. He needed a drag but could use something stronger than nicotine. The bottle of Macallan 15 stuffed in his footlocker under his bed came to mind. He knew that wouldn't be his smartest move, instead he proceeded outside. Before he reached the northern staircase, Evelyn's voice echoed down the narrow, dimly lit hallway.

"Where you headed?" she asked.

Sir turned around. "Need a smoke. Care to join me?"

"No," came her reply in a curt tone. "Where are we with The Body Man?"

"The third round of drugs worked."

"And?"

"He's blabbering, which is somewhat good while also bad."

"How so?"

"It's always a challenge to separate fact from fiction."

Evelyn's gaze narrowed. "Go on."

"I did get him to confirm he printed off four copies of the documents."

"You didn't prompt him?"

"No, he did it on his own, and since it backs up what they found on his laptop, I tend to think he's telling the truth. At least somewhat."

"And what did he do with the other three copies?"

Sir paused. "He either gave them to Rose, the next-door neighbor, or Danny Frazier."

"Well, which one?"

"I think he's trying to protect Rose, but I have the feeling she didn't get anything. It's too obvious."

"So, Danny has them?"

"Yes, and no."

"What the hell does that mean?" Evelyn's expression turned into a scowl.

"He talked in circles, with elements of truth twisted between the lies. Nick Jordan is good, really good. He was trained by the best to withstand interrogation and it shows."

"We're being paid for answers, not excuses."

"I know."

Evelyn pressed Sir. "If he gave Danny the documents, does he still have them? Maybe they are at his apartment in D.C.?"

"Possibly, but I'm not sure. I need to get back in there and keep pumping him for answers. I really feel like we're getting closer."

"Skip your nicotine break and get back in there. Break him. I don't give a shit what's required. Just do it."

Sir's upper lip curled. "I will."

Evelyn turned and under her breath muttered, "You better."

37

WASHINGTON, D.C.

GEORGE WASHINGTON UNIVERSITY HOSPITAL

Marcus and Merci walked into the front lobby of the hospital and toward the bank of elevators. Ten feet separated them, with Marcus leading the way. He spotted two Secret Service agents in the lobby and looked straight ahead to avoid unwanted eye contact. Several people entered the elevator while Marcus stood closest to the door and pushed the button for the fifth floor. After two stops, they arrived. Another person got off with them, turning right while he and Merci took a left.

It looked like a white-coat-and-blue-scrubs convention as they made their way down the hall. Shift change began as the doctors, nurses, and half the Secret Service agents swapped out staff. Marcus chose this time since things turned a little chaotic. The plan was simple enough. He would enter Danny's room and administer the drugs intravenously through the IV port.

Another med drop, right on schedule.

Merci acted as his backup if things went south. Marcus knew she could handle herself against a Secret Service agent.

The drugs Marcus would inject into Danny's bloodstream worked slowly. The deadly cocktail would shut down his vital organs over twenty to thirty minutes. A thorough blood panel done during his autopsy would likely find the abnormal chemicals, but by that point, it would not matter.

Danny would be dead, and he and Merci long gone.

The first step was to get past Danny's guards.

As they approached the ICU room, the agent to the right of the door put out his arm to block the doorway. "Need to see your ID," the surly man in a navy-blue suit said as he stared at Marcus and blocked the doorway.

"Of course, officer." Marcus handed over his hospital identification.

The agent took the badge and ran it through a small device he removed from his suit jacket. The LCD screen turned green, and the word *APPROVED* appeared.

He did the same for Merci, then said, "We'll need to pat you both down."

The agent on the left side of the door stepped toward them.

"Absolutely," Marcus said.

Merci winked. "Highlight of my day." Her response garnered the slightest bit of a smirk from the agent closest to her.

After the search ended, the agents moved aside. Marcus and Merci entered Danny's room where they found two more agents on either side of the bed near the headboard. Their faces were stoic as they sat up straight and eyed them wearily.

"Med time," Marcus said as he approached the bed.

Both agents remained quiet; the one on the left side gave a subtle head nod.

Merci stood to his left.

Marcus reached the footboard as his cell phone vibrated in his right front pocket. Only one person had the number. He pulled out the phone and didn't need to look at the display.

Why the hell is he calling? This can't be good.

He considered ignoring the call but knew that wasn't an option. "I'm with another patient. Can this wait?" Marcus asked as he answered the phone.

The voice on the other end said one word. "Abort."

His stomach tensed. "What was that?"

"Abort."

"Not possible."

"Did you already administer the meds?"

"No."

"Don't give him those drugs, damn it. And get the hell out of the hospital, now."

"Understood." The line went dead, and Marcus put his phone back in his pocket. He pivoted close to the footboard and faced Merci, careful not to change his expression.

He used a prearranged phrase to let her know they were in imminent danger and needed to terminate the hit. "Mr. Brown took a turn for the worse. We need to go ASAP."

"OK. Got it," Merci said.

Marcus nodded but said nothing.

She turned and started for the door with Marcus on her heels.

The Secret Service agent sitting to the right of Danny spoke. "Hold up."

"Yes, officer," Marcus said as he turned back, careful to keep his tone even keeled, his expression friendly.

"I know you," the agent said.

"Well, I've been taking care of Agent Frazier the past few days."

"No. That's not it. I saw you yesterday near the elevators, but you looked different. It's your eyes ..."

Connected to the footboard, a white plastic clipboard dangled from a hook. It contained Danny Frazier's chart. Marcus didn't have time to think, only react. With one smooth motion, he grasped the clipboard, pulled it from the hook, turned it horizontal, and whipped it through the air at the agent's head.

Merci reacted in tandem with Marcus. She spun around and lunged for the agent on the left side of Danny.

The agent on the right drew his gun and raised it toward Marcus as the clipboard struck him above the bridge of the nose with the corner of the hardened plastic. His left hand reached up to protect his face as a sharp pain spread across his eyes and momentarily made him unsteady. Marcus dropped his shoulder like a linebacker trying to drill a receiver, and he hit the agent square in the solar plexus, sending him off the ground. The agent landed against the wall behind the hospital bed with a dull *thud*.

Merci had achieved the *sam dan*, or third-degree black belt, in Taekwondo by the time she turned twenty. Her scissor kicks were vicious and served as her go-to move to immobilize any threat. She moved through the air with the grace of a swan but the ferocity of a hawk. The kick struck the agent below his throat, and the force of the kick rendered him unconscious immediately.

They both knew the agents outside would enter within seconds.

The first agent shoved the door open and stepped inside, but made a tactical error of not drawing his weapon. Marcus reached full stride and hit him with a closed fist punch to the side of the head, causing the agent to crumple like a rag doll onto the floor.

With his weapon drawn, the second agent breached the door ready to fire.

Merci swept hard at his legs and cut them out from under him. He discharged his weapon, the deafening sound inside the small area causing a tremendous ringing in both Marcus and Merci's ears. The round sailed high over Merci's head and lodged into the ceiling. The back of the agent's head hit the floor, and he lost consciousness.

Marcus and Merci knew they weren't out of the woods. As planned, they split up as she took a left and he took a right. They both exited Danny Frazier's room in full sprints.

Merci ended up with the easier escape route, as she encountered only one security officer before she reached the south stairwell. The glorified rental cop didn't stand a chance as she delivered a vicious throat punch and he fell to the ground. Two minutes later, she arrived at the predetermined rendezvous point without incident.

The electric grinding of the dumpster as it crushed the latest batch of trash caused her to turn around. In her head, she kept track of the time since she fled the chaotic room.

Where the hell is he?

They'd planned to meet at the trash compactor located in the rear of the building on the ground floor within five minutes of their escape.

Seconds dragged on, and before long, the five minutes expired. Her escape within sight. All she needed to do was run down the alley, take a right-hand turn, then a sharp left. She would be at the Foggy Bottom-GWU Metro station in less than three minutes. From there, she would blend in and disappear like a ghost.

Marcus had told her not to wait if he didn't make it. To go and not look back.

Merci didn't follow the rules.

Never had.

Never would.

———————————◦○◦———————————

Marcus found himself trapped in the north stairwell.

Not the escape plan he imagined.

Within fifty feet of Danny's room, the heat found him. The first bullet had screamed past his head close enough for him to feel the air displaced next to his cheek. The round had struck the wall before him and sent pieces of drywall into the air like a puff of smoke. There had been no "Freeze and put your hands up." With four agents down, there were still six more on the premises. Three had formed a protective bubble around Danny Frazier while the other three went on the hunt.

Marcus pushed his strained muscles to the max and reached the nurse's station, a chest-high counter filled with paperwork and various items. Pushing off with his right foot, Marcus had plowed through the north-facing stairwell door to the left of the nurse's station, but not before his outstretched hand had grabbed a black stapler from the counter. As he cleared the door jamb, another round had hit inches from the door frame.

Man, these bastards don't give up.

He assumed the stairwell would afford him some measure of cover, but Marcus needed to make it down three flights of stairs to his hiding place for the Glock 19. Finding a groove, he took three steps at a time before pivoting at the platform between levels to catch the next series of steps. After he hustled down two sets of stairs, he heard the agents. There was just enough time to dive into a rounded alcove on the platform as a hail of bullets tore up the concrete wall before him.

He was trapped like a rat on a log floating down a rushing river, with only his wits and a black Swingline stapler to save him. With his death assured, the only question he pondered was would it be best to dive for the next flight of steps and likely die in a hail of bullets or charge the approaching agents and meet his end facing them head-on?

◄O►

Merci heard a barrage of bullets as she opened the glass box containing the firehose mounted to the second level stairwell wall. She reached behind the large, wrapped hose and wiggled free the hidden Glock 19. With the weapon cradled in her left hand, she took two steps at a time. On the way up, she racked the weapon.

As she arrived at the top of the stairs between the second and third floor, she saw him. Huddled in the corner, with a black object in his hand, Marcus looked relieved to see her. They exchanged a brief series of hand signals.

He lowered three fingers, one at a time. When all three fingers were down, she watched as he lunged from the sliver of wall that provided him limited shelter, armed with his black stapler extended out away from him. The darkened object appeared to be a gun. Merci leaned out from the stairwell, exposing only her arm, and pointed the Glock toward the top of the stairs, which led to the third floor.

As fast as possible, Merci emptied the magazine, spraying bullets all around the top of the stairs. She grabbed Marcus by the white lab coat, pulled him toward her, and moved down the steps to the lower level.

Fifteen seconds later, they both sucked in fresh air as they emerged from the stairwell on the ground floor. Without looking back, they ran all-out down the alley toward the main road. Marcus shed the white lab coat while Merci took off the blue scrubs that covered a black t-shirt and form-fitting leggings. They tossed the clothes toward the side of the alley behind a dumpster along with the gun. With no fresh mag, the Glock was nothing more than an expensive paperweight.

With the coast clear, they emerged from the service road and, not wanting to raise suspicions, walked at a brisk pace until reaching the Metro station several blocks away.

———◦———

Hand in hand, they took the Blue Line Metro train and got off at the third stop, Metro Center. Before switching to the Red Line, Marcus retrieved a small duffel bag hidden in a trash can at the end of the platform, and they quickly changed clothes and removed the facial disguises.

Next, they boarded another Red Line train for two stops and got off at Judiciary Square.

They still hadn't said a word since they'd left the hospital. After walking up the stairs and exiting at Fourth and D Streets, Marcus paused.

"Where we headed?" Merci asked.

Marcus smirked. "I need a drink. A stiff one."

"Now you're talking."

"Ever been to the Billy Goat Tavern?" Marcus asked.

"Um, no,'" Merci said with raised eyebrows. "It sounds shady."

Marcus laughed. "Worried about your reputation, are we?"

"A girl only has her reputation and her good looks."

"Not sure about the former, but as for the latter, you've got that in spades." Marcus gave her backside a not-too-subtle pat. "Pretty sure you'll fit right into the place."

38

— • —

SANTA MONICA AIRPORT

Peter Casha climbed aboard the Gulfstream G280 jet. Each step caused a slight jar to his shoulder, sending pain down his arm and across his upper torso. The morphine he injected on the boat no longer dulled the damage from Hector's bullet.

The attractive flight attendant, Cindy, met him at the door and could tell from his ashen face he wasn't well. Peter normally remarked on her chestnut hair, the smell of her cocoa butter lotion, and her warm smile. She worked many of the flights the company arranged for him, and they both engaged in harmless flirting with each other.

Cindy asked if everything was OK, but when Peter didn't reply, she disappeared into the galley.

Unbeknownst to him, she picked up the phone for the pilot.

"You OK, Mr. Casha?" The pilot came out of the cockpit and approached the seat Peter plopped into as he entered the plane.

Peter looked up, a smirk that clearly masked pain formed in the corner of his lips. "I've been better, Ted." With his one good arm, he struggled to remove his polo shirt and reveal his thick gauze-wrapped shoulder. The white bandages revealed deep-red blood stains.

"Jesus. Have you been stabbed?"

"No. Shot." Peter said.

"We need to get you to a hospital immediately."

"Not here. I need to get back to the city."

Ted shook his head in protest. "You're in no condition to fly across the country, Mr. Casha. It looks like you've lost a lot of blood."

Peter didn't want to get into a pissing match with the pilot, who he thought was a good guy just trying to do his job. But a gunshot wound meant paperwork and a call to the local authorities. That wasn't an option for him. "Trust me; I'll survive. Just need to clean out the wound, get some more morphine, and apply a fresh dressing on the shoulder. I'll be OK after a couple of drinks."

"Are you sure?" Ted didn't look convinced.

"Sadly, yes," Peter said. "Peel some paint and get me back east as quick as possible. We have people that can patch me up."

"If you say so, Mr. Casha." Ted shook his head. "Wheels up in five minutes."

"Roger that," Peter said. He gave himself a shot of morphine and settled into the seat.

Cindy returned and helped him clean the wound. Her gentle touch and reassuring voice helped calm Peter's nerves as they removed the bloodied bandages.

"Hope you don't faint at the sight of blood."

"You're in luck," Cindy replied with a wide smile. "In a former life, I was an ER nurse and worked in the trauma bay. Few things faze a girl like me."

"Why leave that to fly assholes like me around in a tin can at crazy hours?"

Cindy laughed. "Well, for starters the pay is better for far fewer hours. And until right now there was no blood."

"Sorry, I screwed that up."

"For you, it's really no trouble, but can you make it coast-to-coast like this?" Her softened features revealed a genuine concern for his well-being.

"It looks pretty bad, but I'll be fine."

Cindy helped him clean the wound and put on a fresh shirt.

"We have any Tito's on board?" he asked.

"Of course. We always keep a bottle on hand when we know you'll be joining us. A tumbler on the rocks, or maybe mixed with some lemonade?"

Peter smiled from ear to ear. Maybe it was the morphine kicking in. "The bottle will do, Cindy."

Cindy returned with the bottle a minute later. "Any food?"

Peter raised the bottle level with his head. "A liquid dinner for me, but I do need one more thing."

"Of course. What?"

"I need a cell phone. Lost mine earlier."

Cindy returned with a new iPhone still in the packaging. "We keep a box of burners on the plane. The battery is charged, and I'll dispose of it when you're done."

He thanked her and took a few long drags from the bottle. The liquid warmed his throat. He dialed the number from memory.

"Hello?"

"Joe, it's me." Peter said.

"Bro, I didn't recognize the number. Plus, you sound different."

"Had a rough night."

"Where are you?"

"On the jet. We took off from Santa Monica."

"What happened? Your phone went straight to voicemail each time I called."

"Hit a snag."

"Is the job done?" asked Joe.

"Yes," said Peter. "But I got shot."

"Fuck. How bad is it?"

"Going to need to go under the knife. He got me in my shoulder."

"Who?"

"Hector."

"Tell me exactly what happened."

Peter spent the next twenty minutes telling Joe everything.

"Look. I'm in D.C. but can make a few calls and get a team to meet you at Teterboro."

"Why are you in D.C.?"

"Junior wants me to meet with someone."

"Who?"

"The prince."

"Are you going to deliver the zip drive to him?" Peter asked.

"No, not yet. At least not all of it."

"Where are you meeting him? The embassy?"

"No, they want to meet somewhere away from prying eyes."

"Who's going to have your six?"

"I was thinking at first of asking you, but you're not up to it in your condition."

"The prince isn't to be trusted, Joe, under any conditions. You need more than the standard security detail if you're going to meet with him."

"Suggestions?"

"Is Marcus available?"

Joe sighed. "He almost got his head blown off by the Secret Service at the hospital."

"He OK?"

"Yeah, he made it out alive because Merci saved his ass."

"What about Frazier? They get him?"

"No, the hit was called off at the last minute. Their evac went all to hell."

"Called off? Why?"

"New intel received from Nick's interrogation."

"But I thought they were afraid Danny knew something and might talk if he regained consciousness."

"That was the case, but now they believe Danny might be the only person that has the info needed."

"Jesus, what a clusterfuck. I'm gonna tell the pilot to take me to D.C.."

"But the doctor is in New York."

"Either get him to D.C., or we can make other arrangements."

"What other arrangements?"

"The Sanctum has a facility near Washington."

"But I thought you didn't trust them?"

"I don't, but they're a money-making business, and if we pay them what they want, they'll come through with the services we need."

"You sure?" Joe asked.

"Yes, get Marcus to go with you to meet the prince. What time is the meeting?"

"In ninety minutes."

"Perfect. When that ends, you can meet me in Manassas at the airport. I'll feel better knowing I've got you to watch my six when the Sanctum patches me up."

"If you say so."

"When have I steered you wrong?"

"Which time you want me to start with?"

Damn it, he has a point. Joe thought.

39

Vienna, VA

Wes Russell pulled in front of Nick Jordan's townhouse and rolled down the window of his magnetic-gray Ford Fusion. He grabbed a wooden strike-anywhere match from the center console, scraped it fast against the steering wheel causing a flame to dance off the end of the match, and lit the Marlboro red. The cigarette dangled from his lips like he was Humphrey Bogart. With his gaze fixed across the street, he sucked in several long drags as the bitter taste of sulfur filled his mouth.

Nothing looked out of place. Even though it was only seven at night, the street appeared empty. He grabbed his cell phone and dialed Eli. The phone rang four times before it rolled to voicemail.

"Hey Payne, it's me. I'm at Rose's house. The street appears quiet, and I'm about to head in. I expect the Dew and smokes on my desk when I get in tomorrow morning. Oh, and don't be such a dick to Stone. Later, dogface."

Wes hung up the phone and finished the last few puffs. He knew he needed to quit, and the guys in his squad gave him a hard time for the habit. "But I'm addicted," he would always retort. Wes rolled up the window, climbed out of the car, and dropped the smoking nub on the asphalt. He ground the last dying embers into a pulp with the heel of his brown shoe.

Out of force of habit, he drew his Glock 19, checked the mag, and confirmed he had one in the chamber. With the weapon hot, he slid it back into his right hip holster and crossed the street. As he reached the bottom step, he tapped the Kevlar vest he wore under his short-sleeve shirt. After four tours in Iraq, Wes knew firsthand all it takes is some jackass with a gun and a lucky shot to ruin a perfectly good day.

He took the nine steps three at a time and approached the door. Before he raised his hand to knock, he reached into his front pocket and pulled out the sticky note to confirm the address. Left of the door on the siding were the numbers 2207.

Good, right place.

Few things embarrassed him more than rolling up on the wrong house and flashing his credentials to the wrong person. As Wes raised his left hand to pound on the solid door, his eyes glanced down, and he noticed the slight gap between the door latch and the frame.

Something's not right.

His right hand reached down and withdrew the Glock while his left hand went from a balled fist to an open palm as he slowly applied pressure to the ajar door.

Old people sometimes forget to close their doors all the way.

With little pressure, his palm pushed the door open. The hinges hadn't been greased in years, and they gave a not-too-subtle creaking sound as it crept open. With the Glock raised and level with his chin, Wes stepped into the house. His eyes darted back and forth as he looked for anything out of the ordinary.

⸻◦⸻

Don stood over Rose and berated her with one question after another.

Ryan was getting sick of his shit. "Dude, she knows nothing about the documents," he said.

With a shake of the head, Don said, "I don't believe her. The Body Man must have told her something."

"Stop using that reference in front of her," said Ryan.

"The Body Man?" Don scowled. "Whatever."

Confused about what was going on, Rose looked back and forth as the two men bickered.

"Look, I told you, she doesn't know anything," said Ryan.

"Then what are we going to do with her?"

"You should have thought about that before you kicked in her door, asshole."

Don shrugged. "Man, I reacted; it's as simple as that."

"Come with me," Ryan said. He exited the living room and walked toward the adjacent dining area.

"What are you going to do to me?" Rose asked from the chair. A level of panic clear in her voice gave Ryan a dull ache in the pit of his stomach.

"Gag her," Ryan said as he left the room.

Ryan and Don walked into the kitchen. They stood on either side of the island in the center of the room facing one another. Ryan nervously tapped on the glass cooktop with his index finger. Don said he wanted to put a bullet in her head, but Ryan tried to figure another way out. The conversation became heated, and neither man wanted to budge.

"Look, I need to grab her some water," Ryan said as he turned toward the kitchen sink.

"You hear that?" Don asked as his head snapped to the left.

"Hear what?" Ryan asked.

Don didn't wait for a response. The creaking sound from the front of the house drew his attention. He paused and raised a finger towards Ryan. Silence returned and he listened for about twenty seconds before he took three long strides and reached the galley-style door that separated the dining area from the kitchen.

―――――◄O►―――――

Wes cleared the foyer, his gun raised, eyes scanning the room for threats. Once he turned the corner into the living room, he saw an elderly woman taped to the patio-style armchair.

Rose Lewis? Damn it. I should have called for backup.

It was too late, and he knew it.

Rose saw his movements and looked toward him. Her eyes grew wide pleading for help. She tried to talk, the inaudible sound muffled by the sock dangling from her mouth. Wes raised his left hand and brought his extended index finger to his mouth, indicating she needed to stay quiet as he approached the chair. Rose nodded, and he got within a few feet as the door in the adjoining dining room swung open.

Fifteen feet away, an armed man took a step into the room.

Wes shifted his weight, pivoted his arms, and had the man sighted in before his body fully cleared the doorway. The gun the man gripped in his right hand swung up.

With a firm voice, Wes said, "FBI. Drop your weapon."

Jesus, this wasn't worth Dew and a pack of smokes.

His mind flashed back to Mosul where hajis popped out from behind doors, windows, and cars parked on the side of the road without warning. You name it, they hid behind it. Back then you didn't announce who you were. As a soldier, once you engaged a hostile threat, you fired. Questions arrived during the debrief later, but survival always came first.

The man continued to raise his gun, and Wes entered autopilot mode.

Wes didn't hesitate. The man with the gun posed a threat, not only to himself but also the innocent woman taped to the chair. With smooth trigger pulls, two consecutive rounds fired from his Glock in rapid succession. Both bullets struck the man in the forehead within an inch of each other. His head lurched back as the rear of his skull exploded. Blood and brain matter splattered all over the white ceiling and beige wall behind the mahogany buffet.

Before Wes had time to process what had occurred, another man emerged through the galley door. The second target froze as the body in front of him dropped to the ground in a heap of twitching flesh.

<hr />

Barely two steps behind his partner, Ryan watched as the back of Don's head exploded.

He froze.

Ryan's legs felt like two pylons surrounded by hardened concrete. His eyes darted to the left, where a man with an FBI badge on his left hip stood behind Rose. The FBI agent's gun moved from Don's lifeless body and was now pointed toward him. Ryan turned his body, raised his gun to hip level, and fired off two quick rounds.

With no aim, the first bullet passed to the left of Rose's head and slammed into the far wall of the living room, sending shards of drywall and white plumes of dust into the air. The second bullet somehow found its mark and struck the man on the upper left side of his chest.

Before Ryan's mind recognized the successful shot, he felt two rapid smacks to his chest. The Kevlar vest was the only thing that saved his life. His left hand clutched at his vest while his legs gave way and he fell to the side. With his right hand still raised, he squeezed off two more rounds, although he could tell from his angle of descent both bullets flew far to the left of his intended target.

Wes felt as if a sledgehammer hit his chest as the round struck his body armor. It all happened in a split second. He reached for his chest at the same time he squeezed off two rounds from his Glock. Two more muzzle flashes burst from the barrel of the man's gun. The deafening sounds of the retorts in confined space caused his eardrums to burst. He didn't hear the ricochet as the second round struck a thick antique plaque hanging on the wall behind him.

Wes muttered two final words as a searing pain burned his neck below the hairline.

"Oh shit!"

His left hand moved from the dime-sized hole in his shirt to his throat which suddenly felt on fire. The bullet punctured between his sixth and seventh vertebrae and exited his windpipe, causing an exit wound below his Adam's apple the size of a golf ball. Blood flowed from the wound, and his legs buckled with his spinal artery punctured. He watched in slow motion as the second man fell in unison with him. Wes's brain commanded his index finger to pull the trigger again. Two final bullets spat from the barrel of the Glock and found their intended target as they struck the side of the man's head.

As Wes dropped to one knee, his body convulsed, and a steady stream of blood sprayed from between his clutched fingers. Involuntarily, he dropped the Glock as his right hand joined his left and gripped his throat. His last conscious thoughts flashed rapidly, like a movie playing in fast forward. He saw Beth Ann's face, thought of the first time they spoke, followed by the sound of his boy's laughter.

God, I'll miss them.

The light faded until only darkness.

40

WASHINGTON, D.C.

J. EDGAR HOOVER BUILDING

Eli stepped off the elevator, took a sharp right turn, and walked down the hall toward the director's suite.

"You ever been up here before?" Kat walked next to him and kept his hurried pace.

"His office or this floor?"

"The director's office."

"Nope."

Arriving at the desk, Eli handed one of his cards to the director's assistant, Annie.

She took the card and looked up with a warm smile. "Go ahead inside, Agent Payne; the director has been awaiting your arrival. Yours as well, Agent Stone."

As Eli stepped inside the office. It looked smaller than he expected. A large cherry desk sat near the far wall, and several stacks of papers near a simple brass reading lamp adorned the desk. A small round table sat in the corner closest to the entrance, with four chairs and two leather couches facing each other near the center of the room. Lining the walls were shelves filled from floor to ceiling with books, plaques, and other keepsakes. Several pieces of artwork hung on the walls, the most vivid an epic five-foot-long landscape oil painting of Monument Valley. A fireplace on the wall crackled and hissed as a fire roared.

Director Ludington stood as Eli and Kat entered, and he walked around the desk to meet them between the couches.

"Director, good to see you again. May I introduce Probationary Agent Katherine Stone."

Ken had a firm grip and gave Eli's hand a solid shake. His eyes left Eli and looked at Kat, whose hand he shook as well. "Ah yes, a pleasure to meet you, Agent Stone. You go by Kat, correct?"

"That's right, sir."

"Hope Eli is treating you well?" The director shook her hand. "He's got a reputation of being slightly, umm, challenging." He said with a wink.

Kat laughed. "You know each other?"

"Yes, we do. Eli didn't tell you?"

Kat jabbed her elbow into Eli's right rib, and he winced in discomfort. "No, he failed to mention that on our long drive here." Her piercing eyes revealed her displeasure.

"I was going to tell you," Eli said as he darted his gaze away from hers.

"Tell her how we met, Eli." The director said.

"Well, we played on the Bureau's softball team."

"The FBI has a softball team?" Kat asked.

The director nodded. "Several."

"And you played together?"

"Nooo," Eli said in a drawn-out manner. "We were on opposite teams. The director has a C-level team made up of all the big dogs."

The director let out a deep laugh; his voice inflection sounded like an old engine as it sputtered back to life. "We played against each other for the league championship three years ago."

"That was one hell of a game, sir." A wide smile covered Eli's face.

"And I still have the scar to prove it." The director pulled back a tuff of hair, revealing a one-inch scar on his scalp.

"Yikes," Kat said. "You got that playing softball?"

"I got that from Agent Payne. It felt like I got hit by a freight train."

"What?" Kat asked, unable to hide the surprise in her voice.

With a sheepish grin on his face and raised shoulders, Eli said, "The director rounded third, and he should have stayed on base. Let's say by the time he reached home plate, he ended up a few feet short."

"You took out the director of the FBI?" Kat gave his upper chest a not-too-playful shove.

"No. I stopped an opposing player from scoring the winning run."

Kat looked at the director. "And you didn't fire him?"

The director laughed. "No. Actually, I almost promoted him about a year later."

"But?" Kat's eyebrows arched upward.

"That, my dear, is a story for another day, another time." The director pointed to the couch closest to the fireplace. "Take a seat, you two; I want to discuss the Webb/Jordan case. I've read through the file, but hope you have more to tell me after today."

"We have lots to share, sir," said Eli.

The director took a seat opposite them. "OK. Read me in."

It took Eli and Kat almost thirty minutes to lay it all out.

A Coke-bottle-thick glass coffee table with an outer metal frame separated the two couches. When they'd first sat down, Eli had put his cell phone face down on the table and set it on vibrate.

As Eli finished the update, the phone shook in quick pulses, sending short tremors through the table. He reached over and hit the side button of his phone, silencing the call. "Sorry about that." Eli looked embarrassed.

"Can I see the pictures?" The director asked.

"Of course." Eli handed over his tablet.

The director flipped through them one at a time and even zoomed in, using his thumb and index finger on the ones that might depict Nick Jordan.

"I mean, it looks like the guy in the photo, but it's hard to say with certainty."

"We're pretty sure it's him, sir," Eli said. "And I think this photographic evidence proves his abduction."

"So, where did these men with Russian accents take him?"

"I made a few calls on the drive here," Kat said. "We requested the flight plan and should have the details from the ATC within the hour."

The director nodded. "I have some contacts within the FAA. If anyone gives you a hard time, let me know. If you track where the plane went, maybe you'll find him."

"That's the plan, sir," Eli said.

"Question is: why would they abduct a Secret Service agent?"

"The White House won't even admit he works for them," Kat said.

The director rubbed his chin. "Yes. Well, speaking of that, I had an interesting conversation with the president at the White House today regarding this investigation."

Kat tapped Eli with her left hand on the leg, and she looked over at him.

"The president called me into a private meeting and said he wanted to discuss an active FBI investigation looking into a missing Secret Service agent. He told me he wanted the Bureau to stand down."

The phone vibrated again. Eli looked perturbed as he leaned over and muted the incoming call once again.

"He asked you to back off an active investigation?" Kat asked.

The director nodded. "Correct, and I told him in no uncertain terms the Bureau excelled at missing-person cases, and we should take the lead on this."

"And what did he say?" Eli asked.

"He agreed, but suggested we let the Secret Service find him."

Kat sighed. "But that doesn't make any sense. Why wouldn't they want us involved?"

"He wouldn't even tell me the missing agent's name. That's why I had Annie pull the file."

"They're hiding something," Kat said.

The director and Eli looked at Kat, and they both nodded.

"The president wouldn't give me a name, but he did admit the agent was on his protective detail."

"Then I may be able to help," Eli said.

"How so?" The director asked.

"I have a, well, let's just say contact on his detail."

"Can you approach him discreetly?"

"Maybe. But it's not a he."

"Uh-oh. A friend or a *frieeeend*." The director intentionally let the word drag out. A slight smirk formed at the corner of his mouth as he looked at Eli.

"Currently she's neither."

"Well, that doesn't bode well."

"Look. It's time I shake the tree hard and see what falls out," Eli said.

"Hold up." Kat said. "The president wants us to back off the investigation."

The director cleared his throat. "Let's get one thing straight. The President of the United States doesn't call all the shots. He might be my boss, but he has no authority to tell me how to run our investigations. If a Secret Service agent is missing, it's the job of the FBI to find him."

"And what do you want us to do?" Eli asked.

"Your job," the director said. "For the record, I want you to continue the investigation as you would any missing-person case. I want you to find this man and get him back safe and sound while following bureau procedures. But off the record ..." The director paused.

After almost half a minute of silence, Eli responded. "Yes? And off the record?"

Ken reached into his pocket and removed two business cards, handing one to Eli and the other to Kat. "My personal cell. Only a few people have it. Off the record, you can have carte blanche access to whatever you need. I don't know what game President Steele is playing, but something isn't right. My intuition says he doesn't want him found. If he did, he wouldn't interfere. Or if he does want him found, he doesn't want us to be the ones to do so." He paused and looked at both Eli and Kat, giving each of them a hard stare. "We on the same page?"

"Yes, sir. Find him, but don't get caught if we need to bend protocol."

Ken smiled and said nothing, but gave a not-too-subtle wink.

Eli's cell phone vibrated for the third time.

The director pointed at the phone as it shook on the tabletop. "Someone really wants to talk to you, Payne."

"Do you mind, sir?"

"No. Take it."

Eli flipped over the phone and recognized the number. He answered in a gruff tone. "Where's the fire, Miller? I'm in an important meeting."

The director and Kat watched as all the blood from his face drained.

"When?" Eli said. After a brief pause, he replied, "I'm on my way." He tried to stand, but his legs appeared weak.

"What is it, Payne? You look like you've seen a ghost."

Eli shook his head in disbelief. "My squad supervisor, Wes Russell, was just killed in a shootout. He was checking in on a witness at my request. She's the one who placed the missing person call."

"Is Rose, OK?" Kat asked, her voice cracked as she spoke.

"She's being transported to the hospital, but she's alive. Sounds like she's pretty shaken up." Eli tried standing once more, and this time made it to his feet. "I'm sorry, sir, but I have to go."

Kat was already on her feet as the director stood.

"I'm coming too. My security team will get us there faster," the director said.

Kat leaned forward and hugged Eli. She pulled him in close to her and let his head fall on her shoulder. "I'm so sorry, Eli."

Tears formed. "It's all my fault," mumbled Eli. He stared at the fireplace and watched the flames as they danced.

41

— ∘ —

WASHINGTON, D.C.

THE LINCOLN MEMORIAL

Joe told the driver to stop at the corner of Constitution Ave. and Henry Bacon Drive NW. As the Mercedes S 560 pulled up to the curb, Joe climbed out of the passenger seat. He leaned toward the open window and told the driver to sit tight. Marcus and Merci emerged from the back seat and fell in behind as Joe walked down the sidewalk.

The pathway split and to the left was the Vietnam Veterans Memorial, also known as "the wall." Even at this late hour, it still had a steady stream of visitors.

Joe veered to the right, and as they got close to the rounded metal barricades surrounding the entrance to the Lincoln Memorial, two men stepped out from the shadows. Both men wore finely tailored Armani suits and A. Testoni Italian shoes. With dark hair and short, neatly trimmed mustaches, they could have passed for twins. The only distinguishing feature was one man wore a red tie, the other a charcoal gray.

"Good evening, gentlemen," the man with the red tie said. He looked back and forth between Joe and Marcus and eyed the latter suspiciously. He then looked at Merci. "And ma'am."

Merci uttered the word "asshole" under her breath. She had some deep seeded issues with men from certain middle east countries, primarily because of their abhorrent treatment of women.

The man in the red tie either didn't hear her or chose not to respond.

"Has the prince arrived?" Joe looked around but didn't see him.

"He has, but before we can escort you, I'll need to check the three of you for weapons."

Shit. Joe immediately realized what he had on his right hip.

The man with the red tie approached Joe and pulled back his suit coat, exposing the hilt of the Omega dagger. The steel was a work of art designed by Half Face Blades, an outfit in San Diego founded by a former Navy SEAL. Peter Casha knew the owner personally and purchased himself and Joe matching knives the year before. After checking Joe's pockets and running his hands up and down his legs and torso, the guard pointed to the weapon. "May I?"

"Of course." Joe nodded as he looked down at the hilt.

The man removed the weapon from the sheath and examined the craftsmanship of the seven-inch-long knife. Above the trident on the hilt, an engraved Spartan with the words *Never Forget* were etched into the steel. The guard smiled. "That's a damn fine-looking blade, Mr. Lagano, but I can't let you near the prince with it in your possession. Nothing personal, just protocol."

"I understand. As long as I get it back, we won't have a problem."

"You will. My associate here will hold onto it for safekeeping."

Next, the two men searched Marcus and Merci, who were unarmed.

"Follow me," the man in the red tie turned and walked away.

A full moon hung low in the night sky and appeared to hover atop the Washington Monument, bathing the structure in a subtle glow. Streetlamps illuminated the sidewalks and beams of light shone upon the thirty-six fluted Doric columns of the memorial. A lone figure stood on the fifty-eighth step at the chamber level, his gaze toward the painted sky dotted with stars.

Two guards led the way and climbed the steps with Joe, Marcus, and Merci following. The guard in the red tie tapped the shoulder of the sharply dressed man, who faced Lincoln's statue, his back toward the reflecting pool.

He whispered something into the sharply dressed man's ear.

Prince Abdul bin Salman turned around slowly and looked down at the three visitors several steps below. Unlike his bodyguards, the prince did not wear a fancy suit. Instead, he wore a white button-down long-sleeve shirt, a light-gray pair of pants, and a pair of black shoes with a dull finish. A Piaget Polo S watch adorned his wrist.

"Please, my friends, join me."

Joe approached the prince and extended his hand. "Your highness, my name is Joe Lagano."

Prince Abdul took the extended hand and gave it a firm shake. "Please, no need to be formal here; you may call me Abdul."

Joe said, "This is Marcus and Merci. They ..." He paused for a moment.

"Are here to keep you safe." Abdul finished the statement.

Joe nodded.

"Well, it's a pleasure to finally meet you," Abdul said. "Your boss is quite passionate about his business and appears eager to see our deal finalized."

"I agree," Joe said.

Abdul turned to his right and looked out over the reflecting pool and toward the Washington Memorial. The United States Capitol loomed large in the distance. "I've traveled the world but can say without a doubt, the National Mall is without equal."

"I read your bio. A bachelor's at Columbia in NYC and a master's in international business from Georgetown University. You've spent a lot of time in two of our largest cities."

"And loved every minute of it. Growing up in the House of Saud affords one many privileges. One of them is an excellent education. We are encouraged ... well, I should say *required*—to attend the most prestigious schools in the West. If you want to be the best, you have to learn from them, or so I've been told."

"And you took that education back home where you've recently been named the minister of commerce and investment."

"Yes. Crown Prince Salman, my cousin, has found favor with me. I'd like to think he saw my talent for business and used it for the betterment of the kingdom. Our hope is this agreement will benefit not only our regional interests but also prove to be a profitable venture for your organization."

"That's Junior's intent as well."

The prince, in a subtle motion, pulled back his shirt sleeve and checked his watch. "It's late, and I'm sure you've had a long day in New York before coming. Should we get down to business?"

"Yes, let's," Joe said as he placed his arm behind his back. Marcus placed the seven-inch-wide tablet in his hand while Merci continued to watch the two guards with a wary glance. "Here it is." Joe brought his arm around his body and handed the tablet to the prince, careful not to drop it. "You'll find everything you're looking for on the device."

Abdul took the tablet and swiped on the screen with his finger. For several minutes, he said nothing and merely looked through the data provided. Several times, he pursed his lips and nodded slightly as his eyes narrowed. "Well, I'm no engineer, but everything looks to be in order. Although I must admit, the crown prince will be happy when he can have the full schematics and not only this partial version."

"Show the crown prince what we've provided when you get back to Riyadh. Consider it a good-faith gift and preview of what is coming once we conclude our business."

With a glance over his shoulder, Abdul indicated to the guard with the red tie to hand him a thick bundle of papers folded three times. "Here is a copy of the agreement with the Kingdom of Saudi Arabia. Please have Junior and his legal team review the documents thoroughly and let me know if you find any discrepancies."

"Of course."

"The crown prince is eager for the shipping container to arrive in Jeddah."

"We've got several people on the ship. The weaponry is safe, and we will continue to provide updates on its progress. Transporting them undetected via a container ship was our best option."

"Agreed, but the slowness of the ocean crossing is frustrating."

"We understand, but there was no way to use air transport, and fortunately our port system has enough security lapses that we could procure safe passage with little risk of detection."

Abdul nodded and snapped his fingers. The guard with the gray tie stepped forward and handed the knife to him. "Do you mind if I take a look at this?"

Joe nodded. "Not at all."

The prince looked over the weapon, careful to not brandish it in a flashy way and attract the attention of the National Park Service police, who monitored the memorial.

"Handcrafted?"

"Yes, only a few made."

"I would love to get one like it."

"I'll make a few calls."

"Money is not an issue. I can pay whatever the designer asks." The prince checked the balance of the blade. Perfect. "Do you carry it with you often?"

"Always," Joe said. "I'd be naked without it."

"Have you ever had to use it?"

Joe smirked. The left side of his mouth curved upward as the right side remained still. "Let's say the blade has pierced flesh, and its steel teeth have tasted blood."

"I find knives fascinating. Too often, men resort to firearms. Effective, yes, but impersonal. But to use a blade such as this one against an opponent, now that is the sign of a true warrior."

Joe reached out with his right hand, and the prince placed the knife in his palm. "I completely agree, Abdul."

42

FALLS CHURCH, VA

INOVA TRAUMA CENTER

Eli's eyes sprang open. He looked around the drab hospital room, unsure where he was or how he got there. With his mind in a fog, he tried to focus. His hands gripped the armrest hard enough that his fingers turned pale.

Then he saw Rose. She lay in the hospital bed to his right and appeared to be asleep.

The memories of why he was there flooded back like a torrential rain.

Eli looked at his watch; the display read 12:15 a.m. He had arrived at the hospital three hours earlier with Kat and Director Ludington. Kat had wanted to stay until Rose woke up, but Eli had insisted she go home and get some sleep. They planned to meet at seven sharp to follow new leads.

After arriving at the hospital, Eli had called his friend Dony, a detective with the D.C. Metro Police Department. Eli planned to meet him at Café Bonaparte in Georgetown at nine for breakfast. Eli knew enough cops to realize a free breakfast was the way to any LEO's heart. One good meal could pay dividends when trying to crack a case.

Now fully awake, a fresh feeling of guilt washed over him like a towering wave as he thought about Wes lying on a metal slab four floors below in the morgue.

It should've been me.

An hour passed in silence before Rose stirred. Eli sat at the edge of his seat and cupped her hand in his. As her eyes opened and she looked over at Eli, a slight smile formed at the corner of her burgundy-colored lips.

"Hey, Rose. It's me, Eli."

"Hello, Agent Payne." Rose glanced around the room, and a concerned look spread over her face. "Where am I?"

"You're at the Inova Trauma Center in Falls Church. But trust me, you're ok. The doctors are keeping an eye on you to make sure everything looks good. You had one hell of a night, didn't you?"

"I had a visit from two men claiming to be FBI agents that worked with you. Clearly, they were imposters."

"That's right, Rose. The men who assaulted you died, as did the agent I sent to check on you."

"Who was he?"

"My supervisor. His name was Wes."

Tears welled up and flowed down Rose's wrinkled face. "I'm sorry for your loss, Agent Payne. His actions most certainly saved my life."

"I believe you're right, Rose. So, can you tell me what happened?"

"Of course."

Eli fished his recorder out of his pocket. "If you don't mind, I'd like to record your statement."

"Of course. By all means, dearie, record away."

For the next hour, Rose recounted the events inside her house. Eli stopped her when she started talking about the documents they wanted. "Go back a second, Rose. They called him what again?"

"The Body Man," said Rose. "The one named Don, the vulgar one, he called Ralph The Body Man several times."

Eli felt the hair on the back of his neck stand up at the reference. He thought back to the mysterious text messages he received. "Are you sure he said it just like that?"

"Yes, I'm sure. Is it important?"

"Right now, everything is important."

Rose continued.

Around 3:00 a.m., he and Rose wrapped up, and she drifted back to sleep.

Eli walked down the hall to the waiting area and took a seat in a worn leather chair. He took out his laptop and logged into the FBI server using his encrypted VPN access. Over the next forty-five minutes, he added what Rose told him into Sentinel, the Bureau's case-file database system, being sure to include the term "The Body Man" as well. The three words were seared in his mind as he sank deeper into the chair and finally gave in to the sleep his body craved.

⚬

At 5:00 a.m., the alarm on his smartphone went off, and he awoke. He felt groggy; the ninety minutes of sleep hadn't been enough. Eli stood up, stretched his back, and walked down the hall to the nurse's station. He was on the prowl for a decent cup of java. One of the nurses noticed his bloodshot eyes and took pity on him. She smiled and grabbed him a cup of piping hot coffee from the break room. Eli thanked her and headed back to the waiting room after a brief stop by Rose's room to confirm she was still asleep.

Back in the waiting room, he knew whom he needed to call. The minute he heard Rose say "The Body Man" regarding Nick Jordan, only one name came to mind. It took all his strength to dial her number. Based on how they'd left things, he wasn't sure she would be too excited to hear his voice.

Will she be up?

He knew the answer to that question. *She's the only person that sleeps less than I do.*

Eli dialed the number from memory, and she picked up on the second ring.

"Hello?"

He had not heard her voice in almost six months.

"Mila. It's Eli."

There was a slight pause. "Not the voice I expected to start my day."

An awkward pause ensued.

"I'm sure," he said.

"How are you, Eli?"

"I'm OK. It's been a while."

"I'll say."

Eli cleared his throat. "Sorry to call this early."

"You knew I'd be up at this hour. After all, I've been up since 4:30 working out. I'm guessing it's important."

"Might be life or death."

"What do you need?"

"We need to talk about a case. Somewhere private, away from prying eyes."

"Is this something that could get me in trouble?"

"Let's say it needs to be off the record." There was a brief pause. Eli almost asked if she was still there.

In almost a whisper, she said, "Meet me at the usual place in thirty minutes."

Eli looked down at his watch. "Roger that."

"Park a couple of blocks away and no electronics. Got it?"

"Thanks, Mila. I wouldn't ask if I had someone else I could go to. You're the only one that can help."

"Yeah, we'll see about that."

The line clicked off.

43

PENTAGON CITY

Peter opened his eyes to see Joe standing at the foot of the bed. He looked around; the space appeared to be a standard hospital room. In addition to the white tiled floor, beige walls, and an adjustable bed with vital-sign monitors to the right of the headboard, there was also the unmistakable smell of a bleach-based cleaner.

He recalled the drive at 1:00 a.m. to the industrial park in Pentagon City slightly southwest of downtown Washington. It was dark, and the metal buildings lining the road looked like your standard series of warehouses. Very few people knew that hidden within one structure, the Sanctum operated a level-one trauma center. It served as a hospital for hire utilized by those who required discretion. Given minimal warning, the facility could handle any emergency, including open heart surgery, reconstructive surgeries, or even an occasional craniotomy, to name a few. The procedures were performed by world-renowned surgeons, a regular who's who of medical professionals. Unlike on television shows where off-the-book procedures are performed in rat-infested, filthy conditions, the Sanctum ran a facility so clean, you could eat off the floor minutes after a surgery concluded.

It all came down to one thing.

Money.

With enough of it, anything could be purchased, including exceptional health care.

Peter tilted his head slightly and narrowed his eyes as he looked at his best friend.

"You good?" Joe asked.

Peter shook his head. "You can't hurt steel, bro." The shoulder throbbed, but he knew whatever narcs they'd given him masked the pain.

"Doc said we could leave whenever you're ready," Joe said.

Peter smiled slightly. "I'm ready to bounce. Never been a good patient."

The doctor walked into the room a few minutes later. "How are you feeling, Mr. Casha?"

"Like a million bucks, doc. I'm heading straight to the golf course to go kick Tiger Wood's ass after I leave here."

"You let me know how that works out for you, Elin," the doctor said with a smirk. "I wanted to stop by before you left and let you know what I found."

"I'm all ears."

"The damage to your shoulder was minimal, based on where it struck. I removed the slug. There's limited damage to the muscle around the shoulder, but you'll heal in time. I don't foresee any permanent damage."

"That's good news."

"Only one last thing before you leave."

A man stepped into the room. He wore dark pants, a white shirt, and a navy-blue tie. At a glance, he looked like a bean counter.

"I take it you want to get paid," Joe said.

"Yes," the man with the navy-blue tie said. "We don't run a charitable organization here, sir."

"This isn't universal healthcare?" Peter asked.

"Someone always pays the piper." The doctor replied.

The man with the navy-blue tie held a small digital pad in his hands and switched between several screens with his fingers. "That will be seventy-eight thousand dollars, please."

Joe reached down to the briefcase at the foot of the bed, entered the six-digit rotary combination, and pushed the silver button. The latches clicked open, and he took out three stacks of hundred-dollar bills and placed them on the table near the bed. From a fourth stack, he slipped off the bill strap and counted out thirty additional bills.

The bean counter, pulled out a small machine no bigger than a toaster and fed the stacks of bills into the device. It took only a few seconds for the digital readout on the front of the machine to display the number "$78,000."

"We're good," the doctor said. "That concludes our business tonight. We're open just like 7-Eleven, gentlemen on the off chance you need our services again."

Safely in a black Suburban headed down Interstate 385, Joe drove toward the Jefferson Memorial.

"We're not going to Manassas?" Peter asked.

"No, Junior wants us to stay in the city tonight."

"Where?"

"You know his preference." Joe said.

"The Hay-Adams?"

"That's right."

Peter changed the subject. "How'd everything go with the prince?"

"Fine," Joe said. "No issues."

"Marcus had your six?"

"Yes, he and Merci kept me safe."

"How much longer before he's tapping that shit again?"

"He told me that ended a long time ago."

Peter raised his eyebrows. "Marcus is a red-blooded man. Everything circles back around again, including old tail if you put it nearby for long enough."

Joe smiled. "You would know all about that, Casanova."

44

---•---

WASHINGTON, D.C.

THE DINER

Eli entered the front door and immediately found himself overwhelmed by déjà vu. Here he was once more, not just at any place, but their place. As he walked past the small receptionist stand, he glanced at the sign attached to the front of the wooden podium that read, "WELCOME TO THE DINER." Back when they were an item, The Diner, a twenty-four-hour restaurant on 18th Street, served as their daily meet-up spot. With her unpredictable hours at the Secret Service and his at the Bureau, it became a constant in a relationship fraught with dysfunctionality.

As he walked past the twelve chrome barstools that lined the counter, he knew where to find her. Two people blocked his view to the back of the restaurant, but when they moved, he saw where the high-backed, red-cushioned bench seats curved. Mila Hall chose the spot for one reason: her back would face neither the front nor the rear door. A creature of habit, she never sat where she didn't have a clear line of sight for all the exits.

Their eyes met, and Mila slid out of her seat and stood as Eli approached. Her straight raven colored hair was pulled back in a ponytail and hung low, about six inches above the curvature of her lower back. The black pantsuit hugged her toned legs, and she wore a long-sleeve white blouse with ivory buttons, the top two noticeably undone. The necklace that hung above the top of her cleavage was in the shape of a heart. Eli recognized it since he gave it to her the previous Christmas.

God, she looks fine. Eli wasn't sure what to expect as he got close enough to smell the strawberry crème lotion she used daily.

Mila answered the question as she reached her arms around his broad shoulders and pulled him in for a firm, yet tender hug. He felt her heartbeat against his chest as the embrace lingered.

God, I've missed her. Emotions and feelings washed over him like a blast of hot air.

Mila let go and slid back behind the table. Eli took the wooden chair opposite her and turned it around, the back butting up against the tabletop.

"You look good, tough guy," Mila said.

"As do you," Eli unable to hide the slight change in his voice.

She snapped her fingers. "Six months went by pretty quick."

"Life moves at a fast pace, especially for people who've chosen our type of careers."

Seven months earlier, while lying in bed after a marathon session of love-making, Eli had done the unthinkable: he brought up marriage and kids. Mila clammed up. It took her a while to open up but when she had, everything felt different. She explained to Eli that the Secret Service was her life, and marriage and kids didn't fit into the lifestyle. The rest of the night became a blur. They'd tried to work things out for about a month, but the magic faded. In the end, she said it would be best if they both moved on. It had felt like a sucker punch and hurt like hell.

They hadn't spoken or seen each other since.

"Ever come by here and grab a bite?"

"No," Eli said. "I don't have a reason to visit this part of town anymore."

She nodded. "Makes sense. I still come by for the apple pie."

"You mean for the whipped cream on top?"

"Yeah, that too." A smile formed at the corner of her lips.

A few seconds of awkward silence occurred. Not something typical when they were an item. Breaking the silence, a waitress came and took their orders.

"You said this was about a case?" Mila took a sip of coffee and stared at Eli.

"Yeah, it's pretty important."

"I'm listening."

"It's regarding an investigation for a missing Secret Service agent." Eli watched as her body tensed. Even the muscles in her neck and jaw constricted.

"You don't say," Mila said through gritted teeth.

"Does the name Nick Jordan ring a bell?"

For as long as Eli had known Mila, she was a terrible liar. "Never heard of him," she said.

Eli pulled the White House ID for Nick Jordan out of his pocket and slid it across the table toward her with the picture and name right side up so she could see it. He leaned in closer. "You and I both know that's bullshit. Nick is on the presidential detail. You are on the presidential detail. I might not be part of Mensa, but I'm not a dumb shit either. That being the case, don't tell me you have no idea who he is."

Mila started to slide her body to the side of the seat. "I'd better go."

Eli reached out and grabbed her hands, coupling them in his own. "Look, Mila. I wouldn't come to you if there were another way. I'm here because the people who took Nick killed Wes."

She paused. "Say what?"

"He's dead, Mila. They killed him."

"Wes is dead? Your Wes?"

Eli nodded. "He died last night. I asked him to check on a witness, a woman named Rose Lewis who lives across the street from Nick. She reported him missing and was the one who told me Nick worked for the Secret Service. I went to the White House, and Brandon Walker lied to my face, said he didn't have a clue who I was talking about."

"Brandon's an asshole. I could have told you that. What happened to Wes?"

"Two men showed up last night impersonating FBI agents, said they were working on the case with me. Rose didn't buy it. She tried to call me, but they busted inside her house, tied her up, gagged her, and gave her a thorough grilling. Wes came thirty minutes later and had a gunfight with the two scumbags. He took a slug to the neck and bled out. Rose said the two men wanted to know what Nick did with the documents. Who he had given them to."

"What documents?" Mila asked.

"I don't know. That's why I'm here with you. Trying to figure this shit out."

Mila's eyes darted around the restaurant. "Did you leave your phone in the car?"

"I did."

"This conversation is off the record. As in, I'll deny it ever happened to my dying day. You got that?"

"Yeah, I understand."

"I'm serious; I'll lose my job if anyone finds out we even spoke."

"Why all the secrecy?"

"We've been told to talk to no one, not even each other. But you know how it goes."

Eli looked puzzled. "Why would the senior brass not want you to talk with anyone?"

"Because they are trying to find Nick themselves." Mila said.

"I heard, but they don't appear to be doing a bang-up job."

"Agreed. The whole thing is fishy. Something isn't adding up."

"You want to tell me what Nick does for the Secret Service?"

"What do you mean?"

"I was told personally by the director of the FBI, who was told by the president in a private one-on-one meeting, that Nick was on the presidential detail. Something is not right here, and my gut says it starts with Nick's real role with the Secret Service."

Mila shook her head. "Look, Eli, I want to help, really, but I can't say any more."

"Can't or won't?"

"Can't."

"You want to tell me why Nick is called The Body Man?"

The stern expression she displayed faded as her lips moved back to a smirk. "So, you finally figured out I was the one who sent you the text."

Eli's brow furrowed. "What?"

"The Body Man text. You figured out it came from me."

"Wait. You sent that text?"

"Yes. But if you didn't know then why are you here?"

"When Rose said the two men who assaulted her called him The Body Man. It confirmed I needed to talk with you. But if you sent the text, why didn't you use Nick's real name instead of saying The Body Man?"

"Over electronic communications? Really? Come on now, Eli. I expect more from you. I sent the text from a burner phone I bought at a convenience store. Figured you might ask questions and with your investigative skills, I hoped you could piece together The Body Man was really Nick."

Eli paused and leaned in close. "No more games. I need you to read me in, Mila."

She withdrew. Her eyes darted around the room.

Eli knew the look. Like when a witness is about to reveal secrets but clams up and changes their mind at the last second. He was this close and couldn't lose her now. Eli lowered his voice and used a softer tone. "Look, Mila, we go way back. I know somewhere inside you still trust me. Believe me when I tell you I need to know who Nick is and why somebody would want to kidnap him. You texted me The Body Man reference for a reason. I suspect it's because you want Nick found and you realize the Secret Service is no closer to finding him now than the day he went missing. I'm the guy that can do it, but I need your help. Please, Mila." Eli's tone turned to a plead by the time he spoke the last few words.

Mila's hard-as-steel exterior softened as her body relaxed. "I do trust you, Eli. But ..."

"But what?"

45

WASHINGTON, D.C.

THE DINER

Mila looked into Eli's eyes. The glare pierced deep within. "I have a question." She said.

Eli looked back with an intense stare, but almost immediately he looked away. She always had a way of disarming him with a single glance, and Mila always won an argument. Sure, she used her feminine charms from time to time, every woman does, but mainly her arguments were sound. And if Eli had the upper hand in a debate, it only took one look from her, and he melted.

"Yeah, what is it?" he asked.

"What is the primary job of the Secret Service??"

Eli's face contorted into a puzzled look as he pursed his lips and scrunched his brow. "Are you serious? Is this a civics test?" he asked.

Mila frowned. "No, Elijah," she said in a stern tone. She only pulled his given name out when she grew irked. "Just answer the question, since you want me to answer yours. Trust me when I say it's a relevant question."

Eli relented. "The Secret Service has many responsibilities, including investigating counterfeiting, forgeries, and other financial crimes. But the primary objective is to protect the president and various leaders within the government."

"Protect the president from outside threats, correct?"

"Umm, yeah," Eli said. "Everyone knows that."

"Well, the job of The Body Man is to protect something much more important than the physical body of the president."

"What's more important than his safety?"

"The Body Man is tasked with protecting the office of the presidency, which is more than one man or, one day soon, one woman's well-being."

Eli's eyes narrowed. "Sorry, I don't follow."

Mila smiled. "You will," she said before adding, "I know you love history."

"I do."

"Well, it all started in 1963 during the last few months of the Kennedy administration. As most of the world knows, JFK was quite the lothario. The Secret Service spent almost as much effort trying to protect him as it did ushering women into the White House for the president's, umm ... amusement, you could say."

"Yes, I've heard the stories of Marilyn Monroe."

"Please. Marilyn was only the tip of the iceberg. The director of the Secret Service, James Joseph Rowley, and several key members of the White House leadership were concerned about the president's behavior. They also realized the world was changing rapidly and the media's infatuation with the president was growing at an unprecedented pace. JFK was the first television president. His good looks and swagger were far more appealing than his legislative experience. It was only a matter of time before the president's private escapades became public fodder and someone raised legitimate concerns about what would happen to the office if the stories got out. It was at that point the powers that created a new position we internally refer to as The Body Man."

Eli interrupted. "And this new role was supposed to keep the president out of trouble?"

Mila shook her head. "Not exactly. It's much more complicated than that. If they can keep the president from doing something that will damage the presidency, they intervene. But most of the time they step in after the president screws up. The Body Man's job is to clean up the mess and make it go away."

"The Body Man is a cleaner for the office of the presidency?"

"In many ways, yes."

A slight laugh slipped out of Eli. "Well, you know whose Body Man really screwed the pooch."

Mila rolled her eyes. "You don't know the half of it. Poor Jacob. He really was a superb agent, but he never lived down the fact he let that goddamned blue dress leave the White House."

"So, he should have done what?"

"Let's just say the dress should have never left the grounds." Mila paused, "Or she shouldn't have."

Eli raised his eyebrows.

"That screwup," Mila continued, "led to Jacob's replacement."

"You mean firing?"

"Not exactly."

"What do you mean?"

"The Body Man is part of our team but not in the ways you think. They offer the role to an agent with at least ten to fifteen years of experience, but he or she has to fit a certain profile."

"What kind of profile?"

"For one, they need to be single with no kids and not much family."

"Why?"

"Because of the nature of the role and also because it's the last position they'll hold within the government."

Eli's gaze narrowed. "How so?"

"They must leave when their term comes to an end, as in leave the United States, for good. The government sets them up with a more than generous retirement package, and they disappear into unknown parts at the far end of the world forever. They'll die one day, hopefully of old age, and the secrets they acquired on the job will die with them."

Eli threw his hands up in the air like an animated New Yorker watching the Yankees lose a double header to the Sox. "What?" He asked in a dismissive tone. "And people sign up for this bullshit?"

"Absolutely." A perturbed look spread over Mila's face. "And this isn't bullshit, Eli. It's an honor to be The Body Man. This person is the protector of the presidency."

"Can't say I see it that way." A growing frown on Eli's face grew more pronounced. When he walked into the Diner, he had no idea the conversation with Mila would follow this path. A dozen questions flew through his brain at once, but he settled with asking her, "how does it work exactly?"

"It's a two-person role; there's always a Body Man and an apprentice. After all, one man can't be with the president 24/7, and when The Body Man's term ends, the apprentice steps into the role, and a new apprentice is appointed."

"And if you fuck up big enough, you get replaced?"

"Correct, but that's pretty rare. It's happened only twice."

"There are lots of stories floating around about President Steele within the alphabet agencies, and some aren't flattering."

"Some are probably true, most are nonsense. He's not overly difficult to protect. His business dealings raised some flags, but up until Nick's disappearance, nothing major occurred. But I must admit Danny's shooting the same day has everyone freaked out."

"Who's Danny?"

"Danny Frazier, Nick's apprentice."

"Never heard of him."

"Didn't his name come up in your investigation?"

"No, I told you, the White House is stonewalling us, and the president said nothing about Danny to the director."

Mila didn't say anything.

Eli continued, "if The Body Man disappeared the same day his apprentice is shot you've got a major problem at the Secret Service."

"Agreed."

Eli took a deep breath and exhaled slowly as he rubbed his temples. "OK, my brain is hurting. Back to how The Body Man cleans up the messes. Explain. What does he do exactly?"

"Whatever needs to be done."

"Are you trying to be intentionally vague?"

Mila leaned in closer. "The Body Man is tasked with making problems for the office of the presidency go away using any means necessary."

"That sounds arbitrary and open for interpretation."

"Purposefully so. I'm not saying anything else, other than it's The Body Man's job to protect the office of the presidency at all costs."

He needed to press for info a different way. "How did you find out about the role?"

"I worked with Nick for several years before he became The Body Man. We were buddies. He started as the apprentice but quickly took over the main role when The Body Man at the time took ill and had to step aside. Since I knew Nick pretty well, he filled me in on some specifics."

"And I never heard a word about him?"

"I wasn't allowed to reveal to anyone what he told me. Even to you, the man I was sleeping with," she said with a crooked smile.

"Let's take a step back," Eli said. "If Nick Jordan, The Body Man, is part of the Secret Service, he has to abide by your code of conduct."

Mila shook her head. "Well, he's not exactly a Secret Service agent once he takes the position."

"What do you mean?"

"He reports to the director of the Secret Service, but technically he works independently of our rules."

It didn't make sense to Eli. "But someone has to tell him what to do."

"Not really. The directive is to protect the office of the presidency. How they achieve that is solely up to The Body Man's discretion."

"So, The Body Man can do whatever the hell he wants to cover up the president's acts without fear of reprisal?"

"For the most part, yes."

"What about prosecution? If The Body Man screws up and someone at the justice department gets wind of some illegal acts performed on behalf of the presidency?"

She sat back slightly in her chair. "Each new president signs a PPD reaffirming the role."

"A what?"

"Presidential policy directive."

"Yeah, OK. I think I've heard of them."

"They're like an executive order except they can be kept secret from virtually everyone, including congress. They have the same authority as an executive order, which becomes public knowledge."

"And the PPD affirms the role, but is vague on what it does?"

"Correct. Also, each Body Man is provided a blank presidential pardon. In theory, they could use it for any prosecution brought against them."

Eli shook his head in disbelief. "No way. The president can't sign a secret PPD saying someone can break the law whenever they want. I mean hell, they'd be breaking the law to protect the person who signed the directive in the first place. That's nonsensical. And then a blank pardon, like a get-out-of-jail-free card? The Supreme Court would tear that thing to shreds, Mila. Give me a break."

She nodded her head. "You're probably right, but it would never come to that."

His eyebrows raised. "Meaning?"

"They'd adhere to one of the few rules The Body Man agrees to follow."

Eli put his hand out away from his body. "Hold up. Let me guess. The first rule of fight club is you do not talk about fight club?"

"Kinda sorta. But it's not about being quiet. Each Body Man agrees to take their secrets with them to their grave."

"What do they do, like off themselves if it ever comes to that?"

"Precisely."

"You're making this all up, right?"

"No, everything I told you is the God's honest truth."

"This is seriously fucked up. You get that, right?"

"It's unorthodox, I agree," Mila said.

"Unorthodox? You know what the alt-right would do if they got wind of this role. This is like a deep-state conspiracy on crack. You're sitting here telling me the President of the United States can break any law on a whim. A government employee who technically doesn't exist covers up their illegal acts."

Mila remained quiet, stoic even.

"Doesn't that bother you?" Eli asked.

"I understand your trepidation about the role, but our country needs it. Absolute power might corrupt, but we don't elect eagle scouts. Most presidents are deeply flawed yet charismatic individuals who know how to do one thing better than anyone else."

"And what's that?"

"Make people they will never meet, nor do they care about vote for them. Even if it's all smoke and mirrors."

"I still think it's unconscionable we have someone with that much power who is unelected and virtually invisible."

"Trust me. We are better off having a Body Man versus not."

Eli rightly figured arguing that point would get them nowhere. "Well, we're still left with the question if someone abducted Nick, is he already dead, I mean by his own doing?"

"It's certainly possible, but if someone snatched Nick, in theory, they must have known who he was."

"And if they knew who he was they would know about the directive to kill himself?"

"In theory."

"And they'd prevent him from doing so."

"Bingo. Especially since nobody has been discovered so far."

Eli wiped his forehead, perspiration formed as the conversation continued. "Nick's role. It's a lot to process ..." Eli let his words hang out there.

"Trust me. When I heard about The Body Man, I figured it was some lame-ass story from a fiction writer with way too much time on his or her hands."

"OK, now that you've blown my mind while making me think the Internet conspiracy wackos might be the sane ones, next question is who took Nick, and why?"

"The list of who would want him is endless. Any foreign intelligence agency who learned about a person with that much raw intelligence would kill at the chance of snagging him and bleeding him dry."

"But I thought few people know about the role."

"Yes, that's true. But this is D.C. after all, and people talk. Some talk too much." She stared at Eli for a couple of seconds as she said the last few words. "I do feel confident few people outside the Secret Service know the full breadth of the role. You're now part of a small circle. I trust you, Eli, and assume you'll keep what I told you on a strictly need-to-know basis."

"I'll have to read in the director, Mila. At least give him the cliff notes version."

"If you must."

"Any chance the Russians know about The Body Man?"

The question surprised her. "I'm not sure. Why?"

"Because the men who kidnaped Nick and flew him out of Manassas on a private jet spoke Russian."

"Are you sure?"

"I have a witness who confirmed it."

"I think it's time you did the talking and filled me in on your investigation," Mila said.

"OK," Eli said, "here's what I know ..."

46

Washington, D.C.

The White House

Charles D. Steele II, or as everyone called him, "Junior," strode up to the east security checkpoint of the White House. A stiff breeze blew from the west, and he pulled his overcoat closer to his body as a chill ran up his spine.

It pissed him off royally that he had to show a security badge to pass through the checkpoint like every other visitor. A nuisance he bemoaned to his father with no sympathy in return.

The guard on duty, Willy Daley, blocked the entrance with his imposing six-foot-four, two-hundred-thirty-pound frame. He smiled as Junior approached. "Good morning, Mr. Steele. I didn't know you were back in D.C.."

"Hey, Willy, I got in last night for some meetings. How are you?" Junior came to a stop and presented his security badge.

Willy scanned it, and only after the digital display on his console read "Approved" did he step aside. "Fine, sir. No car this morning?"

"No, I decided to walk."

"Exercise will keep you feeling young, Mr. Steele."

"I've heard," said Junior as he nodded and started down the pathway that led to the east entrance. Seven minutes later, he entered the Oval Office. His father sat motionless at the Resolute Desk, reading papers arranged horizontally atop the desk laid out from left to right.

The president briefly glanced over the top of the reading glasses that teetered on the edge of his nose as his son entered, and he turned his attention back to the papers.

Junior pulled out his phone and checked a few emails while he waited for his father, who was a notoriously slow reader.

After five minutes, the president finished, removed his reading glasses, and placed them on the right side of the desk. When his glasses touched the desk, he yelled out, "Dolores, clear my schedule for the next fifteen minutes and close the door, please."

His secretary stepped in far enough to grab the door handle and close the door.

Charles Steele Sr. looked at his son but said nothing once the door clicked shut.

"Mr. President," said Junior as he placed his phone back in his pocket. Most, if not all, children of presidents call their father "Dad" when they visit the White House, or anywhere else but this wasn't the case for Junior. No, Charles Steele Sr. insisted his son call him "Mr. President" after the election.

"Anything new to report?"

"Not yet, Mr. President."

"Really?" Charles's tone rose sharply. His muscles tensed, and he snarled as he stood up. "Then tell me why the Jack D. Fuck your guys killed an FBI agent last night in Vienna?"

The sudden outburst startled Junior. His father had a propensity for anger but rarely raised his voice.

"Give me a chance. I can explain everything."

In a swift and violent motion, the president picked up one of the two small busts shaped like Abraham Lincoln's head that served as bookends on the table behind his desk. The president played baseball in his college days and still had quite the arm as he threw Lincoln's head across the room. It sailed several inches over Junior, who ducked down on the couch. The heavy object slammed against the door leading to the secretary's office and waiting area, striking hard enough to shake the door and leave a deep brown gash on its otherwise flawless white surface.

Junior had never seen his dad display violence in such a way.

The bust lay on the floor for mere seconds before three Secret Service agents burst into the Oval through two separate doors. Their faces appeared hardened, and their eyes scanned the room as they entered with hands on the butts of their service weapons.

The president raised his own hands outward and did his best to lower his enraged voice. "Stand down, fellas. We're good. I lost my cool, that's all."

"You sure everything is OK, Mr. President?" The Secret Service agent looked back and forth between the president and Junior.

"Yes, yes. I'm fine. We're fine." His gaze shifted away from the agent and towards his son. "Right, Junior?"

"Of course, Mr. President." Junior sat up from his slouched position. He adjusted his tie and straightened his suit coat, but his wide eyes screamed, *Save me.*

The agent raised his sleeve and spoke into the end of his shirt. "Mogul is fine. Repeat no threat to Mogul. Only a false alarm." As he said the last words, he backed out of the room but looked back at the president. "We're outside if you need us, sir."

"I appreciate that. I'm good. We're good."

With the agents gone, the president looked back at Junior almost as if the incident had never occurred.

"You were saying?" he asked, his voice back to a calm tone.

Junior took a thick glass from the set on the table between the two couches and poured himself a cup of water. He actually needed a scotch, but that would have to wait. After several large gulps, he said, "Look, Mr. President, the guys were supposed to impersonate FBI agents and ask a few questions. That was all. We got some intel from the interrogator, and I acted on it."

"So, they busted into the witness's house and tied her up?"

"You're right. They fucked up."

"Who hired them?"

Junior lied. "Marcus."

"Why did he hire two pieces of shit that acted like rank amateurs?"

"It was a mistake on his part."

"I'll say, and because of their careless actions, an FBI agent lost his life."

"The two men paid for that mistake with their own lives."

The president raised his upper lip. "I don't fucking care about them."

"And you're going to tell me you care about an FBI agent?"

"No, I care about the magnifying glass it'll place over this case. I've been trying to get the FBI to back off, but you can sure as hell bet that won't happen now. Not with one of their men dead."

"Again, these guys went rogue; they were not to harm her."

"Why not use Casha?"

"Peter was still on the west coast."

"And then you had the incident at the hospital."

"Marcus made it out."

"He almost got caught by the Secret Service." The president said.

"Hold up." Junior raised his hand and voice. "You authorized the hit, then pulled the plug at the last minute. Marcus followed your orders."

"Well, that bitch of his messed things up to start with."

"And you gave her another mission," Junior replied.

"That was before I knew Danny Frazier was still alive." The president paced circles around the Resolute Desk, his standard procedure when the stress weighed on him. He paused in front of the desk and glared at his son. "You've exposed us."

Junior shook his head. "The guys who died in Vienna were nobodies with no connection to our company or us."

"My company," the president replied in a vitriolic tone.

Junior rolled his eyes. *It's only his company when it's successful and raking in the money.*

"And what's this about Casha getting shot?" The president asked.

"Who told you?"

"Joe. I spoke with him."

"Peter will live," Junior said. "We used one of the Sanctum's facilities outside the city to patch him up this morning. He's at the Hay-Adams resting."

"Should we be concerned about Casha being injured? Is he a weak link?"

"No, Peter is solid. We're close, Mr. President. The deal will go through."

"This is your deal. You negotiated with the Saudis."

"You thought it was a good idea. And everything I'm doing is to grow the business."

Charles changed the subject. "Updates from the Gulf?"

"Nick is talking. The drugs did the trick, and Nick confirmed he printed off additional copies. We believe he gave them to Danny Frazier."

"Believing isn't good enough, Junior. We need hard proof as to what he did with those copies. Simply killing Jordan and Frazier won't do. God knows if they've set up some way to release the evidence he collected once they're dead."

"I understand."

"Solutions, not excuses going forward."

Junior pivoted. "The other day, I asked you about Merci."

"What about her?" The president asked.

"Where did she go after the hit on Danny?"

"France."

"Why?"

"Because someone needed to die."

"Who?"

"Someone powerful."

Junior considered the recent deaths he read about online. Then it dawned on him. "She killed James Fowler? I read he dropped dead in France, according to the front page of the *New York Times*. But I thought it was a heart attack?"

The president looked away for a moment before his eyes locked back onto his son. "Don't believe everything you read in the Times or see on CNN, Junior."

"Why Fowler?"

"Well, for starters he's one of our biggest competitors."

"And with him gone, someone else will step into his role. It will only be a brief blip, and I don't see Fowler's death helping the Steele global brand in the long run."

"You fail to see the bigger picture."

"Please, enlighten me." Junior said.

"All in due time. Before Merci killed him, she retrieved his biometric signatures, specifically his fingerprints and a retinal scan."

"For what purpose?"

"She and Marcus are on their way to New York this morning. James kept a safe deposit box at the bank in NYC, and I need them to retrieve the contents."

"His bank will change all the access codes upon his death, standard protocol. The biometrics are worth jack shit with him dead."

"At his bank, I agree."

"I don't follow."

"His bank will make changes, but the box is not in his bank. James was far too clever to hide something in plain sight."

"Then where is it?"

"Our bank."

"Which one?"

"Our flagship branch."

Junior thought about the setup at the branch. "We have biometric access to the top-level boxes at that location, and it's open 24/7. Our clients can even slip in and out without interacting with bank personnel by using the biometric access area."

"Exactly."

"And we won't change that for some time upon a person's death." Junior said as the realization dawned on him.

"I know. I designed the protocols."

"What does James Fowler have in his box?"

"Files containing dirty laundry. Lots of dirty laundry."

"On whom?"

The president put his extended arms out from his body and moved them away like he was reaching for the distant horizon. "Everybody, including myself and the senior members of my administration."

"You didn't tell me about these files before?"

"No, no, I didn't." The president's voice trailed off as a thought occurred to him.

Junior noticed the change in his body language. "What is it?"

"Casha. He was black ops, right?"

"Correct?"

"Any experience interrogating?"

"Of course."

"Send him down to the Gulf. Instead of him sitting around with his dick in his hands, maybe he can get useful intel from Jordan."

"You think he'll get something out of The Body Man that the interrogator hasn't?"

"Only one way to find out."

"And if Casha fails as well?"

"Maybe I'll get the military to blow up the entire platform. Destroy all the evidence in one swoop. We could claim drug runners used the platform as a smuggling distribution center. Heaven knows it probably served that purpose before they took it over anyway."

"If you destroyed the platform, you'd be starting a war with the Sanctum. Especially with the Chief."

"Fuck the Sanctum and fuck the Chief."

"He's a powerful man. Plus, you know who he reports to."

"And what am I?" The president spewed out the words and shot Junior a look of disdain, including a snarled upper lip.

"You're the leader of the free world."

"Damn right I am. And regarding the Chief, when you make a deal with the devil, you'd better anticipate the flames."

47

TORRANCE, CA

HARBOR–UCLA MEDICAL CENTER

Hector Fuentes lay motionless in the Harbor–UCLA Medical Center hospital bed. An IV ran from his arm to the clear plastic bag above the headboard, as a steady drip of narcotics entered his bloodstream in a timed release. His vital signs remained stable, and his broad chest moved up and down in a rhythmic motion.

He looked serene.

Special Agent Darius Gabel stepped into the room without making a sound. A nurse stood next to the side of the bed, charting Hector's vitals on a tablet. The woman with auburn shoulder-length hair turned around and gasped as the shadowy figure entered her line of sight.

"Oh, you startled me." Autumn reached up and clutched her heaving chest.

"Sorry, didn't mean to give you a scare." Darius gave her a warm smile. "I'm Special Agent Gabel from the FBI Los Angeles field office. I was told a patient asked to speak with us, and the info I received implied it was an urgent matter. Am I in the right room?"

Autumn smiled. "Yes, Agent Gabel. My name is Autumn Salazar, and the patient has been in and out of consciousness since they brought him in."

"You've been his nurse since he arrived?"

"That's right."

"And he asked you to call the FBI?"

"Yes, earlier when he was conscious."

"What can you tell me about him?"

"His name is Hector Fuentes; he claims to work at the Port of Los Angeles."

Agent Gabel nodded. "Who brought him in?"

"He was found in the Pacific between Santa Monica and Catalina by some fishing boat. The captain saw flames on the horizon, but by the time he arrived, the boat sank. He found Hector clinging to a life ring, barely conscious. The captain notified the Coast Guard, who transported him to the shore, and an ambulance brought him to the medical center."

"Injuries?"

"Besides almost drowning, he was shot in the left knee. Another round struck his shin, and a third hit his upper back. The knee is the biggest concern. It's pretty messed up and will need surgery to try to repair it. Hector is lucky to be alive. He was shark bait out in the water. I'm not sure why Jaws didn't snack on him."

"Understood. So, what did he say that would merit a call to the FBI?"

"A lot."

Darius pulled out a pad and pen, slowly tapping the point of the pen on the white notepad. "I'm listening."

Autumn recounted the story while Special Agent Gabel interrupted her from time to time with questions.

"Did he say what was in the shipping containers they loaded onto the cargo ship?"

"He said they were weapons, military-style weapons."

"So, was this some sort of arms sale?"

"I don't know if it was a sale. He said it was more like a theft."

"Someone stole these weapons?"

"Yes." Autumn said.

"Did he say where the cargo ship was headed?"

"The Middle East."

"Which country?"

"He didn't say. I didn't ask for specific details. He did most of the talking."

"OK, go on."

She talked for another five minutes before he held up his hand.

Darius knew he only received part of the story and needed to talk with Hector. "Did he say what the other job was that this Peter Casha asked them to perform?"

"No, but something else he said was odd."

"And what was that?"

"He used the phrase The Body Man."

"The Body Man?"

"Yes."

"That's an odd phrase."

"Yeah, I agree. Like something you'd hear about the mob. Maybe it's because I saw the movie *Goodfellas* recently."

"A classic," Darius said.

"Strange story he told, right?"

"Not the norm, for sure. Do you believe him?"

Autumn pondered the question before she replied, "Yes, I think so."

"He could be some junkie jacked up on something and making it all up as he goes along."

"No, I've dealt with a lot of those types of patients. Hector wasn't on anything. His drug panel came back clean."

Special Agent Gabel shrugged. "Well, when he wakes up, I can fully question him."

Autumn finished recounting Hector's story, and Darius thanked her for the attention to detail. Before he left the room, he handed over his card and asked her to call him the moment Hector regained consciousness.

⸺◆⸺

Darius drove back to the office on Wilshire Boulevard and sat down at his desk. By 6:20 a.m., he opened a case file in Sentinel and filled out the basics of what he knew, which wasn't much. As he clicked through the date fields in the secure system, he thought about The Body Man phrase. On a whim, he performed a keyword search with those three words. Although he didn't expect to find anything, he got one hit, an open file from the WFO in D.C.. A few clicks later, he pulled up the contact info for the agent handling the case and placed a call. It went straight to voicemail.

I hate leaving messages.

At the sound of the beep, he said, "Eli, this is Special Agent Darius Gabel with the L.A. filed office. When you get this, give me a callback, please. It's about the Nick Jordan case. The Coast Guard fished a guy out of the Pacific Ocean, and he went on about a military weapons shipment headed to the Middle East and some reference to The Body Man. The terminology struck me as odd, so I did a query, and you have the only other reference in Sentinel to an active case with that phrase. Might be a crazy coincidence, but let's talk."

48

GEORGETOWN

CAFÉ BONAPARTE

Eli and Kat arrived outside Café Bonaparte in Georgetown about twenty minutes early for the meeting with Dony, the Metro PD detective. As they approached the café, two black Chevy Suburbans pulled up to the curb only a few feet to their left. The heavily tinted back passenger window slid down, and the director of the FBI called out, "Quick word with you two."

A burly man in a blue suit with a white coiled earpiece walked around the back of the vehicle and opened the rear door. Eli and Kat climbed into the back row of seats with the director in the second row.

"How did you know we'd be here?" Kat had a perplexed look on her face.

The director glared at her. "Your cell phones are nothing more than a glorified tracking device. We followed you via the enabled GPS chip. We track the movements of all our agents 24/7."

Kat's mouth hung open. "You follow us?"

"Of course."

"I can't ..."

The director smiled. "Only kidding, Kat."

Eli let out a deep laugh. "I texted the director last night about the meeting this morning."

"Look, I have a conference call at nine sharp." The director glanced at his watch. "We need to keep this brief. What updates do you have?"

"We heard back from the FAA," Kat said. "The plane landed at the Houma-Terrebonne Airport."

"Where's that?" The director asked.

"Louisiana."

"What's down there?"

"Not much from what I know. It's right on the Gulf."

"And what happened to the plane?"

"It stayed at the airport for two hours before it headed back north and landed in New York City," Kat said.

"Who owns the plane?"

"The plane with tail number N781MF is owned by an LLC in the Bahamas."

"How am I not surprised?" The director shook his head. "What entity is it registered under?"

"That's where things get murky," said Kat. "We've still got people digging, but the LLC name is listed as J. Higgins Enterprises."

"A shell company?"

"Yes, sir."

"Well, it's a start. Who's down there checking out the airport in Houma and shaking the local trees to see what falls out?"

"No one yet. We only got this intel an hour ago," Eli said.

"Sounds to me like you need additional manpower."

"Well, it's only Kat and me at the moment."

"That's not good enough anymore. I'll send down a handful of my best agents to Louisiana ASAP."

"Is this still ..."

The director could tell where Eli was going. "This is still your case. Nothing changes. In fact, you'll be running point going forward. Think of it as a promotion and you will get some much-needed assistance. I need you at full capacity for us to find Nick Jordan. I'll have my people report directly to you with, of course, a dotted line to me. That work for you?"

Eli smiled. "Of course."

"As I told you yesterday, unofficially you have whatever resources you need. Just ask. Capeesh?"

"Understood, sir."

"Anything else you need at the moment?"

Eli hesitated to say anything, but to withhold what he learned from Mila felt misguided. "There is something else, but it may take a while to discuss."

"Give me the cliffs notes version, less than sixty seconds."

"You ever heard of The Body Man?" As the words rolled off Eli's tongue, he recognized an instant change in the director's countenance.

The director was quiet for a few seconds as he collected his thoughts. "I ...um, have, yes. At least I've heard of the terminology."

"Roger that. Do you know what the role does?"

"Officially, no. But off the record, I've heard the rumors. People talk. Are you telling me Nick Jordan is The Body Man?"

"I'm afraid so."

"You sure?"

"As much as I can be at the moment, yes."

"How do you even know about it?"

"I don't want to say at this point, but I trust my source."

"This source. Are they on the inside?"

"They are."

"Well, if your source is correct, this case is now infinitely more complicated. And it might explain why the White House is stonewalling us."

"I agree, sir."

The director shook his head. "Look, I've got to go. But you need to find Nick Jordan, and I mean now. If he is The Body Man, it's a national security threat to have him abducted. Call my cell around noon. I've got a lunch appointment, but I'll be able to slip away for a few to get an update."

Eli nodded. "Thanks for having our back on this, sir."

"Just watch your front, Payne, and also your back." The director diverted his eyes. "You too, Kat."

49

NEW YORK CITY

The four-room apartment Marcus rented in D.C. was small by most people's standards, but at least he splurged on a nice California-king-size bed, which took up most of his living room. He used the actual bedroom as an office. After dropping Joe off at his hotel, Marcus and Merci made good use of the plush mattress for about an hour. He might have said things were over, but the harrowing events in the hospital brought up long-buried emotions and desires. The neighbors on the floor below banged on their ceiling with a broomstick more than once to no avail.

After the marathon sex session ended, they continued their tryst in the shower, where Marcus let the hot water run long enough that it felt like a sauna. One redeeming feature of the apartment building was that the owner had installed tankless hot water heaters, and Marcus felt it more than made up for the over-priced rent. Once dried off, they climbed back into bed and collapsed. Both fell fast asleep within minutes out of sheer exhaustion. At 4:20 a.m. the alarm clock went off, and they were out the door ten minutes later to catch the 6:00 a.m. Delta shuttle from Reagan to LaGuardia.

After the driver picked them up outside baggage claim in New York, they stopped in Manhattan at Lexington Brass for breakfast. One of the few places Marcus was sure to visit every time he made it back to the city.

Marcus climbed out of the black Lincoln Town Car on Fifth Ave. and took in a deep breath of the rank city air while Merci slid out of the passenger seat and stood next to him. The street vendor on the corner hung a fresh batch of oversized pretzels, and the smell drifted to where they stood.

"Ahh, nothing like the smell of shit, piss, and body odor to start a day," he said as he glanced at her.

"I smell pretzels." Merci cocked her head toward the Pakistani vendor.

"After all these years, you're telling me I was wrong and you're a glass-half-full kind of gal?"

She reached out and grabbed his large, muscular hand and gave it a not-too-subtle squeeze right at a pressure point.

"Oww," he said as the pain radiated up his arm.

The feel of a ring on her finger gave him pause as she held his hand. Merci typically eschewed jewelry of any kind unless a job called for it. He looked down and saw the oversized ruby ring surrounded by tiny diamonds. If it had been real, the ring would have been quite expensive. Marcus wondered how he hadn't noticed it earlier. He knew the ring well since it was a gift from him for one of their jobs years prior.

"Wearing the ring, I see."

Merci looked at him with a devious smile. "I am."

"Expecting trouble?"

"A girl never knows what rascals she may bump into in the big city, now does she?"

"Touché."

They held hands and walked to the corner of Fifth Ave. and 57th Street. Most New Yorkers simply referred to it as the First Bank of Steele. The location, the flagship branch opened by Charles Steele Sr. four decades earlier, served as the crown jewel in his banking empire. The façade of the building constructed from mirrored glass and brass-plated metal reflected the rays of sun that crept down the grand boulevards of Gotham.

A man with white gloves, a long black coat, and matching top hat opened the heavy brass doors for them as they approached. Marcus nodded, and the two of them entered the ornate lobby. The center of the room contained black leather couches and high-backed white leather chairs, while oversized elephant ear plants dotted the area, forming an oval shape.

They walked past the lobby and turned left, where they entered a wide hallway lined with neo-Gothic artwork. The hall split, with the right side leading to a large vault containing safe deposit boxes from floor to ceiling. Marcus and Merci stayed to the left, and the hall continued before it dead-ended at a plain steel door with a biometric hand scanner to the right of the entrance.

Already wearing the manufactured glove containing James Fowler's fingerprints, Marcus raised his hand and placed it palm down on the electronic reader. The beam of light went from right to left and read the fingerprints. After a few seconds, the small light to the left of the door illuminated green, and the door opened. The next hallway was less than twenty feet long, with another steel door at the end. This time a small box to the right of the door contained an optical reader. Marcus had the contact in his right eye and put it up to the retinal scanner. The locking mechanism disengaged with a slight hiss, and the door swung open.

As they entered the expansive room, Marcus looked around. The hardwood floors were made of hickory, while the center of the room contained several long tables with high-backed leather upholstered chairs. Two of the three walls were lined with floor-to-ceiling cherry cabinets similar to those found in the locker room of a high-end country club, and the third wall contained small rooms the size of department-store dressing rooms. Red velvet curtains provided privacy for anyone who required discretion while examining their items.

Marcus examined the cabinets and saw the numbers for each in small black letters on the bottom left corner. Each separated compartment measured eighteen inches high and two feet wide. The door to his left said, "No 1" on the bottom, while the one closest to the small rooms read "No 100." Marcus approached cabinet "No 34." As he opened the cherry cabinet door, he noticed the shiny surface of the safe deposit box had no markings except for a single keyhole.

Marcus turned to Merci. "The key."

She looked into his eyes as the tip of her tongue came out and gently rubbed against her lower lip. "You mean this key?" Merci reached down between her breasts and pulled the one-inch-long bronze key from her bra with a drawn-out movement.

"You're incorrigible," Marcus said.

Merci winked. "You've awoken a lioness." She placed the key in his extended open palm.

He spun the key around in his fingers a few times and rolled his eyes, but did glance at the small, curtained-off rooms to his right. The thought crossed his mind as his eyes wandered to her cleavage, but he quickly pushed the thought aside.

Merci read his thoughts. "I'm game."

Marcus smirked. "Business before pleasure."

"OK, Mr. Responsible. You better hope I'm still willing to jump in the sack after we're done."

He looked her up and down and gave her a devilish grin. "You will be."

Marcus placed the key in the hole and turned it clockwise. The sound of the lock disengaging made a distinct *click* as the door swung open. Marcus grabbed the thick metal panel and opened it all the way. The ambient light inside the safe deposit box illuminated the four shelves inside. His eyes saw the black over-the-shoulder bag crammed into the bottom shelf, the item the president had sent them to retrieve. The top shelf contained bound stacks of currency in various denominations from over a dozen countries, while the middle two shelves held identical metal boxes four inches high and twenty-two inches wide.

Marcus looked at Merci, and she returned the curious stare.

She slid out one of the metal boxes and flipped open the lid. Inside were hundreds of neatly folded white envelopes. They looked like wedding invitations without any addresses. Merci pulled out one envelope, opened it, and let the contents slide into her open palm. The lone two-carat pear-shaped diamond sparkled in the light as she rocked her hand back and forth. Her body gave a natural quiver.

"You think all these envelopes contain diamonds?" Marcus asked.

"Guess so," Merci said as she checked several other envelopes and her heart rate spiked.

"But why are they in envelopes? Thought they'd be in suede bags with a nice ribbon tying them shut?"

Merci let out an audible sigh. "You're cute but dumb. That's how they do it in Hollywood, dear, but this is real life. Only a diamond can cut a diamond. Anyone with a serious understanding of the industry would know you keep precious jewels separated for transport. Jamming them into one bag would damage them."

"If you say so."

"President Steele said to bring him the files, and the rest was ours." Merci looked around the expansive room and saw the black cylindrical canvas bags measuring eight inches wide, eighteen inches long, hanging from pegs on the wall. She hurried over and grabbed one, then walked back to the safe deposit box. Using both hands, she emptied the contents of the top three shelves into the bag as fast as possible. We could take this and disappear. Start fresh. There's enough here with the diamonds alone to set us up for multiple lifetimes."

"What about the contents in the bag?" Marcus asked.

"Toss them," Merci said.

Marcus frowned. "I don't think the president would appreciate that."

"To hell with him. We don't owe him anything."

"I was hired to do a job, and I intend to complete it. Then and only then can we disappear."

"Always the Boy Scout, aren't you?"

"I was an Eagle Scout."

"Whatever. Pretty sure the scouts might frown upon your career choice."

"And my choice in women."

"Well, at least you have one redeeming quality."

"Look, I told the president we would bring him the bag, and we will. After that, our obligations to him are over."

"Until he asks for something else, and trust me, he will."

Marcus frowned. "I'll say no."

"He's not used to people telling him that."

"Tough," Marcus said.

50

GEORGETOWN

CAFÉ BONAPARTE

Eli and Kat climbed out of the director's black SUV and walked to the front door of Café Bonaparte.

"After you." Eli opened the door and stood to the side.

"Wow! Who says chivalry is dead?" Kat curtsied and slipped past Eli.

"Oh, it's dead all right." A smile crept over his face. "Dead as a doornail. I figured if there were an active shooter situation inside the restaurant, you'd be the lead stopper instead of me."

"The lead stopper, huh? Sounds about right, dickish renaissance man."

Eli followed behind her and even gave her a good-natured poke between the shoulder blades with his index finger.

Several steps inside the café Eli saw Dony sitting at one of the back tables. "There he is." He stepped in front of Kat and walked towards his friend.

"What's up, G-man?" Dony stood up and gave his friend a firm handshake and a hard smack on the shoulder.

"Living the dream thirty-six; how about you?" Eli used Dony's law enforcement call sign in response.

"Wife and kiddos are good, and my caseload is quieter than normal. I really can't complain."

"Ahem." Kat cleared her throat in a not too subtle way.

Eli got the hint. "Dony Harbaugh, meet Kat Stone."

Dony extended his hand. "Pleased to meet you, Kat. You must have screwed up somewhere to get stuck with numb nuts here."

Eli shook his head. He heard variations of the same joke, no matter who he was around.

Kat smiled. "My parents always told me if it doesn't kill you, it makes you stronger."

"They sound like morons to me," Eli said.

The waiter came by to take their drink orders as they continued to look at the menu.

Dony smirked. "Kat, order as much food as possible. With G-man here paying we don't walk out hungry. I plan on eating for two today." He gently patted his stomach.

Eli cut him off. "It already looks like you have been." He pointed to his friend's paunch. "Hitting up Dunkin' every day, I see."

"Hardy, har, har." Dony said. "A tired cop joke."

Eli shrugged. "It's what I do."

The waiter came and took their food order. True to his word, Dony got enough for two people.

"Since you didn't call me here to buy me a fancy breakfast and chew the fat, Eli, what's up with the case?" Dony asked. "What do you need?"

"I kept it intentionally vague when we spoke on the phone, but here's a little more backstory," Eli said.

He took the next ten minutes while they waited for their food to give Dony a high-level overview of what they'd discovered until that morning. He said little about what Nick did with the Secret Service, and when Dony asked for a physical description, Eli pulled out the picture from Rose.

"No ransom demands?" Dony asked.

"None. Nobody has stepped forward or said anything. If it weren't for Rose reporting him missing, the Bureau wouldn't be involved."

"How about motive? Why would someone want him?"

"I believe for the info he's privy to," Eli said.

"And who do you suspect took him?"

"Not sure. Possibly the Russians, but no hard proof to corroborate that."

"Well, you were vague about his role. Is he on the investigative side or a protective detail?"

"Left that out intentionally. I can't read you into his actual duties. Let's say his eyes and ears are around lots of classified data 24/7."

"And this sensitive information comes from the tippy top, I take it."

"Roger that."

Dony nodded. "Then there are a lot of people who would like to know what's in his head."

"Agreed, especially foreign governments. This is a matter of national security."

"Well, if that's the case, I think we're getting outside my wheelhouse."

Eli frowned. "Not what I was hoping to hear."

Dony raised a hand. "Don't worry. I know a guy who specializes in this type of thing."

"I'm listening."

"He's eccentric but knows everything there is to know about international kidnapping, spycraft, toppling governments, you name it."

"Who does he work for?"

"The agency."

"What's the chance he would talk with us?"

"Zilch," Dony said.

Eli frowned.

"Unless he knows Dagger sent you."

"Who's Dagger?" Eli asked.

Dony pointed at himself but didn't say anything.

"New nickname?"

"Not really, but it's what he calls me."

"Why?"

"I met him a few years back on a metro investigation that turned into a full-blown international affair regarding a foreign embassy."

"The Qatar affair?"

"Exactly. We spent a lot of time together, and I told him one of my favorite spy movies as a kid was *Cloak and Dagger*."

"The old '80s movie?"

"The one and only."

Eli smiled. "You are a dork. You know that, right?"

Dony smiled. "And proud of it."

"What's this guy's name?"

"Zed."

"First or last?"

"That's all he goes by."

"How do I get in touch with this, Zed?"

"You don't. I will. Hold tight." Dony reached down toward the floor and hauled his army-green backpack up to the empty seat next to him. Within a minute, he had his laptop out and connected via the free Wi-Fi offered by the restaurant.

"We're in luck; he's online."

Eli pulled his chair around the table in order to see the screen. "Zed, some super-secret-squirrel guy, uses an internet messenger app?"

"Of course. What did you think? I'd send a carrier pigeon with a note written in invisible ink attached to its foot?"

"Maybe."

Dony exchanged a dozen plus instant messages. To the casual observer, it looked to be a random chat, but for two trained professionals, it was a cryptic discussion. "All set, you'll meet him at the Denny's on the corner of State Highway 123 and Fairfax Boulevard."

"Denny's? Are you serious?" Eli asked.

"Yeah, he likes Denny's." Dony said. "You got a problem with that?"

"Will he want an all-American breakfast?"

"More than likely."

"I've worked with enough spooks over the years." Eli let out an elongated sigh. "They do breed some weird ones at Langley."

"Keep in mind, he's hyper-paranoid about everything, but more so about people. Especially feds."

"But he is a fed."

"Right, but don't remind him of that little factoid," said Dony as he winked. "And whatever you do, don't bring anything electronic with you."

"You sure he can help?"

"If someone took Nick Jordan, and especially if it were a foreign government or agency, Zed would be the one to help you find out who it was and where they took him."

"If you say so," Eli said.

"Watch out for his tics, and please for the love of God, don't point them out."

"Tics? Really?"

Dony nodded. "Yes, lots of them."

"Great, just great. Anything else I need to know?" Eli asked.

"Yes, he's big into conspiracies."

"Like, he believes in them?"

"Oh yeah. Roswell, the Kennedy assassination, even 9/11 and the controlled implosions at WTC 7."

"And they let him have a top-secret clearance?"

"You'll understand when you talk with him."

"OK."

"Sometimes you've got to pass through the darkness to appreciate the light."

Eli rolled his eyes. "Whatever the hell that means."

Dony chuckled. "As I said, you'll see."

Eli shook his friend's hand and grabbed the check. "Next one is on you, cheapskate."

Dony nodded. "The dollar menu at the golden arches it is, then."

They got up to leave, and Dony shook Kat's hand. "Nice to meet you, Kat. Keep my boy here safe, OK?"

Kat smirked. "I'll do my best."

"Oh, no. You did it," Dony said.

In full Sean Connery accent, Eli quoted the famous line from the movie *The Rock*. "Your best?" Eli asked. "Losers always whine about their best. Winners go home and ..."

Dony cut him off mid word. "Eli! There are children in the restaurant, you bonehead."

51

WASHINGTON, D.C.

Peter listened to Junior's pitch but didn't buy what he was selling.

"Why would I have more luck than the interrogator already grilling Nick?"

"The president has faith in you," Junior said.

Peter frowned. "Wonderful. But you deflected and didn't answer my question."

"JoJo tells me you have interrogation experience, right?"

"Some, but I'm not a trained professional like the men employed by the Sanctum."

"Their results have been less than impressive. Especially considering how much money we've paid them."

"Look, Junior, I'm not the sharpest tack in the drawer, but I'm pretty sure me showing up isn't going to go over well."

Junior's gaze narrowed. "I don't give a shit what they think, and neither does the president. We need to know what Nick Jordan did with the files. The Sanctum hasn't delivered and we are out of time. It's cut and dry."

"Nobody likes it when the neighbor's dog comes and drops a big shit in their front yard."

The comment elicited a smirk from Junior. "Then make sure it's a small turd that doesn't smell terrible and keep it under a bush out of sight. Understood?"

"I don't get a say in this, do I?"

Junior snickered. "What do you want to do, Peter? Sit around and stream shows on the Internet from that shitty apartment you call home?"

"Might not be a bad idea." Peter rubbed his shoulder. "I did get shot, after all."

"It's not in your blood, Casha; you're a doer. The president needs you, and he'll reward you accordingly for your loyalty. You're not going to say no to him, are you?"

Peter had no problem telling the president, or anyone else for that matter, no. But Junior was right. No way could he sit around and do nothing. "Guess I'll get back in the game."

"That's the spirit. I've already called the airport. The plane that brought you to D.C. from Cali is fueled and ready to take you to the Gulf." Junior paused as if he were contemplating his next words. "Do whatever you have to, but get us actionable intel. We must know what The Body Man did with those documents."

Peter nodded but didn't verbalize a response.

"Oh, and one more thing."

"Yes?"

"When you get the intel, I want Nick Jordan sleeping with the fishes in the Gulf. Give him an oil-platform burial. The bin Laden special."

Peter looked surprised. "I thought the Sanctum was going to take care of him?"

"They've been a disappointment up to this point, and the president feels Jordan needs to be neutralized by someone we trust. He could be a massive liability if what he knows went for sale to the highest bidder if the Sanctum reneges on our deal."

"Let me make sure I have this straight. Go down there, figure out what he hasn't told them, and then make sure he's dead before I leave."

Junior nodded and said, "Bingo." He walked to the door and left the suite without another word.

"You sure going is a good idea?" Joe waited until Junior left before he said anything.

"No, but I'm not sure saying what I thought would have mattered."

"Valid point."

"Besides, Junior might be a fucking dick, but he's right. What am I going to do? Sit around and do nothing while I recoup?"

"You could binge-watch Netflix or a ton of porn."

"Not my style."

"I know, but you still need to rest the shoulder."

"It's not like I'm going down there to waterboard the son of a bitch or punch holes in his hands and feet with an electric drill. It won't be physical. Besides, if I have a cot, a hot shower, and some food, I'll be ok."

"Think you can get him to talk?"

"Not really. But guess I'll find out, won't I?"

52

—— • ——

FAIRFAX, VA

As they drove to the restaurant, Eli peppered Kat with questions. Eli wouldn't admit it, but he enjoyed having Kat around. There was something unique about her, a perspective he rarely saw with new recruits. Probationary agents straight out of Quantico universally have a determination, some might say even an arrogance. After all, it takes a special breed to serve as an FBI special agent, and rarely does one lack in confidence. Kat may have had the confidence found in others, but she also had a fire deep down, a hunger that set her apart. It didn't hurt that she was sarcastic as hell, a quality Eli not only understood but respected.

"Your folks call you Kat when you were a kid?" He looked towards her as she appeared to stare out the passenger window, oblivious to his gaze.

She turned her head in his direction. "No, it was Katherine until high school. We moved around a bit since my dad was in the military."

"Really? What branch?"

A grin formed at the corner of her lips. "I was an army brat."

"How did I not pick up on that before? Let me guess, Miss Popular, top of the class, and never got in trouble."

Kat laughed. "Not quite. More like a loner, halfway decent grades, and only got suspended once."

"You got suspended? Bullshit. You're a miss goody two shoes if I ever saw one."

Kat shook her head. "Hardly. We were living down in Fayetteville while Pops did a stint at Bragg. That year the kids at school called me Kat, which before long was turned into Kitty by some jocks."

Eli sensed where this was going. "Ruh-roh."

"Oh yeah," Kat said. "So, there I am in homeroom one day, and the captain of the football team, a real douchebag, starts meowing at me incessantly. Well, I nicely tell him to buzz off, and he ups the ante and starts calling out, 'Here, pussy, pussy, pussy.'"

"Wrong move, douchebag." Eli shook his head.

"You got it. I snapped. I walk over to him with the biggest grin I could muster."

"And?"

"What do you think? I cold cocked that motherfucker into first period. Split his lip in two and broke his nose. He ended up sprawled out on the floor out cold with blood all over the place."

"You go, girl. It sounds like that little shit deserved exactly what he got."

"Well, not everyone agreed. It turns out his dad was on the school board."

"Yikes, that's not good."

"Nope. They tried to expel me. That is until Pops pays the principal a visit."

"Bet that guy got an earful."

"The principal was a woman."

"Even better."

"You could hear my dad screaming at her with his drill sergeant voice from the other side of the high school. After some tense discussions, they settled on a three-day in-school suspension, on account of I did lay him out. They agreed not to press charges after his father heard what he said to me. Apparently, his dad decided it might harm his chances for re-election to the school board if his son's filthy taunts made the local news."

"You're like a freaking rock star, Stone." Eli jabbed her with his elbow. "Minus the groupies."

Kat laughed. "Men be warned. Don't mess with the Kitty."

Two minutes later, Eli pulled into the Denny's parking lot and parked between a blue 1984 Datsun 720 pickup and a green 1991 Plymouth Acclaim. Both vehicles showed more rust than paint. As Eli climbed out of his car, he glanced at the two vehicles and let out a loud, elongated whistle. To the right of the Denny's restaurant, a dilapidated 7-Eleven looked like it had seen better days. Big Bite hot dogs, Munchos and orange Hostess cupcakes were a staple for Eli in his younger days.

Kat let out a "whoa" as she walked around the side of the car and looked toward the entrance. "I've not been to one of these places in years. I can't even recall the last time I had a Rooty, Tooty, Fresh 'n Fruity."

Eli grimaced. "That's IHOP, Hawking. Wrong chain."

"You sure?"

"Uh, yeah."

"Whatever. Wait? Who's Hawking?"

"You serious?"

"Yes, why?"

Eli smacked his forehead with his open palm. "Never mind."

"You think this Zed guy will show?" Kat asked.

"Hope so. If Dony says he'll be here, then I assume he will."

As they walked toward the door, Kat turned toward him and poked her finger into his chest. "By the way, don't make fun of Stephen Hawking again."

Eli laughed. "Oh, you got that dig?"

"I did. Stephen Hawking was freaking brilliant."

"Yeah, I tried reading *A Brief History of Time* once."

"And?"

"It took me some time, and it was a brief read, as in I made it halfway through the first chapter before it became history."

"And you went back to what? A Vince Flynn novel?"

Eli's eyebrows turned downward. "Don't knock the master."

"Right, I don't want to piss you off."

Eli said nothing, opened the glass door, and stepped into the restaurant.

The hostess desk was empty. Instead of a worker, a hand-written sign on a white folded piece of paper taped to the counter read, *Pleaze Seat Yourself* in thick black letters.

"Figures," Eli said under his breath, unsure if the word please was misspelled on purpose or not.

"See him?" Kat asked. She stood close enough that her breath blew against the scruff of his neck.

"I don't know what he looks like. Dony said he would come to us."

Eli scanned the mostly empty restaurant. To his left, a mother with two children sat in the booth closest to the front door. She wore a tired expression, and Eli could tell from her appearance that she was part of the lower-end working class who did their best each day to provide for their families. Further down the row of high-backed booths and toward the back of the restaurant, a man with a long gray beard sipped at a cup of steaming coffee while his free hand twirled the end of his beard and twisted it around his finger. Eli thought the man looked frazzled, on edge.

As Eli looked to his right, he saw the row was mostly empty except halfway down the aisle a FedEx worker dressed in the standard black-and-purple polo shirt appeared to be finishing his meal.

"Which one is Zed?"

"My money is on gray-bearded dude."

Kat nodded. "Mine too. He looks psychotic."

Eli stepped to the right and walked down the aisle, taking a booth two down from the FedEx guy, who gave them no notice as they sauntered past. Eli sat closest to the window, and Kat took the aisle side of the narrow booth. At the end of the row, a sign hung from the ceiling panels that read *Restrooms*.

"Why are we sitting on this side if Zed is over there?" Kat gestured toward the other side of the restaurant.

"Dony said he will come to us. So, we'll wait for him. I don't want to scare the guy off." He looked down at his watch. "Old graybeard will be over here in two minutes flat. Just you wait and see."

As the FedEx guy stood and started down the aisle, presumably for the restroom, neither Eli nor Kat could suppress their surprised looks as he slid into the seat opposite them.

Kat looked startled. "Can we help you?"

"Pretty sure I'm the one here to help you." The FedEx guy replied in a raspy voice. "By the way, you might as well be wearing matching jackets with the white letters' *FBI* stenciled across the back. You both stick out like sore thumbs."

"Zed?"

He ignored the question. "One-word response, or I bail. Who sent you?"

"Dagger," Eli said in an even tone.

Zed nodded. "I've been told you need to find someone?"

"What's with the FedEx outfit?" Eli asked.

Zed leaned in closer, squinted his eyes, and stared at Eli. His right cheek twitched, followed by his eye rapidly blinking for several seconds. "It's called a disguise. You should try it sometime."

"Got it," Eli said as he watched the strange movements and remembered Dony told them to expect some tics.

"Back to my question. Who are you looking for?" Zed asked.

"A missing person. He's a federal agent."

"Which agency?"

"Secret Service." Eli said.

Zed sat back and grew silent. The facial tics appeared to increase in intensity and length, and he replied with one word: "Interesting." Next, he placed his left hand on the table and tapped his fingers, beginning with his pinky and moving down to his index finger as if he were playing an imaginary piano. Each time, the movements became faster. "This missing agent has a name?"

For a moment Eli considered not saying the real name.

Kat could see his hesitation and kicked his foot.

"The agent we're looking for is named Nick Jordan."

Zed made a clicking sound with his tongue against the roof of his mouth. "So, the rumors are true?"

"What rumor?" Eli asked.

"The Body Man went AWOL."

"You've heard of The Body Man?"

"Of course," Zed replied in a matter-of-fact tone, as if everyone knew about the role.

"I was under the impression few people outside the Secret Service were aware of him."

"Dagger did share with you what I do for the agency, right?"

"He did," Eli paused. "Somewhat."

"It's my job to know things that I'm not supposed to know. If I didn't know them, I wouldn't be good at what I do."

Eli decided against refuting the statement or saying, "What the hell does that even mean?"

Zed's eyes darted back and forth. His body slouched down in the booth slightly. "Is he missing of his own accord, or was he taken?"

"The evidence we've collected leads us to believe the latter," Kat said. "But the White House has been stonewalling us, making it hard to get the facts."

Zed looked back and forth between Kat and Eli. "Who took him?"

"Not sure yet, but we have an eyewitness that indicated the men who took him spoke Russian. They forced him onto a private plane at the Manassas Regional Airport in the middle of the night," Eli said.

"Destination?"

Kat spoke up. "Houma, Louisiana."

Zed's eyes grew wide. "Houma? Are you sure about that?"

"One hundred percent confirmed it with FAA," Kat said. "The plane stayed in Houma for several hours before it flew to New York City."

Zed said nothing for almost a minute, and merely rubbed the bridge of his nose while he made a dull humming sound. "Are you familiar with black sites?" he finally asked.

Eli scrunched his nose. "You're referring to secret prisons, right?"

"Correct. Know much about them?"

"Very little. I know the last president got rid of them, which caused a lot of murmurings within the DOD and other agencies. From what I heard, it pissed off the agency."

"It did for a time, yes, but we're a resilient bunch."

"Are you insinuating the practice is still alive and well?"

"Well, I can most assuredly tell you the changes instituted by that administration remain in place. The United States government no longer runs any black sites."

"I have a hard time believing the practice ended," Eli said.

Zed's voice rose noticeably in pitch and volume. "Listen to me carefully. We no longer control any black sites. Period. End of story."

———◦○◦———

"Then why bring them up?"

"The key word in what I said was *we*."

"Meaning?" Kat asked.

"If a person with an intimate knowledge of our presidential secrets has gone missing, we must assume someone took him."

Eli and Kat looked at each other, perplexed.

"I agree," Eli said as he looked back at Zed.

"And they must be holding him somewhere. Plus, you said it's likely men who spoke Russian took him."

"That's our working theory, yes, but why did you bring up black sites?" Eli asked.

"Because when the government took away that option, the free market stepped in. That's why I said *we* no longer maintain any sites. I didn't say black sites no longer exist."

"Then who runs the sites now?"

"A crime syndicate out of Russia. They've placed facilities around the world to fill the vacuum created when we shut down our locations."

"When did they start to do this?"

"As soon as we got out of the business of secret prisons. This criminal syndicate goes by the name, the Sanctum. They offer highly illegal services at a premium cost. It's a vicious organization that operates outside of any laws or jurisdictions."

"And they engage in torture?"

"Torture, interrogation, murder. Hell, on the opposite end of the spectrum, they even run hospital facilities for criminals who can't walk into a regular hospital."

"Great. They rough people up, then might make money fixing them up after the fact?"

Zed grimaced. "An astute observation."

"And you think this group has Nick? Why?"

"Because the men spoke Russian. Plus, where they took him."

"Houma, Louisiana?" Eli asked.

"Correct."

"What's so special about Houma?"

"The Sanctum operates a facility in the Gulf. An old decommissioned oil platform south of Houma."

"How do you know this?"

"Because the agency sends people there from time to time."

There was a slight pause.

"Unofficially, of course," Zed said.

"What the hell? You're saying the US government pays a crime syndicate to torture and interrogate people?"

"Don't be naïve, Special Agent Payne." A powerful wave of tics slowed Zed down for a few seconds. Now, both hands were on the table and drummed rapidly as he continued to talk. "The agency and others, even some at your illustrious Bureau, do what is needed to keep the populace safe from external threats. That includes paying for services with questionable legality."

"Questionable? What you're suggesting is downright illegal."

"It's a moral quandary for sure, depending on your perspective."

———————◆◇◆———————

Eli didn't have the energy to get into an ethical argument and rightly figured he wouldn't get far with someone like Zed anyway. "If what you're saying is true, how can we determine if this facility has Nick Jordan? I mean, who says the plane didn't stop in Houma and they moved him via another mode of transportation? If the Russians grabbed Nick, he could be in a gulag by now, and the Russian president could be torturing him for everything he knows. Hell, he could be in any number of countries, or even in a condo at Del Boca Vista for all we know."

Zed smiled. It was the first time he cracked even the faintest of smiles since he sat down. "Seinfeld reference. Clever. I like it."

Eli wasn't sure what to say.

Zed continued. "True, he could be anywhere. As for how we can find out if the Sanctum has him, leave that to me. I have a hunch he's there since I don't believe in coincidences, and nobody has a reason to go to that part of the country."

"I'm sure lots of people have a good reason to visit Louisiana," Kat said.

Zed frowned. "Not likely. Have you ever been to Louisiana?"

"Yes, I have," Kat said. "Mardi Gras is quite fun."

"Sure, if you want to drink, see lots of titties in every shape and size, and vomit by the end of the night."

Kat looked irritated. "I stayed sober at Mardi Gras, and I kept the girls covered up, thank you very much."

"I'm sorry to hear that," Zed said as he glanced at her chest. "What I'm telling you is that the primary reason a plane would leave Manassas, Virginia, in the dead of night and fly to Louisiana is not for crawfish or to celebrate a pagan holiday."

Eli tried to steer the conversation away from the train wreck it was about to turn into. "How long will you need?"

"Give me an hour, two at the most. I'll turn over some rocks and see what tries to slither away."

"And if your hunch is right, and the Sanctum has him?"

"What do you mean?" Zed asked.

"How do we get him out?"

"The agency pays to use the Sanctum's facilities, not break people out."

"Then what do you suggest?"

"The FBI is resourceful. You'll think of a way to get him out if he's being held in the facility."

Eli shook his head. "How do I get in touch with you?"

"I'll contact you directly."

"But you don't have my info?"

"Don't need it. I work for the CIA, not the county library."

"How will I know it's you?"

"You'll know."

"Are you sure you don't want my business card?"

Zed put his hands out to rebuff the card Eli thrust in his direction. "Keep it," Zed said. "I don't like taking things from people's hands."

"Who are you, Tony Stark?" Eli withdrew his hand and put the card back into his wallet.

Zed reached into his pocket and produced a long, thin piece of paper. "This is for you," he said as he stood up and walked toward the front door. He walked with a slight limp on his right side, exited the restaurant, and continued outside without turning around. Zed climbed into the blue Datsun. The engine fired up;

it sounded like a lawnmower as it dragged out of the parking lot and disappeared down the road with a high-pitched whine.

Eli smirked and looked down at the piece of paper. It was a receipt for an all-American breakfast. "Well, Dony called that one, didn't he?" Eli handed the bill over to Kat.

"You expecting me to pay or something?"

"Yeah, we can go dutch. I paid for Dony's breakfast; you can pay for Zed's lunch."

Kat handed it back. "A senior agent always pays; it's in the handbook."

A perplexed look spread over Eli's face. "What handbook?"

"Mine." Kat stood up and walked out the front door.

Eli sat alone in the booth. A lone voice broke the silence as the gray-bearded man from the other side of the restaurant held a bill in the air and said, "You can pay for mine too while you're at it, sonny boy." A crooked smile revealed blackened teeth and more than one that appeared missing.

With a shake of the head, a wide smile formed, and Eli retorted. "Bring it over, Gandalf The Grey. I'll pay it."

53

---•---

THE GULF OF MEXICO

Nick lay flat on his back and opened his eyes. A dense fog lifted from his mind as if he had awoken from a deep slumber. His brain was no longer cluttered with the drugs that had pervaded his waking thoughts and ran wild as he slept. He didn't know what chemical cocktail they'd used, but he knew for certain the drugs no longer held sway over him.

Nick sat up slowly and looked around the sights of his sparse cell as he rubbed his temples. *How long have they held me?* He really couldn't be sure. Several days at a minimum, but deep down he knew it could be longer. Much longer.

The uncertainty of not knowing what he told Sir nagged him. Memories flooded back like waves pounding the rock face of a towering cliff. He resisted, even concocted all kinds of disinformation to confuse Sir and muddy the waters. But was it enough? Thankfully, he didn't know the specific banks where Danny hid the documents. But did he tell Sir they were in a safe deposit box? He couldn't be sure.

The sound of the electronic lock on the steel door disengaging made his head snap to the right. His eyes fixed on it as it opened. Two large men entered the room one after the other. They said nothing but approached Nick with a set of shackles.

Binding his hands and ankles, the two men pulled Nick to his feet and ushered him out of the room and down the hall. They passed through two secured doors that required outside intervention to buzz them through before they arrived at the interrogation room. It was the same room they'd brought Nick to every day.

Sir sat at the familiar stainless-steel table but didn't look up as the men fastened Nick to the table and floor. The routine questions started, but after a few words, something caught Nick's eye. An item protruded from inside the thick file under Sir's folded hands.

A number-two wooden pencil protruded from the center of the file, stuffed between several sheets of paper. As Sir spoke, Nick formulated a plan in his head.

The questions dragged on while Nick did his best to evade, deflect, but never give Sir what he wanted.

After ninety minutes of conversation that got them nowhere, Nick made his move. Even though they had his hands secured to the table, he still had eight inches of play, and he lunged for the file. Sir reacted and pulled the file from the firm grasp while Nick held the corner of the thick stack of papers and yanked hard. The ensuing struggle caused the thick manila folder to open, spilling the top third of its contents over the table while the rest fell to the floor. Sir's attention turned away from Nick and toward the scattered pages long enough for Nick to grab the pencil, which landed serendipitously on the table within his grasp. Once secured, he kept it hidden in the palm of his hand.

Sir looked up. "What the hell was that about, prisoner?"

"I wanted to see my file." Nick said in a defiant tone.

Sir's face turned red. He glared at Nick, and his hands visibly shook.

Nick knew the mirror had to be a two-way type, and he wondered how many others watched his movements. As Sir reached down to pick up some papers, Nick carefully used the index finger from his opposite hand to slide the pencil down past his elbow and worked it toward his torso. Carefully, he finagled the pencil toward his body before he hid it in the waistband of his pants, which resembled scrubs used by hospital staff.

After the file was reassembled, the interrogation continued for another forty-five minutes. When Sir had had enough, the two same guards came back into the room, undid Nick's binds, and ushered him to his room. Fortunately for Nick, neither man patted him down before they left the interrogation room or after he returned to his cell.

Now alone, Nick hid his newfound tool in the far corner of the bed between the mattress and the wall. The tip was dull, but he figured a way to make both ends of the pencil sharp enough to serve as a deadly weapon.

Sitting on the edge of the bed, Nick knew he needed an opportunity. Personal survival required freeing himself. The information held in the files he gave Danny and what he stored in his mind needed to see the light of day. At all costs.

54

WASHINGTON, D.C.

Eli and Kat said little as they drove from Denny's to the office. They made a few stops along the way and found traffic was light, something abnormal in D.C. most days. His cell phone vibrated. A text message read, *Are you in your office?*

The number on his caller ID read *999-999-9999.*

Who is this? He typed.

Thanks for the all American, the reply said.

Eli typed. *Headed to my office.*

The phone vibrated a second later. *Meet me at the WWII memorial in 20 minutes.*

Eli looked at Kat. "That was fast," he said.

"Zed?"

"You got it."

They circled the memorial twice, and dodged a fair number of visitors enjoying the national mall amid a sunny day.

Kat saw him first. "There he is." She pointed to the far end of the fountain.

"Where?"

"Under the Connecticut pillar. Yellow shirt, green hat," Kat said.

Eli squinted, but it didn't help. "How can you see that far? People look like blobs from this far away."

"Younger eyes. What can I say?"

"Yeah, rub it in. Why don't you?"

"I will," she replied over her shoulder as she started around the pool.

Zed looked past them as they approached. He fidgeted as he bounced on the balls of his feet. "Come alone?"

"Yeah," Eli said.

"Good. What I'm about to give you didn't come from me. Got it?"

"Got what?" Eli asked as a wry smile formed at the corner of his lips.

"Catching on faster than most feds, Agent Payne. Fantastic."

Eli wanted to remind Zed whom he worked for, but decided against it.

Zed held a cell phone in his right hand. With his left finger, he swiped across the screen, and immediately Eli's cell phone buzzed.

Eli looked at the message, which included several photos. "Is this what I think ..." But he didn't get to finish the thought.

"That first photo was taken as they processed Nick Jordan at the Sanctum's facility in the Gulf of Mexico. The images came from their in-house security system."

"And how the hell did you get them?"

Zed shrugged his shoulders, but didn't respond.

Eli didn't ask a second time and examined the photos. Kat stood close enough he could smell her perfume. A subtle scent of lilac and strawberries. She was almost leaning on his broad shoulder. "The diagram is of the entire facility? Schematics are accurate?" he asked.

Zed nodded amidst several twitches. "Correct."

"And it's up to date?"

"The facility is not old. The Sanctum moves around quite often. Complacency doesn't serve anyone well in their line of work."

"Why do they use oil platforms?"

"The real question you should ask is why not? There are thousands of abandoned structures in the Gulf, and they are almost impossible for agencies like the Bureau of Safety, and the Environmental Enforcement to keep tabs on them. Old, abandoned platforms have been used for illicit activities for decades. Most often by drug runners and sex traffickers, but now the Sanctum uses them as well."

"Sex traffickers? Are you serious? The drug runners don't surprise me, but I had no clue the sex industry utilized structures in the Gulf."

"Absolutely. It's a brave new world, Agent Payne. The traffickers come to the Gulf via Mexico and Central American countries and have sorting facilities on abandoned platforms. Then they are sent to Atlanta, Georgia."

"Atlanta? What's in Atlanta besides The Varsity?"

Zed's expression revealed he didn't get the joke.

Kat interrupted. "I've read some of the official briefs the Bureau puts out. Atlanta is a hotbed of the sex-trade industry on the East Coast." She looked at Eli. "Maybe you should read your email from time to time. Lots of interesting factoids are sent out."

Eli ignored the dig. "Oil platforms run by crime syndicates, and major cities used as sex trafficking hubs. What are we? Some backassward third-world nation?"

"Quite the opposite. We are the land of the free and home of the brave," Zed said. "Meaning the brave criminal elements realize they have free rein to do whatever they want as long as they bribe the right person and manipulate our loopholes. Power in the money, money in the power. It's the tale as old as time."

Eli was hung up on the platforms and missed the references that jumped from Coolio to Beauty and the Beast. "And our federal agencies know about the activities on the platforms?"

"I'm not saying the United States is complicit, but we certainly turn a blind eye to them, yes."

Eli shook his head. "Why?"

"It's complicated."

"That's bullshit."

"It's all you're getting right now, Agent Payne," Zed said. "Corruption has always been a part of life and always will be. Those who believe in justice have to work hard to save a ship with far more holes than buckets."

Eli shook his head but didn't reply.

"Regarding the platform operated by the Sanctum ..." Zed motioned to the images on Eli's smartphone. "Everything you should need is right there. Including longitude and latitude coordinates."

"Look, Zed. Don't take this the wrong way, but why help us? Certainly you're taking a risk by talking to us and then taking more chances by sharing this intel with us. I want to know why."

Zed's tics started anew as he flicked his thumb and index finger together in rapid succession. "I'm a smart guy, see. OK, I'm borderline genius, a card-carrying member of Mensa. And, I know for a fact our government uses my intellect for unethical means. I could have gone to the private sector and made more money than I could have dreamed of, but instead, I decided to serve a higher calling. I think this guy you're looking for, Nick Jordan, The Body Man, is doing something similar. Protecting not one man, but the Office Of The President is a noble calling. Covering up someone's indiscretions to spare the country undue pain and disgrace is admirable. I'm not sure why the Sanctum has him or who ratted him out, but it bothers me to the core that he's in this predicament. It might sound corny, but it's the right thing to do. Sometimes my analytical skills are used to take a life, and this time maybe they can help save one." Zed paused and took a slow, measured breath. "Does that make sense?"

Eli nodded. "It makes perfect sense."

Zed turned to leave. "Oh, and by the way, to answer your question before you ask it, platforms like that need to be resupplied. Think about that."

Before Eli or Kat could respond, he was gone.

No goodbye. No good luck. Just gone.

Eli said the words, "Thank you," but couldn't be sure if Zed even heard him. With a shrug of the shoulders, he looked over at Kat, and she gave him the look. The stare. "What?" he asked.

"Next?" Kat asked.

Eli took a deep breath from his nose and exhaled it slowly out his mouth. "Follow me."

55

Washington, D.C.

Eli's feet felt like lead weights as he walked to the car. The director wanted them at headquarters for a debrief. He looked at Kat as they walked the gravel path. "This is a hard job, Stone. Mentally, physically, and even emotionally. I hope you don't plan to have a family."

"Well, that's random." Kat stopped along the pathway, placed a hand on her hip, and stared at Eli.

Eli stopped as well. "I just want you to know what you've signed up for. Especially if you decide to make a career out of it."

"I'm still getting my feet wet, Eli. I don't want to commit to anything long term until I'm in it for a while. See what it's like."

"That's smart, Kat. And take it from me, the job is hell on a relationship. No set schedule, lots of time away. It's pretty hard to maintain any semblance of anything normal with a spouse or, God forbid, kids."

"Is that why you're single?" Kat started walking again.

"Probably. Well, that and my bubbly personality." A wide grin formed on his face as he followed her and tried to catch up.

"Is that what killed the relationship with the Secret Service agent?" Kat looked over at him. "Your job was too hard?"

"Kind of, but so was hers." He grew quiet for a moment before he continued. "You can get by sometimes when one partner has a stressful job, but when both do, it gets tricky. Plus, I think fate stepped in."

"Fate's a bullshit excuse people throw out there to ignore the true issues that doom a relationship," Kat said with a forceful tone. "Let me ask you this," she continued. "Do you still love her?"

"That's sort of personal."

"You brought this conversation up, Payne, not me."

"Valid point." Eli grew quiet. An entire minute passed before he replied, "Honestly, Kat, yes, I do."

"Then maybe it's meant to work out after all?"

"Doubt it."

"Why do you say that? Is she with someone else?"

"Not that I know of. Like me, she's married to the job."

"Maybe you should give it another shot."

"It ended badly."

"Jesus, Eli. Lots of relationships end badly. What are you? Twelve?"

"Hey, watch it! Most guys are twelve, at least in their heads."

"Truth, but that doesn't mean it has to end for good. Relationships are hard, especially the really good ones, and God forbid if there's a penis involved. Those things fuck up everything they come in contact with. Literally." She jabbed him in the side as she uttered the dig.

Eli let out a guttural laugh. "Point taken. And by the way, you might be more of a mess than me, Kat."

"Is she hot?"

"Pffft. Of course," Eli said as he pursed his lips.

"Got a nice rack?"

Eli smirked as he glanced down at her chest, then back up. A devilish grin formed on his lips. "Better than yours."

Kat laughed. Louder than he had ever heard. "Then get back on that pony, you perv, and take her for another ride around the ring."

He shook his head. "You're not like most women, Stone."

"Yes, I know. I'm God's gift to the female race," she said and rolled her eyes.

His eyes narrowed.

"That's sarcasm, Payne. False bravado."

"I'll miss our banter when this case is over."

"Believe it or not, I will as well. You're growing on me."

<hr>

They arrived at his vehicle and climbed in. Eli's cell phone buzzed, and he fished the phone from his pants pocket. The display indicated he had four voicemails.

Eli handed the phone to Kat, and he pulled out of the parking space. "You mind playing these messages for me while I drive?"

"Sure," Kat said. "Even though you made fun of the size of my tits. No problem."

Eli shook his head. "I said better, not bigger, Miss Insecure."

Kat played the messages. On the second playback, she smacked Eli on his right arm, which caused him to jerk the wheel slightly.

"What gives? I'm trying to drive over here, Stone."

"Eli, you've got to hear this."

"OK, put it on speaker."

Kat replayed the message. When it finished, she asked, "Do you know this Special Agent Gabel?"

"Never heard of him."

"What do you want to do?"

"I need to call him back. Mind dialing his number for me? Put it on speaker?"

Kat gave him a crooked glance. "Sure, as long as you don't start thinking I'm your secretary or any such nonsense."

Eli smirked. "Nah, if I had one, my secretary would be really, really old."

"Um, why?"

"Would save me a bundle on the sexual harassment litigation."

"Figures."

<hr>

The phone rang two times before a baritone voice answered. "Special Agent Gabel."

"Darius, it's Eli Payne from the Washington field office."

"Eli, yes. Thanks for getting back to me."

"Your message said you got a hit in Sentinel with the words *The Body Man*, and you saw it referenced in my case file?"

"Sure did. Pretty unique phrase, and I wondered if this guy they fished out of the Pacific might have something to do with your active missing-person case?"

"Can you tell me more about this person you spoke with?"

"I haven't talked with him yet. I'm on my way to the hospital now; Hector regained consciousness a few minutes ago. The nurse spoke with him last night, and she relayed the info to me. He asked to speak to a member of the FBI when they brought him to the hospital."

"That's unusual."

"I agree."

"I don't believe in coincidences. But I'm not sure how some possible arms shipment may have to do with my missing-person case," Eli said.

"Neither do I," Darius replied.

"Tell you what. I'm less than ten minutes out from headquarters, and I'm about to walk into an important meeting. It could be a while, but call me when you're in the room with Hector, and I'll see if I can step out and be on phone."

"Works for me. I'm about thirty minutes out from the hospital."

"Thanks, I'll talk with you soon." As the call ended, he glanced over at Kat and gave her a questioning look with one eyebrow arched higher than the other.

Eli and Kat tag-teamed the conversation with the director. Tension filled the air as they got into the specifics. The lines on the director's face became more pronounced as the story unfolded.

When they pulled up the schematics on Eli's smartphone, the director held a hand up in the air. "We need to complete this in the Strategic Information and Operations Center." Ken walked over to his desk and raised the receiver on his phone. "Annie, call down to the SIOC and tell them I'll be there in the next few minutes. You know which room I want." He hung up the phone and turned back to Eli and Kat, who sat on the edge of the couch. "We're about to see if what this Zed says is legit intel or utter nonsense."

"I believe Zed," Kat said.

Eli agreed. "As do I."

The director shook his head. "You're probably both right. I guarantee after what the last president did to restrict our intelligence gathering capabilities, someone stepped in to fill the void. I didn't want to tip my hat earlier, but I'm familiar with the Sanctum. They are a massive international crime ring. I wasn't aware of any facilities stateside or in the Gulf, but their reach is far, and their grip is tight."

"What will happen if we confirm what Zed told us?" Kat asked.

The director considered her question. "Well, then the real fun stuff begins, Agent Stone. And you're about to be the first probationary agent to step foot into the lion's den."

56

WASHINGTON, D.C.

J EDGAR HOOVER BUILDING

Eli stared at the four oversized hi-def screens that lined the far wall of SIOC Operations Room One. His eyes narrowed as real time intel flashed across the screens in a dizzying array of images.

Located on the fifth floor of headquarters, the space serves as a crisis management center where global events are monitored, and operational initiatives are created. Those who work inside the secretive room refer to it as "the lion's den," and for a good reason. Each screen measures four feet high and six feet wide, with less than an inch gap between the corners of the four screens. It almost looks like an IMAX screen from the rear of the room.

The bottom left image held Eli's attention as it showed a satellite upload from the Gulf of Mexico. Three screens displayed various images uploaded from Eli's case file.

A feed showed live, real-time images above Pike 84, an oil platform located in the Gulf of Mexico at the coordinates provided by Zed. The warm Gulf waters appeared still, the platform a stoic figure alone in a vast expanse of blue. According to the data acquired by the SIOC analysts from the Bureau of Ocean Energy Management and its sister agency, the Bureau of Safety and Environmental Enforcement, the platform had been decommissioned a year prior. However, like many other abandoned platforms, its fate hasn't been determined, and the structure remained intact, albeit officially abandoned. While the BSEE periodically inspected decommissioned platforms, the backlog and lack of resources made a physical inspection of most virtually impossible.

Eli absorbed the constant activity inside the Operations Room and processed the sights and sounds. To his right sat the director in the center seat of a crescent-shaped wooden table that sat five. High backed leather chairs sat spaced beside the table and the room contained four identical tables all facing the wall of hi-def screens.

Eli watched the director lob instructions at various staff members who scurried around the room like cockroaches after someone turned on the lights. Even at sixty-eight years old, an unmistakable sharpness was present in the older man's eyes as the data flickered from numerous sources simultaneously. The tone of the room had changed twenty minutes earlier after the director walked in and told everyone to "Lock it down." Each man and woman present knew that meant: "Get to work, keep the chatter to a minimum, and shut the hell up about whatever you see or do in this room."

Kat sat to Eli's left, and a total of fifteen senior analysts and various support members present inside the secure room. A palpable tension filled the air as none of them knew what was at stake, and each member treated the situation like someone's life depended on them doing their jobs to the best of their abilities.

"What have the eyes in the skies revealed? Do we know how many people are on the platform?" The director asked.

"Hard to say as of right now, sir," a senior analyst answered. "We need thermal images from the drone, to be sure. We've been compiling images from several satellites making passes over the platform."

"I thought you had images from the WorldView satellite?"

"We did, and it appeared to show at least two people outside the structure on the seventh level. But we can't be sure; the satellite was only in range for a few minutes before we lost the signal."

"How long until we get thermal images and real-time video transmissions?"

One of the other analysts, with a phone placed to his ear, cocked his head toward the director. "I'm on with Joint Reserve Base New Orleans. They fitted the drone with a thermal imaging camera, and it should be airborne within fifteen minutes."

"That's the best they can do?"

"We're lucky they even had one, sir. The Gray Eagle is only on base as a training tool, and they hadn't expected to use it for the purpose we requested. If you hadn't gotten on the horn, we would be tasking a bird from much farther away."

"Yeah, well, Captain Paulson and I go way back," the director said. "Although I may need to hand out a marker before the day is done." The director looked around the room. "Tell me, ladies and gentlemen, do we have the right spot?"

Micah, one of the senior analysts, replied, "Based on the intel we've collected, whoever is running the place didn't set up a Club Med. The drone images should fill in some gaps, but I'd agree with the assessment that this platform is used for illicit activity. Can't be sure what they are doing on the platform, but they assuredly shouldn't be there."

The director stayed silent for several minutes.

"What are you thinking, sir?" Eli asked.

Ken rubbed his chin and looked away from Eli and toward the image of the platform on the far-left screen. "Think it's time to call Quantico and get the HRT ready for a trip to the Gulf."

"How long do they need?" Eli asked.

"They can be ready to deploy globally in four hours. I'll tell them they have two. I want the TOC set up in Houma by dinnertime."

Eli's phone vibrated. He looked down at the number. The area code showed a 310 number.

"This is that call I need to take, sir."

"Yes, of course," the director said. "Take it. I'll get the ball rolling with HRT and coordinate the trip to the Gulf."

Eli answered the call but covered the microphone with his hand. "Kat and I want to go with the HRT team."

The director smiled. "I wouldn't dare leave you here and miss out on all the action."

Eli gave the thumbs up and removed his hand from the microphone. "This is Special Agent Payne ..."

57

THE WHITE HOUSE

THE OVAL

President Steele shook the hand of the speaker of the house as she left the Oval. He noticed her wide smile twist into a menacing frown before she even made it past the doorway.

"Bitch," he said in an audible voice, not even waiting for her to exit the Oval. Unsure if she heard him or not, he really didn't care.

Dolores peeked in the doorway seconds after the speaker left. "Sorry to interrupt, Mr. President."

The president half smirked, half frowned. "What is it now?"

"Director Kline is in the waiting area. He has some urgent news regarding Agent Frazier."

The president's posture stiffened, and his heart rate increased. "Send him in."

"Is this a good update or a bad one, David?" The president asked as he gestured to the leather chair positioned in front of his desk.

Director Kline strode in and took a seat as instructed, taking in a deep breath before he spoke. "It's good news, sir."

"Go on," the president said.

"The hospital called to inform us Danny is conscious."

President Steele appeared startled. "He's awake?"

"Yes."

President Steele could not hide his surprise. "Is he talking?"

"No, he's still intubated and heavily medicated."

"But he's aware of his surroundings?"

"It appears so. He scratched a few things on a pad, but they're illegible."

The president felt the room spin. David continued to discuss what the doctors said as the president's mind went into overdrive.

As David finished his update, the president said, "I want to see him."

Director Kline looked perplexed. "You want to see Danny, sir?"

"Correct."

"I guess we could arrange a visit. When?"

"Now, if he's awake. I want to spend a few minutes with him."

"I didn't realize you two were that close?" The director eyed the president with a perplexed look on his face.

"David. I've been worried sick ever since he was shot and want to see him with my own eyes."

"That will take some time to secure the floor and configure your motorcade route, Mr. President."

"Bullshit." The president spoke in a firm, boisterous tone.

The director appeared taken aback by the outburst. Although the president was known for his temper and vile mouth, the director hadn't expected it directed at him. "Pardon me, sir?"

"What did I say that was unclear? The floor is secured by agents, and we don't need to go with a full entourage. Send me with the same manpower you use on Saturday nights for poker at Al's house in Georgetown."

"That's different, sir."

The president rose from his seat and leaned his heavyset body toward the director. "I'm not asking you if I can go, David. I'm telling you I'm going. Make the calls; I want to be on my way to the hospital in less than thirty minutes."

The director swallowed hard and nodded. "Yes, Mr. President. I'll tell the team to travel light."

"See? That wasn't hard." The president dismissed the director with a wave of his hand.

Once the director left, the president lifted the receiver on his phone. "Dolores, get me a secure line."

Marcus looked down at the caller ID of the vibrating phone as it shimmied atop the nightstand at the Plaza Hotel in mid-town Manhattan.

He looked away from the phone and toward Merci as she crept toward him on all fours from the far corner of the California king-size bed. "You better not answer that goddamn phone," she said, her upper lip snarled as she uttered the last two words.

She looked as sexy as hell as she glided across the bed in the French maid outfit they'd bought an hour earlier at Abracadabra on West 21st Street. Her ample breasts hung almost completely out of the black-and-white laced top as her body swayed with each movement. Never any issues turning him on in the past; it was the turning-off part that became a problem.

Marcus looked at her voluptuous body and then back at the vibrating phone. *Fuuuuuck,* he thought.

"I've got to, babe. It's him."

"Charles Steele can burn in hell." Merci paused halfway across the bed.

"Oh, he will. But I still got to answer his call." Marcus grabbed the phone.

"Yes, sir," Marcus said as he clicked the "accept" button on the phone's display.

"Where are you?" The president asked.

Merci could only hear one side of the conversation, a large frown displayed on her face. Within a second, the frown turned into a full-on pout.

Marcus mouthed the word "sorry," then placed the call on speakerphone so she could hear the conversation.

"Still in Manhattan, Mr. President."

"And did you retrieve the file already?"

"Yes."

"Is Merci with you?"

"She's here."

"Having fun screwing her in the Plaza?"

"Wait. What?" Marcus was unable to mask the shocked tone of his voice.

"I'm the President of the United States. Kind of hard to keep secrets from me, Marcus."

"We're together at the moment, yes," Marcus said.

"Good. All I care about is the file. Did you look at it?"

"Absolutely not."

"Keep it that way. I take it there was money or other stuff in the box?"

"There was. The box included ..."

The president cut him off. "I don't give a shit what else was in there. It's all yours. I only want the file."

"Thank you, sir," Marcus said.

"And by the way, Danny Frazier woke up."

Marcus felt like Mike Tyson had slammed him with an uppercut. "Is he talking?"

"Not yet, but that will likely change soon. I'm on my way to the hospital to have a word with him."

"Regarding?"

"I'm going to get the location of the three remaining files. I need you back in D.C. tomorrow afternoon with the file. Both of you."

"Understood."

"Junior sent Casha down to the Gulf. He'll have a few words with Nick Jordan."

"And after we deliver the file to you?" Marcus asked.

"Your services will no longer be needed. You'll be free to go." The president said.

"No strings attached?" Marcus asked.

"None whatsoever."

"See you tomorrow, Mr. President."

The line went dead. Marcus tossed the phone back on the nightstand. "Where were we?"

"You're a real dick, you know that?" Merci's face scrunched up into a snarled expression. "I can't believe you answered the fucking phone."

A twisted grin spread across Marcus's face as he grabbed her bare arm. "And you wouldn't have it any other way, babe," he said as he pulled her toward him.

Merci's arm cut through the air like a scythe through grass and hit his arm away while her free hand knocked him back against the headboard with a loud *thump*.

The action startled Marcus. "What the ..."

Like a lioness to her prey, Merci was on him in an instant with a full-on straddle. "It's my turn to show you some tricks." Her legs wrapped around his thighs like a python as it slowly constricts its victim.

58

— • —

Houma, Louisiana

Peter's shoulder throbbed constantly with each bump and jostle on the two-hour flight. The eight hundred milligrams of ibuprofen and two shots of Gentleman Jack did little to dull the ache.

Peter stepped off the plane exhausted as the Cajun heat and stifling humidity greeted him like a Turkish steam bath. His clothes clung to his skin like a wet rag, and the area around his wound itched as he sauntered across the tarmac.

The helicopter rotors came to life as he approached. Peter carried a small duffel bag with essentials, including several changes of clothes, although he hoped to complete the task in less than twenty-four hours. Two men greeted him at the left rear door of the Robinson R44 Clipper II helicopter. One took his bag while the other leaned in close and spoke into his ear loudly enough to compensate for the rotor wash. Peter nodded his head in response and climbed in as the helicopter rose and made a rapid ascent into the air.

———— ❖ ————

Special Agent Fred Simmons watched the man with his left arm in a sling climb out of the Gulfstream G280 and proceed to the waiting helicopter.

He concealed himself behind a large steel door while the rest of his team set up equipment in the empty hangar, which they turned into a de facto command center. The team arrived around lunchtime, and Fred dispatched two of his men to the marina in Port Fourchon while the others organized the command post.

With his binoculars raised, he watched as the mystery man climbed into the waiting helicopter. Fred immediately made a call.

"Rich, it's Freddy."

"Hey, Uncle Freddy," Rich Knappick, an analyst back at headquarters said. "What can I do you for?"

"I need you to contact the FAA and track a helicopter."

"You still at the Houma airport?"

"Yes. It looks to be a four-seater. Tail number is N as in November, two, zero, four, C as in Charlie, T as in tango."

"Got it. N204CT. Confirm?"

"That is correct. The helicopter looks to be headed south toward the gulf."

"I'm on it. We'll track and provide a flight path ASAP."

"Thanks, Rich. Let me know where it lands."

"Will do."

Next, Fred called the SIOC. His partner in crime, a woman he worked with for almost twenty years, answered. "Kathy, it's Freddy."

"Hey, Freddy," said Kathy Sanders.

"A Gulfstream landed at the airport in Houma. Can you look up the registry info for me?"

"Sure thing. Go ahead with the tail number."

"N as in November, one, nine, zero, N as in November, B as in bravo."

"Copy that. N190NB, correct?"

"Affirmative."

"I'll ring you back when I've got something."

"Appreciate it, Kathy. Pull me a comprehensive flight history as well."

"Will do."

"Is the rest of the team on their way?"

"Yes, they left Quantico. The director is even joining the HRT."

"Really?"

"You bet, and when the big dog joins in ..."

Freddy cut her off and finished the statement. "Forget the bark and fear the bite."

59

THE WHITE HOUSE

PRESIDENT'S PRIVATE STUDY

President Steele leaned back in his chair. Large bags had formed under his eyes.

The office door swung open fast and startled him. Charles looked up to see Junior in the doorway.

"I didn't hear back from you. How did the visit go with Danny?"

The president looked perturbed, an emotion he did nothing to hide. "You're not planning on sleeping in the Lincoln bedroom, are you?"

Junior knew he wasn't welcome in the official residence. His father had made that clear soon after he moved in. "Of course not. I have my normal suite down the road."

"Good."

"The visit?" Junior asked again.

The president's cheeks rose, and his mouth puckered. Slowly, he moved his head from one side to another. "Not as I hoped."

"Was he conscious?"

"Yes, for a few minutes."

"Did he talk?"

"No, he's still intubated."

"But he knew you were there?"

"Yes. I could see the recognition in his eyes. I asked how he felt and if he knew who I was. He nodded his head. The nurse gave him a notepad and pen, but what he wrote was illegible, gibberish really. Nothing more than a series of lines and dots."

"What did his doctor say?"

"There's a team of doctors now, and they're being vague. The consensus is that after a brain trauma, patients will sometimes have to learn to speak and write all over again."

"Anything else?"

"They might remove the trach tube later tonight. If so, I want to be the first one to talk with him."

"Won't the Secret Service want to question him first?"

"Of course, but I've said it would be better if I tell Danny about Nick's abduction. Director Kline is on board."

"And you think he'll tell you what he knows?" Junior asked.

"If he's able to communicate, yes."

"What if Nick already told him the truth, or if he looked at the documents Nick gave him?"

"I'll improvise."

"Meaning?"

"Just what I said. I'll roll up my sleeves and do what is needed."

"You normally have others do your dirty work." Junior observed a snarl form on the corner of his father's mouth. "Mr. President." He added.

"You'd be surprised what a man is capable of when the fate of his presidency and legacy rests in the hands of others less capable."

Junior changed the subject. "Casha arrived at the facility."

"When will he see Nick?"

"In the morning."

"If he fails at cracking him, well, let's say the circle of who knows what you've done is too big. I think it would be best to thin the numbers."

"What I've done?" Junior's voice rose an octave.

"We're not having this discussion again, Junior." The president raised his open hand and closed it fast into a fist.

Junior seethed. Through gritted teeth, he said, "And how do you suggest I *Thin the numbers* as you put it?"

"However you see fit, but I don't want to know or be involved anymore. There's already enough blowback on me."

"Cleaning up a mess can get expensive and bloody. And depending on who I involve, they might not appreciate retribution for fellow operators."

Charles Steele glared at his only son. "Everyone has a price. After all, how do you think I got elected?"

60

— • —

AT CRUISING ALTITUDE

Eli peered out the window at what looked like a snow-white down comforter covering the horizon contrasting with the deep blue sky above. He had never been on a private jet, and a G550 served as one hell of a first time.

A full contingent of HRT operators from Quantico followed in two trailing planes. Formed in 1983, the elite FBI Hostage Rescue Team formed due to the 1972 Olympic Games, when eleven Israeli athlete hostages were murdered by the Black September Palestinian terrorists. The FBI vowed not to allow a similar incident to occur during the 1984 games held in Los Angeles and created the HRT in response.

Eli was lost in thought as Kat walked down the aisle. He didn't notice her until she cleared her throat and snapped her fingers several times. Finally, he looked away from the window.

"Jeez, you zoning out or what, Payne?" Kat asked.

"Sorry, a lot on my mind."

"Penny for your thoughts?"

"Part of me doesn't like the idea of bringing a full contingent of HRT down there to rescue Jordan."

Kat took the seat next to him. She looked puzzled at his comment. "Then how would you suggest we get The Body Man back?"

"I know some guys."

"Who?" Kat asked.

"They are called The Omega Group. Purely off the books outfit. Much less of a footprint and probably a better chance of succeeding."

"Better chance than the HRT?"

"Knowing my pal, Troy Evans, who leads the team. Yes."

Kat shrugged. "Then why didn't you suggest this Omega Group friends of yours to the Director?"

"Because I might look kinda stupid, but I'm really not. Besides, I like my career. It would not have gone over well if I suggested to the Director we should operate outside the proper channels."

Kat shifted in the seat and pulled out a book wedged between the seat cushion and the armrest. She wiggled the book free and a broad smile spread over her face. "*The Escape Artist*, huh? You trying to find a way to ditch me?"

"Why did you sit next to me Stone and disturb my brooding?" A scowl formed on Eli's face.

"Well, Mr. Moody, I got a call when you were on with Darius."

Eli perked up. "Yeah? Who called?"

"WFO. The tech guys used facial recognition software and matched two of the guys from the photos we got at the Manassas airport manhandling Nick with the footage we retrieved from the Days Inn."

"Guess we now have proof the same guys who dumped the car were at the airport with Nick."

"That's correct. They said the match was 95 percent certain."

"I'll take those stats," Eli said.

"You going to tell me how your call went earlier?"

Eli rubbed his eyes. "Oh, where to start?"

"From the beginning. We've got some time before we land in Houma."

He recounted the conversation before Kat cut in.

"And you spoke with Hector Fuentes?" Kat asked.

"Yes, but only after I gave him immunity."

"Immunity? From what?"

"His illicit activities that may or may not have something to do with Nick Jordan."

"So why did he use the phrase 'The Body Man?'"

"Hector works at the Port of Los Angeles. A man named Peter Casha hired Hector and six other men to transfer shipping containers delivered by General Atomics from a ship bound for one of our bases in Italy to another ship. Hector and his men were paid to switch the containers."

"And where was this other ship headed?"

"Saudi Arabia."

Kat pursed her lips. "General Atomics. They're a defense supplier, right?"

"That's correct."

"And what was in the containers?" Kat asked.

"According to Hector, a dozen high-end military drones. State of the art technology."

"That's it?" Kat asked.

"Isn't that enough?"

"Well, sure, but ..."

"Besides drones, there were missiles. Lots of them."

"So, someone is giving Saudi Arabia high-tech weapons of war?"

Eli nodded. "Sounds that way."

"And how does The Body Man tie into this?"

"Not sure. Hector didn't know anything about Nick; he only knew the term 'The Body Man' as a reference made by this Peter Casha guy."

"And is this Peter Casha his friend or a business associate?"

"He appears to be a business contact and nothing more. According to Hector, Peter Casha lured Hector and his men out to the Pacific with the promise of another job, but it was simply a ruse to kill them. Casha killed everyone except Hector. During the melee, Hector said he shot Casha in the shoulder and escaped."

"Can anyone collaborate what he said?"

"Analysts back at SIOC are running down what they can and hope to have some proof in the next few hours that Hector wasn't blowing smoke out his ass. General Atomics has already confirmed the shipment, although they swear it's still on a container ship bound for Italy."

Kat considered what Eli said. "What if Nick learned about this transfer of material to Saudi Arabia?"

"You mean as part of his job?"

"Bingo."

"Are you thinking the president had something to do with this?"

"Not sure, but if he did, it would be the perfect reason to get rid of The Body Man, wouldn't it?"

Eli laughed. "Sounds like you're buying into Zed and his conspiracy theories."

"Truth can be stranger than fiction more times than not."

"Yes, but that's an enormous leap."

"I agree. That's why we need Nick Jordan AKA The Body Man. He'll blow this whole case wide open."

"If he's still alive," Eli said.

"He is."

"How can you be sure?"

Kat pursed her lips. "It's quite simple. Because he has to be."

61

HOUMA, LOUISIANA

Eli and Kat stepped into the expansive hangar. The waxed concrete caused their shoes to squeak as they moved against the smooth surface. Eli headed straight for the back corner of the building, where he found the command center composed of seven folding tables, a dozen laptops, and two sixty-inch flat-screen televisions. Special Agent Fred Simmons turned as Eli approached, a cell phone pressed against each ear. Agent Simmons looked at Eli and gave him a slight head nod. When the first call ended, he placed the phone on the table and held his index finger up in the air letting them know he needed a minute.

As the second call ended, Eli extended his hand. "Good to finally meet you. I'm Eli Payne."

"Eli, yes. The team's been waiting for you to arrive. My name is Fred Simmons, but everyone calls me Uncle Freddy."

"Sound like you've been busy."

"Sure have. Did you get the intel on the private jet?"

"Yes." Eli scratched the side of his face.

"The jet is owned by a shell company," Freddy said. "There are some loose threads that tie it back to the Steele Corp."

"How loose?"

"Well, whoever set up the legal entities was good, really good. And trust me, they covered their tracks well, but unfortunately for them, the FBI hires the best and along the way someone screwed up and left a trail our team could follow."

"And the analysts are sure those loose threads point to the Steele Corp."

"Correct." Uncle Freddy nodded.

"That's troubling," Eli said.

"Also, SIOC just got back with us. They ran the image of the man from the jet through the FBI national facial recognition database and got a hit from passport control at LaGuardia."

"And?"

"His name is Peter Casha ..."

The name startled Eli, and he put his hands up to interrupt. "You sure?"

"Yes. SIOC confirmed his identity." Freddy noticed the recognition in Eli's eyes. "Why? Does the name ring a bell?"

"It does." Eli's mind kicked into overdrive as he tried to piece together the growing evidence and form a cohesive storyboard in his mind.

Freddy continued. "SIOC determined it's an alias, and they're running down everything they can on him, including a list of known associates. Only a matter of time until they get his real name and figure out his connection to the Steele Corp. A chartered helicopter transported Mr. Casha out to the Gulf. Based on the coordinates, it landed on the abandoned platform."

"Anything else?" Eli asked.

"We have another interesting development."

"I'm listening."

<hr/>

"Regarding the platform, your source from the agency said to look at how it's supplied."

"That's right. What did you learn?"

"Most boats operate out of Port Fourchon to resupply the Gulf platforms, and we connected each supplier and their ships to one of the major companies that operate platforms in this area. That is all but one."

"Let me guess." Eli didn't need to finish the thought.

"You got it. The platform in question is resupplied by a single boat that operates under an LLC named P. Logan Enterprises. And get this, all the payments for their resupply business originate from an offshore bank account."

"Which one?"

"They run through a Cayman account, but the bank of record is Danske Bank, a branch located in St. Petersburg."

"Russia?"

"You bet."

"Well, since the Sanctum is supposedly a Russian outfit, that makes sense. But I'm surprised they would be sloppy like that."

"I agree but think about it. How many people are looking into resupply ships operating in the Gulf?" Freddy asked.

"Yeah, good point," Eli said. "And considering how many electronic transfers occur, the criminal element understands few get looked at with much scrutiny."

"Anyway, I have two agents watching the resupply ship right now. They look to be stocking it. My men asked around, and the locals say the ships normally depart in the a.m."

"How many men onboard?"

"Five not including the owner, who is also the captain."

"His name?"

"Bradley Taylor. Locals say he's new to the area. Moved here about six months ago, but they don't know much about where he's from or what he did before he arrived. Keeps to himself. There's a rumor floating around he has a military background, maybe army, possible a former operator, but nobody knows for sure."

"Anyone approached him?"

Freddy shook his head. "No. Not yet."

The director arrived halfway through the conversation without saying anything.

Eli turned to face him. "What do you think, sir?"

"Sounds like we need to pay Captain Taylor a visit."

"Are we playing good cop or bad cop?" Eli asked.

The director shrugged. "If he's former military, it might not matter. I say we go in, ask some poignant questions, and then lay down the law. Tell him cooperation is not a choice and articulate what we need. He either goes along, and we forget the fact he's abetting a crime syndicate, or we force his cooperation and then throw the book at him."

"When do we go?" asked Eli.

"Now," the director said.

62

HOUMA, LOUISIANA

Eli watched the full contingent of HRT operators enter the hangar in a single-file line.

One word jumped to the forefront of his mind.

Overkill.

Ten rows of chairs were set up to house everyone. The television monitors in front showed real-time imagery beamed straight from the drone circling high above Pike 84, where thermal imaging confirmed fourteen people on the platform.

On the flight from D.C., Eli went over the intel from Zed several times. Although he hadn't shared it with anyone, a plan formed in his mind.

The director walked to the front of the space, but before he could say anything, Eli spoke. "Are we planning a full-scale assault on the facility?"

The director looked back at Eli with a quizzical look. "We don't have a plan yet. That's what we're here to figure out."

"Well, with all due respect, sir, if the consensus tonight is to go balls to the wall and hit the facility with everything we have, I think we'll have a problem."

"How so?"

"We need a small tactical team to conduct a precision strike, not a full assault team."

The director arched his eyebrows. "I'm listening."

"I mentioned when we were in the SIOC that Zed's intel indicated the facility was only staffed by at most a dozen people."

"Yes, I read the intel on the flight as well. Thermal imaging confirmed his data. Your point?"

"My point is if we send in a bunch of boats or helicopter in and fast rope down, they'll spot us from miles away. Once that happens, they'll kill Nick Jordan."

"How can you be sure they would do that?"

"Because that's what I'd do. I would not let someone take back a hostage with so many secrets."

The director frowned. "And I take it you have a suggestion on what we should do?"

"Absolutely. We only need a small team, six HRT members at the most. Since we already vetted Captain Taylor, we use his resupply boat and breach the facility undetected as part of the scheduled supply drop set to occur in the morning. With the schematic of the facility, the HRT team can use it to plan a small-scale assault and snatch Jordan."

The HRT commander, Austin Chapin, shook his head. "That's not our standard operating procedure, Agent Payne. We normally breach with a superior force, including overwhelming firepower."

"I know your SOP commander, and you need to adapt," Eli said. "A superior force approach will get Nick Jordan killed."

Commander Chapin's face turned two hues of red, but before he could protest, Uncle Freddy stood up. "Excuse me. I know I'm not a part of the HRT team, but I think Agent Payne makes a valid point. In my previous life, I was part of SEAL Team 5 and conducted many missions, including hostage rescues, on land and at sea. I agree we need to hit them hard, but the coordinated attack needs to be small. Above all, we must have the element of surprise, which is something we can achieve only by utilizing the resupply vessel. The only other option besides the resupply boat would be to use submersibles and come up under the platform undetected. For that we need the SEALs."

"We don't have time to bring in the SEALs. Besides, this is an HRT op, and we'll conduct the raid. No other agency is getting read into this operation." The director's tone was stern, his face stoic.

"Then Eli is on the right track," Freddy said.

The director shook his head. "Isn't using a commercial vessel and going in with a small team risky?" He turned, raising the question to Chapin. "Commander, your thoughts?"

"My team can execute that type of raid, sir." His gaze focused on Eli as his eyes narrowed. "I'll admit coming in heavy could be problematic in the open ocean. Agent Payne makes a valid point."

"For argument's sake, let's say we went with what Eli suggested," the director said. "Do you have five men besides yourself you'd take, commander?"

"Of course."

"All I care is that we lay out a plan that works for all of us and mitigates the chance of Nick getting killed during our recovery. Light or heavy makes no difference to me; I care about a successful retrieval." The director looked at Chapin. "Assuming we go light and use the resupply boat, what would that look like?"

Commander Chapin stood at attention. He placed his hands on his chin and rubbed the stubble slowly. His mind whirling like a weathervane in a fierce gale. "Well, the six of us would penetrate the facility ..."

"Eight. The eight of us." Eli sat in the last row of chairs with Kat and stood up suddenly.

"Eight? What do you mean, eight?" Chapin asked.

"You're implying Kat and I would remain on the boat with the captain?"

"Who said you'd even be on the damn boat?"

"We didn't come all this way to twiddle our thumbs in this hangar while your team breaches the facility."

"Yes, you did," Chapin countered. "Neither of you are qualified ..."

"Director?" Eli shook his head and protested.

"I don't see a problem with them being on the boat," the director said.

Commander Chapin shook his head. "Sir, I think this is a bad idea."

"We want to breach the facility with the team," Eli said.

"Out of the question." Chapin turned away from Eli and stared at the director. His eyes ablaze and left hand clenched into a fist. "Look, sir, you can make an argument that Agent Payne is qualified to join us. Several of my men have trained with him. He's proficient with firearms and HRT tactics. But there's no way on God's green earth we can let a probationary officer come out into the open water with us."

Eli could see where this was going and changed tactics since he knew an argument would get him nowhere. "Look, commander, according to the FLIR images the platform has fourteen heat signatures. One of them we're certain is Nick Jordan, which leaves at most thirteen hostiles. A handful of those are support staff who probably don't even know how to hold a gun, but let's say for argument sake they're not. You have thirteen people to deal with. Now, I know your guys well, and can say without question they are the best of the best. You guys can take them out using a team of six. Kat and I will stay out of your way. We simply want to ensure Nick is taken alive, not be heroes, and steal any of your credit."

"Flattery will get you exactly dick in this scenario, Agent Payne." Chapin shook his head. "My answer is still no on taking her with us."

Kat glared at Eli as her eyes shot daggers, and Eli knew what that look meant. A shitstorm was about to brew, and he had to stop it from erupting.

"Can I speak?" Kat asked.

"Hold up." Chapin held up his hand and looked toward the director, then back at Kat. "No offense to you or your abilities, Agent Stone, but we train for years to learn our craft, and this isn't a normal building we're about to breach. An oil platform is a logistical nightmare even for my guys, who know what the fuck they're doing. I don't want the responsibility of an inexperienced agent on her first assignment. That would be you, dying on my watch." He paused, then looked at Eli. "I mean shit, Eli. Besides the course at Quantico, has she ever even cleared a room?"

"Yes, she has with me, in fact." Eli conveniently left out the fact the house was empty.

The perturbed look on Chapin's face only intensified. "That's not good enough."

"But I vouch for her." Eli knew full well he had never witnessed Kat fire a weapon.

"Whatever. Still doesn't fly with me, Payne." Chapin gave a dismissive wave of his hand.

"She'll be on my six, and we'll both be staying back as your team clears the facility."

"Doesn't matter. I still see her as a liability, not an asset."

Eli wasn't interested in getting into a pissing contest, but he sure as hell wasn't about to back down. He looked at the director. "Sir, we're a team. You told me from the first time we talked this was my case. I call the shots. Well, I say she goes. We didn't come down here to watch someone else go out and rescue Nick Jordan."

The director stayed quiet.

The commander eyed Eli suspiciously, then looked back at the director. "Sir. You're going to have to make the call on this. Payne and I will get nowhere, and we really need to plan this mission."

"I know in these situations you're normally granted tacit authority, commander, and I'd be remiss to supersede you, but I think given the unique circumstances they both should go. If Eli trusts Kat, then so do I."

Shaking his head, Chapin looked at Eli and made direct eye contact. "I don't like this Payne, don't like it at all." He paused and stared at the front of the hangar, his eyes darting back and forth between Eli, Kat, and the director. Finally, he spoke after what seemed like several minutes. "If something happens to her out there, Payne, it's on your conscience, not mine. You got that?"

Eli nodded. "She'll be fine. Trust me."

Commander Chapin said nothing. The look on his face made it clear. He was pissed off.

Over the next three hours a plan came together. They reviewed it ad nauseum until everyone on the team became comfortable with its execution.

The director wrapped up the night and said, "Godspeed to all of you. At dawn, bring back Nick Jordan and yourselves in one piece."

As the meeting broke up, most the group went to the far side of the hangar where cots had been set up so the team could sleep.

Eli and Kat lingered.

Commander Chapin approached and got right in Kat's face, close enough that she could smell his breath, feel the heat from his nostrils. He thrust something toward her. Kat's hand reached out and felt the cool touch of metal. "You know how to use this thing?"

Kat held the H&K MP5 in her right hand. "Yeah," she said, "you take the pointy part and aim it at a bad guy and pull the trigger thingy. Bang-bang, he's dead."

"Don't fuck with me, Stone." Chapin stared her down, and a snarl formed on his lips.

Eli almost stepped in, but he instinctively knew Kat could handle herself. Instead, he looked at Chapin with an icy gaze.

Kat returned Chapin's glare and without looking down pushed out the rear pin, removed the stock, and the lower. Next, she pulled the bolt and carrier assembly away from the frame. Her eyes never left Chapin's as she put the weapon back together and handed it to the commander. "Look, I get it. You don't want any weak links on your team."

He looked down at the weapon, a surprised look on his face. He said nothing.

"I'm not a weak link," Kat said. "I know my stuff."

He shook his head. "It's not only about the equipment, Stone. Trust takes time to build, and while you might be a fine agent people freeze in active shooter situations. I don't know how you'll react when the shit hits the fan. But I know exactly how my men will react. That's why I trust them with my very life. I've built no such rapport with you, or even Payne."

The director approached as the commander said the last few words, but he remained quiet.

Kat nodded. "Trust must be earned, not given. I get it. I want Nick back alive. Period. End of story."

"I don't want you coming back in a body bag," Chapin said.

"Well, we have that in common." Kat displayed a slight smile.

"As long as we're on the same page."

"We are."

As Chapin left, the director stepped forward. He put one hand on Eli's shoulder and the other on Kat's. "Commander Chapin and the other five operators are the best of the best. Yes, he has a chip on his shoulder, but his main concern is the safety of his team, including you two. I'd go to hell and back with any HRT member anytime and trust them with the lives of those dearest to me."

"We know, sir," Kat said.

The director said nothing else, squeezed their shoulders, and left.

Eli leaned toward her. "After what you said when we cleaned out Nick's safe, I didn't think you were into guns? How'd you know how to field strip the MP5?"

"You assumed I don't know guns only because I asked about that one weapon. Never assume, Eli. Like the saying goes, it makes an ass out of you."

"Valid point."

Kat looked at Eli. "Thanks for covering for me."

"You're welcome, but if someone busts a cap in your ass, I don't want your mommy and daddy giving me a hard time. You got that?"

"Sure. But what'll happen if it's me having to save you out there?"

"Guess I'll eat crow, won't I?"

Kat winked. "You like it hot or cold?"

Eli raised his middle finger. "On a stick."

63

PIKE 84 - SANCTUM FACILITY

THE GULF OF MEXICO

Pete Casha woke up with his shoulder feeling like George Foreman used it as a punching bag the night before. As he walked across the hall to the bathroom and gazed into the mirror, the reflection revealed he looked worse than he felt. After a fast shower, he walked back to his room and got dressed. The sling provided by the doctor hung on the chair in the corner of his room. He decided against using it when he saw Nick. The sling conveyed weakness, something Peter could not afford to project when he faced The Body Man. After he got dressed, he left the room and took the narrow hallway to the cafeteria. Breakfast wasn't half bad, considering they were over twenty miles from dry land. As he ate, he overheard two workers complaining about the leftovers and how the resupply ship was scheduled to arrive within the hour.

As he walked back to the room, his phone rang. It still amazed him he got reception inside a big tin can in the Gulf. He looked down at the caller ID. "Yeah, what's up?"

"You talk to him?" Joe asked.

"No, headed that way in a few. Why?"

"Change of plans."

"Don't say I came down here for nothing and they want me to leave without putting him through the wringer?"

"Well, yes, and no."

"Meaning what exactly?" Peter asked.

"Go see him, but there's nothing to talk about."

"Kill him?"

"Exactly." Joe said.

"What changed?"

"The president spoke with Danny a few minutes ago. He fed Danny some bullshit story saying the files Nick gave him contained evidence implicating the vice president in a series of crimes. The files used for safekeeping before charges would be brought against the vice president."

"Seriously?"

"Yes."

"And Frazier fell for it?"

"Yes, but don't forget, he was pretty jacked up on pain meds. The president can be a dick, but he knows how to sell a bag of powdered milk to a dairy farmer."

"So, he has the files?" Peter asked.

"Not yet. I'm on my way now. Frazier stashed them at three banks around the D.C. metro area in safe deposit boxes."

"Clever."

"Agreed. Look, bro, take care of The Body Man, and get the hell out. I got a bad feeling about this."

"In what way?"

"Frazier is dead."

"Since he talked with the president?"

"Yes."

"He crashed?" Peter asked.

"All I know is he was alive. He spilled the beans. And now he's dead."

"Did someone hasten his demise?"

"Not sure."

"You think Junior or the president are about to double-cross us? Maybe tie up loose ends by putting us in the crosshairs next?"

"Don't know, but I think we need to get this whole thing wrapped up and watch our six at the same time."

"Should I bounce? I can walk out of this facility and leave Nick to rot in his cell."

"No, finish him off. We'll be ok."

"Or we'll be saying we should have bailed right before someone puts a bullet between our eyes."

"I think we should stick to the plan," Joe said.

Shit, Peter thought. He struggled for a moment, but finally relented. "Fine. I'm on my way to the interrogation room now."

"You going to use a gun?"

"No, I decided to use something a little more personal."

"The Omega?"

"Precisely."

"Is that wise, considering your shoulder?"

"Nick is chained to a table. What can he possibly do?"

"A caged tiger is always dangerous."

"I got this," Peter said. "I'm no snowflake."

64

THE GULF OF MEXICO

It was Eli's first time in the Gulf. For all his trips to Florida over the years, he never ventured to the west side of the state. The closest he ever got was Legoland in Winter Haven with an old flame and her son. He didn't miss that broad.

He heard the Gulf waters stayed calm most days with relatively little swells. Someone fed him a line.

The resupply vessel bobbed up and down as it struck one wave after another. The boat heaved up and down like a rubber ducky in a bathtub with an irate toddler thrashing about. According to the brief they received, the winds picked up overnight, and the normally calm Gulf waters acted more like the Atlantic with a heavy chop.

A storm was brewing, and the timing could not be worse.

As the waves rolled, Eli caught himself staring at the operator next to him. The HRT operator slipped a coverall over his uniform as Eli looked at the patch on his left shoulder that read *"Servare Vitas"* with an eagle holding a broken chain. The motto exemplified the reason the HRT exists, *To Save Lives*.

In the distance, he saw the towering oil platform as it appeared to rise out of the sea like a Kraken emerging from the deep. Relatively small compared to newer platforms, it was the first one Eli ever saw with the naked eye.

To him, it looked big.

Nine levels comprised the structure. When in service, the lower six floors were used for oil extraction, while the upper three acted as living quarters, maintenance rooms, and a control center. A helicopter pad sat atop the southwest corner of the top level.

As they got close to the platform, Eli thought about Peter Casha and what brought him to the facility. The analysts back at SIOC pieced together a rough bio but still could not locate his real identity. Facial recognition software placed him in various countries around the globe over the past year, and several of those flights were on jets tied to the same shell company. A security camera near one of the loading docks at the Port of Los Angeles caught Casha's image a few days earlier, which corroborated Hector's story about the containers. The rough dossier compiled on Casha revealed a list of known associates. Flagged communications took place between Peter and Joseph Lagano, the global head of security for the Steel Corp. Also, calls traced to Marcus Rollings, an information technology analyst based in the D.C. area. SIOC included a full bio on Mr. Lagano, but the analysts failed to complete one for Rollings before the resupply boat left the dock.

The operator to Eli's left tapped him on the shoulder and held up two fingers. *Two minutes out.*

Eli rarely felt nervous, but his stomach tightened as the ship approached the platform. Out of his element, Eli took several deep breaths, which helped, at least for the moment.

Ahead, Kat stood next to Commander Chapin. Eli regretted giving her such a hard time. Kat proved herself more than capable, and he already knew the sky would be the limit for an agent of her caliber. Besides that, she grew on him, like the little sister he never had. Sure, she could get under his skin, but he would do anything to protect her.

The captain turned the boat around as the vessel approached the oil platform. Protocol dictated he back the stern up to the platform. Some of the larger platforms required compact cranes to unload gear, but the boat was a smaller crew transport style vessel that pulled close to the platform to offload supplies and men. The transfer required the help of several crew members using some cleverly designed rigs.

When they were close enough, Eli could see two men on the lower metal walkway who awaited their arrival.

The captain gave a wave as the men recognized him, and they returned the gesture. "Thirty seconds!" He yelled over the rumble of the engines. Captain Taylor's voice was loud enough for everyone to hear.

The six HRT operators, plus Eli and Kat, wore identical dark-blue jumpsuits with the resupply ship's insignia on the upper right chest. The same outfit the captain and his men wore each time they delivered supplies twice a week.

Commander Chapin turned around and in his booming voice said, "Let's do this!" as the boat idled next to the platform.

65

— • —

PIKE 84

THE GULF OF MEXICO

Nick Jordan finished his hundredth pushup as he stood up in the center of his cell. With his head clear of the narcs, he needed the burn from the exercise to course through his muscles. The endorphins released naturally from his body flushed the last traces of the chemicals the Sanctum pumped into him.

The sound of footfalls echoed down the hallway, which caused him to move back to the cot, where he hid the pencil. Using the metal in the corner of the bed frame, he sharpened it as best he could until it had become a finely pointed weapon. If the opportunity presented itself, he only would have one shot with the homemade shiv.

As the steps got closer, Nick stuffed the weapon in between his waistband and skin, careful to pull his shirt loose to conceal the shiv. Moments later, the door unlocked, and two guards entered the cell. The man to the left held leg and ankle restraints.

"You have visitor, prisoner," the man who held the restraints said in a thick Russian accent.

Nick frowned. "Please tell me it's Amal Clooney. I've been waiting for her to show up and get me out of this godforsaken shithole."

The two guards looked back and forth at each other and shrugged.

"Who?" The guard who held the restraints asked.

"George's wife." Nick said.

The blank expression on both guards' faces revealed they didn't get the joke.

"She's an international lawyer and human rights activist."

"We give no shits about rights here, prisoner."

"Of course, you don't," Nick said as he held out his arms.

Nick waited inside the interrogation room. Shackled to the floor and table, there wasn't much for him to do but stare at the wall. After the guards left, he confirmed he had enough slack in the restraints to reach his waistband.

After several minutes passed, the lock disengaged, and a man walked in. Nick didn't recognize the man held a set of keys in his right hand while his left hand pushed the door closed.

"Well, you're not Amal," Nick said.

"Nor are you, George." A slight smile appeared on the stranger's face.

The man was six feet tall, with thick, dark hair and several days of stubble down his face and neck. Sharply dressed and sporting an expensive watch, he spoke without a Russian accent, which set him apart from the others except Sir. Behind the polished exterior, Nick sensed a man in physical pain. The bulge under the man's shirt at the left shoulder looked to be the source.

He walked behind Nick and paused.

Nick felt a set of burning eyes bearing down on him. After several seconds, the mysterious man continued around and took the seat opposite him. Nick got a good look at the hilt protruding from the man's right hip as he sat down. The blade looked lethal. Versus the pencil tucked between Nick's waistband and bare skin, not so much.

He placed the keys on the steel table, and Nick looked at the keys out of the corner of his eye. Judging by their location, they were out of reach of his restricted hands.

"Hello, Nick. At last, we meet. I've heard an awful lot about you." The man stared straight into Nick's eyes as he spoke.

Nick was surprised to hear his actual name. They hadn't uttered it once since his ordeal at the facility began. "They normally call me 'prisoner.'"

"Well, I'm not them."

"Then who the hell are you?" Nick asked.

"My name is Peter Casha."

"Are you here to free me, Mr. Casha?"

Peter's left eyebrow arched higher than the right. "Yeah, Nick, I guess you could say I'm here to set you free."

The sudden, ear-splitting sound of automatic gunfire echoed down the hallway, and both men reached for two vastly different forms of weaponry.

66

THE OVAL OFFICE

Charles Steele knew he should feel relief. After facing certain disaster, he would soon have all the damning evidence and could begin the arduous process of cleaning up the collateral damage. He came close, too close to not only losing his company but also his presidency.

As he circled around the Oval Office, something felt wrong. A nagging suspicion from the pit of his stomach gnawed at him. He considered every angle and wondered if there was still a loose end requiring his attention. But with Danny dead and Nick Jordan joining him momentarily, the president came up with nothing.

Dolores interrupted his pacing. "Sir, your son would like a word."

With a perturbed tone, Charles stopped and walked back to his desk. "Send him in."

Junior entered and started talking before the president fully sat down. "Joe told me Danny provided the location of the files."

"That's correct." The president leaned back in the chair. "Joe is on his way to retrieve them."

"How about the other file? The one Marcus and Merci recovered?"

"On its way as well."

"Looks like everything is coming together."

"It almost became a clusterfuck." The president shook his head and balled his fist.

"But it didn't."

The president looked up and made direct eye contact with Junior, but said nothing.

"What's next?" Junior asked as he diverted his gaze and looked out the windows toward the Rose Garden.

"I've instructed everyone to meet me here at nine tonight. I've got a fundraiser in Charlotte that will take up most of the afternoon. Once I'm back, I'll wrap up all the loose ends."

"Meeting here at the White House? Is that a good idea?"

With a sharp glance, the president replied, "Not in the building. Underneath it."

"The tunnels?"

"Yes. There's an incinerator on the lower level. Once I have all the evidence, I'll destroy it myself. Frankly, I'm sick of amateur hour." His eyes bore down on Junior as he enunciated the last few words. "It's time to put an end to this nonsense once and for all."

Junior ignored the jab. "I'll see you at nine."

"No. You won't."

"And why not?"

"You started all this when Nick learned of your deal with the Saudis, and now I'm cleaning it up."

Junior felt a pulse of rage shoot through his body, causing his hands to constrict. "What do you expect me to do?"

"Go home. And don't make any more fucking messes." The president's tone reinforced the anger his face displayed. "I've placed you in charge of a highly respected and enormously profitable company. With Nick Jordan eliminated, the files destroyed, and hopefully soon the weapons transfer to the Saudis complete, the Steele Corp. will thrive in a new and profitable market. We'll get a foothold in a part of the world that few American companies can enter."

Junior did not protest. "Thank you for all your assistance, Mr. President," he said through gritted teeth, not meaning a word of it.

"That's the least you can say."

67

PIKE 84

THE GULF OF MEXICO

Eli watched the stern move closer to the platform. He felt his pulse quicken as his right foot tapped several times on the deck in a rhythmic beat.

Two guards met the boat from the walkway on the lowest level of the platform. They tossed over thick, braided ropes to the boat crew. Captain Taylor swung over first with Commander Chapin on his six. The two Russians bristled as they saw Chapin, clearly someone they did not recognize. Taylor said something and pointed first toward the commander and then toward the boat. The two men nodded; whatever he said appeared to assuage the men's concerns. Both the captain and Commander Chapin swung back to the boat and grabbed supplies, then the rest of the team came over two at a time.

As Kat landed on the metal walkway and passed by one guard. The towering figure gawked and leaned toward her. She could smell a foul odor of salted herring and pickled mushrooms in his mouth.

In broken English, with a clearly Russian accent, he said, "So, you captain's hot sister-in-law, huh? You know how to lift something heavy?"

Kat smirked, looked down toward the man's crotch and back into his eyes. "Well, I don't see anything heavy around here. But sure, I can handle the big ones."

The man let out a hearty laugh and looked toward the other guard. "I like this one!" He stepped out of Kat's way.

Two large canvas duffel bags and a pallet holding a half dozen plastic crates filled with essential supplies moved over via ropes and pulleys attached to the structure.

As Eli started up the steps, he turned to Kat. "What the hell was that about?"

"Apparently dick jokes are funny in Russia too."

Eli shook his head. "You have a way with men."

"If you can deal with a toddler, you can handle a man."

Eli smirked.

The supplies were divided up, and the eight members trudged up the fourteen flights of stairs, two sets for each level, until they reached the seventh floor. Within duffel bags were legitimate supplies, but concealed under a false bottom were the team's weaponry and breaching material.

As the team carried the bags, the two Russians said nothing, nor did they volunteer to help huff anything up the steps.

The lower stairwell was slick with water, but as the team climbed higher, the conditions improved. Within several flights, Eli and Kat's legs grew tired, their arms ached.

As they moved higher, the stairway ended on the seventh level at a solid steel door. With no handle or visible lock, Eli saw the closed-circuit security cameras above the door pointed downward. The two guards moved from the back and approached the door, and the larger of the two waved at the air. A buzzing sound came from the thick handle, and the door partially opened.

In a single file line, they entered a dimly lit space.

Eli looked around the room; he didn't see any closed-circuit cameras. The room appeared to be used for storage. As one of the canvas bags hit the ground, it made a loud *clank* sound. The two Russians exchanged glances.

The larger one said, "What in here?" He lumbered toward the bag.

Commander Chapin was on him as the man bent over to examine the bag.

One of the HRT operators, Riggs, secured the other Russian.

Both Chapin and Riggs already had syringes out and jabbed them into both men in a synchronized fashion. With the needles deep in the Russians' necks, the two operators pressed the plungers, sending enough drugs into their systems to ensure neither man would be a problem. They flex-cuffed the guards, even binding their ankles bound. Both Russians were stuffed in a closet of sorts in the room's corner.

As Chapin and Riggs took down the two Russians, Dirk Benedict, the IT guy on the team, removed his laptop and plopped down on the floor to hack into the platform's network.

Dirk had expected at least a minor challenge but found as he ran the IP scanner that there was a guest entry point.

He let out an audible laugh that caused the others to turn and stare.

"They didn't change the default login," Dirk said as he shook his head.

"Meaning?" Chapin asked.

"The login is 'admin' and the password is ... you got it, the word *password*."

"What the fuck? Are these guys amateurs?"

Eli spoke up. "Told you guys that Zed said they didn't put too much into security features since we're out in the open water."

"Yeah, I know." Dirk shook his head. "But to not even change the factory password is just plain lazy."

"Russians don't have the best reputation when it comes to smarts," Kat said.

Dirk touched the screen of his laptop. "And the proof is right here."

<hr />

Within thirty seconds, he identified the system file that controlled the security cameras and gained access to all the video. He recorded a minute-long loop of all the cameras currently online. Next, he set those videos to continuous playback in order for the teams to move through the floors undetected.

At least, that was the plan.

"We own video," Dirk said.

Chapin nodded. "Good deal. Let's poop or get off the pot, team."

They split into two preassigned groups. The A-team comprised Commander Chapin, Operator Riggs, and Operator Duncan. While the B-team included Operator Peppard, Operator Schultz, Operator Benedict, Eli, and Kat. Everyone removed the resupply ship coveralls, revealing matching black BDUs. With the canvas bags emptied, Commander Chapin handed out H&K MP-5/10A3 10mm submachine guns with suppressors. Besides the submachine guns, Riggs and Benedict each carried Benelli M4 twelve-gauge shotguns slung over their backs. The weapons acted as door breaches in lieu of explosives. All members carried Glock 22 .40 cal pistols on their hips. Everyone carried flash bangs (also called stun grenades), knives, and explosive breaching charges for the numerous doors they would encounter.

The two teams would search levels seven, eight, and nine, even though the intel indicated Nick Jordan was on the eighth level. Stairwells in the corner of each floor were the easiest way to move between levels.

Both the A-teams and B-teams stayed together to clear level seven. Besides the storage room, the floor contained a laboratory, a medical bay, and a dozen other rooms. After they cleared floor seven, the teams would split, with the A-team searching level eight and the B-team level nine.

All three levels contained identical floorplans. A narrow hallway in the shape of a square allowed access to each floor. Rooms filled the center and lined the outer portion of each square, with four stairwells allowing access between the levels.

The team moved down the hall in standard file formation, with Eli and Kat in the rear. Briggs reached the lab door first. With his MP5 raised, he turned the handle with his left hand and nuzzled the door open. Across the room, a chemist in an oversized white lab coat turned from his barstool as Chapin, Briggs, and Peppard made their way inside the long, narrow space. Briggs saw the movement as the startled person jumped off the stool and lunged for a box with a red button in the center on the opposite wall. A former SEAL before he joined the HRT, Briggs let his MP5 drop, his sling keeping it aloft, and reached to his right leg. In one smooth motion, he unfastened the Ontario MK3 Navy knife and let it fly at the intended target. The knife stuck into the side of the tech's neck a foot before he reached the alarm box. His body crumpled to the ground and twitched uncontrollably for several seconds. Briggs calmly walked over to the body, removed the knife from the man's neck, and wiped the blood dripping from the blade on his BDUs before he sheathed the weapon.

It took the team six more minutes to clear the entire floor.

With the seventh level secure, the teams split up, with the A-team taking the north stairwell and the B-team taking the south. They stayed in constant contact with their comm units and planned to meet up when one of them acquired Nick Jordan.

The A-team ascended the stairwell and arrived in the hallway on level eight. According to the intel, Nick was in one of the three rooms to the right as they exited the north stairs. The element of surprise disappeared as two guards turned the distant corner and saw the darkened silhouettes of the team as they stepped into the hall.

Both hostiles raised their weapons and fired bursts of automatic fire toward the shadows. Commander Chapin, Riggs, and Duncan ducked into an open room as the bullets struck the surrounding walls. A deafening sound filled the hallway as the shots reverberated down the narrow-enclosed space. As the sounds of the bullets abated, the wailing of an alarm took its place. Commander Chapin clicked the stopwatch on his wrist; they all knew minutes if not seconds separated Nick Jordan from certain death.

The ear-splitting sound of bullets and the high-pitched alarm startled Sergei from the monotony of watching the cameras. A minute before, he returned from his morning constitutional in the bathroom down the hall, stopped at the cafeteria, and poured himself a fourth cup of coffee on the way back to his closet-sized server room. Sergei glared at the array of images on the screens before him. The four monitors were split into six small screens, each showing various images throughout the facility. As he looked at the video, he saw no movement.

Something felt wrong.

Then the gunfire erupted.

With a few clicks of the mouse, he found out someone had gained access to the system and run a continuous loop of empty images across the system. Thirty seconds later, he disabled the unauthorized access and live images from the platform flooded his screens.

"Shit," Sergei said as he struggled to pull his cell phone from his skin-tight pants pockets.

68

PIKE 84

THE GULF OF MEXICO

Nick watched as Peter reached for the protruding hilt on the right side of his pants. Nick's mind slowed the events down.

At least it isn't a gun. Nick knew he stood no chance against a bullet fired at point blank range. With his hands and feet bound, he would have no way of defending himself against a firearm.

Nick grabbed toward his waistband and removed the number-two pencil.

It sounded like a lazy joke, a knife versus a pencil. But Nick was keenly aware, based on his extensive training, that the ability to improvise often determined life or death in an impossible situation.

Nick watched as Peter pulled the knife out of its sheath. Peter's motion revealed this wasn't his first rodeo. Their eyes locked, and Nick saw Peter stare intently at his neck as he lunged across the table.

Mistake number one, Nick now knew with certainty the intended target. He now had one and only one job. Defend his life.

With the pencil gripped tightly, he swung it up and away from his body at a forty-five-degree angle. The sharpened pencil moved in an arc motion while he twisted his body to dodge the impending steel blade.

Nick took fencing lessons as a teenager, and his fast reflexes and ability to parry came as second nature to him.

The move barely worked, as Peter's blade missed his neck by less than a quarter of an inch. It was close enough that he felt Peter's hand brush past his neck hairs.

Nick finished the arcing motion of his swing in a downward stab, thrusting the pencil into Peter's chest. Crude but effective, the pencil pierced skin with ease and slipped between two ribs, lodging almost halfway into the chest cavity.

Peter's eyes grew wide as the pencil burrowed deep into his flesh. His body stiffened, and too late, his hands shot out in a defensive position. The knife he swung fell from his hand and made a metallic sound as it bounced several times along the floor, as it came to rest along the wall.

With the air rushing from his chest, Peter fell backward and landed with a dull *thud* back into his chair. A shocked expression overtook his face as a blood spot formed around the wound and spread down his shirt toward his navel. The gunfire from the hallway sounded intense and right outside the interrogation room door.

Nick reached for the keys. He was now close enough to grab them, as Peter's lunge across the table had pushed them toward him. With the keys in his hands, Nick located the one for his restraints and started first with the handcuffs and then the shackles.

Peter watched intently with labored breaths as his hands clutched his bloodied chest.

With the restraints removed, Nick turned toward the door.

"I never saw that coming, bro," Peter said. A faint trickle of blood started at the corner of his mouth before he added, "That was a slick move."

"The pencil is in your aorta, Peter. If you remove it, you'll bleed out in minutes. Leave it in, and you may survive if you get immediate medical attention." Nick paused as he cocked his head toward the hallway and the sound of gunfire. "It's your choice," before he added, "bro."

A half smile formed on Peter's face. He had to admit he got beat at his own game. "You know who sent me, don't you?"

"Same person who sent me to this shithole for torture and death at your hands."

"I might have failed, but he won't rest until you're dead. What are you going to do about that?"

Nick walked toward the door, opened it, and turned back toward Peter. He smiled. "I'm going to burn his fucking house down, Casha."

69

PIKE 84

THE GULF OF MEXICO

The gunfire woke Sir from a deep sleep. At first, he thought the clanging sound of lead on metal was a nightmare, but dreams fade to black when your eyes open.

This one didn't.

Sounds of bullets fired in rapid succession a floor below, impossible to mistake.

He ran across the hall into the server room and watched the images as they flashed across the screen from the closed-circuit cameras.

He yelled at Sergei. "Who the hell are they?"

Sergei shook his head. "No clue. But they're good. American special ops, I think."

"We need to get out of here." Sir scanned the facility and flipped between several cameras. Then he caught something on the arm of one soldier. He pointed to the screen and told Sergei to pause the image.

Servare Vitas. Sir knew that patch. The military were not on the platform, it was the FBI, to be more specific a Hostage Rescue Team.

He needed an escape plan and realized the next few seconds may determine whether he lived or died. Without hesitation, he told Sergei to flee and ran back to his room. Sir grabbed a go bag and headed down the hall to Evelyn's room.

The sound of more gunfire erupted below.

"We've got to get out of here," Sir said as he burst into her room.

"What's going on?" Evelyn was already getting dressed. As Sir stood inside her room, she hastily pulled on a shirt over her red bra and buttoned the ivory-colored buttons on her navy-blue shirt.

"An FBI HRT has breached the facility; it appears they're coming for The Body Man."

"We've got to stop them."

"Us and what army? I'm an interrogator, not a soldier."

Evelyn stuffed clothes and belongings into a gray bag.

"We've got to go now," Sir said as he gripped her by the elbow and practically pulled her out of the room.

"Get your hands off me." Evelyn spoke in a deep, almost growling tone.

"If we stay here, we die." Sir yanked on her arm harder.

They were on the fifth-floor landing before she came to a sudden stop. "We've got to go back," Evelyn said as she stopped.

"For what?"

"Him."

"Look, I told you, a team breached the facility to rescue him. We can't stop them."

"Then we do what we were paid to do and kill him."

"The Steele Corp. guy, Casha, will do that. It's why he came. We're in the clear."

Evelyn drew a weapon from the black Chanel purse draped across her right shoulder. "We need to make sure he takes care of The Body Man before we leave."

Sir raised his hands. "Hold up, Evelyn. What are you doing?"

"If we leave here and he's still alive, we're as good as dead."

Sir didn't respond.

"If the chief finds out we let him live, he'll skin us alive." Evelyn's face had a determined grit to it.

Sir shook his head, and he pointed above. "I'm not worried about any of that. You need to focus on the here and now. This is simple, Evelyn. If we go back up there, we will die, or they'll arrest us, which is worse than death." Perspiration formed on his forehead as he wiped off beads of sweat with his left arm.

She trained her weapon on him. "That's a chance we'll have to take."

"You're fucking crazy." Sir's face grew red.

Evelyn gripped the gun harder. "Move it, Sir. I don't want to shoot you. But I will. Get up those stairs, now."

Sir turned and took a step, with a feign attempt to place his hands up in the air. He felt certain imminent death awaited them if they went back in. It took him two flights before he decided on his course of action. Less than six steps from the last level, he missed a step and fell hard on to the metal grated steps.

It wasn't accidental.

Evelyn lowered her gun and reached with her free hand to help.

A fatal mistake.

Sir pulled the concealed SIG 365 from his ankle holster and removed the safety with his thumb as he stood. He brought the weapon up to chest level, took a step closer, and stared at her. "Sorry, Evelyn, but I've got a family that needs me to live." Sir jammed the barrel of the SIG between her breasts and pulled the trigger three times.

Her eyes grew wide in surprise and the life left her body as she fell backward, tumbling down the steps with one sickening thud after another until her body came to rest upright in a sitting position against the rail. Her head rested back against the middle rail and her arms spread out away from her body and rested on the metal floor.

Sir grabbed his bag and ran down the steps, not even bothering to look down at her lifeless form as he passed. When he reached the bottom level, he moved toward the center of the structure and the silver control panel on one of the steel girders. He pressed the green button, which started the mechanism, lowering a motorboat suspended ten feet above the water. There were three boats, used only in case of emergency.

Sir figured this qualified.

The entire process was supposed to take less than two minutes.

Two minutes till I'm free.

As he waited for the boat to lower, he saw the resupply ship idling just beyond the lower walkway. A man cloaked in darkness stood at the helm, his back toward Sir, who hoped the sound of the stationary resupply vessel drowned out the sound of the mechanism lowering the boat.

70

PIKE 84

THE GULF OF MEXICO

Eli and Kat acted as the rear guards while the B-team moved up the south stairwell. They arrived on the ninth-floor landing, and the team lead, Peppard, held up a closed fist indicating a full stop. With gunfire erupting, the floor below any element of surprise vanished. Peppard saw movement down the hall through the glass pane and opened the door quickly, tossing two stun grenades as far as he could throw them. Even hidden behind a steel door, they felt the concussive shockwave as it carried down the hallway and rattled the door, splintering the glass like a spider web.

Peppard, Schultz, and Benedict opened the door and rushed inside, sending three-round bursts from their MP5's toward the two hostile targets left dazed after the stun grenades. Their rounds found flesh and eliminated the threats.

Eli and Kat waited and entered when Peppard announced, "All clear," over the comms.

Then it happened.

Eli heard a sound to their right around the corner, down a darkened hallway. He followed the noise with Kat on his six. Eli didn't make it two steps down the hall before a figure hidden in the shadows leaped toward him from a concealed doorway.

Eli played Pop Warner and high-school football as a younger man. He knew how to take a hit and instantly remembered what it felt like to have a two-hundred and fifty-pound linebacker nail him on the field. His legs flew out from under him and turned up as he came down hard on his back and shoulders. The attacker landed on top of him as thick, python like arms curled around his body and squeezed.

With no leverage, Eli only had one thing close enough to grab. With his left hand, he reached between the man's legs and squeezed his scrotum until his attacker screamed out in pain. The man responded with two lightning-quick punches to Eli's face, which did the trick as Eli release the man's testicles from his vice-like grip.

Disoriented, Eli didn't see the man reach to his side and remove something silver from his waist.

━━━━◄○►━━━━

Kat raised her MP5 as the man tackled Eli, but in the melee she didn't have a clear shot. Her pulse raced. A slight tremble started in her shoulder and worked its way down her arm. She took a deep breath, letting the air out slowly as she waited for her moment. When the man dressed in all black thrust himself back and pulled a large Bowie knife, her window of opportunity opened.

Kat didn't hesitate.

She reacted.

A three-round burst spat from the end of the H&K MP5 and drilled the man in his chest. A nice half dollar-spaced grouping. The man's body slumped forward as Kat stepped closer and put three more insurance rounds into his head forehead between his eyes. The lifeless body dropped onto Eli as blood flowed onto Eli's tactical vest.

Kat pulled the body off Eli and helped him to his feet. Peppard, Schultz, and Benedict were at her side by the time Eli stood up.

Peppard looked concerned. "Holy shit! You both good?"

"Yeah," Eli said as he looked at Kat, "thanks to Kat." He then looked at Peppard. "I guess that plan did not come together."

Peppard smiled. "At least he didn't break your nose." He looked away from Eli and glanced at Benedict. "Right, Face? I mean, Benedict."

Benedict smiled. "Better noses broken than rules, Hannibal, I mean Peppard."

The voice of Commander Chapin came over the comms. "We've got the package. Repeat, we've got the package. What's your status, B-team?"

Peppard replied, "Still clearing the ninth floor."

"Well, get a fucking move on it. Time to evac."

"Copy that, commander," Peppard said.

"Package says there's a man in interrogation room three on the eighth floor," Chapin said. "Check on his medical status after clearing floor nine and bring him with you if he's still alive."

"Roger. On our way."

⸺⊶⊷⸺

As they moved down the hallway, Eli grabbed Kat by the arm with a firm grip. "Thanks."

With a slight pause she said, "Yeah, no problem."

Eli could see her eyes were dilated and her eyelids were open wider than normal. He figured she must be in shock. "You good?" Eli asked.

"I think so," Kat said. "That was fucking intense."

"You weren't the one about to be filleted."

It took them five more minutes to clear the floor, engaging and killing three more hostiles. Descending one flight of stairs, they arrived at interrogation room three and found it empty. A bloodied chair and what appeared to be half broken pencil dripping with blood lay on the stainless-steel table. But no person.

"Commander," Peppard said into his comms.

"Go ahead."

"Interrogation room three is empty."

"Say again, B-team?"

"Room is empty."

"Roger that. Proceed down to the boat. Watch your six in case we overlooked any hostiles."

"Copy that."

Three minutes later, the two teams met up on the lowest level. They passed one body, an African American female on the sixth-level landing. Another dead body lay on the walkway on the first level.

Nick Jordan spoke loud enough for all of them to hear. "That guy went by the name Sir. He's the one that interrogated me."

Commander Chapin looked at Peppard, Schultz, and Benedict. "One of you take him out?"

They all shook their heads, and Peppard responded, "Negative, not ours."

Kat pointed to the two boats suspended from the floor of the second level. "Commander, I think we're missing a boat. There were three hanging from the roof when we arrived."

"Looks like a rat got out of the drowning ship. Maybe it's the guy with a pencil in his chest?"

"If it is, he shouldn't get far in his condition," Briggs said.

"What was his name again, Jordan?" Chapin asked.

"Casha. Peter Casha."

"We know who that is," Eli and Kat said at the same time.

71

HOUMA, LOUISIANA

The humid Cajun wind blew as Eli stood at the hangar door and wiped beads of sweat from his forehead. He watched as the HRT team loaded gear for the flight home.

Kat approached and stood close enough to brush up against his left arm. Eli saw Nick Jordan, Director Ludington, and Uncle Freddy in the background over her shoulder engaged in an intense discussion.

When the conversation ended, Uncle Freddy jogged over. "I might have something, Eli."

"What's that?"

"SIOC called while you were on the platform." Freddy said.

"And?" Eli asked.

"They got a hit on one of Peter Casha's associates."

"Which one?"

"Marcus Rollings."

"Huh," Eli said, "Where is he?"

"New York City. Facial recognition software placed him outside the Plaza Hotel on Fifth Ave."

"Interesting."

"There's more. He was with this woman." Freddy handed over a manila folder that included a full bio and several photos.

Eli scanned the pages. "Merci De Atta. Who is she?"

"One badass bitch." Freddy caught himself and looked sheepishly at Kat. "Sorry, Agent Stone."

Kat laughed. "No offense taken. In fact, I'm a fan of badass bitches. As long as they are on the right side of the law."

"Since Merci is a hired assassin, she's clearly not. Miss De Atta is wanted by more agencies than I know how to count. Interpol, FSB, Mossad, you name it. Lots of global agencies have warrants out for her arrest."

"Any idea why they are together in the city?" Eli asked.

Freddy shook his head. "None."

"Hmmm." Eli rubbed his chin. "Thanks for the intel, Freddy."

"You got it, bud. Safe travels to you and Agent Stone."

Eli turned away and stared off into the distance. His mind swam with possibilities. Presently there were too many variables, but he knew somehow it all connected. They needed to keep digging. He only had a few minutes before he boarded the plane, but knew who to call.

Mila answered on the second ring. "Eli?" she asked in a slightly hushed voice.

"A bad time?" Eli asked.

"Kinda sorta. I'm on Air Force One on our way back from Charlotte. Grabbing a quick bite to eat."

"Eating a salad to watch your figure?"

"Yeah, right. A pastrami on rye. Screw that I've-got-to-look-pretty bullshit most women obsess over. I need fuel, plain and simple. Kale and quinoa don't cut it in my line of work."

"I forgot how perfect you were," he said in a half mocking, half serious way.

"You call to butter me up or share intel?" Mila asked.

Eli chuckled. "We got him."

"Who?"

"Him." He let the word linger.

"Nick? You got him?" Her voice raised several octaves.

"Keep your voice down, but yes, he's alive."

"Where are you?" Mila asked.

"Louisiana, on the Gulf, headed back to D.C. soon. We'll debrief him on the flight back with the director."

"Does the White House know?"

"No, not yet. And Director Ludington doesn't want it to get out."

"Why not?"

"Because the director and the president already got into a pissing contest about investigating Nick's disappearance. He wants to de-brief Nick and try to figure out what happened before we let the cat out of the bag. I'm letting you know because of what you told me, and I don't want you blindsided if ..." He paused.

"If what?"

"Nick shows up at the White House later tonight."

"You serious?" Mila asked in a hushed tone.

"I think so. He wants to have a word with the president."

"Well, depending on when he does, we, and by we, I mean the president might be unavailable. He has something going on later."

"And what is that?"

"I overheard a call earlier that I don't think I was supposed to. Something about a meeting tonight down in the tunnels on Broadsway."

"I don't follow."

"Tell Nick; he'll get it. Anyway, the president is meeting several people."

"Who?"

"Only heard first names. Marcus, Merci, and Joe. They are meeting President Steele at nine. Something to do with files they retrieved."

Eli grew quiet for several seconds. His mind raced. "You sure about the names Marcus and Merci?"

"Yes, why?"

"Catch the last names?"

"No, do you know who they are?"

"Maybe. Got some intel a few minutes ago that is helping connect the dots. Not sure how the president factors into all this, but the meeting sounds suspicious."

"I agree. The funny thing is, I'm not even supposed to be working today. A stomach virus made its way around the detail this week, and three of his normal agents are taking turns either praying to the porcelain pony or shitting their brains out."

"That's a nice mental image. Well, I'll pass along what you told me to Nick."

"Give him my best. Tell him I'm relieved to know he's alive and well."

"Will do. Just remember to keep it on the down low, for now."

"I don't need to be told the same thing twice, Elijah." Mila's tone sounded stern.

She could not see it, but Eli rolled his eyes in response. "Yes, I know."

"Does he know about Danny?"

"That he's in the hospital?"

"No. He's dead."

"Wait. What?"

"He crashed at the hospital this morning. I figured Nick would want to know. He died shortly after the president visited him."

"Wow, I had no clue. I'll let him know when we board the flight. Look, not to cut this short, but I'm getting a wave from the director. Think it's time for us to go."

"Maybe we can meet up again soon. It was good to see you," Mila said.

There was a longing in her voice, something he hadn't heard in a long time, manifested itself in her tone. Eli smiled as an image of her from a weekend in Tahoe suddenly appeared in his mind. Some images he wanted to forget, but this was one he wanted to remember always. "Yeah, I'm glad we caught up. Let's make it happen. Drinks are on me next time."

"You've got my digits, cowboy."

———◆———

Eli caught up to Kat as she walked toward the jet. With a firm squeeze, he gripped her left shoulder and stopped her in mid-stride. "You got a sec?"

"Sure." Kat said.

"Look, Kat. I wanted to say thank you for saving my ass out there."

"Sure thing, Payne. No biggie."

"No really. It is a big deal. That guy got the drop on me, and if you hadn't reacted, well, we wouldn't be having this conversation." He extended his hand for her to shake. "I want you to know you proved the commander wrong out there on the platform and I'll never forget what you did."

Kat's smile grew wider as she pushed his hand away, and with both out-stretched arms pulled him in for a hug.

He never saw it coming.

"That's how we say you're welcome where I come from." She let go and took a step back. "That's what partners do, Eli. Through thick or thin they've got each other's six, twelve, nine and three. No matter what."

"Thanks, Kat," Eli said. As she turned away and continued towards the jet, he said, "You'll hold this over me for as long as we know each other, won't you?"

Without breaking stride or looking back, she replied, "Hell, yes." The words were followed by a loud laugh that had a sinister quality to it.

72

AT CRUISING ALTITUDE

Nick Jordan sunk into the plush leather seat, closed his eyes and felt his body relax. Compared to the past week's accommodations, the seat felt like Club Med. He promised himself that after the current shitshow came to an end, he would sleep for a week straight.

The long, slender fingers of a dream state enveloped him as the constant hum of the jet engines made a rhythmic, soothing sound, pushing the ordeal on the platform into the recesses of his mind.

The distinct sound of a cleared throat brought him back to the present.

Nick opened his eyes to see the director eyeing him, and in particular the outfit he wore. It was the same shirt he had on after they left the platform.

"I can get The Body Man a clean shirt if he would like," the director said with a genuine grin. He snapped his fingers, and an agent brought a black polo shirt with white FBI initials on the left sleeve. The director handed it to Nick, who shook his head in protest.

"Sorry, boss, The Body Man doesn't wear polo shirts."

"Seriously?" the director asked.

"We saw his closet. He's a Magnum P.I. type of guy," Kat said.

"Damn straight," Nick replied.

"Is there anything you want before we get started?" The director took a seat, as did the others. He sat in the chair directly across from Nick. Kat sat to the left of Nick and Eli next to the director.

"Guess a quick siesta is out of the question?" Nick raised his arms over his head and gave an elongated yawn.

"Sorry." Director Ludington's face displayed a look of genuine concern. "Business first, rest later."

"In that case, a stiff drink would be nice." Nick smiled. "To awaken the synapses."

"Of course. Pick your poison."

"Since I doubt you have any Old Düsseldorf on board," he looked around, but it appeared nobody got the beer joke. "A bourbon, any brand, please. Light on the ice, heavy on the bourbon."

The director snapped his fingers again, and this time a flight attendant came down the aisle. "My friend would like a triple shot of Blanton's with a touch of ice, please, Amy."

The flight attendant smiled and nodded. "And everyone else?"

"Just water," the director said.

Eli frowned.

"You're on the job," the director said as he observed Eli's expression.

Amy disappeared down the aisle in her form-fitting blue dress and returned a few minutes later with a silver tray, which included a three-quarters full tumbler of amber liquid and three crystal glasses of ice water.

"Cheers." Nick raised the thick glass and then took it down in two large swallows.

"Not one to sip on it?" the director asked.

"Not after the bullshit week I had," Nick said.

"You ready?" the director asked.

Nick nodded. "I am now."

<hr />

"Before we begin, Eli, you had a phone call right before we got on the plane that you wanted to share."

Eli nodded, "Yes, sir. I did." Eli looked towards Nick. "I spoke with Mila Hall before we boarded the plane. First, she wanted me to tell you she was relieved you're alive and safe."

"Mila's a sweetheart," Nick said. "And one hell of an excellent agent. Wait ... you're not *the* Eli, are you? The special agent she dated?"

Eli blushed slightly. "Guilty as charged."

"Mila never told me what happened between the two of you, but I hope you realize how much she adores you. Everything is still always Eli this and Eli that."

Eli ignored the compliment, although it caught him slightly off-guard. "I told Mila you might head to the White House when you get back. Is that still your intention?"

"Absolutely. I plan to confront President Steele face to face. Why?"

"Mila is on the president's detail today, and she overheard a call the president had about a meeting tonight with three individuals on Broadsway. She said you'd know what that meant. I think I misheard her, and she meant Broadway."

Nick smirked. "No, you heard her correctly. It's Broadsway, not Broadway. It's the not-so-subtle name of the tunnel that leads from the basement under the White House north under Lafayette Square and connects with the St. Regis Hotel. The tunnel got its name during the Kennedy administration since it was used to bring in women for the president's," Nick paused before he added, "pleasure."

"This was a regular occurrence?" Eli asked.

"Yes. The tunnel didn't get much use after Kennedy, but like some of the other tunnels, it's still used to usher people in and out of the White House who don't want to be seen."

"According to Mila, it sounded like the people who are meeting the president are bringing files to him. I'm assuming they're the ones you tried keeping from the president."

"That's likely why Peter Casha came to the facility to kill me. With access to the files, they clearly didn't need me anymore, and the time came to shut me up permanently."

"What can you tell us about the files?" The director put his hands on his knees and leaned in closer.

"Let me take a step back, since I'm not sure the three of you know what my role is."

"I have a pretty good idea, based on what Mila told me," Eli said.

"Well, let's make sure you got the entire scoop."

For the next thirty minutes, Nick gave a concise yet extremely detailed account of what it meant to be The Body Man. Mila's description to Eli was spot on, but the details provided by Nick were extensive and on occasion disturbing.

After some time, the director interrupted. "So, what did you find that caused you to confront the president?"

"The president's son, Charles Steele II, or as everyone, including the president, calls him, Junior, bartered a deal with the House of Saud for a dozen of our Gray Eagle drones."

"And what would he get in return?"

"The Steele Corp. would be allowed unrivaled access to the Saudi's finances. They'd become one of the premier lending institutions not only in Saudi Arabia but throughout the Gulf region."

"That's certainly corrupt," Eli said. "But we sell military technology to the Saudi's already, and besides, several former presidents gave special deals to organizations that benefited their interests while inside and out of office."

"True. But this is much bigger than the Steele family trying to acquire more wealth. You need to understand what they were selling. These are prototypes drones, the newest and most sophisticated UAVs designed by General Atomics. We don't even employ these in warfare. This is next generation tech we don't want anybody, even our closest allies, to have. These particular UAVs utilize stealth technology and are virtually invisible to conventional weapons. Besides the drones, Junior is selling schematics to build their own UAVs as well as our most lethal missiles. Ones specifically designed for the Gray Eagles that make Hellfires look like M80s."

"Look, I'm not mitigating what Junior is doing here, but your job is to make problems go away. Am I right? Why gather all this evidence? Why not bury it? Or even prevent the sale?"

Nick looked lost in thought before he responded. "My job is to protect the office of the presidency at any cost. Even if that means I protect it from the person who occupies the Oval Office. This weapons transfer is for the ongoing Yemen conflict with Saudi Arabia against the Houthi rebels, who receive funding from Iran. What's going on between Saudi Arabia and Yemen is nothing more than a proxy war between Iran and Saudi Arabia. Given the technological advancement, this sale would ensure the Saudis would be in a position of power and likely use that tech attack Iran. That could start World War III since we're in bed with the Saudis, and Iran aligns with Russia. What I was trying to do was not merely stop the Steele family from benefiting financially from an illegal arms sale. I'm protecting the office of the presidency from a global war. And trust me, if the Saudis get these weapons, we will be one step closer to that occurring."

Eli nodded, but before he could respond, Nick added, "And to answer the other part, I couldn't stop the transfer. If I could, I would."

"So, you collected this evidence and did what?" Eli asked.

"I confronted the president."

"Clearly that didn't go well."

"He denied any involvement even after I showed him the proof of the Steele Corp's involvement. I wasn't aware until I was kidnapped how good of a liar the man really is. Anyway, he deflected and said Junior wasn't capable of such a betrayal."

"But how could he deny it if the evidence implicated himself?" The director asked.

Nick shook his head. "But it didn't. No evidence I uncovered points back to him."

The director raised a furtive brow. "How could that be?"

"There are several hundred pages of documents I collected, but everything points back to Junior. Nothing implicates the president," Nick said.

"But if the transfer benefits his company ..." Eli said.

"*Was*. It *was* his company," Nick replied. "When he took the oath of office, he signed everything over to Junior. On paper at least he no longer has any interest in the Steele Corp."

"But if Junior is implicated, it would still come back to haunt him."

"You're right. There's no way his presidency could survive a scandal like this, whether he still owns the company or not. But trust me when I say his ego is tied to that company, and there's not a chance in hell he would let it be tarnished."

"So do you think it was all Junior?" The director asked.

Nick shook his head. "Hell no. Junior isn't smart enough to concoct a scheme like this on his own. It has Charles fingerprints all over it."

Nobody said anything for a minute. The hum of the jet engines the only sound filling the cabin.

———◦———

Nick looked out the window as billowing clouds passed by the wing. His face turned stoic, even a slight frown forming on his lips. "Look, you can't protect the office of the presidency with blinders on. You observe all of it: the good, the bad, everything. Sometimes you make a judgment call whether or not to intervene. Other times you cover up shit that nobody should ever get away with. In the end, the office of the presidency is bigger than one person, and it above all else must be protected. As for the person who acts as The Body Man, we're all human and sometimes we make the wrong call."

"Are you saying you should have covered all this up?" The director asked.

"No. Unequivocally, no. Going after Junior and by default, the president, was the right call. As for your question of why he's not implicated in any evidence, it's simple. The president is paranoid about putting anything in writing. That's why none of the evidence I collected points back to him."

"But how did he run his business without written correspondence?"

"Face-to-face meetings and phone calls. He would sign legal contracts, of course, but he never sent texts or emails. Ever. Nothing can be traced back to him. He's technologically illiterate. Most of his presidential directives are verbal. He signs very little besides what he must. Nothing he's signed as president can point back to this arms deal."

"But I take it Junior doesn't have his father's misgivings?" Kat asked.

"Not at all. Junior has no such qualms. He's a technology whore, and tracking down evidence against him was easy."

"Regarding the documents, you printed off four copies, right?'

"Correct. One was in my safe ..."

"Which they got the day after they grabbed you," Eli said.

"I figured as much, based on the interrogation questions I received. The other three I gave to Danny Frazier. He was supposed to put them in a secure location. They took me the day I was going to read him into what was going on."

"What did Danny know?"

"Very little. I hadn't shared what I'd discovered yet."

"You kept this close to the vest?" Eli asked.

"Of course."

"Did the president know Danny was in the dark?"

"Not that I'm aware of. After I confronted the president, he proclaimed ignorance and said he would confront Junior and get back with me. Well, the president ignored my follow-up inquires. I knew something wasn't right, and that's why I printed off the additional copies and decided to get Danny's assistance. Hindsight is twenty-twenty, and I should have realized even though none of the evidence implicated the president, he was really the one behind this deal."

Eli cleared his throat. "I hate to tell you this, but Danny's dead."

Nick's expression didn't flinch. "I figured as much. But based on the questions they asked me during the interrogation, I believed they hadn't recovered the other three documents."

"It appears that changed recently, and the president will have all the copies at the White House tonight."

"He'll destroy all the paper copies," Nick said.

"That's all the evidence you have?" The director asked.

"I only printed off four copies," Nick said. "There's an old incinerator in the hub. That's the name of the central room where all the secret White House tunnels converge. He'll likely destroy them there."

"We need to stop him," Kat said.

"No, it's not as simple as that. I'll need to go alone."

"I'm not sure that's a good idea," the director said.

"Look, I know Charles well enough to say he won't let any of you near the White House tonight. Especially if he has all the evidence."

Eli disagreed. "He can't stop us from coming."

"He can, or at the least, he can delay you until he destroys the files. But he can't stop me," Nick said.

"How are you so sure?"

"Trust me. Inside 1600 Pennsylvania Avenue I'm safe, while outside I'm susceptible to the assets who work for Junior, but they can't lay a finger on me in the White House."

"What do you need from us?" Director Ludington's expression appeared stoic.

"I need to shower and swing by my townhouse in Vienna to get a change of clothes."

"That's it?"

"Yes, I can do the rest."

"You're sure?" The director asked.

"Without a doubt."

Kat did not look convinced. "What about backup?"

"I'll have all the backup I need inside the people's house."

"Well," Eli said. "Would you like to know what Kat and I learned during our investigation?"

Nick nodded. "Read me in, buddy."

73

— • —

BEAUMONT, TEXAS

JACK BROOKS REGIONAL AIRPORT

Each breath felt labored, shortened, and painful.

The tip of the broken pencil protruded from Peter's skin, and he could feel it shift inside his rib cage with every gasp for air. He looked down at his blood-drenched shirt. Time was working against him.

He reached over to the passenger seat of the Oldsmobile Cutlass he stole in Port Arthur near Pleasure Island Boulevard and grabbed a fresh t-shirt. A half-dozen shirts lay neatly stacked on the seat, shirts he bought at the Walmart across the street from the airport.

Going back to Houma after he fled the platform wasn't an option. He knew the feds would scour the airport based on its proximity to the coast. Sailing west, he settled on Beaumont, based on the charts found on the boat. Once on land, Peter used his smartphone to track down a charter plane at the Jack Brooks Regional Airport and reserved it online. Before leaving the Cutlass and getting on the plane, he placed a call.

"Hey, bro, it took you a long time to return my call," Joe said. "I got worried. Everything go OK with Nick?"

Peter groaned, "No. No, it didn't."

"Uhhh, you ok?"

"Not really. As I was about to finish him off when the facility was attacked, and Nick got the drop on me."

"Wait, Attacked! By who?"

"Feds. An FBI HRT team, based on their uniforms."

"Did they rescue Nick?"

"I believe so."

"Fuck."

"But I can't be sure. I broke off the pencil in my chest, and I got the hell out of there."

"Wait. The pencil? What?"

"When I went to stab Nick, he got me first. Apparently, he made a shank out of a pencil."

"And he stabbed you in the fuckin' chest?"

"Afraid so."

"That sounds serious."

Peter looked down at the wound; he knew it was only a matter of time with or without medical attention. "Nah, I'm all good, bro."

"Where are you now?"

"Beaumont, Texas."

"What about the jet?" Joe asked.

"There was no way in hell I was going back to Houma. I chartered a plane that will take me to D.C.."

"You mean New York?"

"No, I'm coming to you."

"Negative, I'm good. No need for that," Joe said.

"I insist," Peter said. "I'll be at the Manassas airport tonight." He then changed the subject. "You get the files?"

"Yes. Danny hid them in three different safe deposit boxes, but I've got them. I'm headed to the White House soon."

"And after that?"

"I'm supposed to catch a flight with Junior back home. We'll meet at the Manassas airport at 10:00 p.m., sharp."

"What about Marcus?"

"He's with Merci in Washington at his apartment. Why?"

"I need to warn them."

"You think he and Merci are in danger going to the White House? I mean, shit, I'm meeting them there."

"Not sure, to be honest. I can't convince you to not deliver the files personally, can I?"

"No way. I've got to do it. You know how Charles can be."

"Sure do," Peter said. "That's why I don't think you should deliver them without me."

"I'll be careful. Anyway, I might not be a badass like you, but I can handle myself."

Peter knew arguing wouldn't get them anywhere. Joe didn't realize the danger he was in, and, chances were, convincing him of the risk would be damn near impossible. "Be safe, Joseph. Watch your six, and I'll see you later tonight."

"OK, bro."

"If things go south, you know where the money is. You've got the access code for the Cayman account."

"Bro, nothing's going south. See you at the airport. Deal?"

"Yeah, bro. Deal."

The call ended, and Peter made one more call.

Next, he gathered the plastic bag of shirts and climbed out of the Oldsmobile. Pain pulsated in rhythmic shots out from his chest to his extremities as he lumbered across the parking lot and onto the tarmac.

Can I make it? He wondered and climbed inside the Cessna Citation M2.

The pilot walked back to greet him. "I'm told we're taking you to Washington, D.C. tonight, Mr. Casha. Is this a business trip or pleasure?"

Peter smiled as best he could and tried to hide the pain. A blanket he removed from the overhead covered his chest and concealed the blood. "Let's say it will be a pleasure for me to put some unfinished business to rest."

"Sounds like the best of both worlds."

"Oh, it will be," Peter said.

74

THE OVAL

Rage flowed through the president's body like heroin circulates through the veins of a strung-out junky. A scarlet hue formed on his cheeks and grew in intensity as he took a deep breath of air in through his nose, and slowly exhaled it out his mouth. Charles needed several repetitions before he told Dolores through gritted teeth to call his son.

Thirty seconds later, Junior was on the secure line. "Yes, Mr. President."

"Junior." He paused a moment and took another deep breath before he continued. "Did you hear about it?"

"About what?"

The president bit the side of his cheek hard enough to draw blood. "The raid."

"What are you talking about?" Junior asked.

What a worthless piece of shit, thought the president. "I got off the phone with a contact at the FBI. An HRT team raided the Sanctum facility several hours ago."

Silence greeted him.

"Did you hear what the hell I said? They hit the facility. Hit it hard."

Junior paused before he said, "Yes, sir. I heard you."

"And? You don't have anything to say about it?"

"Do they have Nick?"

Unbelievable. "I don't know. Details are sketchy. The director kept this operation close to the vest, and few people knew about it outside of his inner circle. That son-of-a-bitch wanted to keep the White House in the dark. Even the deputy director had no clue, or we would have known about the raid."

"Who else can tell us if Nick is alive?"

"You know someone that should know. Haven't you heard from Peter?"

"No. Radio silence."

"That should tell you something."

"You think he failed?"

"I think he's dead. If an HRT team raided the facility, I doubt they took any prisoners. Peter sure as hell doesn't strike me as someone who would lay down his gun and let himself be taken alive."

"What do we do?" Junior asked.

"Are you home?"

"No, not yet."

"Where are you?"

"Still in D.C.. I had a few things to wrap up. Joe is catching a ride back with me after he delivers the files. Should I alter the plans?"

The president grew quiet as he paced around the resolute desk. "No, I need time to think. I've got a few hours before they arrive."

"What are you going to do?" Junior asked.

"I don't know yet."

"If Nick is still alive ..."

"I'll handle The Body Man," the president said.

"And in the meantime, you expect me to do what?"

"Clean up this mess, starting with Joe after he brings me the documents."

"As in eliminate, Jo-Jo?"

Charles Steele ignored the question. "Marcus and Merci need to be neutralized as well. They all know way too much." His voice steadily transitioned to a guttural growl.

"They're professionals. How do you expect me to take care of them?"

"With others who share their unique skill set."

"And where do you expect I find them?"

"Be resourceful, but in God's name, be discreet."

"What about Director Ludington? He must know what's going on." The panic evident in Junior's voice.

"I'm not sure what Ken knows, but I've got another way to keep him quiet."

"Meaning?"

"I have leverage over him."

"How did this all go to hell?" Junior asked.

"I let inferior, weak people do my dirty work instead of shoving my hands down into the shit and doing it myself. Never again. Do you hear me? Never!"

"I trusted these people and paid them handsomely for their services," Junior said.

"Not talking about them," the president said. "I'm talking about you. I place the blame for this failure squarely on your shoulders, Junior."

Junior didn't respond.

The president disconnected the line, walked into his study, and poured a tall glass of Macallan 1947 Highland single-malt scotch whisky. He sat down and took the first sip to clear his mind and subdue his shaking hands.

75

WASHINGTON, D.C.

ST. REGIS HOTEL

Joe sat on a plush red sofa in the lobby of the St. Regis Hotel and looked up at the gold-inlaid ceiling. Decadent was the word that came to mind as he counted the chandeliers and marveled at the opulent display of wealth. He glanced down at his watch.

They're late.

As if on cue, Marcus and Merci walked into the lobby and approached where he sat. Joe stood, the three of them made their way over to the concierge desk.

"George is expecting us," Joe said to the sharply dressed African American who sat behind the desk. The man nodded, said nothing, and slipped out, using a door to the right of his desk.

The concierge returned a minute later without a word and motioned toward his left by tilting his head.

A tall man with a dark bushy beard, dimpled chin, and rugged good looks advanced to the desk. Dressed similarly to the man behind the concierge desk, he walked towards them with a purpose, his footsteps firm yet light. Joe thought he looked more like an operator than a hotel worker. The dark, wraparound sunglasses looked entirely out-of-place indoors.

"Follow me," the man said in a voice devoid of inflection.

"Are you George?" Joe asked.

"I am," he said and glanced down at the black-and-silver Rolex watch on his wrist. "You're a few minutes late, and he's expecting you."

George, if that was really his name, led them down a series of hallways until they came to a nondescript door at the end of the hall identical to every other door they passed. Instead of a key card, the door had a touchpad to the right of the doorframe. After George entered a six-digit code, the lock mechanism disengaged, and the door swung open. They descended four flights of stairs that ended at another door. Unlike the door upstairs, this one resembled a bank vault door with another keypad on the left this time. A light above the door turned green when the valid code was entered. Next, a *hiss* sound emanated from around the doorframe as a seal of sorts released. He stepped aside as the door pivoted and waved his arm, indicating Joe, Marcus, and Merci should step inside. "He's waiting for you on the other side," George said.

"Who is?" Joe asked.

George didn't respond to the question. "Please enter," he said.

Reluctantly, the three of them stepped inside the darkened space as the heavy door closed behind them. They were all alone in a mysterious tunnel with only one direction to go.

Before they could say anything, a figure emerged from down the tunnel and approached. The spaced-out lighting above made it difficult to see much more than ten to twenty feet with clarity.

Nick Jordan emerged from the shadows as a surprised expression formed on all their faces. "Welcome to Broadsway." The Body Man said.

"Guess you're not dead after all." Joe wasn't sure what else to say.

"No, but the three of you will be if you're not careful."

"Is that a threat?" Merci's eyes darted around the tunnel, looking for a weapon, or something she could wield.

"No threat. It's a fact. The three of you are smart, intelligent enough to know when someone is cleaning up after themselves."

"I take it you know who we are?" Joe's eyes narrowed.

"I do. I read all of your bios in the dossier created by the FBI on the flight from Houma."

"You came here to what? Warn us?"

"The enemy of my enemy is my friend."

"Who says we're the president's enemy?"

Nick shook his head. "In any logical scenario, we would be against each other. However, Charles Steele is systematically eliminating all the evidence. Trust me. He's your enemy. Underestimating his capabilities would be unwise."

"And if we told you this was all Junior's plan," Marcus said.

"Oh, Junior is guilty for sure. But a dog always has a master. And the four of us know who pulls the strings. Pinocchio only goes where Geppetto leads."

"Do you know what we're bringing him?" Joe asked.

"I do. You have the files I compiled and possibly other things."

"And do you think you'll take them from us by force?" Merci's body tensed, ready to attack.

Nick shook his head. "No. Quite the contrary. I want you to hand deliver the evidence to him personally."

The Body Man had a calm, almost uninterested demeanor. It confused Merci. She kept waiting for him to snap and come at them. But he didn't. His tone remained even, almost serene.

"What do you want?" Joe asked.

An unmistakable fire suddenly burned inside Nick's eyes. "To light the powder keg."

"You're coming with us?" Joe asked.

"I'll be along shortly after you conclude your business with Charles. But I'd prefer he not know I'm here. At least not yet."

"What assurance do we have that you won't kill us or have us arrested after we meet with him?" Merci's head swam as she listened to Nick.

"You have my word. No harm will come to you by my hands or actions." Nick answered truthfully. "My word is my bond. The three of you should be more worried about Charles. You're merely pawns on his board. I'm not interested in pawns. I want to take down the king."

76

— • —

BROADSWAY TUNNEL

BENEATH THE WHITE HOUSE

President Steele and two Secret Service agents rode the elevator from the West Wing down to the hub. Abnormally quiet, the president stared at the red carpet and mahogany walls of the elevator as the squeak of the pulley and slight jerk announced their arrival to the basement.

Charles walked out with an air of confidence in his step, like a prizefighter as he struts into the ring against an opponent who stands no chance.

A relic of a bygone era, the twenty-five-by-forty-foot hub contained an old boiler, several large printing presses, and an incinerator. The latter item still functioned and currently spewed forth enough heat to turn the expansive room into a sauna.

Earlier in the day, the president requested the incinerator be fired up. The White House staff thought the request was odd but did as the president requested without question. Early in Charles Steele's presidency, the staff learned to question very little of his actions. Poking a bear rarely worked out well for the one with the stick.

The president stood in the center of the brightly lit room with his arms crossed and slowly tapped his left foot against the tiled floor. Beads of perspiration formed on his forehead as he looked down at this watch. With a smug expression plastered all over his face, Charles looked down Broadsway as the sound of footfalls approached from the direction of the St. Regis Hotel.

Marcus, Merci, and Joe came into view as they turned the corner. They each walked toward the president with pensive looks clearly displayed on their faces.

The president looked at the agents on either side. "That will be all for now, gentlemen."

"Mr. President?" The senior agent looked concerned.

"I'll take it from here." He pointed toward the gold eagle cufflinks on his white dress shirt. "If I need you, I'll let you know."

"We can be here within seconds, sir."

"I know. It will be fine. The meeting won't take long, and my guests will show themselves out the same way they came."

"As you wish, sir."

They were all alone. Only five feet separated the president from the others.

"Welcome to a place few people see. Needless to say, it's not on the self-guided White House tour."

None of them responded.

Charles almost felt like he could smell the fear. Except from Merci, her eyes looked like they could shoot daggers. He smirked. "Did you bring what I requested?"

All three nodded.

"You're up first, Joe."

Joe stepped forward, removed three brown legal-sized folders from a black briefcase, and handed them to the president.

"You open any of the folders?" The president tapped the top file with his index finger.

"No, sir, I did as you instructed and retrieved them from the three safe deposit boxes. They never left my sight."

A devilish grin formed at the corner of the president's lips. "Not even a peek inside? After all, curiosity can get the best of anyone."

"No, sir. I know what that did to the goddam cat."

Charles Steele let out an audible chuckle. "You and your sense of humor, Joseph. Well done. I won't forget your efforts and will reward your loyalty."

"Thank you, Mr. President."

The president took the three brown file folders, undid the clasp, and flipped through the contents one at a time. It took several minutes, but once he felt confident everything was in place, he put them down on the floor next to his right foot.

"And the other item?"

Marcus stepped closer and handed the president the black over-the-shoulder bag they'd retrieved in New York City.

"Same question Joe got."

"We didn't look, Mr. President. Never opened the bag," Marcus said.

"Good to hear."

The president tapped the bag as a wide smile spread over his face. "This one will come in quite handy in the coming days and weeks. Thank you both for retrieving it."

Marcus and Merci nodded, but said nothing.

"And you, Merci," the president continued. "Good job taking care of James Fowler. The man was a prick and got what he deserved."

The president said nothing about her failure to kill Danny Frazier.

Merci smiled on the outside, although on the inside she seethed. "All in a day's work, sir," she said through gritted teeth. She could read people well. The president was placating them, all of them, as his true intentions writhed below the surface. "Are we free to go?"

"Of course." The president said.

Merci's bullshit meter flew past the number ten as she saw the deceit in his eyes.

"But before you all leave," the president said. "Let's put these files where they belong." Charles placed the bag from Marcus on the ground, picked up the files from Joe, and walked over to the incinerator. As he got close to the heat source, the elevator made a screeching sound as it descended to the basement. The president held the files tightly as it reached the bottom and the doors slowly opened.

—◦—

Nick stepped out of the elevator and with a slow stride and walked toward the president. He wore a pair of brown leather shoes with wooden heels, a three-button blue suit, a white shirt, and a red tie.

"Ahh, the prodigal son returned," the president said in a mocking tone. "I was wondering when you'd join our little soirée."

"Your biblical doctrine is off, as usual, Mr. President. The prodigal son left of his own accord. I did no such thing."

"Ahh, but he came back."

"I came back not out of desperation, but out of necessity."

"Was it necessary to betray me, Nick?"

Nick shook his head. "My oath is to the office, not the occupant. You know that, sir."

"And that loyalty nearly got you what you deserved."

Nick ignored the dig. "Based on your smug look, I take it you're not surprised to see me alive."

"Of course not. I've got eyes and ears everywhere." The president looked away from Nick and toward Joe. His face muscles tensed as he spat out the next few words with a vitriolic tone. "I learned earlier his best friend failed."

"Next time send someone that isn't wounded," Nick said.

"I won't make the same mistake twice."

"No doubt, Mr. President."

"You're here just in time." The president took the additional steps toward the incinerator.

Nick kept walking until he got even with Joe, Marcus, and Merci before he paused.

"I've already destroyed the copy we found in your safe." Charles slid on a pair of heat-resistant gloves and opened the thick incinerator doors. They made an awful sound, like fingernails down a chalkboard, as the rusty doors crept open.

Even fifteen feet away, a wave of heat licked everyone's faces.

"Bon voyage," the president said as he tossed all three brown folders into the flames.

He looked back at Nick and the others, but received only blank stares. After closing the incinerator doors, he walked back to where the black bag lay on the floor.

"It's done then?" Nick said.

The president smiled, but it wasn't a warm, friendly smile. "Not quite. I don't like loose ends, and there are still many to tie up."

"Are you planning to kill me here in the White House, sir?"

"Of course not. But I can assure you these grounds are where you will take your last breaths."

"Do you think my fellow agents will finish me off?"

The president nodded. "I didn't say that."

"Mr. President, I did my job. And the thanks I got was a trip to the Gulf of Mexico, where I was tortured and almost killed."

"It's likely we'll agree to disagree, Nick."

"My job wasn't to make all of your sins go away. It's protecting the office of the presidency. Even if that means I must protect it from a man like you and your piece of shit son, sir."

"We can go back and forth all night, Nick. The bottom line is you and others without the foresight to see several moves ahead have failed. I'm still in power, and without any evidence, the deal will go through. You can't stop it at this point."

"Is that so?" Nick asked.

"Yes, it is."

Nick shook his head before a smile formed. "Mr. President, I'm not sure who is feeding you intel, but the transfer of the drones and missiles won't happen. As we speak, a tier-one unit is on route to the cargo ship. They'll board it and take possession of the containers. The Saudis won't be getting our drone tech. Meaning the Steel Corp. will not be entering the lucrative banking industry in that part of the world now, or ever. It also means the Middle East won't catch on fire when the coming war between Iran and Saudi Arabia turns into a full-scale global conflict."

The president's smile receded as his face tensed. "Whatever, you're bluffing. You couldn't possibly know which container ship the weapons are on."

"You're right. I didn't get intel on that before you ordered my abduction. But Peter Casha knew. And he paid Hector Fuentes to make the switch. Peter was supposed to kill Hector but failed."

"Bullshit." The president's lower lip snarled.

Nick continued, "Hector survived the attack in the Pacific. The FBI interviewed him yesterday, and he sang like a canary. All it cost was an immunity deal. A small move in a large game of chess."

The smug look the president's face wore most of the time now disappeared. "That isn't possible."

"You're finished, Charles." Nick said. "I can direct you to the room Nixon wrote his resignation letter in, if you need."

The president's face grew crimson with rage as he swung his pointed index finger toward Marcus and Merci. "This is your goddamn fault. If you had killed Danny Frazier like you were supposed to, none of this would have happened."

Merci's hands were behind her back, her body tensed as the president blamed her errant shot for the entire mess. She turned the ring on her finger so that the jewel faced her palm and flipped back the ruby to reveal the small needle.

Nick saw her hands move behind her back. He read her expressions earlier in the tunnel and knew what she was capable of when cornered. At that moment, he let things play out. "I should snap your neck right here for killing Danny." Nick's voice raised to a thunderous level as he took a step toward the president.

The president's reaction surprised them all.

He laughed.

A maniacal sound from deep down coming not from a place of confidence but desperation. The tone reverberated down the corridors leading from the hub. "You are nothing more than a junkyard dog looking for a reason to pounce."

Nick lunged toward the president and shouted, "Arf!"

President Steele's resolve faded as he reacted to the sudden movement. He stumbled and lost his balance, falling backwards.

Merci moved with the speed of a cat evading water as she caught the president and broke his fall. The palm of her hand cupped the back of his neck as an imperceptible pinprick broke his skin.

That's all it took.

The president didn't notice the small puncture to his neck and quickly gathered himself as he pushed Merci away and stood up. "Get out. All of you. This is my fucking house, and none of you have the right to be here."

None of them responded.

Nobody moved.

"I said get out!" The president screamed louder as spittle formed on his lips and flew out of his mouth.

The four of them turned away, and Nick motioned for them to follow as he walked to the elevator.

"No!" The president pointed toward the Broadsway tunnel. "You'll leave the same way Kennedy's whores left my house."

They ignored him and continued toward the elevator.

Nick turned around to face the president as he reached the elevator doors. "Like hell we will, Charles, and this isn't your house. It's the people's house. You're only a temporary guardian of the office. You don't deserve the honor and privilege to call the people's house your home. Besides, we'll walk right out the front door, and there's not a goddamn thing you can do about it."

President Steele's lip snarled, and his hands shook. The rage within him grew to a level where he couldn't find the words to respond.

"And another thing." Nick stepped into the elevator with the others and turned to face the president. He bent over, removed his left shoe, and slid the wooden heel to the side. Next, he removed a small flash drive. "A piece of advice. When you destroy evidence that you think can bring down your family business and possibly your presidency." He held the flash drive up for the president to see clearly. "Make sure you destroy all the evidence, you dumb motherfucker."

The president stood in a paralyzed state as the doors closed.

Nick looked at Merci inside the elevator. "How long does he have?"

Merci looked back with an icy glare. "For what?"

"Don't bother with the act, Merci."

Her eyes grew wide.

"Yes, I saw what you did with the ring. How long does he have?" Nick asked again.

"Maybe fifteen minutes if he's lucky."

"Is there anything that can reverse the poison?"

Merci shook her head. "Not according to the agency."

Nick paused for a moment. "I'll escort the three of you out the east gate, then go back to have a final word with Charles."

Five minutes later, at the east security entrance, Nick waved to the guard. The man looked like he saw a ghost.

"These three are with me. Let them go, Frank."

The guard looked down at his clipboard.

"Their names aren't on there. They are with me," Nick repeated.

"But how did they ..."

Nick cut him off. "You heard me, Frank. Lincoln's ghost let them in, and you're letting them out."

Frank nodded and waved them past the checkpoint.

Joe, Marcus, and Merci paused and looked back at Nick.

"I don't want to see any of you again. Ever. Understood?" Nick said.

The three of them nodded.

"How long of a lead time do we have?" Marcus asked.

Nick ignored the question. "Have a good life somewhere far, far away from the United States." He said before he turned and walked back toward the door leading into the White House.

⚬

Charles Steele stood in the west sitting hall of the official residence and took several large gasps of breath, each one harder to draw than the last.

What the hell is happening to me?

The agent closest to the doorway leading to the center hall took a step into the room as he saw the president grab his chest.

"Mr. President, are you okay? Should I call for your doctor?"

A voice startled him, and the agent pivoted on his heels to turn.

"That won't be necessary, Tom." Nick walked into the room and put his hand on the agent's shoulder.

Special Agent Tom Brady's eyes grew wide in disbelief.

Charles Steele slurred his words. "Get this son-of-a-bitch out of here. Call my doctor. That bitch poisoned me ..."

Tom looked back and forth between the president and Nick Jordan.

"Tom," Nick said as he squeezed his shoulder a little firmer. "Alpha seven."

The phrase surprised Tom, and he protested, "But the president ..."

Nick cut him off. "Alpha seven, Tom. I'll take it from here."

"Yes, sir," Tom said as he turned and left the room.

Charles Steele tried to call out, but his voice failed him. Unable to draw a breath, he fell to his knees, with both arms now clutching his chest. Sweat poured from his brow and flowed from the pores all over his body.

Nick Jordan approached him and leaned down. He came face to face with the man whose presidency was about to meet an expeditious end.

"You stood too close to the fire, Charles. But fear not. I guarantee you won't be alone for long."

Charles eyes grew wide as the last bit of oxygen escaped from his lungs.

Nick continued, "Junior will join you soon enough and taste the same flames. I'll be sure of it."

The president fell forward to the ground, and his body jerked about like a fish thrown onto the shore. After a minute, his erratic movements stopped, and his body grew still. The piercing eyes filled with life seconds before now stared toward the wall in an empty gaze.

"Godspeed, Mr. President," Nick whispered into his ear as he reached down and closed Charles Steele's eyes for the last time.

77

---•---

Manassas Regional Airport

A thick fog settled over the airport as Joe stepped out of the car and looked around. Like a dark blanket, the haze obscured everything within view. Joe turned back to the driver.

"You going to be, ok?" Marcus asked. A hint of concern evident in his voice.

Joe paused and glanced toward where the veiled plane idled. "Yeah, I'll be fine, and you?"

Marcus exchanged a glance with Merci before turning to Joe. "We're good. A jet is waiting for us at Hyde Field, someone Merci knows who can get us out of the country easily tonight. There's room on the plane, Joe."

"Appreciate the offer, but I'm supposed to meet Peter here tonight."

"Well, best of luck to you, Joe," said Marcus as he shook his hand. "If you need us, we'll be ..."

"In a non-extradition country sipping fruity drinks." Merci sounded like a teenager about to sneak out the bedroom window to meet her boyfriend.

"Take care, you two." Joe turned away and headed to the jet.

---◆---

As Joe walked down the tarmac encompassed in darkness on all sides, only the lights from the jet cut through the absolute fog as he approached the hangar. About twenty-five feet away from the now visible airstairs, he paused. A gnawing feeling inside took over. At that moment, he realized meeting Junior was a mistake and he should have left by some other means, even if that meant going with Marcus and Merci.

But he couldn't leave. Peter said he would meet him here.

Junior and two men from his security detail, men Joe had hired personally, descended the airstairs.

"Well, well, well," Junior said. "You finally made it, Jo-Jo."

"Yes, I'm here."

The look on Junior's face confirmed his suspicions. Joe froze, but he knew going back wasn't an option. With the 1911 tucked in his waistband against the small of his back, he calculated his odds of drawing and dropping all three of them.

The odds were not in his favor.

"If only Casha didn't fail." Junior said.

Joe knew where this was going. He looked around, but there was no sign of Peter.

Where are you, bro? He thought.

"We can talk about this back in New York." Joe said as he tried to stall. "I'm sure we can work something out, and I can make things right."

"You don't get it, do you? Peter failed, which means you failed."

The two security guards stepped to either side of Junior, raised their carbines, and pointed them at Joe.

Shit.

"My father said don't leave a mess on the tarmac, but I figure we can clean everything up and bury you out at the Quantico tank course. You won't be the first body rotting in those woods, nor the last."

The first bullet rang out with a loud *crack*. Joe watched as blood sprayed across the side of Junior's face while the guard's face exploded. The body dropped to the ground, and Joe reached behind and gripped the 1911 as he pulled it from his waistband. Another shot followed a fraction of second later, and a massive hole appeared in the throat of the other guard. The man reached up to the wound as blood streamed out like the flow of water from a drinking fountain.

Joe watched the blood for a fraction of a second before another slug struck the guard's forehead.

———◦———

Peter stepped partially out from the darkness directly behind Joe.

"To your knees, Joseph." Peter's voice sounded raw, his tone gruff.

Joe dropped without hesitation.

Junior panicked, unable to move. He closed his eyes as a sudden wetness covered the front of his pants and worked its way down his leg.

A third guard emerged from the plane and fired a burst from an AR-15 in the direction of Peter and Joe. Most rounds missed wildly to the left, but two rounds struck Peter in the upper chest. Joe's life was spared on his knees as the rounds flew over his head.

Peter stumbled and almost lost his balance as air rushed from his lungs, but somehow raised his weapon and fired three rounds at the guard. One sailed high, but two of the bullets struck the guard in the chest as he summersaulted down the airstairs landing on the tarmac motionless.

As the shots ceased, Junior knew it had to be Peter. He yelled out. "How much money do you want, Casha?"

Peter stumbled forward and emerged from the darkness. With each step, his coordination got worse as he walked like a drunk trying to keep a straight line during a sobriety test. The arm that held the raised gun pointed toward the pavement.

Unsure if Peter heard him, Junior yelled out with more force. "I said how much money, Casha? Name your price. It's yours."

With surprising speed, the gun came back up.

"Fuck you and your family's money, Junior."

Three retorts from the pistol lit up the darkened sky as the muzzle flashed brilliant hues of reddish orange.

Junior's face exploded, and his body crumpled to the ground like a heavy sack.

As the last round split the sky, Peter fell to his knees. His white t-shirt turned crimson with the blood stains grew larger.

Joe turned and ran to his friend. "No, no, no," he pleaded. "Don't do this, bro. You can't go out like this."

A bubble of blood escaped from Peter's mouth and dribbled down his chin. Within seconds, his head slowly leaned back toward the dark sky.

Joe kneeled and brought Peter's head to his chest.

Peter pointed past the plane to the vast darkness above. "I see him, bro. I see the warrior."

Tears flowed down Joe's face. "Go to him. Go to the warrior. Go home."

Joe held the lifeless body of his best friend for several minutes. Long enough to say goodbye, but not long enough to process what happened. The distant sound of sirens pulled him away from the overwhelming grief.

He lay Peter's body down gently and removed the pistol from Peter's hand. The 1911 his friend carried a duplicate of his own. He stuffed Peter's weapon in his belt and cradled his own pistol. Quickly he climbed the airstairs of the idling jet.

Joe knew the pilots, and a look of fear covered both men's faces as he stepped into the cockpit.

"Where to, Mr. Lagano?" The one pilot asked.

"We have enough fuel for the Caymans?"

The pilot nodded. "Yes, sir."

"Head there."

"But our flight plan is for New York?"

Joe clicked back the hammer of the Kimber and pressed it to the back of the man's skull. "Change of plans, Matt. Make it happen."

The pilot gulped hard. "You got it, Mr. Lagano."

Epilogue

Old Ebbitt Grill

Three days later

Eli and Kat sat on the bar stools of the Old Ebbitt Grill on 15th Street east of the White House. The bartender handed both of them a Guinness, and they clanked the necks of the bottles together.

"To Wes." Eli pointed his bottle skyward.

"Absolutely," Kat said as she threw back a large swig of beer.

"Room for one more?" A figure approached from the side.

Eli turned around and saw Nick. "For The Body Man? Anytime."

Nick frowned. "Hey, man, watch how loud you say that."

Eli looked around the half empty bar. "No one cares. Your secret is safe here."

Kat moved a stool to the left. "Ignore him, Nick. I do." She patted the empty seat. "Here, I kept this one warm for you."

"Well, thank you, pretty lady."

"Are you're sweet talking my partner, Jordan?" Eli asked.

"Oh, so now I'm your partner?" A surprised look spread over Kat's face. "Say what?"

"That's the first time you've ever referred to me as your partner, Payne."

"Seriously?" Eli gave her a quizzical stare.

"Yes." Kat said.

"Well, it must have been a Freudian slip." A wide smile formed on Eli's face.

Kat rolled her eyes. "You're such a dick."

Eli laughed loud enough to turn a few heads from the uninterested patrons scattered around the bar. "I'm only kidding, Stone. You became my partner the moment you climbed into my car."

"Oh, really?"

"Ok, maybe when you saved my ass on the oil platform."

"Jeez, let's not relive that moment again. You going to cry on my shoulder?"

Nick laughed, a hearty guttural sound from deep within. "I love it. She's a real ballbuster, Payne."

"Tell me about it," Eli said.

Kat pointed to Eli. "And as a probationary agent, I learned from the best."

Eli shrugged. "OK. She might have a point there."

"What's your poison?" The bartender asked as he put a napkin down in front of Nick.

"Oh, I'll have what they're having."

"I've got his drink." Eli said as he tossed his credit card to the bartender. "Plus, add three Irish car bombs to my tab."

"Wait a minute. How the hell will we get home if all of us get shitfaced?" Nick asked.

"I'll be the DD." Mila slid onto the empty bar stool next to Eli.

"Is this a double date or something?" Nick asked.

Kat kicked Nick in the shin and wagged her finger back and forth.

Eli laughed and spat out half a mouthful of beer. "Told you not to trifle with her, Jordan."

Nick rubbed his shin. "Yowzah, I got the message loud and clear. I can get you a job on an abandoned oil platform any time you need it, Stone."

The sight of the new president on the television screen behind the bar caused all four to stop.

"After what went down with Steele, how is he?" Kat pointed to the screen.

"Who preacher?" Nick used the Secret Service code name for the man elevated from vice president to president three days before. "Jury's still out, but after Charles, I can't imagine he could be much worse."

Eli raised his glass. "I can drink to that."

––––––––◆––––––––

"Not to mix business with pleasure," Nick said. "But you guys have a lead on Marcus and Merci?"

Eli shook his head. "You mean after you let them walk right out of the White House? The most secure eighteen acres in the world."

Nick frowned. "I like to say I gave them a professional courtesy. Anyway, I knew the FBI could track them down in no time. Like they did me." He rolled his eyes at the last phrase.

Eli smirked. "Trail went cold. They took a chartered jet from D.C. to Paris. From there we got a probable match via surveillance cameras that placed them on a commercial flight from de Gaulle to Singapore. But they fell off the grid once they arrived at Changi airport. No hits in the past twenty-four hours. Interpol is looking for them, but we all know how well that typically goes."

"How about Joseph Lagano?" Nick asked.

"Same deal. He forced Junior's pilots at gunpoint to fly him to the Cayman Islands, and once they landed, he knocked both of them out. When they came to, he was long gone. It appears Mr. Lagano emptied a bank account held in Peter Casha's name and disappeared. The working theory is he fled by boat, but no hard evidence to substantiate that yet."

Nick nodded. "How much money did he get?"

"Several million. Enough to fall off the grid for now, but he'll turn up. Sooner rather than later, he'll mess up since everyone does eventually. Oh, and this morning we got a positive ID on the female body found on the stairwell outside the platform. Her name is Evelyn Rhimes. And get this, up until six months ago she worked in the communication department at ..." Eli tapped his fingers quickly on the oak countertop. "Drum roll, please. The White House."

"Really?" Nick looked surprised.

"Yeah. Ever heard of her?"

Nick pondered the name. "No, name doesn't ring a bell."

"The Sanctum either had or has a mole inside the White House."

Nick stroked the side of his face. "I'll flush them out if there's any left. Thanks for the heads up."

"What about the Sanctum?" Kat asked. "What will happen with them?"

Nick's eyes narrowed. "The preacher started a task force called Operation Red Star and placed me on it."

"Its purpose?"

"To find the members of the Sanctum and take them down."

"That didn't take long," Eli said. "He's only been POTUS for a few days."

"He realizes the existential threat we face with a crime syndicate with their reach operating in the United States so brazenly."

"Interesting," Eli said. "And has a new apprentice been named to replace Danny?"

The serious expression faded, and a thinly veiled smile crept over Nick's face as he cocked his head towards Mila.

Eli saw the look. "Oh, hell, no."

Mila reached over and rubbed her palm over the top of Eli's right hand. "Don't worry. I'm not interested."

"I might convince her otherwise," Nick said.

"Watch it, Jordan. You were growing on me."

"Only playing, man. So, what's on the docket for you two?" Nick looked back and forth between Eli and Kat.

Eli smiled. "Tell him, partner."

"New case," Kat said. "We just got a call on the way over here. A United States senator is missing."

"Then why are you in here drinking with me? Shouldn't you be out finding him?"

"We have a few questions for you."

"How so?"

"You're privy to intimate details regarding the senator," Eli said.

"Am I?" Nick asked as his right eyebrow raised.

Kat nodded. "That's why we're here."

THE END

The Body Man will return ...

ACKNOWLEDGEMENTS

It's been a long and strange journey. *The Body Man* (TBM) originally published on November 11, 2021. I had finally reached a goal I set for myself seven years earlier. Fast forward to mid-2023 and the publisher informed me he was closing down his business and I would get the book rights back. Instead of starting the process to find a new publishing home for *The Body Man*, I utilized my established book imprint to re-release *The Body Man* under the **BruNoe Media Publishing** brand I created in 2023. Not the path I expected, but one I welcomed with open arms. Always remember, life is what you make of it.

A novel might come from one person's imagination, but others lurk under the surface and are involved in the overall creative process. I am humbled, grateful, and happy to share in this lifelong achievement with so many who have supported me. I often remind my kids, others, and especially myself, "Life's a Journey, Not a Destination."

Above all, thank you to **I AM** for the gifts you've bestowed upon me.

Bruce and **Noelle**. My loves. Being your father is my joy, my sacred honor, and above all my greatest privilege in life.

My **Mom – Patricia (Patty)**. My first fan and biggest supporter. I love you, always.

My **Dad – Thomas (Tom)**. You gave me my 1st **Tom Clancy** novel.

Jackie, **Shawn**, & **Brett**. Family first. Always.

Aunt Sue. I love you.

Ray & Barb Tanguay (Gramm & Grumpaw). My second parents.

I miss you **Nanny.** Pike 84 is for you.

To the rest of my **Family.** Much love.

Max Council. The Pope. My closest friend and brother.

TC Thompson. Mr. President. My sounding board.

Kathy Lubin. My very first editor and dear friend.

Adam Hamdy. You championed *The Body Man* and believed in me.

Laurie (LA) Chandlar. One of the strongest people I've met on life's journey.

Brad Meltzer. My favorite author and supporter of all writers.

Lori Twining & **Colleen Winter.** The first scribes I befriended at Thrillerfest in 2017.

I write novels thanks to the mesmerizing tales told by both **Tom Clancy** and **Vince Flynn.** Two of my literary heroes. #RIP gents.

The Body Man protects the office of the Presidency. The current **Body Man** and those that came before would like to thank these men: **#46 Joseph Biden, #45 Donald Trump, #44 Barack Obama, #43 George W. Bush, #42 Bill Clinton, #41 George Bush, #40 Ronald Reagan, #39 Jimmy Carter, #38 Gerald Ford, #37 Richard Nixon, #36 Lyndon Johnson,** and **#35 John F. Kennedy** (the man who started it all).

Bono. Your music has been the soundtrack of my life.

John Guarnieri. Humbled by your constant support and grateful for our friendship. Bring on THE REAPER!

Eric Bass from **Shinedown**. Quite simply you are inspiring. Your generosity towards my son is beyond words. Keep writing, making music, and being you.

I'm beyond blessed to have an amazing group of friends who've encouraged me on this journey: **Dave Richards (Ravid Dichards), Jim Latina, Fudgie, Brian Wohnig, Bill Esch, Andrew Reinertsen (Rino), Simon Fraser, & Noah George.**

I do have a day job. Special thanks to my work family: **Carolynn Tolbert, Shawn Cassidy, Kathy Lubin, Kim Marquez, Loretta Uribe, Cynthia Ehlers, & Diane Torres**

Joe Lagano and **Matt O'Hara**. We met after the **Warrior** left you, but **Terry** is still here in spirit. Sorry you weren't "playboy billionaires" in this tale Casha & JoJo.

To my **Troop 610 Dad's**: **Bud McCall, TC Thompson, Marty Thomas, Scott Taylor, Mike Webb, Radar,** and thanks to the "Mountain Dew Man" **Wes Russell.**

Thank you to the review team at **Best Thriller Books www.bestthrill erbooks.com. Stuart Ashenbrenner, Chris Miller, Todd Wilkins, Derek Luedtke, Steve Netter, Kashif Hussain, Ankit Dhirasaria, David Dobiasek, & James Abt.**

Plenty of authors provided advice, ideas, & kinds words over the years: **Scott Swanson, Jack Carr, Brian Andrews, Brad Taylor, Tony Tata, Don Bentley, JT Patten, Joe Goldberg, David Darling, Kyle Steele, Dony Jay, Jeff Clark, Ama Adair, David Temple, J.B. Stevens, G.P., Kyle Mills, Jamie Mason, Steve Stratton, Ben Coes, Simon Gervais, Steve Urszenyi, Dr. Jason Piccolo, & Jeremy Miller.**

My sincere thanks to amazing Beta readers who read a very rough version of *The Body Man*: **Jim Cooke, Vikki Faircloth, Debbie Sabatini, Austin Chapin, Mike Goodwin, Julia Hogenmiller, & Frank Mentis.**

In memorial: **Doug King.**

Thanks to **Adam Sydney** for the initial edit of *The Body Man*.

Thank you to **Momir Borocki** for the amazing new cover on this second addition of TBM.

Brandi Fugate for my author photos.

Beyond blessed to be the owner/operator of a small "Indie" press, **BruNoe Media Publishing**. Not the path I planned in 2014 when I wrote my first novel titled *Vengeance*, but grateful for the path I have found myself on. Life is what you make of it, folks.

———◄O►———

To you the **Readers** ... I'm grateful for every person who took a chance and reads my words. Above all, I want my literary journey to reinforce my belief that anyone can accomplish any task they put their mind to. No matter what you try in life, the only thing standing in the way of success is **You**. Don't be a hindrance to your dreams. Life is short, and our book has a first page and a last. Nobody knows how many pages are included. Fill those blank pages to the best of your ability.

The glass really is half full, don't see it the other way.

One more thing.

NEVER QUIT!

EVER!

Onward and Upward my friends,

Eric P. Bishop

(January 2024)

SUPREME JUSTICE

A MERCI DE ATTA NOVEL

Chapter 1
Asheville, NC
The Grove Park Inn

———◆O◆———

Merci De Atta's legs wrapped around the torso of the overweight man and squeezed with the ferocity of a serpent as it crushes life from an unsuspecting prey.

The mark gasped for breath, but his vain attempt to inhale life giving oxygen only resulted in more intense pain as Merci exuded compound pressure on his chest. Careful not to break any ribs or leave visible signs of a struggle, she positioned her body in such a way to deliver maximum pressure with a minimum effort.

This asshole liked it rough, and Merci intended to deliver on what he paid for, even if it didn't result in the happy ending he might expect.

Laying in the center of bed and with his arms pinned, the man's sole focus became a struggle to breathe. With her thighs like a vice around the side of his chest and her shins pinned his arms into the mattress. The move immobilized his arms. He struggled for sixty seconds and tried to throw her from atop, using his bent legs and waist as leverage.

But to no avail.

Years of poor diet and a lack of motivation to exercise caught up to him as his mid-section girth prevented his thrusts from effectively dislodging the petite woman less than half his weight.

Merci weighed one hundred and twenty-five pounds, but what she lacked in body mass she made up for in lean muscle, agility, and innate skill. Her toned body sculpted over years of focused work and dedication to her craft. She used her figure as a weapon, both the physical strength it exuded and the shapely features which enticed weak-minded men to fall into her traps.

Her skill set allowed her to administer death wherever and whenever necessary. For the right price.

The man's eyes darted around the hotel room. The cherry-colored bedside nightstand and brass lamp caught his eye as he entered a death spiral. Although the life slowly left his body, his gaze stopped at Merci's glossy black bra. Her pert, overflowing breasts, in the two size too small bra, momentarily distracted his fight-or-flight struggle for life.

Even with the icy hand of death engulfing him with each gasp of air, the man still turned to the wrong head for guidance.

She used the weakness of the opposite sex to her advantage countless times. In fact, she counted on it to not only extinguish life, but to save hers.

Merci saw his eyes focus on her breasts.

She smiled, then gave him a not-so-subtle wink.

Leaning over and close to his ear. "Men are weak," she said in a sultry tone.

The mark gasped a large gulp of stale hotel room air and as he exhaled with a strained voice as he uttered the word, "Omaha," just loud enough to be heard over the sound of the hotel room air conditioning.

Their pre-arranged safe word.

Shit, thought Merci before she said. "You know you're not Peyton Manning, right?" Seconds later, she climbed off his chest.

The man nodded, grabbed at his sternum once she got off and the pressure abated. "That ... was ... intense." He spoke between gasps of precious air. "I thought ... you ... were actually ... gonna kill me." The words cut in and out between jagged breaths.

Merci smiled as she slid off the bed. "You got off easy that time. The fun stuff hasn't even started, big guy."

He coughed a bit of phlegm. "I ... I can't wait."

"Want a drink?" Merci asked as she walked towards the bar in the corner of the room.

"Of course." He said.

Merci smiled warmly. "Pick your poison."

"I'm a Jack man."

Before she got behind the mahogany bar, Merci turned to see him staring at her pert ass, covered in barely there black laced panties. "One Doctor Jack on the way, baby."

"Pour one for yourself, darlin'." He replied.

"Don't mind if I do."

The man turned to adjust the oversized pillows and straighten out the down comforter on the bed as he re-positioned where he lay. Merci used the brief interlude to remove two shot glasses from under the bar, careful to pour a small vial of clear liquid she hid in the back corner of the shelf into the man's glass before she filled the rest with Jack Daniels.

She carried both shot glasses towards the bed, his in her left hand.

Before she reached the side of the bed, she tossed down the amber liquid in her right hand in one quick motion, licked her lips, then tucked the other shot glass between her voluptuous breasts. It proved to be a tight fit in the way too small bra and her overflowing breasts.

"What, no test tube?' He asked.

Merci smiled warmly. "These puppies are big enough to hold a thick shot glass. I don't use a thin test tube like those tramps in strip clubs, baby."

He laughed. A deep, guttural laugh trailed by a wheezy cough.

Merci climbed up and slowly slithered across the bed towards the mark. Careful not to spill a drop of the liquid as her body glided across the bedspread like a viper. She climbed atop him and slowly rubbed her body on his.

"Bottoms up." He said as he sat up and buried his face between her breasts.

She leaned over, and allowed him to shoot down every drop within the glass. The man fell back onto a fluffy pillow. A content look spread over his face as he looked like he had just witnessed all the majesty of the next life to come. His eyes slowly closed, and he almost appeared to drift off to sleep.

Merci counted to ten using the old one Mississippi, two Mississippi methodology before she climbed off him.

He lay there motionless for several seconds as his eyes suddenly opened. The content expression replaced by a look of sheer terror as his body convulsed. The tremors started slow, like the motion when a washing machine starts the spin cycle. Within seconds, the jerking movements became intense as his body flailed about all over the bed.

Then, as quickly as it started, he went still and his deer in headlights eyes rolled back into his head.

His body went limp.

Merci waited two more minutes and watched his chest intently. She then checked his pulse.

Nothing.

She dressed, put the same black cocktail dress on she slipped off thirty minutes earlier, and next put on surgical gloves. It took her twenty minutes to wipe the room down and erase any DNA she may have left in the room or on his body.

Before leaving, she removed the hair samples and fingerprints from her handbag and staged the scene as instructed by her employer.

As she opened the hotel room door, she looked back at the lifeless body with a piercing, deriding glance. Fucks like him disgusted her, and even the scalding hot shower she would take would not eradicate his body oils or the smell of his skin fast enough.

Another mark against her already tattered soul.

Yet.

She had a job to do, and she did it better than virtually anyone who walked the planet.

⸻◈⸻

Merci climbed into the car next to Marcus.

"Well, hello honey. How was your day?" Marcus said in a sarcastic tone as he reached over and patted her thigh.

Merci rolled her eyes and pushed his hand off her skin. "Not in the mood. I need a scalding hot shower. I can still feel him on me."

"You know you just killed the husband of a Supreme Court Justice, right? How did that feel?"

With a deep sigh, Merci shrugged her shoulders. "About like the rest of them. He got what he deserved. There's one less asshole out there who will cheat on his wife and enrich hookers."

"Win-win." Marcus said with a toothy grin.

"Get me to the hotel." Merci's only response.

⸻◈⸻

The blond-haired man sat in the driver's seat of the metallic gray sedan, his back stiff, nerves frayed. He watched as the woman with raven colored hair in the black cocktail dress leave the inn. The grand stone façade and deep red colored roof of the structure reflected the nearly full moon from above. The woman walked with a confident stride, and gave off no hint she just committed a murder.

He tracked her as she continued past the parking lot and crossed over to a side street. He started the car and moved forward, careful not to give away the tail.

Sure to stay a safe distance back, he observed the woman climb into the passenger seat of a silver Audi R8 three blocks away from the hotel. Once inside, the car sped away.

The man reached to the empty passenger seat, picked up his cell phone, and placed a call.

"Yes?" A voice said after the second ring.

"She left the Grove Park Inn," the blond man said.

"It's done?"

"Presumably."

"Let me know when the staff finds the body. You might want to prod them along so we don't have to wait till morning."

"She left with Marcus. What do you want me to do?"

"Tail her."

"In Asheville, that may be difficult."

"Look, I don't care how you do it, but keep eyes on her."

"I've got a way to track her."

"Don't lose her. We've got too much on the line."

He audibly signed, "This isn't my first rodeo."

"Good. Be smart. Make sure it isn't your last."

The line disconnected and the blond-haired man watched as the Audi's taillights faded away into the darkness of Innsbrook Rd.

He put the car in drive and followed Merci and Marcus as they cut through the darkness of the night.

ABOUT THE AUTHOR:

———————◄O►———————

Eric P. Bishop grew up in Connecticut, and relocated to the South after college. Moves to the Rockies and the Pacific Northwest occurred before finally heading back East to raise his family. Part of him never left the West, and he is always grateful to make it back as often as possible.

After many years in corporate America, Eric turned his passion for the written word into reality and chased his dreams of crafting novels.

Eric lives in Western North Carolina with his children, where they explore the great outdoors most weekends, all the while he dreams up his next great adventure. See www.ericpbishop.com for more about Eric, his novels, and pictures of splendid journey.

Printed in Great Britain
by Amazon